Praise for
Redeeming Eve

"It is the modern woman's challenge to juggle career and family, and Bokat's likable, amusing characters struggle gamely to survive the contemporary conundrum, attempting to fit messy life into neat little packages. Bokat serves up an ably written tale complete with an Austenesque happy ending." —*Publishers Weekly*

"When a literature scholar tries to model her hectic Manhattan life on the elegant world of Jane Austen, chaos ensues. A juicy book." —*McCall's Magazine*

"A scrumptiously witty, suspensefully woven story full of sharply drawn characters, calamities, and a surprising measure of hope." —Leah Cohen

WHAT
MATTERS
MOST

Nicole Bokat

 NEW AMERICAN LIBRARY

NAL Accent
Published by New American Library,
a division of Penguin Group (USA) Inc., 375 Hudson Street,
New York, New York 10014, USA
Penguin Group (Canada), 90 Eglinton Avenue East, Suite 700, Toronto,
Ontario M4P 2Y3, Canada (a division of Pearson Penguin Canada Inc.)
Penguin Books Ltd., 80 Strand, London WC2R 0RL, England
Penguin Ireland, 25 St. Stephen's Green, Dublin 2, Ireland (a division of Penguin Books Ltd.)
Penguin Group (Australia), 250 Camberwell Road, Camberwell, Victoria 3124, Australia
(a division of Pearson Australia Group Pty. Ltd.)
Penguin Books India Pvt. Ltd., 11 Community Centre, Panchsheel Park,
New Delhi – 110 017, India
Penguin Group (NZ), cnr Airborne and Rosedale Roads, Albany, Auckland 1310, New Zealand
(a division of Pearson New Zealand Ltd.)
Penguin Books (South Africa) (Pty.) Ltd., 24 Sturdee Avenue,
Rosebank, Johannesburg 2196, South Africa

Penguin Books Ltd., Registered Offices:
80 Strand, London WC2R 0RL, England

First published by NAL Accent, an imprint of New American Library,
a division of Penguin Group (USA) Inc.

First Printing, October 2006
10 9 8 7 6 5 4 3 2 1

REGISTERED TRADEMARK—MARCA REGISTRADA

LIBRARY OF CONGRESS CATALOGING-IN-PUBLICATION DATA:

Bokat, Nicole Suzanne, 1959–
    What matters most/Nicole Bokat.
        p. cm.
    ISBN 0-451-21948-1 (trade pbk.)
    1. Mothers and daughters—Fiction. 2. Consolation—Fiction. I. Title.
    PS3552.O566W47 2006
813'.54—dc22   2006010765

Set in Monotype Dante
Designed by Elke Sigal

Printed in the United States of America

For Jay, Noah and Spencer,
the loves of my life

ACKNOWLEDGMENTS

I need to extend my deepest thanks to my agent, Elaine, first and foremost. Without her hard work on my behalf and her belief in this novel, it would not have gotten into the very capable hands of my editor, Kara Cesare. I am indebted to Kara for being such a pleasure to work with and for her keen eye and excellent suggestions. For believing in and recommending the book, I am grateful to Stephanie Lehmann.

Much gratitude to all those who were generous with their time and attention in reading the manuscript in its various incarnations and for acting as cheerleaders along the way: Lynne Lisa, Sasha Troyan, Tess James, Naomi Rand, Deirdre Day-MacLeod, and Susan Shapiro. For their insight and excellent suggestions, my appreciation goes to Sally Arteseros and Melanie Fleishman. For his help and sensitivity through the toughest of times, thank you to Jed Rosen.

Thank you to my family, for being there for me. I owe so much to my husband, Jay, whose love, support, encouragement, and unwavering faith carried me through my most insecure moments. He read draft after draft when he should have been sleeping. Finally, I have to acknowledge my children, Noah and Spencer, who were always there with a hug and to remind me that J. K. Rowling had lots of obstacles to overcome too. Every single day—without exaggeration—they have made motherhood a joy and a privilege.

PROLOGUE

Estelle held the letter from Spain in her hands. It was the night before her wedding, the last time she'd sleep in her childhood room on Morris Avenue with the sagging twin beds, the chipped dresser made of faux wood, and the faded pink curtains that had yellowed around the edges. She sat in her old rocker that her mother had decorated with rose bouquet decals a decade before, boxes, taped closed, filled with her first-year medical texts at her feet. Across the narrow room, the largest container was positioned with its sides up, filled with her poodle skirt, a few jumpers, and her old dungarees; the rest her mother was to donate to B'nai B'rith. She envisioned the plain brown moving carton as a gigantic jack-in-the-box, its lid open, with a jester in a tricolored hat primed to pop out: surprise.

The real surprise was that this message should arrive this week, after years of no contact. With all the preparations for the wedding—the final fitting of the dress after Estelle had dropped five pounds from nerves, the rehearsal dinner at the Pierre Hotel, compliments of her future in-laws, the bachelor party at Peter Luger's Steakhouse—she hadn't allowed herself a moment to ponder the significance of the letter's timing.

Until the moment when she glimpsed its crinkled presence in her apartment's mail slot, she'd felt invincible, having taunted the fates: *See, even a* kurveh, *a whore, can start a new life!* For three days she'd carried this missive in her pocketbook, along with her red lipstick compact with the tiny mirror and a coin purse. She gazed now at the envelope adorned with colorful airmail *España* stamps, addressed to her in his swooping black calligraphy.

Carefully, she ran her fingernail under the lip of the envelope to loosen its hold. She could hear herself breathing above the sound of her mother washing the dinner plates and her father listening to *The Huntley-Brinkley Report*. Before reading, she glanced at the door to her room, then at her closet, as if expecting one of her parents, primed to catch her in this illicit act, to jump out of the shadows.

> *Estella*, mi querida,
> *I have lost some of my English being so long out of*
> *your wonderful country. Forgive me. A long time*
> *passes since we saw each other but I have not forgot-*
> *ten. I am hoping that you have not forgotten either. I*
> *have not heard from you years ago when I sent you let-*
> *ters. I am giving you the place I will be when I am*
> *coming to New York in two months' time. If you write*
> *to me I will know that you want the same as me.*
> *I am looking forward to that, Estella.* ¿Tú recuerdas?
> *My love to you, belleza.*

His name was scribbled and would be indecipherable to anyone not familiar with his script. The signature, self-important in its illegibility, was inconsequential to Estelle. She planned to ignore this correspondence, as she had the others. She would never confess the significance he'd held, how the memory of him was one she'd never have the luxury of discarding, how their relationship had left a residue in her heart clear enough to be detected by an X-ray or a loved one.

PART ONE

───

GEORGIE, 2000

ONE

Her father's funeral was packed with patients, those clever thieves whom Georgie had imagined faking stomachaches and fevers all those years, in order to steal him—his sepia eyes, half-cocked smile, and warm hands—away from her. One of the taller girls, with little buds of breasts, stepped up to the rabbi's pulpit to read a eulogy in a fluty voice. In one hand she clutched the satin ribbon of her black purse, while with the other she busily tucked her scotch-colored hair behind her flushed ear.

"Dr. Merkin wasn't like the doctors who stick a cold stethoscope on your chest and call you by the wrong name. He actually talked to *me,* not to, you know, my mom while *pretending* to talk to me. When I got really sick with pneumonia last year, he showed up at my house with the Narnia series, which, you know, is something doctors just don't do anymore these days."

The girl shook her head and took a big, dramatic breath. "I'll never forget him."

So earnest. Of course she'll forget, Georgie thought, jealousy aching like an old scar that should have healed decades ago.

A month before he died—when he'd received the ominous news that the cancer had spread to his liver—Adam Merkin had set out to write a letter to each and every one of his pediatric clients. None of the letters contained instructions about caring for their bodies once he was no longer there to do it for them. Instead, they were wistful reminiscences of his youth—tales of canoeing in the lakes of Vermont during summer break, or stories about camping trips with his boyhood friends—mixed with encouragement and good wishes.

Johnny, don't give up the violin when the going gets tough, as I know you have it in you to persist. Ashley, thank you so much for the beautiful drawing of my waiting room. The daisies you added were an excellent touch. I'm sorry I never placed a vase of them next to the tank of guppies.

Georgie had secretly longed to receive a missive too, yet could barely admit this wish to herself. She couldn't permit the childish thought to mingle in her brain with its more sophisticated rivals.

She remembered now her father's reaction to the death of a terminal patient, a girl who died of leukemia at age seven, Georgie's own age at the time. That night she'd awoken to her father's gulping sobs, and had imagined baby seals being clubbed to death, their skulls crushed even as their animal screams rang into the arctic air. Her second-grade teacher had been lecturing their class on cruelty to animals all that week. Georgie heard her mother cooing, "Ssh, now, Adam. You did everything possible for her. No one could have done more."

Georgie had tiptoed to the hall bathroom and, once in the narrow space, slipped and banged her knee on the pipe that curled like the bottom of an S under the sink. She'd lain, balled up on the floor, legs close to her chin, and licked her wound. Her mouth had gone dry and had a metallic taste in it. She must have fallen asleep on the black-and-white tiles, because, in the morning, her mother propped her into a standing position.

"What are you doing here?" Estelle asked in a tired voice.

"I heard Daddy crying last night. I was scared."

"I'm sorry about that, Georgie. But your father was very upset."

"Me, too. He was crying because a little girl died."

"C'mon, out of here now." Her mother had sighed. "You're fine. This isn't about you."

In the most literal sense, her mother had been right. Now her father's death was not about her either. So it shouldn't have mattered that Georgie read nothing, wrote nothing in commemoration. Or that she did not, could not cry, that it took all her energy just to breathe. Still, both the rabbi and her aunt Lily had questioned her about saying a few words. "Darling, you should get up there and memorialize Adam. You're the writer in the family, after all," Lily had said. "You're looking wonderful, so thin."

Georgie's mother, Estelle Merkin, ob-gyn, did deliver a eulogy, imposing in her Donna Karan mourning suit, her hair slicked back in the tightest of ponytails, her inky eyes staring fiercely at the back of the room, her mouth a red circle emitting perfect diction.

When the services were over people flooded around both mother and daughter, some weeping, others shaking their heads. "Why should such a lovely man, such a wonderful, caring doctor, be taken while my father-in-law, the nastiest man alive, is still in excellent health at eighty-five years old?" asked a woman with mottled skin.

A nurse in Adam's office—a zaftig woman with blond curls and dimples—squeezed Georgie's forearm so hard she left a faint mark. "This was far and away *the* best funeral I've ever been to. Believe me, honey"—the fat woman clucked, bearing down on her flesh—"I've been to more than my share, and this was a class act."

Luke Carter, Georgie's ex-husband, kissed his former mother-in-law. He was all dressed up in his Prada wing-tip shoes and black Italian suit with the starched white shirt, the too-tight collar causing a web of rash to spread.

"Call me tomorrow, Georgie," Luke said, paler than usual, with his feathery hair rising up in the wind. He shifted his weight from one leg to the other and squinted into the sky.

"Are you okay, Mom?" Georgie and Luke's son Jesse asked. His round-eyed face scrunched up in concern, this nine-year-old protector of his mother's heart. The lifted eyebrows, the steady, piercing gaze were birthrights, as noted by several maternity nurses. "He's so intelligent, but a little worrier," was the standard line. After her divorce, Georgie joked that her son assumed the role of E.T. to her Elliot, an empathetic, perceptive being, wise for his age and in sync with her every mood. She needed to tread lightly when in pain, to never forget her maternal responsibility to shelter her son, both physically and emotionally.

Georgie nodded now. Her head felt fuzzy, as if wrapped in cobwebs, and her sinuses were clogged. She touched her boy's silky skin and smiled. "Sure, honey. Go home with Daddy. Watch *Episode I* and order up Chinese. I'll be over to get you first thing in the morning."

"Okay," he agreed, his brows still knitted together.

Out of nowhere Estelle appeared and sidled up to Jesse. "I'm glad you were here, and I know Grandpa would be too. You're the only one I wanted to see today," she whispered loudly.

Georgie's cousin Nina accompanied her to the limousine that would drive them to the cemetery. "Everyone is saying that this is the best funeral they've ever been to," she said.

"In our family, competition is brutal even in death," Georgie said, floating above her feelings like a slab of ice on water. "Wait till we get back to my mom's. There will be a can-you-top-this race for the most brilliant accomplishment of the year."

"Don't forget the bathing suit competition," Nina said.

"It's the number one draw, bigger than the talent show. Cousin Alex's a shoo-in to win in a bikini; that is, if you're partial to the Holocaust-survivor look, very big in our circles."

Georgie looked at her and smiled. Nina was all hair, hands, impossibly long legs, and size-ten feet. She was well dressed, five-foot-ten, and model-thin no matter how many calories she consumed. Pink-complected, freckled Nina the Good: mother of two sweet girls, wife to gastroenterologist Elliot Shulman, and eagerly sought-after psychologist. Her client list included CEOs, fashion models desperate to keep their prisoner-of-war look, and teenage anorexics whose parents spent much of their million-dollar salaries to keep them out of trouble. She was Georgie's best friend and her lighthouse. Two years ago Nina had beckoned Georgie out to suburban New Jersey with promises that if she and Jesse moved there from Manhattan they'd have a saner life. It was a promise that had been fulfilled until the evening her mother called; in a voice drained of all expression, she'd said, "I have some bad news." The two knuckle-size tumors her father had discovered in his groin were "malignant," the worst word in the English language.

Knollwood Park Cemetery was New York's equivalent of a rush-hour subway for the dead. It was overcrowded, with a view of the Brooklyn-Queens Expressway. As several Merkin women hiked up to the family plot, the damp air whistled its chilly tune. The sun was nowhere to be seen, but the moon hung, a wafer in the gray afternoon sky, on a day so bleak and ashen-colored you could almost hear the trees sigh in despair of ever again turning green.

Estelle vowed, "I'll get my husband out of here. Adam should be someplace beautiful, restful, someplace he'd like. A little churchyard in New England." She was as spectacular as Scarlett O'Hara, who'd never go hungry again.

"Ma, we're Jewish."

"Never mind. I'll figure it out. You wait and see."

"Okay," Georgie said, and grabbed her mother's elbow to steady her. "Let me help you. I'm worried about you." Finally, after the long, rolling years of childhood in which she'd prayed for her mother's approbation, maybe now there would be a way in, a niche into her soft crevice of sorrow.

But Estelle's eyes snapped furiously. "I'm fine," she said, letting her daughter close only for the brief stint uphill, wind crackling in their ears. Then she pulled away. "I meant to ask, what's with the pants? Couldn't you have found a dress this once for your father's funeral, even one of those shapeless smocks Eileen Fisher makes for old widows like me?"

"Ma, what do you want me to wear at my age, miniskirts? I'm not twenty-two anymore."

Suddenly Estelle gasped as if asthmatic. Georgie wanted to scream, *Get a doctor*, but, of course, almost everyone there was one. Estelle whipped around to face her daughter. She said, "I see you *did* have the presence of mind to get a pricey haircut with highlights."

Georgie felt herself blink too quickly as she replied, "You just said I looked shabby."

"I did not say that. I said that pants are too casual. Do you think Dad would care if your hair was streaked?"

"Do you think Dad would care about our clothes right now? You look like you just went shopping at Saks."

It had always been this way. Her mother insisted on perfection in body as well as in mind, performed almost magically, without makeup or mirrors. Hard work was paramount, but only if it was noble and of service. Beauty was something that should shoot through a woman, as it had Estelle, like a waterfall, iridescent and sugar white.

"Lily bought this suit for me. She tossed things at me and I got dressed." Estelle shook her head. "I don't want to argue with you now. It's disrespectful."

At the burial site Georgie stood apart from the crowd at first, eyeing the tombs of her dead relatives. There were the tasteful granite stones commemorating her paternal grandparents, Ruth and Eddie Merkin, who had lived long, purposeful lives as a high school French teacher and an otolaryngologist, respectively. They died quickly and without fuss, within a year of each other—her grandfather of a stroke, her grandmother of a heart attack—missing their son's first battle with cancer.

To the left, Georgie's great-grandparents were buried, Eddie's *shmegeggy* of a father and his whiz of a mother. She'd sold newspapers to Wall Street brokers at a kiosk for thirty years, scribbling down the stock tips she overheard and slowly building up an inheritance for her two thankless daughters and the star of her life, her doctor son. To the right were Georgie's maternal grandparents, uneasy in their patch of earth, perpetual outsiders in their adopted country's soil. The Russian inscription on their tombs reflected Grandpa Jacob's bitterness for all he had forsaken, his dream of becoming a professor of mathematics in Taras Shevchenko University of Kyiv, to be stuck behind a deli counter all day, slicing kosher meat and scooping potato salad into plastic tubs.

Georgie walked over to join the others and saw that Saul Lieberman, her father's second cousin, was passing out his card to shivering guests. He was standing far enough away from the rabbi so as not to disturb the Hebrew prayer he was reciting, which few of the clan could follow anyway.

"Rochelle is done with Princeton law school this spring and will be coming to work for my firm next fall. She made law review again," he boasted, cocking his balding head, the tips of his large, flat ears reddened from the cold. "Gotta hand it to that kid: She's a marvel. I always knew she was smart, but not that she was the smartest damn one in the family."

"Wonder what Rochelle's older brother, cousin Bob, would say to that?" Nina asked as she shimmied up to Georgie. She leaned against some stranger's tombstone, holding one shoe in her hand and massaging her long, narrow toes. "These things are killing my feet."

"I heard through the grapevine that cousin Bob's a drug dealer working the U.S.–Mexican border. Tainted the pure bloodline," Georgie said.

"Actually, he's an orthodontist with three kids, living in Short Hills."

"My recollection is so much more romantic."

The Merkin women were all there, one looking more handsome than the next, as fit and trim as Hollywood's finest, with bright eyes and flawless skin. They glowed with achievement, as did the men, their advanced degrees combed into their coiffed hair, shining from their good leather shoes and straight porcelain teeth. But Georgie knew that there were individual clan members who couldn't manage to snap their lives like clean linen drying in the wind. There were the pill poppers and the bulimics among them. Yet, when they flocked together, she still felt that ancient push-pull of disdain and envy tugging in her chest.

Alex Merkin Grossberg—the plastic surgeon second cousin married to another plastic surgeon—approached the two women in her burgundy suit, her designer pumps poking tiny holes in the ground. "Hi, Nina. Georgie. I'm so sorry about your dad. Everyone agrees he was the nicest man in the whole extended family."

"Thanks," Georgie said.

Through pursed collagened lips, Alex said, "I heard you made contributing editor at *Elle*. That's great. Aunt Lily told my mom." She squinted into the sky as if the nonexistent sun were blinding her. "I don't have time to read *an-y-thing*. But you guys do some pieces on beauty, right? If you ever need to interview me about anything from lipoplasty to breast augmentation, don't hesitate to call."

"Thanks. But my specialty is more psychological these days, along with health and fitness" Georgie said, biting on her mouth. "Has been for years now, actually."

"How you doing?" Nina asked in her shrink voice.

"I'm doing well," Alex said, her pretty cheeks all flushed. "You know, performing lots of lipos and fat grafting. Everyone seems to want a miracle." She threw up her hands. "Whatever happened to good old-fashioned dieting and exercise?"

Nina smiled and shrugged. "I don't know. But it's not bad for business, I'm sure." She raised her eyebrows and widened her eyes at Georgie, just like when they were kids.

The rabbi was wrapping it up, reciting a Hebrew prayer that not one of the reformed Merkins could comprehend. Soon he would request that the family shovel dirt into the grave. "Excuse me. I think I need to get closer," Georgie said.

Later, in the limo—one eye glancing her mother's way for signs of stress fractures—Georgie broke the ice with, "What's with Alex's fat lips? Can't she tell that she's overdone it, that it looks like someone punched her?"

"She's obviously anorexic," Nina responded.

"She is very thin," Aunt Lily, Nina's mother, agreed, as she fussed with the collar of her washed-wool beige coat. She smelled of Shalimar and whatever face powder she'd been using since time immemorial to achieve that French-old-lady scent. Her hair—dyed an orangey red—was tamed into a chignon that she ran her hand over, chronically, to check on its position, her signature gold charm bracelet rattling down her arm. That Lily was Adam's sister was as hard to fathom as imagining Jimmy Carter sharing DNA with Nancy Reagan.

"Ah, leave her alone. Alex is a very pretty girl," said Uncle Art, a high-price gastroenterologist with an office on Central Park West. Georgie and her father used to joke that Art's patients confused the abbreviation HMO with designer initials. From the look of him—this short, stocky man with bushy eyebrows and a pear-shaped nose who wore pinkie rings, raccoon coats, and silk pajamas—one might have guessed he was a professional gambler or producer of "classy" porn. Blinking at the sight of her uncle now, Georgie conceded that she'd never call him in a medical emergency.

"Maybe she thinks starving herself is glamorous," Estelle said. "She should visit Sloan-Kettering if she wants to see glamorous." Estelle turned to gaze out the window at the overcast sky. "What do I care if Alex starves herself? My husband is dead. Adam would have loved to be able to eat these last few weeks. He had no appetite anymore."

Georgie's heart rate quickened. She pictured her father the night before he died, lying on the ER gurney, his face jaundiced, the startled gaze of his yellow eyes, how they darted around, death's fluid running like a river into his irises. For one moment he was able to focus. He raised his fleshless arm and pointed to some piece of equipment, offering his potassium levels to the other doctors, one of the team to the end.

"I know, dear," Lily said, taking Estelle's hand in hers.

"Ma, don't," Georgie said, piling her hand on top of Lily's as if they were gearing up for a game. "Don't even think about Alex. Really. Don't talk to her if she upsets you."

Estelle shrugged and slipped her hand back into her own lap. "Everyone upsets me. The fact that they're alive and Adam's not."

The Merkins' seven-room apartment remained unchanged despite the loss of one of its essential occupants. Everything was in its rightful place, yet the air felt static, centuries old, the living room like a museum exhibit partitioned off from the visitors by a solid velvet rope. The flowery aroma permeated the air, eliminating all traces of dog musk. Cancer had been driven from this house, but its ghost remained, hidden in the wood of Grandma Ruth's Wegner chairs, brewing in the excellent espresso, radiating out of the one-hundred-watt bulbs in the pewter trumpet lamps. Estelle had cleaned out the "cancer room," Adam's den that had been filled with morphine tablets, samples of BuSpar, containers of shark cartilage, NutriVir powder, *JAMA* and Internet articles on breakthrough treatments and books with uplifting titles like *Conquering Cancer* and *The Cancer Diet*. Now, in time for them to sit shivha, the den had no sign of disease or of Adam, not even his red flannel jersey that he'd always flung on the back of his La-Z-Boy chair. Even the scent of him—Mennen deodorant, the original chalky Tums, and a hint of sour dog on flesh—had been banished. "Wow," Georgie whispered under her breath. "Mom's one cool customer."

Charlene, the Merkins' housekeeper and cook for the last three decades, greeted the guests. "Oh, honey." She embraced Georgie in her corpulent arms; her skin was warm and smelled of pot roast and her famous gravy. It felt like a holiday.

"Look at all this food, Charlene," Georgie said, tearing off her gloves with her teeth.

"Yes, miss. There's those biscuits you like and bagels and that lox and whitefish in the living room." She was referring to the Jewish food their family lived on, the attraction of which Charlene still didn't understand after all these years.

"Why don't you help Charlene take some of the trays out?" Estelle asked her daughter.

"No, Dr. Merkin. I don't need Miss Georgia's help. She's been through enough. You too, go rest, ma'am."

Estelle nodded. Charlene was one of the few people in the world from whom she would take instruction.

"Where's Odysseus?" Georgie asked, searching for Adam's old sheepdog mix and sidekick, the beloved mutt she'd adopted for her father at the ASPCA after she'd received the glorious news that his first bout of lymphoma had gone into remission.

"Your mother put him in the kennel for the week, you know," Charlene said, shaking her head. "That dog's a goner. Your mother never did care for him."

Georgie joined Nina in the living room with its grand piano, polished wood floor, sleek Danish furniture, and view of Central Park. "I got us some white wine from the kitchen," Nina said. "Thought you might need a glass."

"Thanks. I will as soon as the cousins arrive and start drumming up patients again."

"If only one of our relatives owned an auto repair shop." Nina sighed as she handed Georgie a goblet. "The Audi is in constant need of attention. I hate European cars. Elliot is pathetic for wanting it, his stout little phallic symbol."

"Being a mechanic is too low-class. Maybe on my mother's side of the family there are still some Ackermans who recall their immigrant status." Georgie took a sip. It was a very dry chardonnay. She felt remarkably light, giddy even. It couldn't have been from the wine, not that quickly and not from so little.

"So should I scope out the food?" Nina asked. "See if there's any of those cheese balls your mom always orders from Marina's?"

"Absolutely. Get me a brioche to shove it into and some cantaloupe slices."

Squeezing her cousin's hand hard, Nina said, "I'll be right back."

Georgie turned to see cousins, friends, and colleagues arriving in a pack and—just for a moment—seemed to glimpse her father skirting around the crowd in his Hush Puppies shoes and old trench coat. He waved right at her, his long, narrow face broken into a plaintive smile, his earnest brown eyes crinkled behind his reading glasses.

Striding past all the MDs and PhDs convened in the hallway, she swung open the kitchen door and beckoned Nina to join her in what had once been her bedroom and was now Estelle's study. They sat side by side on the plush aubergine couch and ate their goodies.

"Do you think it's required of me to talk to any of those people?" Georgie asked before slugging another mouthful of wine.

"Well," Nina said, "your mother might find it rude if you don't, but your dad wouldn't have cared."

When she swallowed, Georgie noticed how dry and tight her throat felt. "He'd have hidden in here with us," she said. How many times had he ducked out of family gatherings to answer the anxious calls of parents or just to escape the "BS floating around the room"?

"You know how lucky you were to have a dad like him?"

"Christ, Nina. I don't feel especially lucky right now."

"But you are, regardless." She shot Georgie a familiar look that meant: Uncle Art was not Adam.

"I never got enough of him, between my mother and his patients. I know I shouldn't complain. Maybe I just expected too much from him, from men in general."

Nina shrugged. "Or too little." She leaned her head on Georgie's shoulder, causing her plate to slide and her bagel to land, cream cheese first, on one of Estelle's prized Persian rugs. "Whoops!" Nina exclaimed, lifting up her lint-filled lunch. "I have to clean this up or she'll kill me."

"Leave it," Georgie said. "My mother doesn't have to know who did it."

"If only there were children here we could blame it on."

"Nina? It's weird, but it seems like my father is still here."

"That's perfectly normal."

"Okay, because I thought I might be freaking out."

Nina inhaled deeply and reached inside her purse. "Want one just in case?" she asked, holding out her hand. Her palm was long, the color of an eggshell. One sad-looking blue Valium sat in the center.

"Oh, my God, Nina. Where did you get that? No one's taken those since 1975."

"My mother, of course. Remember?"

She did remember—it was more than two decades ago, behind Temple Emanu-El on Fifth Avenue.

"You're a shrink. Couldn't you get someone to prescribe something of *this* century?" Georgie asked. "Never mind. I have some Klonopin at home that my father gave me weeks ago. It makes me loopy but not Valium-depressed."

"Loopy is good, kid." A bit sternly, Nina added, "Just don't take it and drink."

"I won't. I took one last night and I think it made me hallucinate, because this morning when I woke up I heard my dad's voice telling me to call my mother, that she needed me."

Nina was nodding, her kinky russet-colored curls bouncing around her face. "She does. Your mom *does* need you now."

Georgie shrugged, the taste of cheese and wine stinging her tongue. "My mother never needed anyone, except maybe my father, in her entire life."

"Hey," Nina said, "she just doesn't show it. You know how prickly your mom can be."

"It's hard to be there for someone who won't let you near her. She seems pretty furious with me, even more so than usual. At the cemetery she criticized my clothes and my haircut."

Nina touched the caramel-brown bob. "Your hair is cute. What's wrong with it?"

Georgie shook her head. "No, the fact that I got it cut."

"Oh. It will get better. It'll take a while but Stellie will come around. She's just losing it right now."

Georgie nodded, but was thinking, When was it *ever* better? At any rate, the adrenaline of rage was less frightening than the alternative: crumbling grief. She had never witnessed her mother in a state of emotional disrepair, and dreaded even the notion of Estelle's noble, imperious face cascading into the wordless horror of loss, a woman no longer able to galvanize herself into action. All of

Georgie's life her mother had been as regal and independent as Queen Elizabeth I, who not only headed the last Tudor monarchy and established England as a major European power, but never married, never had a child, and certainly never went to medical school. Georgie didn't think she could bear it, losing the familiarity of two parents at once.

"She's not falling apart, which is incredible, really. You have to admire her for it," Nina said.

"I do." Admiration and anger were permanently wound around Georgie's heart, intertwined like a pair of socks. "I think that no matter what, my mom is strong enough to be okay."

"Stellie will be right as rain," said Aunt Lily, who had poked her head in, diamond earrings slapping her jawbone. "We were looking for you, dear. Come be polite and say hello to the guests."

Georgie rose, leaving behind her half-eaten brioche, because there would always be requirements to follow.

Vases, pots, and baskets of flowers were everywhere: stargazer lilies, heather, gerberas, snapdragons, delphinium, and yellow roses. Adam would have sneezed, muttered about his "damn relatives"—not because he'd have recognized that displaying flowers was against Jewish custom but because of the allergens—and he would have sneaked out for a walk on Fifth Avenue.

How Georgie wished she could go with him.

For the rest of the afternoon Georgie hovered politely, nodding and smiling and adding little to the various conversations. Looking around, she felt like the scandalous Countess Olenska in *The Age of Innocence,* estranged from her husband while the other members of fine society were all respectably married or—in her mother's case—widowed. No one was divorced. She picked at a plate of noodles in peanut sauce and finished off three large pieces of eggplant sautéed with onions. Nina stayed by her side for much of the day, and, at one point, they insisted on helping Charlene in the kitchen, brewing coffee, and then serving French roast in demitasse cups. The desserts included marble cheesecake, German chocolate cake, and a warm pecan pie with whipped cream. A celebratory feast.

Slightly buzzed, Georgie watched her mother converse with the physician cousins, her fellow veterans of the cause: monitoring and mending other people's private places.

Although an obstetrician, Estelle never fell in love with either the babies or their mothers. It was the mechanical act of childbirth she marveled at, its primitive accomplishment that filled her with satisfaction, the separating of two people who moments before had existed as one. This was the miracle she had recounted over late dinners while a young Georgie imagined her mother's work as snapping the long end off the wishbone. Yet Estelle's favorite tales from medical school ran toward stories of pathology rounds, students playing practical jokes on each other while the bone saw screamed its way through corpse after corpse. One time she'd returned home with a piece of earlobe clinging to her medical bag. Another time a friend had taken a slide of someone's brain, stuck it in an envelope, and slid it into her jacket pocket.

Georgie's parents shared this story with each other every spring, a ritual ingrained in the couple's unique Haggadah.

"It was my first year at Columbia," Adam would begin. "I was friends with an intern in neurosurgery and, for Passover, neither one of us could make it home. Shira invited me to a seder for the patients on her ward."

"How thoughtful," Estelle would say, nodding, bolstering him to "go on, go on."

"What I didn't realize until the day we were doing the service was"—here he would always smile slyly—"that they were all coma patients."

Inevitable as the platter of bitter herbs, haroset, and parsley was Estelle's delighted gasp.

"When we asked why, on this night, do we recline, the answer was because we're comatose!"

"Oh, that's great."

"Shira was an interesting girl. . . ."

"But not as interesting . . . ?" She would nudge him flirtatiously.

Adam would turn to his wife, eyes luminous with love. "She was just a friend taking pity on a new kid on the block, an embarrassingly homesick boy several years her junior."

It was even more than a husband that Estelle had lost, Georgie knew. She had lost the guiding doctrine of her life. Medicine had always been a constant, her companion for the long haul. The only time Georgie had been welcomed unequivocally into her mother's sanctuary, the hospital had been transformed into death's waiting room, sterile and bleached of color. Georgie had accompanied her parents to the oncologist at the last, worst moment. "I'm terribly sorry," the doctor had said quietly, gazing down, his skin an ashy tone, like frayed paper. "The cancer has spread to the liver and stomach." When he looked up, his eyes were sad and tired, a watery blue, leaking a bit out of the corners.

Moments later, the oncologist cornered Estelle and Georgie scurrying to the ladies' room. He'd warned them, "Prepare yourself. It won't be long." "Don't say that to me," Estelle had hissed back, then tumbled into the glare of the bathroom's fluorescent lights. Georgie followed, dry mouthed, as if slapped by winter's frigid hand. In the mirror, Estelle's face had a mustard-yellow cast; her eyes looked cavernous and old. "I never believed this could happen to Adam and me," she whispered, as if unaware of Georgie's presence at the next sink. "I always thought we were protected. Magical thinking. Ridiculous. Old lady," she added accusingly at her reflection. "Widow."

"Ma, Dad's still here," Georgie had said, dizzy, reaching for the porcelain basin to steady herself.

"Don't you go falling apart on me," Estelle snapped, eyeing her daughter. "You're just going to have to keep yourself together this time, Georgia. Focus on your father, not yourself."

Most of the guests had cleared out by nightfall. At Estelle's insistence, Charlene had gone home without finishing the dishes, heaving herself out of her housedress (into what looked like another one) and picking up her fake leather pocketbook with one hand and a canvas bag with the other. Lily was speaking softly to Estelle.

Georgie had collected glasses and was inside the kitchen, unseen. "Have you gotten back to Daniel yet?" Lily asked.

There was something in the tone of her voice that caught Georgie's interest.

"Who's Daniel?" she asked a few minutes later, reemerging into the living room.

"Oh," Lily said, blushing, her already pink cheeks deepening in color.

"An old friend from the Bronx," Estelle said evenly. "No one you've ever met."

A question was weighing down Georgie's tongue. Like confetti, pieces of a recent memory fluttered through her mind, the weekend before her father died. She'd visited with him, and later admonished herself for not foreseeing the inevitable in his bony hands with the skin loosening around the knuckles, the disheveled beard, and the crane legs. Despite his condition he'd been walking around, talking to Jesse about buying him a new fishing rod, his mobility a red herring for Georgie, who'd absurdly convinced herself that a dying man would have to be bedridden. During that afternoon, her mother had mentioned a man named Daniel. Georgie was certain of this.

"I was wondering, would you like me to pick up Odysseus for you, Ma?" she asked. "I don't mind doing it. Tell me what I can do."

"I don't think so. I think I'll leave him for a few more days. I just can't deal with him right now."

Georgie nodded thinking, *Poor boy, poor thing. You've just lost the only one who loved you here.*

TWO

F riday night, a month after her father's death, Georgie was alone in her house in Yantacaw, New Jersey. She felt so lonely without her son. She flipped through her stack of women's magazines, pondering disappointment and the various purposes children might have in inflicting it. Her parents had spent their adult lives viewing the human condition through the lens of disease, bodily fluids of pus and stench, the microscopic survey of epidermal crud. As a teenager she'd peruse their old medical textbooks, gaping at the ugly humiliation of human flesh, cauliflower-shaped warts on the penis, scaly psoriasis under fingernails, oozing basal cell carcinomas on ears and scalps, and deadliest of all, the black moles of melanomas. A part of the body one could cut away but never remove—skin. Soon after discovering these testaments to illness and decay, she became obsessed with *Mademoiselle*, *Glamour*, and *Vogue*, with Carol Alt's glowing cheeks, Christy Brinkley's amber tan.

By sixteen she was compulsively perusing the glossy pages of fashion magazines and seeking out advice—not on sex and dating, but on naturally smooth skin and perfect pedicures for summer. Exfoliation and electrolysis became her catchwords. What interested her were the myriad nonmedical uses for women's bodies, possibilities that had nothing to do with the sloppy agony of childbirth or the dehumanizing mutilation of breast cancer.

When Georgie informed her parents that she was planning on becoming a journalist, Adam proposed that his daughter might hop a plane for Suriname to save the rain forests. Estelle surmised that she'd join the international campaign to halt clitoridectomies in Africa. Instead, her first published piece was entitled, "Are White Shoes Acceptable for Winter?" *Cosmo* on the very first try! Georgie was thrilled. Her parents were bewildered. Who was this lightweight they'd produced who, after six years of higher education (including a master's in creative nonfiction), had settled for concocting such confection? Having written herself off as intellectually inconsequential back in high school, Georgie wondered why it had taken the two superior thinkers of the family so long to catch up.

Her parents questioned her choice of a husband—as did Nina and even Georgie, privately, in her journal. Why, they all wondered, after a long relationship with a liberal, intellectual journalist, was she suddenly engaged to a financial adviser, a gentile with skin that resembled a dalmatian puppy's before its spots came in, whose mother sent him monogrammed handkerchiefs, who had so much platinum and gold in his wallet that when he flipped it open the sun's rays seemed to bounce off the palm of his hand? Was it for revenge against them that Georgie had never outgrown her love of the airbrushed image, that she hankered after *Vogue* the way her fiancé did *Playboy*, pretending to scan the satiny, perfumed pages for tips on cellulite or lingerie, but really just in awe of the pretty girls?

Georgie had long since stopped probing her psyche about her career choice, but she still berated herself about her marriage. In retrospect, her reasons for marrying Lucas Carter seemed simple: a childish yearning for certainty, balance, and adherence to the prescribed plan. This Lucas's clan could provide. For Dorothy and Campbell Carter from Princeton, New Jersey, life made sense the way good copper plumbing did: You paid for the best and it worked without much maintenance or complaint. They had to face death and taxes like all mortals; but for them, *angst* was not a word found in the best standard-English dictionaries. This innate sense of calm was what Georgie hoped to swallow down with Dorothy's strong Earl Grey tea.

Two weeks before the wedding, her father had called Georgie at Luke's place. Her fiancé was trotting through Central Park as he did every morning, despite hail stinging his cheeks or heat that clung to him like cellophane. Georgie watched Luke leave his apartment, eager to greet the pale sky rushing in from out of the darkness. She thought: *There it goes again, moving away from me, this body.* She'd gotten out of the shower and was towel-drying her hair over the sink in the cool marble-floored bathroom when the phone rang.

As soon as she heard his voice, her mouth felt cold as if suddenly full of ice chips. "Dad, are you all right?" This was how all their conversations began of late.

"Sure," he said impatiently. "Hanging in there. Listen, I know this is sort of bad timing on my part, but something's been bothering me. I think you may be rushing into marriage for the wrong reason, honey. I don't mean to question your judgment, because I know you can take care of yourself. Correct me if I'm wrong, but I have a gnawing suspicion that, with everything that's happened, you haven't been so clearheaded lately."

What Georgie wanted to say was: *Breathe deeply, take yoga, meditate, stroll through the park with the whistle of life in your ears. Don't concern yourself with me. Don't concern yourself!*

Instead she said, "You don't need to worry. I'm not making a mistake."

"Please don't take this the wrong way, because I like your young man." He paused. "It's just that you haven't known him very long. You started seeing him on what we used to call the rebound, and with my getting sick . . . Well, no point in rehashing. All I'm trying to say is, a lot of stuff has been happening."

"Dad, I'm right as rain."

Never mind how fast her life was spinning around or the fact that she'd wake up at three a.m. to stuff slabs of matzo and butter down her throat, nearly gagging, as if she were famished, or that sometimes at the Carter estate, the sight of Luke's parents in their white linen pants and emerald shirts made her wonder if she'd woken up in a Bing Crosby musical without her section of the script.

"Okay, good to hear," her father said. "Just looking out for my daughter's interests, her long-term happiness, all that dull fatherly stuff."

"Luke's a great guy, Dad. I plan to be happy," she said a little too emphatically. "Really."

"Honey, I like Lucas. I love you. I want you to have a good life."

Then don't die, Daddy, she thought.

He'd obeyed her wishes for almost a decade.

But now in the aftermath of the worst possible outcome, her monthly magazines could no longer spin their golden magic. Georgie's heart was swollen with absence; Jesse gone to Luke's for the weekend, her dad gone for good. She was too sad to marvel at all that decadent beauty in the magazines. Instead she glanced at an old picture of Jesse that stood on her desk, hands on his hips, grimace on his face, eyebrows a straight line above chestnut eyes. Kneeling behind him was his idol, Grandpa Adam, lean and loving, bespectacled and pale. Since he'd already gone one round with lymphoma, they'd thought him in the clear.

"Hi there, you," Georgie said, lifting up the kitten. Abigail Abyssinian was Jesse's birthday present from Adam, purchased in early February. She watched Abby jump out of her grasp in order to lick her lower regions, blissfully self-involved.

Georgie's hands shook. She walked to her bedroom with its putty-colored walls, polished honey headboard and matching dresser, its fluffy periwinkle quilt. On the nightstand was the vial of sky-blue pills, courtesy of Estelle, and a can of soda. She took a bite of one and left the rest out just in case. She washed the piece down with the Diet Pepsi.

She sank onto her bed and held her down pillow to her face, shutting her eyes, doubting she'd have the tenacity to leave this sanctuary. The weekend stretched out before her like the Dead Sea. Her friends were trying to help. One had brought over a pot of spaghetti marinara with a tossed salad. Another called every few days to check up on her. A third sent a sympathy card in which she'd written, *Please let me know if you need help cleaning the refrigerator or just some company*. Kind gestures all. Yet grief was a raft untethered from the island of life. From her prone position, dehydrated from salt and thirst, Georgie could view but could not touch the busy, productive fray of suburbia with its comforting pool clubs and soccer matches, school fund-raisers and bake sales.

She thought about her mother and what she might be doing. Estelle had hinted at being overwhelmed, of depths of paperwork and phone calling, the utilitarian follow-up to death. Georgie dialed her mother's number and, for the third time that week, reached the answering machine with its stony new message. Her father's voice, pensive and crackling with compassion, was erased. She'd never hear it again.

"Hi, Ma," she said carefully, trying to ensure that each syllable was washed clean of past grievances. "Hope you're okay. Call me and let me know how you're holding up."

A rattle, a click, a low moan. "I was asleep."

Her mother's misery tightened Georgie's gut like a tourniquet. "Sorry. I can call back later."

"Don't bother. Now is fine." Estelle cackled—a sound stuffed with rage. "Once I'm up these days, I'm up for good."

"You aren't sleeping? Can you take something for that?" Georgie stroked her quilt like a child with her blankie.

"That's not what I need."

"Dad gave me Klonopin, and that works really well."

"It doesn't matter. I sleep when I sleep. What's the difference now that your father isn't here?"

"Well, with work . . ."

"I'm not back at work yet, my dear," Estelle snapped triumphantly. "It's next week."

"Sorry, I forgot. Can you get more time off?"

A sigh so huge it could pull a tree up from its roots. "What for?" Estelle asked. "It makes no difference if I'm home or at work."

Fear tickled Georgie right below her ribs with its long, clever fingers. Was her mother's depression deepening? One could go mad from grief; this she knew from the poets. But certainly not her mother, she reassured herself. Estelle had always been as guarded from human emotion as an Inuit fisherman insulated in bearskin pants, snowhare stockings, and sealskin boots.

"Maybe you need more time to rest," Georgie offered.

"Rest? Is that what you think I'm doing?"

"I just meant—"

"I'm not *resting,* my dear. I'm taking care of things. I have the next twenty years to rest."

"What things?" Georgie blurted out, then immediately regretted her tactlessness. "I just meant, can't they wait?"

"There are details that need to be taken care of after someone *dies.* I'm taking care of a great many loose ends by myself."

Georgie felt an electrical humming in her fingertips, like a piano tuner possessing perfect pitch, oversensitive to her mother's sharp keys. "Ma, I've offered to help you every time we talk. You insisted on doing everything yourself."

Estelle missed a beat but quickly recouped, saying in a glacial voice, "There are legal documents that only the widow needs to deal with—so I'm told by my lawyer. Then there are personal effects of your father that I don't feel it would appropriate for you to be going through."

"Okay. But I could come in, take you to lunch . . . ?"

"I'm not really up for doing lunch!"

"Right."

"There is something important I need to discuss with you, just not yet. I'm not ready."

"About Daddy?" Georgie's heart flapped in her chest.

"It has nothing to do with Adam. It's a problem that needs addressing soon, I'm afraid. I put off dealing with it because of your father's illness. Oh, I can't think of that now. I'm too worn out."

"Okay, Ma. I'm here when you're ready."

Georgie hung up and stared out the window at the sun filtering through the trees so that diamonds of light created a mosaic on the cement of the patio. The dogwood was just beginning to blossom, its silky pink and white buds still clutched tight like small fists of hope.

She spent the night battling the vivid memory of her dying father. The emergency room loomed in her mind, how its putrid, urine-colored light pulsated as if trying to regulate her heartbeat. Patients were rolled in, schools of fish wiggling to their doom, lunch meat of predators. Doctors—with ID tags hanging on chains around their necks, like keys to the kingdom of hell—sped by in motorized precision. One patient clutched her abdomen and pleaded in Mandarin; another ancient body clucked nonsensically. A woman with big patches of baldness in her otherwise drab brown hair moaned, "I can't pee where I sit, in the hall, like a dog. A decent person would unhook me." The young nurse on duty gripped her clipboard so hard her fingers drained of color. "I'm sorry; I can't allow you to get up. You'll have to use the bedpan."

Georgie had kissed her father on his sunken cheek and patted his clammy forehead. But she couldn't make herself say good-bye to him. As if standing at the end of a diving board several feet too high, she'd contemplated the downward-falling motion, the anticipatory headfirst landing, that ripping open of the water's skin, followed by total submersion. It had struck her as a shocking request to make of anyone, this leap.

By dawn, the pain of remembering that last day had turned Georgie pallid and gray; anxiety swelled like a fat lip. When she swallowed, her throat hurt. If only she could dial her father's cell phone number and ask him to order her some antibiotics just in case. She called in the hope of hearing his voice. Instead what she got was, "The number you have called is no longer in service."

Not in service. Kaput.

She stared outside her window at the brisk, clean morning in early April, the air hinting of lilacs, at a future for which she was lacking some fundamental adult skills. Grown women of thirty-six didn't call their fathers at the slightest tickle in their throats, did they? They waited their turn, sitting in the overcrowded offices of doctors who barely knew their names or faces, who would not embrace them on the street, who didn't kiss their cheeks before writing out a prescription for penicillin.

"I can always call Mom," Georgie said aloud, testing the notion, and then dismissing it. While she could spread her legs in a stirrup for a stranger with the best of them, having her mother prescribe for any of her orifices seemed too intimate a request. "Or Nina. She could ask Elliot." Shame flooded her the way it might a widow receiving notice that the bank was foreclosing on her home. Who would rescue her?

She remembered three months after Jesse's birth, alone constantly due to a heavy workload at Luke's investment firm, Georgie had been sleepwalking through her life. It was a different kind of misery from what she was feeling now, but still, it offered her a compass, a frame of reference. It was the only other time she could refer to when the world had turned upside down like a snow globe, all the pieces falling on her head. Alone with her infant, she'd been beyond exhausted from wakeful nights and breast-feeding, metamorphosed into an animal state: bloated, weeping liquids, and losing weight at a staggering pace. She'd experienced the world from a distance as her own existence shrank down to hands, mouth, and breasts, to orchestrating the successful merger of these body parts, her son's and her own. Relief finally came from the loud, greedy suckling, until the next feeding, the next demand.

Nights had been an eternity. By the time Jesse was four months old Georgie had stopped sleeping. The baby was sometimes up three times between midnight and eight, so out of protest—to the cheat of a few hours' rest—her body gave up sleep. Her nerves, ever-vigilant soldiers, went on permanent alert. One night Jesse's cries took on a different tenor, urgent shrieks rather than affronted wails, his face flushed a deep mauve, his body stiffening into a rod of anger and pain, his head wobbling frantically against Georgie's chest.

"What's the matter with the little bugger now?" Luke murmured, having fallen asleep hours earlier. Her husband struggled valiantly to wake up, his legs doing a breaststroke motion, his arms reaching out for his wife before he sank back into a stupor.

Georgie tiptoed into the other room and called her father's emergency pager. It was after two a.m. An hour later Adam showed up in rumpled clothes, with his doctor's bag and a sample bottle of amoxicillin. When he looked at his daughter, his eyes penetrated through her despair, like the lights of the coast guard on a lifesaving mission.

"Sounds like my grandson has a little ear infection," he said softly, his voice lulling Georgie into the first state of relaxation she'd felt in days. He kissed her lightly on the forehead, his lips as dry as paper. "It's his mom I'm more concerned about. I've been worried about you. I don't want to interfere, but I think you could use some help around here."

"How can such a teeny person can be so demanding and terrifying?" she asked, her whole body chattering from fatigue, the sight of her father a familiar token from home here on her topsy-turvy planet.

"I can prescribe something to help you rest," Adam said. "I'd like to pay for a woman, a baby nurse, whatever they call it these days, to pitch in for a few weeks."

"Crisis averted," Lucas—suddenly awake and peeking into the vestibule—said in a jocular voice. He was hugging his naked chest, on his way to the bathroom in his boxers. In a quick once-over, Georgie cataloged her husband's worst features: a rather large, egg-shaped head, a chalky Anglo-Saxon complexion, and pointed reptilian toes.

Lucas called out as he retreated, "It's a generous offer, but I can cover the expenses if Georgie needs help. Thanks so much for the house call, Dr. M. You're our hero."

"You're our hero," Georgie whispered into the morning, imagining her slight sore throat as a case of undiagnosed strep, which would lead to rheumatic fever and, subsequently, heart disease, all because her father was not alive now to prescribe her the proper pills.

Without turning on any lights or pulling up the white shades embroidered with crescent moons, she padded into her kitchen with its squares of multicolored ceramic underfoot, its Corian countertop, its glazed backsplash. She poured water into her Mr. Coffee and thought of how her breasts swayed as she moved, how ridiculous she might look to a Peeping Tom, topless in her ex's boxer shorts, the suburban sexpot who hadn't gotten any in a year. While the coffee brewed she took a long, tearful shower, her heart clenching in her chest. She chugged down two Advils in hope that by the time they wore off, so would her sore throat.

Her laptop computer buzzed, signaling her to pay attention. The nutty aroma of Kenyan coffee, one white rose gracing her goose-necked vase, the sun through the back window so long armed it reached her cheek—these earthly touchstones were supposed to pump her with incentive. Sipping coffee out of her dad's old fishing mug, all she could think about was waiting for her parents to call after rounds of chemotherapy and early-morning radiation. She had had many late nights of scanning medical journals on the Internet, becoming well versed in medicine after a lifetime of resistance. Memorizing the vocabulary of war: autologous stem-cell transplants, harvesting, reinfusion, and the newest, sleekest missile in the arsenal, monoclonal antibodies. Hope ignited in all its glorious shades of gold and then diminished, dimmed to a twinkling yellow light before petering out in a blink.

She picked up the phone, hand slightly trembling, as if it had aged three decades overnight, and dialed Luke's number.

"Hey, good-looking," her ex said when he heard Georgie's voice. "Did I forget something? Jesse's toothbrush?"

"No. Where is that boy of mine?"

"In the bedroom sleeping. It's real early, George. What's up?" She imagined him scratching the patch of eczema at his temple where the hair met his face. His one source of mild discomfort, his only vulnerability. She used to tease him. How, she asked, could anyone exist for nearly forty years immune from any real pain?

She replied, "Nothing much. What are you guys doing today?"

"Not sure. Maybe brunch."

"Luke, Jesse's nine. He doesn't do brunch."

Her ex exhaled. "Listen, did you call to rank me out? Not that I couldn't use a good ranking, but I haven't even had my eggs and Ovaltine."

"Right. That's not why I called." Why had she, exactly? Certainly she wasn't hoping for an outpouring of emotional support from a man who was as proud of his powers of repression as other males were of their pectoral muscles or their sports cars. Fiddling with her cereal spoon, she fibbed. "I have to be in the city for a . . . party tonight and thought I might stop by." What was that? Familiarity might breed contempt, but loneliness was certainly breeding familiarity.

"Okeydokey. I'll keep some dessert for you. I've got Ben and Jerry's, three flavors. If I'd known you were coming, I would have bought flan."

"Death by Chocolate."

"Coconut custard pie with whipped cream on top."

She smiled, remembering how adorable Luke had been during their courtship. "There's still time to shop, but no need. Oh, and Luke, don't keep Jess up if I'm late, if the, uh, party runs late."

She hung up the phone, thinking, *I'm a moron*. The glow of nostalgia warmed her cockles nonetheless.

A chilly spring evening. Georgie walked through Soho three times, strolling down its narrow, cobbled streets that hugged and protected, stopping in chic designer shops and makeup boutiques, galleries, and a gay-and-lesbian bookstore. She bought nothing but cherry cough lozenges for the slight sensation of pain still present, contemplating the idea of dating an ears-nose-and-throat man. At nine fifty, she cabbed it up to Park Avenue and Sixty-sixth Street, home of Lucas Xavier Carter.

"C'mon in," he said, eye candy in his worn jeans, blue wool sweater, and moccasins. He looked the same as the first time she'd spotted him at a party, trying to balance a ham brioche with a cannoli on one flimsy napkin. Georgie had thought he looked a bit like a stockier Hugh Grant with even less pigment. She must have been smiling his way, for he glanced up from his complicated juggling act and shot her his dazzling grin.

She fell in love instantaneously—the way you might with a verdant landscape or a pearly beach or an airbrushed magazine spread— his downward-slanting mouth, the right side of which refused to cooperate when he attempted his "got the world on a string" smile, his up-on-the-tip-of-his-toes stride, his muscular calves from years of racquetball and morning runs, his baby-fine hair so light that summers in the Nantucket sun had turned it the color of corn, the lapis blue of his eyes. If only she could have skated on his shiny surface and never cracked the ice with her blade, Georgie would have stayed married to him forever.

Now she barreled her way past him into his three-bedroom bachelor pad. Her former home was a six-room palace decorated mostly in rich autumnal shades, dark leather and wood, raisin-and-charcoal Persian rugs, the walls now repainted a forest green except for the almond-colored bedrooms and terra-cotta-floored kitchen. The living room boasted a working fireplace and mahogany bookshelves that used to be chock-full of Georgie's hardbacks and were now, sadly, working at half capacity (holding Lucas's first editions of unread books and some paperbacks from business school). Since Georgie's departure, he'd installed Jacuzzis in each of his two bathrooms, and a fifty-seven-inch television in his home office.

"Where's Jesse?" she asked.

"In his room. Asleep once again. He tends to do that before seven thirty a.m. and after ten p.m." He smiled.

For a moment they stood looking at each other. "Maybe I should go," she said.

He blinked but didn't answer. "It's your nickel."

"What a strange tribe you come from, everyone clean and well mannered and speaking that weird language," she said.

"Hey, that kid of yours, he's half weird-tribe too. And what about your even weirder tribe?"

"I'm an Ashkenazi Jew with a genetic link to those moaning Russians who prostrate themselves on the temple floor in despair," she'd explained to this unnervingly chipper man on one of their early dates.

"How exotic. Exotic is sexy." Thus, her "exoticness" was what first attracted Lucas to her the way entomologists were drawn to rare scarab beetles.

"Come here," he instructed.

She smiled. Apparently her ex enjoyed backward movement as well.

It took fifteen minutes, from the time of her arrival, until they were in their birthday suits. Lucas's was nice—trim, long, and muscular, with bulges in all the right places. Here he was—this man with a chronically underactive conscience and a clever penis—dating his twenty-five-year-old assistant and still willing to bed ho-hum, middle-aged Georgie. You had to love him, she thought defensively. "Listen," she said, as they lay in precoital anticipation. "This can't mean anything."

"I know," he said, diving headfirst into her breast. "Of course not. Don't want to piss off Zoë."

Zoë was the assistant with whom he'd begun a conjugal relationship about five minutes after his marriage fell apart. This Georgie knew because he was so stupidly honest. ("I only felt her up once while we were married. It was the Christmas party. I was drunk and we were fighting all the time.")

"You two exclusive?" she asked.

"Hmm," he said midsuck. "I guess. *She* is, anyway."

"How nice for you," she answered, arching into his mouth.

"Very," he said, sliding her legs apart and inching two fingers into her.

"You must be very happy," she hummed, palming his ass. Such a cute ass! Had she forgotten? The rest of his nether regions weren't too bad either, she rediscovered.

"I am." He groaned. "Very, very happy."

She kissed him deeply and tugged on his hair.

By the time he entered her, they came almost immediately, in tandem.

Short and sweet, Lucas style.

"You know," she cooed afterward, still drunk with lust and forgetting. "We need to do this more often. It makes for more congenial coparenting. Don't you think?"

He looked at his ex-wife with appreciation shining in his eyes. "I've always thought so. I'm game if you are."

It was ironically perverse, Georgie acknowledged, how much more she enjoyed Luke's company now. When they'd been married she'd been acutely aware of how awkwardly they fit. It was as if they were two images photographed in different time zones and locales, and then pasted together to odd effect. She'd experienced the severity of their mismatch as far back as their honeymoon in pastel blue–and-white Greece. When the pictures had been developed, they told the story of the newlyweds' disassociation. In one they were standing together without touching—she tan and frowning, he gritting his teeth into the Mediterranean sun—the Parthenon, that ancient and majestic edifice, crumbling behind them, a witness to their mistake.

THREE

At six ten a.m., she arose with a start. She'd had a dream that began with her mother appearing in a short black shirt that showed off the long, sleek curve of her legs with just the hint of a blue vein snaking down her right thigh. She'd bent over to whisper in Georgie's ear, "I'm taking your father to the hospital. Charlene will be here to watch you."

On April 9, 1968, Martin Luther King Jr. was buried while her father lay in Columbia New York–Presbyterian Hospital with a bleeding ulcer brought on by some nondescript "emotional problem," as her mother and aunt called it under their breath. All that week, names and phrases muttered by Charlene on the telephone slid apart and together in Georgie's four-year-old mind: napalming in Vietnam; "snick," which, for years, she would confuse with the name of a candy bar; Emmett Till; riots in Watts, Selma, Birmingham, and Memphis. (These last three she'd clumped together, picturing them as old ladies in their church dresses and pillbox hats.) Slouching over in her father's maroon leather chair, Charlene stared at the television, which was mumbling something about an earlier attempt on King's life. After a letter opener had been plunged into his chest, the surgeon had remarked on the blade's proximity to King's heart. "One sneeze and he might have drowned in his own blood," the housekeeper clucked, shaking her head in remembrance.

Charlene shielded Georgie from the television, guiding her away from the procession, from Coretta King's tearstained face, memorialized behind her sheer veil, like the curtain that falls at the end of a Shakespearian tragedy. Instead of Charlene's usual hearty dinners, she prepared peanut butter–and-fluff sandwiches on Wonder bread served on Estelle's favorite Wedgwood china. "You're a good mama, Leeny," Georgie had said, cuddling into the portly woman's embrace. Her own mother was away more than usual that week, either at work or staying past visiting hours with her father. This was nothing new. Most nights, if not Charlene, it was her father who tucked Georgie into bed. He'd read to her from his original copy of *Babar the Elephant* while she slowly dunked her two Oreos in milk, then broke them up to make them last longer. But it was always Charlene who met Georgie at the door after school each and every day, who laid out the coffee crumb cake she loved, and asked how the world was "treatin' you."

Eight nights later Georgie heard her bedroom door creak open just as she was slipping into the long tunnel of sleep. The streetlights shone through the window blinds, forming bright parallelograms on the floor and illuminating the figure of Adam, smiling so that the deep grooves at the sides of his mouth and the vacant look in his eyes were accentuated. "I missed you, Georgie Porgie," he said, bringing his face close to hers, smelling unfamiliar, antiseptic, a mixture of rubbing alcohol and Vaseline. Georgie looked up at him, frightened by his sudden, short-lived drizzle of tears.

"I'm sorry if I scared you, sweetheart. Your old dad was a little sick and a little sad. I know your mother was away a lot this week. You were probably very lonely. I'm sorry about that, too. She's my angel, your mom is. When you're down and out, she's the gal you want by your side, taking care of everything. Don't forget that."

To which Georgie replied, "Okay, Daddy. I'm glad you didn't sneeze."

He smiled quizzically and hugged her to him. "Me too, sweetheart."

Now Georgie blinked into the anemic gray light of Luke's bedroom. She seemed to see her father sidling up beside her, smiling wistfully, scratching his peppered beard, unaware of the awkwardness of his showing up here. He whispered, "Call your poor *mudder*. She needs you more than you think."

Georgie shut her eyes. There she was in her ex-hubby's bed—his birch-white legs wrapped around rumpled sheets, his mouth slackened like a dimwit's—being visited by visions of her father! What Freudian textbook would she find this in?

Oh, and how pathetically redundant to be making this mistake again! She remembered how, years ago, the sight of her fiancé in his starched navy suit and polished wing-tip shoes disoriented her so completely that she felt like an amnesiac waking up in someone else's life. She'd wondered if, to quash loneliness and fear at her father's first diagnosis, she'd been giving a cute, cool stranger blow jobs, like some teenager desperate to be liked. After all, what she and Luke did best was to eat out at expensive restaurants and have the kind of frisky, unabashed sex you had not to get more intimate, but to experience something so utterly foreign to you, so other.

More than a decade later, she was repeating bad behavior. She crept her way into the bathroom, peed, brushed her teeth with Luke's electric gizmo, and rushed to dress. The most important thing now was for Jesse not to learn of her slipup, for him not to be filled with a false, boyish hope. If she charged out of there and into the nearest phone booth, maybe she could slip into her mommy suit before breakfast. Outside, the sky was pissing rain onto the majestic avenue. She pulled her red Windbreaker over her head as her sneakers sloshed through puddles.

As soon as she stepped foot into a diner on Lexington Avenue, the phone was in her hand. "Lucas," she whispered, stealthy as a spy.

"Uh?" She'd woken him. He was wiping the fairy dust from his eyes in preparation for another wonder-filled day. "Hey. Where are you?"

"I left early. I wanted to call and make sure you were okay with what happened. It's understood that Jesse won't find out?"

"Sure. No problem. Do you . . . you know . . . want to talk about it?" He'd learned this line—after much coaching—by the end of their six-year marriage.

"There's nothing to talk about, Lukie. I just regressed, that's all. With everything that's happened lately . . ."

"Gee, thanks. Glad to be of service."

"Excellent service," she said, bowing her head. "Thank you. I'll pick Jess up later. I'm going to hang out in the city. Kiss him for me." And she hung up on the one man who'd seen her disrobed since Clinton's second term in office.

After a quick plate of scrambled eggs in the diner and her required two cups of coffee, she decided—not without misgivings—to
visit her mother without prior warning. She ordered a latte and a
croissant to go.

Twenty minutes later, standing in front of Estelle's white high-
rise, Georgie felt her left shoulder begin to itch; a patch of scaly skin
would grow. "Good morning, Miss Merkin," the doorman greeted
her, the gold buttons on his jacket sleeve winking in the deflected
light of the overhead fluorescents. Everything was the same: the marble entranceway, the toile-covered wing-back chairs, the potted ferns.

Estelle answered the door in her housecoat and bare feet, the
phone perched under her chin, saggy jowls, puffy eyes. During the
last few weeks of Adam's life, she'd begun to gain weight and had
taken to wearing dresses, which she called her "pitiful muumuus."

"What are you doing here?" she asked, although the doorman
had already announced Georgie. "You're soaked. Come in." In a
wholly different tone she said to the person on the other end of the
line, "I promise to call you back about him. I haven't spoken to
Georgie about it yet. Yes, I'll get back to you."

Odysseus waddled to Georgie's side, wagging his scruffy tail
with the last ounce of vigor left in him.

"Hey, fella," she said, petting his matted fur. *Poor old thing.* "Good
to see you." She wanted to ask how he was holding up without his
master but caught her mother's eye first.

"Ma." She handed her the soggy bag of breakfast. "I figured you
could use this."

"I could use a great many things," Estelle said, placing the phone
back in the cradle. *"This"*—she waved her hand in Georgie's general
direction—"is a surprise."

Avoiding scrutiny, Georgie dodged into the kitchen for a glass of
water. The usually immaculate room was shockingly messy: the
countertop riddled with crumbs, a knife pasted to it with butter, the
milk left out without its plastic cap, and a pastry box of doughnuts
opened to reveal four out of a dozen gone, grape jelly from one
smeared on the floor. The table was covered with newspapers, dirty
coffee mugs, and, shockingly, an ashtray filled with cigarette butts
(her mother had never smoked). Estelle had mentioned on the phone

that she'd given Charlene some time off, that she "just couldn't bear her company at the moment." Georgie squeezed her thumbs into her palms as if to turn off the valves to her mounting trepidation.

"Jesse's at Lucas's for the weekend," Georgie called out, playing dumb to this obvious decline. "I decided to come in early to get him. Thought I'd stop by here first and see how you were doing, Ma."

She reemerged, glancing from left to right, noting the cardboard moving boxes lining the living room. They were open, some packed to the rim, some half-full. Peering into one, she saw her dad's things, his crumpled, worn shirts, wrinkled ties, papers, and old medical journals. "But I won't bother you if you're busy . . . ?"

"Busy?" Estelle wrung out that one word like a washcloth. "Your father died four weeks ago. What could *possibly* have kept me busy since his funeral, Georgie?"

"Ma, I didn't mean anything. Whenever I ask you if I can help, you say no."

"You're an adult. You could have decided to come to the city without my coaxing."

Georgie thought for a minute, her mind rooting around for that statement's trapdoor. Would a better daughter have been able to excavate the dense muscle of her mother's heart, to unearth the genuine pearl of her desire?

"I need to be home for Jesse. I need to plan ahead and know if you'll be here. It's hard for me to be spontaneous."

Estelle straightened her posture, her eyes focused ahead, narrow and cold, her body shivering like a tuning fork. "Please! You could come in any morning, like you do to meet an editor. Where else do you think I'd be, at the opera? I've been holed up here sorting things out. I lived with Dad for thirty-eight years. There's quite a lot to do."

"C'mon, I've been worried about you. But you've made it clear that you wanted to be by yourself for a while."

"I'm not exactly in the mood to socialize, to have brunch, Georgia. The truth is, I can't always anticipate how I'll feel from one minute to the next."

"That's why I've come now." She gestured in her mother's direction. "I brought you some coffee."

When she didn't respond, Georgie pointed to the proof in the paper bag.

Estelle shot her a regal, deprecating look and said nothing.

Fatigue settled behind Georgie's eyelids, the back of her neck. During the last few weeks, her mother's determination to grieve in private had echoed the style in which she'd cared for Adam; she had insisted on accompanying him to each and every one of his treatments alone. Her father had acquiesced. When Georgie had volunteered to take him to chemo, he'd say, "Stellie can handle anything, whatever happens. She's an ox, your mother."

The one concession her parents had made during those awful months was to stay in steady contact with Georgie via the phone. Her mother's cell was on day and night. For the first time in Georgie's life there was an umbilical connection between her and her mother, a whisper of fear, although their conversations were always confined to speaking about Adam, how he was feeling after a particular treatment, both his body and his spirits. Mostly what they shared was reportage and brainstorming on how to bolster him up with more Ensure, fewer solids, a list of his favorite old movies on video, such as *Thirty Seconds over Tokyo* and *The Longest Day*, a special visit with Jesse.

They'd clung to the practical details of illness, how to manage the side effects of the toxic juice being shot into his veins: malaise; a metallic taste in his mouth, like sucking on pennies; a profound depression nipping at the edges of his mind. Their mutual project—to save this man—plaited them together, so that father, mother, daughter finally made up the three strands of a thick braid. It unraveled with Adam's last breath.

Walking to the windows, Georgie realized the climate had changed, reminiscent of Indian summer. The heat could stick around until late September, a series of gloriously warm days, until you became giddy at the thought of how you'd cheated Mother Nature into caressing your face with the sunny palm of her hand. It would end, suddenly, with you waking up one chilly, dank autumn morning, shivering under your sheet, goose bumps rising on your skin.

She longed for the forgiveness of the New York streets. She ran her hand through her hair and gazed out at Central Park, her childhood getaway with its tickle of sloping branches, the smell of chestnuts and dog, the green promise of miles away from her mother.

"I'll go out shopping for you," Georgie said. "Whatever you want. That's why I'm here."

"Thank you. It's not necessary." Estelle peeled back the lid on her cold latte and took one sip. *"Please* don't bring Jesse here. I don't mean that I wouldn't love to see him. Of course I would. I'd rather see him than anyone else—any other *living* person, that is. All those new babies being born every day . . . it's horrible for me. I'll be forced to witness that again starting next week." She frowned, her nose flaring in disdain. "I don't want my grandson to see me like this."

"Like what, Ma?" Georgie asked gently. "Sad?"

"I have to be able to tell someone to leave when I need to be alone, and I don't want to do that to Jess. I can't tolerate too much . . . contact."

"I won't stay long."

The pilot light behind her mother's eyes flared up. "I wasn't talking about you. Do you have any idea how much I've had to do here on my own? Packing up all of Dad's things, his papers, his clothes. Going through the piles of unpaid bills—with Dad's name on them—paying them all, calling and informing everyone to change them to my name. We were months behind. Everything, we'd let slide. The death certificate and the will, taking his name off the credit cards, out of the phone book, for Christ's sake, so those awful people won't call asking for him, trying to sell him things. It never ends." She strode across the room to deposit the leaky cup onto the grand piano.

Over the last few weeks, Georgie had imagined her mother curled in her bed, lights low, shuffling to the refrigerator to spoonfeed herself some of Charlene's sweet-potato bisque, then sneaking Hostess Sno Balls, peeling off the cake's marshmallow hat and eating that coconut top first, straggling into the glisteningly clean bathroom, finding solace by soaking in the Jacuzzi. Certainly Estelle had paperwork to complete, but Georgie had assumed that she was besieged by lugubrious heartache, not chaotic commotion. Yet here she was, her mother, so fitfully filthy, so stunningly active!

"Why are you doing all of this now? I mean paying the bills, yeah. But cleaning out his stuff. What's the rush? Maybe you should get away for a few days."

"Take a trip? I'm not really up for that, Georgia. This is what I have to do. I'm the one who has to live with his shirts and shoes, without him." She cleared her throat. "There are other things, things I can't talk to you about now."

"What, Ma?" Georgie asked, panic, in the form of gossamer wings, flapping on her back.

"Oh, never mind."

"Is there something about Dad you're hiding from me?"

"Don't be melodramatic." Her mother glared at Georgie. "You can look through his books and things, see if you want anything."

"Now?"

"If you're in a rush." She shrugged. "I hope it's still here when you want it."

"I'm not in a rush. I don't feel ready to look through his things. Can't it stay here a little longer? I need a little break here."

"*You* need a break? You have no idea how difficult it was for me, your father's illness. I was the one there with him the whole time, not you. Not your aunt Lily, his only sister. Not his only daughter. No one. Just me."

"I saw Dad every weekend! Sometimes more. I spoke to you every day, several times. He didn't want me there at all his treatments."

"Yes, that's what he *said*. He didn't want you to suffer. And Lily . . . well, she was no use to him. *I* was all he wanted. Do you understand the strain all those years of being the only one he wanted, needed to help him—" She stopped abruptly.

Georgie's eyes were fixated on a white patch of carpet, illuminated by the torch lamp's mellow glow.

On opposite sides of the Merkins' huge trapezoidal living room, they retreated into their separate grievances. Georgie remembered waking up in the middle of the night to use the bathroom, and peering into her parents' room. She must have been no more than ten. Her mother and father had lain with their backs facing each other, like inverted parentheses, the vocabulary of symbiotic love concealed inside. The mounds of pillows her father always slept with and the crisp satin sheet, which he had wrenched free from the housekeeper's neat hospital corners, hid his face. Her mother's expression was partially eclipsed by her hair, which swirled around her arms, dusting her chin and cheek. Georgie had had the urge to tiptoe in, to touch her mother's skin and smell her sour night breath, to feel close to that face that was vulnerable only in slumber. Instead she padded quickly back to her own room.

Estelle spoke first. "I don't know if I can stand it, frankly. This is my house. My house. I'm the one who has to live here."

Georgie nodded. Her right eyelid twitched.

Estelle glanced in her daughter's direction, the phone now in her hand, and her finger on the redial button. She walked over to the dining room table and picked up an envelope from her pile of condolence cards.

"There is something you can do for me, come to think of it," she said. "You can take Odysseus. I can't stand having that animal around. He reminds me of your father. I know that sounds cruel, but that's just how I feel right now."

"Okay," Georgie said tentatively. "I'd have to get the car. I can't take him on the train, I don't think."

Estelle waved the request away. "Never mind. It's too much trouble."

"It isn't. I was thinking out loud. It's fine. Jesse would like that. He loves Odie."

In that instant Estelle's face relaxed, her mouth softened. "Yes, it'd be good for him to have the dog around. Just not good for me."

"Okay. I'd better get going. I'll be back by five and pick up Jess a little late. Luke won't care."

As Georgie stepped into the hall, she glimpsed back to see her mother. Estelle's head was bent down over the letter in her hand. She stroked the envelope with her fingers, her expression hidden from view.

By the time Georgie made it out of Manhattan with boy and dog in tow, she felt cracked with exhaustion and sorrow. There was no hammer and nail, no needle and thread, no tool that could repair her. Fitfully weaving her way down the Harlem River Drive in her metallic gold Intrepid, she'd snuffed out her fourth and last cigarette before picking up her cargo. It was the first time she'd smoked since college, but she was a lifelong New Yorker who'd gotten a driver's license after thirty, and driving through metropolitan traffic brought to mind Dante's first circle of hell.

Back in town, Georgie decided to stop at the pet store near her house for supplies. Pet Peeves was sandwiched between Kaput Kafe and a Pilates studio. The streets were devoid of those sleek young things—in black getups, clutching PalmPilots and silver cell phones—and bustling with uncoiffed moms in exercise gear, cajoling their screeching tots into strollers and SUVs. Georgie noted how restful it was to live with the tedium and bedlam of child rearing.

Since the onset of her father's recent illness, Georgie had found solace in the quieter pace the suburbs afforded her, including the two parks within walking distance of her street. One acted as a spacious bridge between her neighborhood and upper Yantacaw and, in the spring, erupted in an orgy of tulips. The other boasted the Champlain Memorial Gardens, with its hundreds of varieties of amethyst, midnight blue, ballerina-pink, and canary-yellow irises. "Am I losing my cool, my New York edge?" she once joked to Nina.

Georgie unlocked the door to her house, bedraggled and stinky from tobacco and sweat, only to find Abigail, the cat, staring at her blankly. Not so much as a meow, not a purr. "Nice to see you too," she said.

Odysseus barked with old-dog glee, then lunged with everything left in him. The cat—too agile to have her butt sniffed—hissed and hightailed it into the bathroom, home of litter box and hearth.

"Hey, Abby, it's okay, girl," Jesse called out, chasing his kitten around the stairs and then cradling her in his arms.

Another kind of person would have poured herself a drink, Georgie observed, but there were no alcoholic beverages in her abode, not a benign bottle of chardonnay, not one lone beer. She remembered the plastic vial of Klonopin now lying at the bottom of her underwear drawer, alluring in its promise to deliver her into a state of obtunded fuzziness. But all the pills did was cocoon her in a softer layer of sadness mixed with a nostalgic comfort made possible by a parent's prescription pad. She settled for kava kava tea and ordered takeout from the nearby Chinese restaurant, typical suburban fare: Hunan Too-Much-Brown-Sauce-Slathered-on-Everything.

Her shoes made a clopping noise against the hardwood floors, and the wind whistled outside her windows, the curtains billowing where she'd left them open on the bottom. It was chilly and damp inside. She sighed and the sound seemed to carry to the back of the house.

Jesse looked up at her with his dark chameleon eyes capable of changing expression in a millisecond. Sometimes Georgie ran her fingers across his cheeks while he slept, to feel the delicious smoothness before adolescence took it from her. "Mom, are you okay?" he asked, shifting his weight from foot to foot.

"Sure." She was clearing the kitchen table of her son's orange, yellow, and blue school memos—most written by a PTA president infatuated with superlatives—to make room for their takeout. "I hate cooking, that's all."

"That's not what I meant. It's just . . ."

Georgie stopped all her gathering and shuffling and stood still. "What? Are you worried about something?"

He bit his lip. "Kinda," he said. "You were so stressed coming home."

"Honey, the dog was whining."

"Yeah." He shrugged, starting to ease back out of the room, lithe as a mime. He moved with a fluid grace few boys his age could boast, without awareness of this advantage.

"I hate driving in the city. Talk to me." She reached out for him. "It's okay."

"It's whenever you see Grandma. I mean . . . why don't you get along with her, anyway?"

Oops, she thought. "We get along okay." She hugged her son and he didn't flinch. If she was lucky, she still had a few good years before he'd reject his old ma.

He glanced down at his sneakers. "Grandma's a formidable woman."

Georgie grinned and nodded, thinking of the *New Yorker* cover that depicted Manhattan as dwarfing the rest of the country, replacing her mother as the personification of that central landmass. "Where'd you learn that expression?"

"From Grandpa," he said, smiling wistfully.

The back of his neck summoned with its sweet vulnerability. She rubbed it gently. "Poor Jesse."

"Nah. I'm okay. Grandma's called me a couple of times on my cell," he confessed. He bit the side of his mouth. They'd discussed the reason for the phone Lucas had purchased for him: emergencies to be used only for having to reach his parents. "I'm sorry, Ma. I guess I gave her the number."

"Hey, it's okay. She can call you at home, though."

"I know. It just seems like she hasn't wanted to see me lately."

Jesse's forehead creased. Estelle and Adam had always adored him, their one and only grandchild. Jesse at his third birthday: shirtless, wearing his grandma Stellie's sunglasses and holding her key ring in his chubby fist, belly and cheeks smeared in chocolate icing from his birthday cake, he sang, "Oh, the shark, babe, has such teef, dear. And it shows 'em pewly white" along with his grandmother. Grandpa had been the nurturer, the warm embrace, but Grandma was a steely constant when everything around Jess was switching orbits: his parents' divorce, the move to the suburbs, Adam's illness and death.

"She needs a little time to herself to figure out some things. You're going to spend a lot more time with her soon, I promise."

Later, after tucking her darling boy into bed, Georgie headed for the living room with its bookshelves, potted plants, faded Persian rugs, and sweeping damask curtains in an amber yellow that covered the huge window facing the back garden. Black-and-white photos of Jesse adorned the walls, charting his growth from babyhood until his ninth birthday. Her father had taken the best of them. She'd chosen the couch for its palomino coloring, golden with creamy white seams and pillows. There she lay, reading *The Age of Innocence,* sipping peppermint tea and petting the dog, who let out a few dry coughs. Finally she began to doze.

When the phone rang, she was startled to view the ID number of her aunt, Lillian Merkin.

"Hi," Georgie said, jolted into full consciousness.

"I just wanted a moment to speak with you, dear. Is this a bad time?"

Sliding into an alert "up" position, she said, "No. It's okay."

"It's about your mother."

"Oh." Knees shaking, she asked, "Is something wrong?"

"Not in that way." Aunt Lily whispered the relative pronoun as if it were too dreadful to voice. "I've never involved myself with your business, Georgia. Whatever's gone on between your mother and you, I've never thought it my place to interfere."

"Uh-huh?"

An exasperated sigh emanated from somewhere deep in Aunt Lily's bony chest. "This time just seems different, considering the circumstances: our poor Adam's terrible illness, our losing him. . . . Everything Stellie has had to deal with since then and even before, much more than you or I were privy to, dear."

"Oh." That syllable, that letter, spilled right out of Georgie, fluid and accessible as water.

"Normally I'd never presume to talk to you about Stellie. But this isn't a normal time, is it? I know we've never been as close as I'd have liked. But I've always appreciated your sweet nature, just like Adam's."

Uh-oh! She closed her eyes and listened to the dog's jagged breathing.

In a histrionic voice, Aunt Lillian proclaimed, "I don't wish to hurt your feelings, dear. Since your dad's passing I've noticed that you haven't been around much to help out in the apartment, in all the organizing, and bolstering up poor Stellie at such a difficult time."

Georgie licked her lower lip, unsure how to respond without sounding defensive or petulant. In a measured tone she said, "I've tried to be. I've offered. I don't know what my mother's told you."

"Not a word! Your mother would never, ever complain about you or encourage me to call. This was all my idea." Lily's voice fell off, as if someone had forgotten to thread the next reel into the projector. A moment later she said, "Stellie's such a strong woman, so admirable. Sometimes you have to ignore what she says and rally around her, do what you know, in your heart, is best. Your mother could really use more support right now, whether she's asking for it directly or not. She's had a lot more on her plate than you realize— emotionally, I mean, more has happened than you're aware of, even more than losing poor Adam."

Fear rustled its leafy hands around Georgie's heart. "I don't understand. Is something wrong with Dad's will, or was he hiding something?"

"Goodness gracious, nothing like that! You can put your mind at ease on that score. It's not my place to say, dear. I don't want you to judge Stellie too harshly. It's been an extremely painful time for her, as you can well imagine."

"Of course I do. I lost my father, too," Georgie squeaked. *Pathetic.* "I'm also in mourning, I mean."

"It's not the same, dear. Estelle lost her other half. She feels *literally* cut in half. You know how your father worshiped her. Adam is—was—so kind, so accepting and so encouraging of your mom's strength. He was her safe place. Now she's lost that."

Georgie was no shrink, yet it was clear to her that her aunt was experiencing a bizarre transference of her own. She'd never loved her husband as much as she had her brother.

"I do know that, Aunt Lily. I know how close my parents were, how awful this must be for my mother."

"Of course you do, dear," Lily said, her voice finally softening into spongy compassion. "All I'm saying is, you and Stellie need to make an effort to come together as a family. I've told her this, too; don't think I haven't. It's what Adam would have wanted. I hope this call didn't offend you. I did this, in large part, for Adam's sake. I won't bother you again like this, dear."

With that, Lily hung up.

Georgie sat in seamless quiet for several minutes, the room bathed in a muted gold. "What was that?" she asked Odysseus. "Did my father have a second family in Utah?" She smiled at the absurdity of her question. "Or was Aunt Lily being her usual dramatic self?" In response, the dog raised his big furry head and opened his bloodshot, dubious eyes—but just for a second. Then, with one cough that sounded more like a clearing of the throat, he conked out.

Georgie had been eight years old when her mother delivered her first stillborn baby, a tragedy that would not be repeated often in Estelle's long, impressive medical career. It happened sometime in the night, because when Georgie woke up, her mother was still asleep and not to be disturbed. Her father led her by the hand over to the sofa. He stroked her hair so tenderly she grew frightened.

"Listen, Georgie Porgie, you should know that your mom had a rough time at work. She might feel kind of bad for a while."

Georgie nodded mechanically. "Is she okay?"

"She's just feeling sad and tired. Would you like to peek in, just to make sure?"

"Yes. Please."

The door to her parents' bedroom was ajar, and her father encouraged Georgie to sneak in without making any noise. In her attempt to be extra quiet, she stumbled over her own feet and fell on the hardwood floor near their bed.

"What's going on? Adam?" Estelle opened her eyes, startled. "I told your father I need to rest. This is a bad time for me, Georgia."

Georgie glanced up to see her mother wrapped in her blue silk sheets reaching right up to her chin. Her face was dun colored, her eyes watery shells empty of expression. Georgie backed up, quickly, in her bare feet; the floor was slippery and cold.

Later that day Estelle was home when Georgie returned from school. Estelle dressed her in the red velveteen coat with the white fake-fur collar and walked her to the children's zoo. They fed pellets to the rabbits and goats and Georgie tried to climb on the sculpture of Alice in Wonderland. That night her mother washed her back with a rubbery sponge that looked like a round hunk of Swiss cheese.

"I'm sorry I snapped at you this morning. It's hard for a child to understand this about her own mother, but I'm a person who deals best with problems alone." Her eyes grew glazed and distant and her voice thin. "I tried to explain it to Adam even before you were born. I'm good at bringing babies into the world, not at raising them."

Estelle's voice caught like a fishing line and she squeezed the sponge firmly so that water cascaded down Georgie's shoulders. "Never mind that. You're used to your dad. Most people are not like him. You'll see when you get older how special he is, how lucky you've been to have him as your daddy." She shook her head and *tsked*. "You're one for two, kid. That's better than nothing."

FOUR

A few nights later Georgie tried to log in a few hours of work before bed. As always, the ribbon of need—to make her own money, to not be too dependent on Luke's wealth—tightened in her gut, the tug more insistent since her act of debauchery with her ex. She sat at her desk, naked toes rubbing against her chenille throw rug, and checked her e-mails. Despite herself, she felt pleasantly surprised when the phone rang and she noted the phone number on caller ID.

"Hell's bells, this is prophetic. I was just thinking of you, Lukie. What can I do for you at this late hour?"

He emitted a strange muffled sound, then said, "The thing is, Georgie, I feel a little bad about that, your thinking of me. Seems there's been a change in my life. A sort of development."

A pang of fear. Could the big C, cancer, have put a pox on his house? This—her brain's misguided clanging of the alarm—was followed by an instant wash of relief. It was Lucas to whom she was speaking! People born under lucky stars were immune to such plagues.

"Spill the beans, Lucas. What good tidings are you calling me with?"

"Right, right. Uh, where's our boy, by the way?"

"He's in bed. Quit stalling. You're making me nervous."

"Yeah, right. Seems Zoë's moving in with me."

That the heart could flip-flop seemed proof of its retentive powers. Loving Lucas was passé, and yet his "news" now rang the final death knell for this love (i.e., no more of her expired spermicidal jelly hidden away in the cabinet under his bathroom sink).

"It *seems* like she is?"

In a contrite voice he said, "Yeah. I guess it does. Anything to get her to back off from all the marriage talk."

"Your commitment just knocks me right out." She laughed.

"You're not all depressed about this?"

"Not depressed, Luke. We're divorced. Remember? Maybe I'm a little hurt that you're letting her manipulate you into this right after our little rendezvous."

"It doesn't necessarily mean no more quickies for you and me," he said with puppyish glee, misunderstanding her. "We just have to be more cautious and plan our little tête-à-têtes for when Zoë's not around."

Georgie took a sip of her cold tea, waiting, no longer sad—thankful even. "I don't think so."

"Are you upset?" he tested.

"I'll get over it," she said acerbically.

"Gee, Georgie. You don't have to get over it so fast."

She hadn't. But he wasn't going to see that. He could no longer have it both ways, years of working ridiculous hours, and putting noisy friends and colleagues all around their relationship when he was with her, then expecting her to grieve the demise of their relationship all these years later, just to stroke his already intact ego. "Anything else, Lukie?"

"Huh? No. That's it. Except I was wondering . . . you want me to tell Jesse, or do you want to do it?"

"Ah, Lukie, such a sense of entitlement, such expectations, someone to do the dirty work for you. Let's see . . . who would be the logical person to tell your son that your girlfriend is moving into your apartment?"

"When you put it like that . . ."

"I'm just a natural wordsmith, Lukie. You can tell him next weekend. It can wait."

Hee, hee, she thought, remembering the last conversation she'd had with their son about Zoë.

"Ma, you wouldn't like her," Jesse had exclaimed. "She dresses like Britney in those magazines you write for. Her belly button shows and it's *pierced.* She wears these itsy bitsy glittery T-shirts"—he inched his index finger and thumb together—"and these tight pants that are so low her crack shows. She's supposed to be a grown-up. I mean, *c'mon.*"

Lucas said, "Well, if there's nothing else?"

"Not a thing. You can go now, Luke. You're the one who called me." Once again, her ex had delivered Georgie from morbidity with his rollickingly idyllic life.

She brewed a new cup of tea, then curled up on the couch, Odysseus at her feet, and glanced at an article in *Harper's Bazaar* entitled "Happiness: Your Life Versus Your Neurotransmitters." She wondered if she, too, might not benefit from swallowing some serotonin, if pills would sheathe her nerves like those inflated snowsuits new mothers encased their babies in whenever the temperature dropped below forty degrees.

"I'm being ridiculous, right, Odysseus?"

No reaction. No quick arching of the eyebrows, no longing look at the door, nothing. Just labored breathing.

"Odie? Honey?"

The dog did not look at all well.

"Oh, please, no. Not now, Odie, please," she pleaded, walking tentatively to the animal's side. She knelt down to stroke him, adrenaline rushing to her fingertips as if to infuse the poor creature with one last burst of energy. Odysseus didn't lift his big head, not even after she'd repeated his name several times. He shuddered, the slits of his eyes pink around the black pupils. Any idiot could see he was going fast.

With a deep breath, Georgie dialed the number of the all-night animal hospital in downtown Yantacaw. She didn't know what she expected the woman with the girlishly high voice on the other end to say when she pleaded her case against waking up Jesse in order to bring a sick dog to the veterinarian. What she wanted to say was, after her experience with her father, even a canine emergency room would give her goose bumps and loose bowels. "You know, I'd rather not alarm my son unless it's absolutely necessary," she said. How was this her dilemma, this receptionist or veterinary nurse or whatever her title was?

But the voice on the telephone said with rabbinic patience, "You might try the Community Clinic. They offer mobile vet care." When she got no response, the voice illuminated, "They make house calls."

"Great." Georgie imagined the library on wheels that used to travel around the Upper East Side when she was a child.

While waiting for a Dr. Ian Weiss of Community Clinic to get on the telephone, she muttered her prayer of pleases.

"This is Dr. Weiss," a man's gentle voice said. "How can I help you?"

"It's my dog—my father's dog, actually. I think he's dying."

"Why do you think that, Mrs . . . ?"

"Georgie. Georgie Merkin. He's just lying here, not responding to anything. He's an old guy, a sheepdog mix, and those big breeds don't live as long. He's over thirteen."

"Uh-huh. How's the dog's breathing?" he asked calmly. "Is it labored? Quicker than usual?"

Georgie bent down to feel Odie's warm, furry chest, to smell his particular dog musk, the stale, wet pretzel odor of his rotten mouth. "I don't know. He does seem to be breathing hard."

"Any fainting? Loss of appetite? Swelling of the abdomen or legs?"

She glanced at his soft white belly. Since he was lying on his side, it was tough for her to determine any changes in its shape or size. "Come to think of it, he hasn't shown much interest in dinner the last couple of days. I've only been taking care of him this week, so I'm not really sure of his habits."

The doctor cleared his throat politely. "It's not easy to assess the situation over the phone, Mrs. Merkin, but . . ."

After she'd explained her situation, Dr. Weiss asked for her address and reassured Georgie that Odysseus's condition could probably wait until morning—and if for any reason it couldn't, there was nothing he could do anyway, short of making the animal comfortable. But he'd try to swing by the house at the end of his shift.

She dozed off under a blanket and dreamed that her father's death had been a case of mistaken identity. Some other poor schmuck was buried in that long cherry box, sandwiched between Grandma and Grandpa Merkin in the overcrowded cemetery off the highway. It was the day of his funeral and the apartment was packed with mourners, everyone in black choral robes, nibbling on Charlene's fried chicken wings. Georgie was the only one who noticed that her dad was in his bedroom, oblivious to the event, sorting through his papers, as usual, clad in his long underwear and bathrobe, his skinny calves peeking above torn slippers. She followed her father, leaving her mother laughing flirtatiously with both Lucas and Georgie's college boyfriend, talking to them as if they were her charges, top students of hers or chief residents whose conversation she found pithy and delightful. Lingering in the archway, unseen and unheard, Georgie observed the look in her father's eyes, one of desperate anguish, and for a moment she had the feeling that his spirit had vanished without him, just lifted up through his neck and shoulders so that only the husk of his personhood remained. Yet in this dream world, his body was not ailing.

In the semireality of waking, Georgie believed the person ringing her doorbell was her father.

"Coming," she trilled. Her heart was bobbing like a toy ball, straight up to her throat. Scampering about, she threw off the covers, slipped socks on her feet, hopped to a standing position, and ran her hands through her matted mop. She almost tripped over Odysseus, who barely moved. On the other side of her door stood a tired-looking man wearing a beige leather coat, boots, and faded jeans, with a shock of dark hair blown into round amber-brown eyes. Everything about his face, she noted, was pleasing: his full lower lip and off-center smile, his long cheeks and narrow nose that widened at the tip, his slight overbite. He was thin and tall—over six feet, she estimated—and was holding a worn doctor's bag.

"You should ask who it is when answering your door at"—he glanced at his watch—"at twelve thirty at night," he admonished kindly.

"Who is it?"

When he smiled, his eyes grew even wearier, crinkled at the corners. "Dr. Weiss, the vet from the mobile clinic." He extended his hand and shook Georgie's firmly. "May I come in?"

"Wow, you're really here." She stepped out of the way, glancing down to check on her attire: sweatpants, a T-shirt, no bra.

She thought of her father and how his oncologist, a fellow doctor with whom he'd had a ten-year professional relationship that bordered on friendship, had never shown up for a house call.

"I live here in town. I figured I'd check in and see how the old boy is doing on my way home."

"That's so nice of you. Call me Georgie, by the way. Merkin is not my married name. My ex-husband's name is Carter, but I never took it." She giggled at the inanity of her chatter. "Can I get you anything, some tea maybe? Or water?"

The man looked askance and she realized he wasn't really listening. He was searching for an animal. On cue, Abby Abyssinian jumped down from her perch atop the center-hall stairway banister and landed close to his feet. She arched her back. When he bent down to stroke her, she relaxed into his hand.

"Hey, there, sweetie," he said in a soft voice. "Who are you?"

"This is Abigail."

The cat purred in pleasure, nudging her ruddy red head into this stranger's palm.

"You certainly do have a way with animals."

"I should hope so." He grinned and stood up. "I take it this isn't your sick sheepdog."

She smiled back. "No. He's in the living room. I'll show you."

Odysseus was still lying on his side, just as he had been hours ago. "Poor Odie," she said, crouching down to pet his head. His eyes were closed, perhaps for the last time, in preparation for his long death sleep.

Ian Weiss knelt down next to Georgie and caressed the dog. "Odie, old guy, how ya doing?" he asked in a soothing voice, stroking behind the animal's ears as he spoke.

Had anyone touched her father so gently when they examined him? "The scan was terribly painful," her mother had reported back to Georgie once, near the end. "The technician didn't seem to grasp how agonizing it was for Dad to have to lie in that position for so long."

For just a second Odysseus seemed to perk up. He looked at Dr. Weiss, eyebrows shifting in question, and wagged his tail halfheartedly, as if he knew this good man was here to help him.

"Let's see what's going on." He unzipped his bag and took out what looked like an ordinary stethoscope. "This may feel a bit cold, buddy," he said. The dog didn't even flinch when it touched his skin.

He removed the instrument from his ears and turned to Georgie. "His heart rate is up. I think you should get some tests done in the morning, a chest X-ray and ECG. Do some blood work."

"Okay," she said, her own heart racing in tandem with the animal's. "Do you know what's wrong?"

He hesitated, rubbing his index finger across his upper lip as if deciding what to tell her. "I'm guessing it's dilated cardiomyopathy, a form of congestive heart failure. But I can't confirm that without tests."

"Oh, God." She couldn't believe it! She was crying.

He reached out, as if by instinct, and patted Georgie's upper arm. "Hey," he said. "It's not as bad as it sounds. I won't lie to you: Odysseus here is not in great shape, but there are medications he can take to help improve his quality of life."

"You mean he's not dying?"

He sighed. "The thing is, Ms. Georgie, he's an old dog and he doesn't have a whole lot of time left in him. But he's not dying, not today."

She wiped her nose on the sleeve of her T-shirt and nodded. "Okay. Sorry about that."

"It's okay. It happens all the time. Losing a pet is an emotional thing."

"It's not that. No disrespect to your clients. Anyway, thanks so much. I'll bring him in to see you after I take my son to school."

"You might want to talk to your father before you do anything, since he's the owner." (She had to give the man credit: He was a good listener.) "He may have his own veterinarian with his own ideas, although I'm pretty certain of my diagnosis."

Georgie's eyes welled up again. "I can't do that. My father recently passed away. Odysseus is mine now." And he *was*, she acknowledged. Her mother had unburdened herself of him as a form of penance for avoiding the rot and stench of Adam's disease, the boat ride to Hades, for standing on the other side of the River Styx and not one inch closer.

"I'm so sorry," the doctor said, his face stricken.

"Thanks. It would be nice to squeeze some more life out of Odie for my son's sake. Jess, my son, he's only nine, and he was very close with my father. Plus, with the divorce, he's gone through a lot in his short life." She babbled away, despite her mounting mortification. "I'd just like to hang on to the dog for a while."

"Of course," he said, rubbing her shoulder. "We need to keep this guy alive."

"Yeah." She licked the briny tears above her mouth, and then wiped her face of saliva. "How about a cup of tea? You came all this way."

"That's not necessary. I live right here on Maple Ave. You're on my way home. So I should be pushing off."

"Of course. It's late. I don't know how you do it."

"It's only two nights a week," he said, stuffing his stethoscope back in his bag. "I don't mind the late hours."

Didn't he have little ones who woke him up before school? There was no ring on his finger, yet Georgie knew the rumor mill—all the gossipy, frustrated, horny, or bored moms in town—would never overlook Dr. Weiss's single status.

"Don't feel that you need to take Odysseus to me," he added. "I'm sure you have someone for adorable Abigail. . . ."

"Dr. Jackson."

"Right. She's very good. She'll be able to fix him up as well as I could."

"No. I'm bringing Odie to you." She walked him into the foyer toward the door. "What time tomorrow?"

"Call the office in the morning. They'll fit you in."

The next day proved Dr. Weiss correct in his diagnosis of poor, weak Odie. Georgie left the clinic with two prescriptions and instructions to feed the dog low-sodium food. By the time she returned home an hour before Jesse was due from school, her workday was shot and she was feeling strung out. Until her father's second bout with cancer, she'd been at home in medical surroundings the way children of undertakers were comfortable with corpses. Now even a vet clinic was capable of setting off her anxiety, as an innocent friend might activate your home alarm. All those yelping pups and hissing cats responding to the sound of the chimes each time the front door opened with another middle-aged mommy bringing in the family pet, and the young woman behind the front desk answering the phone in her syrupy voice, kitchy-cooing even the mutts being sent off to extinction. Georgie had sat in the waiting room, trying to ignore the specters of doom hovering above her dog's head.

She figured it was only right to call her mother about Odysseus—just in case Estelle decided she wanted to be included in the animal's ultimate fate—after all, he had lived with her all his life.

The receptionist crooned in her cheery voice, "East Side GYN."

"Hi, Carole, it's Georgie Merkin."

"Oh, *Georgie,* hello. How have you been, dear? Let me just buzz your mother. She's in with a patient, but I'm sure she'll want to speak with you."

Carole put her on hold to the tune of Barry Manilow declaring, "I write the songs that make the whole world sing!"

"Georgia, what's wrong? I'm in the middle of a vaginal examination."

"Right. It's about Odie. . . ."

"Odie?" Estelle repeated the name blankly.

"I need to speak with you about him. He's not doing well, Ma. The vet examined him, and it turns out he has a heart condition. I think he may be dying." She glanced over at the chronically prone canine, his red-rimmed eyes.

"They all do, most sooner rather than later. You'll have to deal with it this time. Okay, Carole, tell her I'm coming. I need to go, Georgie."

Her mother rang off without saying good-bye.

"Dad," Georgie whispered into the silence. "I really need to talk to you. It's me, the family mutant, the one who has no talent for dealing with sickness."

The dog groaned in his sleep. The world grew still.

Later that afternoon, she drove Jesse to his friend Gus Cowley's house for an impromptu homework fest. "We're doing this really cool weather system," her son explained, bouncing a bit in his seat just like the old Jess.

"Groovy. You'll have to demonstrate for me when you're finished. Don't eat too many chips."

"Ma! We're scientists," he said, as if such exalted beings would never dream of consuming junk food. "And Ma, no one uses the word *groovy* anymore. It makes you sound old."

After kissing him one too many times for his taste, Georgie drove off to the local YMCA for some much-needed physical release. There on the treadmill, she encountered her friend and neighbor Charlotte, a London-born economist who'd given up her career to marry the CEO of an accounting firm.

"Hi there, Georgie," Charlotte waved, her beryl blue eyes smiling. "Come keep me company." She pointed to the free machine to her right.

It had been weeks since they'd seen each other, although a few days after Adam's funeral Charlotte had arrived on Georgie's doorstep with a salmon quiche and a tureen of homemade lentil soup. She called regularly just to chat, never prying, ending each conversation with the refrain, "Please let me know if there's anything I can do." But Georgie didn't because there wasn't.

"Hey," Georgie said. "How's everything with you?"

Charlotte shrugged. "Can't complain. Fred's been traveling quite a bit, to Cleveland, of all places—if you can believe it—poor man. I've been home with the boys. We miss him, of course, but can't complain."

Charlotte almost never complained. She lacked the gift of self-flagellation, the voice in the head that harangued most of Georgie's friends, enticing them with the promise of self-betterment if they listened and obeyed. When Georgie had first met Charlotte, she was in the process of adopting her second child. Her tales of woe: four miscarriages, diagnosed as having an incompetent cervix, her own brief tango with death resulting from complications following the last pregnancy, which ended at twenty-four weeks, the fact that her own mother had been prescribed the synthetic hormone DES, which damaged Charlotte's reproductive system and made it nearly impossible for her to bring a pregnancy to term—all this was recited in a chatty manner to Georgie, in her friend's kitchen, over a cup of Darjeeling tea.

"How've you been?" Charlotte asked. "How's your mum?"

"She's all right, I guess." Georgie looked straight ahead out the window, at a view of the car dealership across the street with its showcase windows of gleaming new Volvos. "I seem to have inherited my father's sweet old dog from her. Turns out he has congestive heart failure."

"How *horrid*. What bad timing! Did your mum foist him on you?" She broke into a jog. "Because she's had her share? It must be terrible for Jesse."

"He doesn't know what's wrong. He thinks Odie's just sad about my dad."

"What a love that boy is," Charlotte said, sweat glistening on her collarbone. "Not a mean bone in his body."

"Yeah, he's a good boy. Last night the dog gave me a real scare." Georgie sped up so that she huffed when she spoke. "Did you know there's a mobile vet clinic where the doctor comes to you at midnight?" When her friend expressed surprise, she said, "The vet was very nice. I wish my internist or Jesse's pediatrician were as attentive as Dr. Weiss. If I even call Essex Pediatrics after six p.m., I piss off Dr. Feldman."

"Oh, I've heard she's a raving bitch. We see Lind. He's excessively boring. But Dr. Weiss . . . I know that name. Kathy O'Connor uses him for that god-awful mongrel of hers. He's supposedly very dreamy." Charlotte shot Georgie her dazzling smile, overbite and pouty lower lip. A bead of sweat shone under her nose.

"I hadn't noticed that. I was busy panicking."

"He's separated from his wife and has a daughter around Jesse's age, I think."

The muscles around Georgie's neck and shoulders tensed. She shrugged. "All I know is he can stick a thermometer up my dog's ass."

"Lovely image. No wonder you're a writer. Maybe when things are a bit better for you?"

"Charlotte, I can't even think about men right now."

"Of course not," she said, blushing a deep coral. "I'm sorry. Who am I to give you advice in that department after my humiliating dinner party fiasco?"

"Exactly," Georgie said, grateful for any excuse to change the subject.

The year before, Charlotte had arranged an intimate gathering for a few couples. Her husband, Fred, had invited a colleague from work to be Georgie's date, a rude man with rosacea on his left cheek, as if his last girlfriend had slapped it there. He spoke in a loud businessman-on-a-cell-phone voice and referred to Georgie as "the lipstick lady." (Fred had described her line of work as "writing articles on makeup.)" The next day Charlotte apologized profusely, promising to buy Fred *The Idiot's Guide to Social Skills*.

No one really understands, Georgie thought. It wasn't as if her friends were suggesting the widow jump back into the saddle.

"The vet *was* very nice, very compassionate about Odie. But this is not a good time for me."

"Speaking of bad times and the wrong man, how's your sexy ex treating you? Is he *deeply* understanding about your loss?" Charlotte had listened to her friend whine about Lucas's emotional impenetrability more than once, about how self-revelation in his presence was far more embarrassing than drooping breasts or thighs pocked with cellulite.

"*Deeply,* although he's a bit preoccupied with his own problems. He's moving in with his so-called girlfriend in order to placate her and distract her from thoughts of marriage."

Charlotte laughed. "Sounds about right. Well, when you're ready, love, I'd call that sweet veterinarian before some other hungry divorcée snatches him up."

FIVE

Georgie was ready sooner than she'd anticipated.

Two weeks later, poor Odysseus died in his sleep. She'd run some errands after lunch, and then picked Jesse up at the bus stop one rainy April afternoon; when she got home the dog's body was stiff and cool to the touch. Gone. His soul en route to join his owner's. Dr. Weiss, DVM, materialized in his forest green van within twenty minutes of her hysterical phone call. He patted Jesse on the shoulder and said simply, "I'm sorry." No platitudes, no "He lived a full life" garbage. Jesse's eyes filled up and his face reddened. He shrugged as if the death of his dead grandpa's dog were "no big deal, man," and slinked off to his bedroom, chewing hard on his bottom lip to prevent spillage of embarrassing tears.

"I can take care of this for you," the veterinarian offered.

"It's okay. I'll talk to him."

Shaking his head, he said, "Of Odie. I can take him." He paused. "Cremation. If that's what you want."

Georgie glanced out the window at her five yellow tulips, lonely amidst the weeds in the unkempt lawn. She imagined dragging the poor beast's body to the backyard, wrapped in a beach towel, digging a massive hole with a shovel purchased at Henry's Hardware until her arms ached, then heaving the decaying animal inside.

"That would be great," she said, nodding, not able to look down at the living room rug at the ever-stiffening mutt near her feet. "Thanks so much. I can't imagine what else I'd do with him."

"Just part of the job." Glumly, Dr. Weiss added, "The worst part."

She reached for her bag, for her checkbook and pen. Her hand, she noted, was trembling. "How much do I owe you?"

Dr. Weiss's eyes were bloodshot, his expression morose. Odie's passing might have been harder for him than for her. "Don't worry about that now," he said, as if the exchange of monies would be sacrilegious at such a time.

The week ended with Georgie insisting that Jess sleep over at his friend Gus's house. He needed levity after the recent chain of events that concluded with the news of his daddy's new living arrangements. ("I can't believe he's letting that Britney Spears clone move in with him! Can't you stop her, Ma! First Grandpa, then Odie, now this! I'm so stressed! Kids aren't supposed to be this stressed!") The atmosphere at home had turned maudlin: Georgie in the same pair of sweats for three days running, not applying a dab of makeup, barely managing to find her shoes, once driving Jess to school in her slippers. The demise of her father's dog had prompted another shivah fest, albeit in more casual attire. She had not attempted to hide this relapse from her son.

After dropping him off at Gus's, Georgie purchased a bottle of chardonnay and cold sesame noodles for dinner. Back home, three glasses of wine later, a warm fluidity ran under her skin, filling her with a mixture of rage and sloppy generosity.

When the phone rang, she didn't hesitate or let the machine answer. The drink coated the passage between her and Estelle, her brain short-circuited by the gray mist wrapped around its crevices, all warning systems shut down. "Hi, Ma. What's up?"

"I wanted to check and see how Jesse is doing with Odysseus's death," Estelle declared imperially.

"He's upset."

"I might not have cared about Odysseus at this point—I'm sorry but that's just how I feel."

"Yes. You've said that. You've been expressing your feelings with refreshing candor these days."

"Excuse me," Estelle replied. "I can't suppose what trauma might have caused such a change in me. I hope you didn't tell Jesse! I certainly do care about how *he* feels. I know how much that dog meant to him."

"I'd let you talk to him, but Jesse is staying at Gus's house until tomorrow afternoon. How are you?"

Estelle sniffed, then blew her nose noisily. "I'm holding up. You know, that's the first time you've asked me how I'm doing in I don't know how long."

"What can I say? I'm just being my typically thoughtless and self-involved self."

"That's *not* what I meant, Georgia. I guess you've been preoccupied."

"Not at all. I'm A-okay."

"You sound . . . odd."

"Thank you." Georgie was having considerable difficulty weaving the noodles around her fork.

"I *meant* peculiar."

"You know me, the neighborhood weirdo."

"Georgia! Did you take too many Benzods? I told you to be judicious in your use of the Klonopin. I explained to you that they are long-acting and can produce psychological and physical dependence."

How adorable, Georgie thought. Her mother couldn't even fathom that she might indulge in something as pedestrian as alcohol. Of course, Estelle also didn't think she was savvy enough to understand the risks associated with medication. "No, ma'am, scout's honor. No drugs for me."

Estelle sighed the sigh of a medical professional being tested by a noncompliant patient. "You sound off. You should rest so that you're able to be there for Jesse when he gets home. I know how busy you get, working on those articles of yours."

Yes, Georgie thought—stabbing the soft flesh between her thumb and index finger with the prongs of the fork—*I've been busy with my cute little life.*

"Losing a pet can be very upsetting for a child. I hope you're doing things to distract him from all this sadness."

"I'm taking Jesse to the circus to ride the ponies just as soon as he gets home."

"Georgie, what is wrong with you tonight? I meant take him to the movies or let him out in the fresh air. That boy doesn't get enough exercise. Let him ride his bike for a change instead of sticking his head in front of a computer screen all day."

Insufficient physical activity was a familiar refrain of her mother's—the one point of intersection between Lucas and Estelle— but certainly not her only dispute with Georgie's parenting style. The divorce had been the pinnacle of Georgie's bad decisions, the smaller ones acting as steps on a ladder leading to this faulty construction. Estelle had not been reticent with her prediction: Georgie's new life was bound to cause Jesse irreparable distress.

"You know how many articles there are these days, in my medical journals, about the dangers of computers to children's physical and mental health?"

"In your gynecology journals?" Georgie asked.

"I would take him to the planetarium if I had any energy at all."

"You go lie down, Ma. Oops, the water is overflowing in the tub."

"Georgie, there's something I've meant to discuss with you for a while, and—"

"Not now. Impending flood. Gotta go."

Georgie shuffled into the living room and plopped down on the couch with her fourth glass of wine. Minutes passed while she stared out the side window at the rain drizzling down onto her driveway. She dialed Luke even as the voice in her head advised against it. *This is exactly why you can't sleep with him,* it said. *You get confused.*

"Hello?" said a bored female. Zoë.

Georgie hung up fast, with a ping of her heart's harp strings.

Normally she wouldn't have skimmed the phone book for the home number of Dr. Ian Weiss on Maple Avenue. Now it struck her as a marvelous idea, as therapeutic as a mood elevator or grief counseling, only wrapped in a much prettier package. She imagined Nina and her husband Elliot, Charlotte and Fred, and Luke and Zoë ascending the plank to Noah's Ark while she stood on the pier with her mother in their respective muumuus.

The thrill that ran through Georgie when she viewed his name in the white pages reminded her of freshman year of college, how she'd sit in her dorm room, torturing her split ends, talking on the

telephone to hunky Dennis Fieldstein, the lucky fellow who'd relieved Georgie of her virginity. The walls pulsated around her and instinct instructed: *Do it now, before sobriety, with its hard slap of sense,
rouses you to a history of wrong choices and bad timing.*

"Hi? Dr. Weiss?" she exclaimed in a perky cheerleader voice. "It's
Georgie, Georgie Merkin."

He hesitated. "Yes, Ms. Merkin. How are you and Jesse holding up?"

He remembered her son's name! She bit down on her mouth to
take the edge off her sudden burst of jubilation. "We're okay. Considering . . ."

"It's often harder than one anticipates. I'm sorry about Odysseus.
I thought we could keep him around a little longer."

"It's not your fault. I wanted to thank you for being so kind, so,
you know, attentive. It's rare nowadays. I mean, you know . . ." *Slow
down there, cowboy.*

"Just doing my job."

"Right. Still." Her wineglass stood half-empty on her end table.
She swigged from it. "Wisten," she said. "Umm. Sorry." She giggled.
"I was wondering if I could, uh, reciprocate, you know, the favor. I
mean, take you out to lunch, maybe. I'll send you a check, of course,
the second I get the bill. It's not that. I thought next Saturday, if
you're not too busy with work or removing doggy gonads." It was a
stretch.

He laughed. "As it turns out, we don't perform doggy gonad re-
movals on weekends. But it's not necessary."

Her spirits sank. She was not a hot babe or a sweet young thing.
She was an intoxicated, middle-aged client whose dog had died. "I'd
like to anyway," she said, her voice quavering.

Pause. "Sure, why not. It would be my pleasure."

Just like that, she had a date. Magic.

My pleasure. My pleasure.

Words to chew on.

The following Saturday dawned in a cloud of gray drizzle. Despite
the discouraging weather, Georgie felt blissfully giddy, as if she were
surfing on top of her emotions—on a lovely, cool wave—above the
gaping, murky ocean. They'd planned to meet in the city after she'd

dropped off Jesse at Luke's place. Ian Weiss would be at Pearl Paints on Canal Street buying his daughter, Ava, an art kit for her upcoming tenth birthday. They had decided to cab it over to Little Italy for lunch. She'd purchased a new sweater for the occasion—lavender with a scoop neck—to wear with her black jeans, little black boots, and silver teardrop-shaped earrings.

That morning she was in the bathroom applying mascara when in walked Jesse.

"Gotta pee," he said, eyes still shut.

"Hello to you, too." Georgie peered at her reflection in the mirror. "Do you think my bangs need trimming?"

"Huh? Ma! I gotta pee."

"Right." She dashed out. "Two minutes! Breakfast!"

"So what are you and Dad doing today?" she asked once her son had shuffled into the kitchen, hair still mussed, goop in eyes. Coffee was brewing. Oreo O's were poured. Milk was on the table. Maybe all could be right with the world again.

Jesse sat down and began spooning cereal into his mouth. "Dunno," he said, slurping.

"I hope you're not planning on sitting around playing video games all afternoon. You could use some physical exercise." Amazing how her mother's anxieties could still slip through the psychological umbilical cord.

"I might. If Dad has work to do." With Jesse's expectant eyes on her, she knew she should snap at this information. "What's up, Ma? Where you going today?"

"Whatta you mean?"

Lapping up the milk in his bowl, he shrugged with forced nonchalance. "You look good for a change, that's all."

"I do?" She leaned over and kissed the top of his sweaty-smelling head. "Thanks. Don't eat like that; it's disgusting," she reprimanded, because he'd earned it. "Into the shower with you!"

Pearl Paints was huge, industrial-looking, and very crowded. College art students—in capri pants, tie-dyed shirts, chunky-heeled shoes, bandanas, everything pierced—mulled about, chattering away about "supplies." An inky smell hung in the air. What pungent scent from her childhood did this recall? Printing press? Ditto machine? While Ian Weiss shopped purposefully, Georgie loitered near the door, fingering the rows of stamp blocks: cats, dogs, fancy letters, rosebuds, sexy ladies, and pursed lips.

"Okay," he said, huffing and puffing, having run upstairs and back within a minute. "I found this advanced mosaic-making kit." He was wearing a light blue shirt that reminded her of a May sky, faded jeans, and shockingly white new sneakers. For the first time in their acquaintance, he looked rested.

"Great," she said, smiling.

He inched his way toward the racks of fancy, overpriced popup cards. "Just let me pick out one."

Strolling toward him, she repeated, "Great."

"Are you always this agreeable?"

"Oh, yes."

He lifted up one card with a beach motif, a curvy woman standing in a bikini while two muscular men leaned on their elbows in the sand. "Hmm. Doesn't seem right somehow."

"You think? How's this?" Barbie in pink Cadillac with white poodle and Ken.

"Nah. Ava's not really a Barbie girl. Stacy, my ex-wife, doesn't like the whole nineteen-inch-waist, forty-inch-bust, perpetually-arched-feet thing."

"But Barb's in the driver's seat here," she said, noting a slight shift in her enthusiasm, wishing to instruct that ex-spouses were verboten.

The checkout line ran the length of the store. Ian apologized profusely while they waited, having settled on a card with a palace theme, a castle with drawbridge and moat, which read: *Today you are royalty. Happy Birthday, Princess.* "It's fine," she said, sanguine because, in this dusty store with its factory layout, the knotty ball in her chest had loosened for the first time in months.

Until Ian's cell phone rang. "Oh, hi," he said stealthily. "Yeah. Uh-huh. I'm there now. Getting her birthday present. Right. It's an art kit, like we discussed. Right. Okay, talk to you later. Bye."

Georgie licked her lips and didn't ask.

Ian smiled sheepishly. "Coordinating presents for the kid," he said.

"I heard."

Twenty minutes later the sky cracked—loud as a jackhammer— and broke loose with rain. By the time they left Pearl Paints, the streets had flooded with pedestrians, hooded and armed with inverted umbrellas that resembled upside-down petticoats. Drivers were furiously honking to no avail. Traffic was backed up for as far as she could see.

Georgie took his hand and tugged. "C'mon. Forget Little Italy. There are tons of Chinese restaurants around here, and I'm in the mood for wonton soup anyway."

Around the corner was a hole-in-the-wall—the Excellent Dumpling—tucked under scaffolding, rave reviews pasted to the windows. Soaked, they peered in, viewing a heavily Asian clientele. They grinned at each other and walked into the teeny, tightly packed restaurant, finding it hard to navigate between chairs to the one available table near the window. The walls and tiled floor were institutional green, but the smells of spicy duck and peppery brown sauce, succulent chicken and pineapple were marvelous.

A speck of dust flew into Georgie's eye and she attempted to root it out with her pinkie nail, ever so discreetly, facing the window so as not to be caught. "So," she said.

"Fine weather we're having," he said. "For a day in the city."

"My name's Georgie Merkin." She swiveled around, despite her runny eye. "Nice to meet you. I'm thirty-six years old, never mind how many pounds, five-foot-five, no communicable diseases, divorced, one nine-year-old son, a freelance writer. And you are?"

"Hungry!"

"I didn't bring any doggy bags of cheese crackers or whole-wheat pretzel sticks along. Sorry."

He laughed, extending his hand to shake hers. The feel of his flesh caused her body to sigh. "I'm Ian, veterinarian by profession, Giants fan, separated, divorce pending, one daughter and . . . what were the other questions in this survey?"

She shrugged, oh-so-flirty. "Standard stuff. Age. Height. Weight. Shoe size. Favorite color. Favorite dessert. That kind of thing." *Divorce pending*. The fluttering in her chest would have to be ignored. This date was just for fun, she kept telling herself, nothing more.

"Hmmm. Thirty-nine. Almost six-foot-two. One hundred and eighty-two pounds last time I checked, about three months ago. Size-ten loafers. Turquoise. Chocolate cheesecake."

"I love chocolate cheesecake! With graham-cracker crust. Good thing you didn't say carrot cake. I would have been forced to mutiny. It's my ex's favorite. It's like when you associate some food with having the stomach flu. It ruins the taste for you."

"Why did I get the impression that you two get along?"

"We do," she said, instantly angry that she'd slipped Luke into the equation. "It's just weird how, when you pick the wrong mate, it doesn't matter how amicable your divorce was; the whole debacle makes you feel like a failure."

"What happened with you guys?" he asked, the color darkening in his cheeks. "You don't have to answer if it's too personal a question."

"It's fine. You're my vet, remember?"

"Right. I've been trying to figure out the relationship."

Georgie smiled into her cup of tea. The room felt hot. She envisioned Lucas watering his plants, an expression of tender reverence on his face, one he reserved for living things that asked nothing of him. She couldn't say that Lucas resembled one of his flowering plants or a cool white tulip encased in glass, beautiful to behold, impossible to touch.

"Nothing exactly *happened*. We made a mistake. The timing was strange on my part or I would never have let our relationship get so serious. Lucas is a nice, light guy." She shot Ian one of her cutest smiles. "He's an hors d'oeuvre rather than a main course."

"A food metaphor!"

"What about your ex-wife?" she redirected, shifting in her seat, wondering if there would be reconciliations, the yellow light of caution flashing in her head.

"She's on the tall side. Five-foot-eight."

"I *meant* something more personal."

His voice lost that bounce of levity and dropped in pitch. "I loved her and she left me."

"I'm sorry." Georgie stared at her feet, which had ended up resting on the green vinyl seat of the chair next to hers. Quickly she repositioned herself into a more respectful pose, legs down, uncrossed, like a parochial schoolgirl.

"She didn't return the feeling."

"Wow, you mean *never?*" she exclaimed, perhaps with less sensitivity than was warranted.

"We got married young. Two years out of college, UC Berkeley. We moved back to New York and I started veterinary school. She got a job as a research assistant at NBC News. She's still working there. She's a staff writer now. It's a good job, flexible hours, conducive to parenting." His eyes beamed with nostalgic pride. "For the first five years we lived in a dump in Little Italy that probably should have been condemned. I didn't mind, but Stacy was homesick for California. Still is, I think. Her family is from Palo Alto; it's a nice life out there. We put off having a baby for the first four years because Stacy just didn't feel settled; finally we decided to move out to Yantacaw. I'm sure she'd go back to California now, if it weren't for the custody agreement and . . ." He lowered his head sorrowfully. "Her boyfriend. Stu Levin."

"Oh. Oh, I'm sorry." *I'm sorry?*

"I don't even know why I'm talking about this."

"Because you spend all day poking around animal innards and need a chance to vent?"

"I have friends other than four-legged ones. But men don't really discuss their embarrassing problems."

"Of course not." Slumped over her bowl of soup, she sipped her Diet Coke through a straw and watched him spear a wedge of bean curd. "It was Stacy who wanted the divorce?"

He nodded and the last ounce of healthy color drained from his face. "Yes. It was her idea. We'd been trying to have another baby, but she was feeling ambivalent about it. She kept at me, goading me. Did I want another? I was content with what we had, so I told her it was up to her." He smiled wanly. "That answer made her crazy. I was so happy with Stacy and Ava and the dogs—our family. Another child would have been great, too. I just didn't need one to be fulfilled. That made her nuts."

"Why?"

He shrugged. "She wasn't happy. She was struggling with figuring out what she wanted when I'd already fulfilled all my dreams. My contentment drove her crazy."

"I don't get it. What's so bad about being happy?"

"She wanted more. More socializing, more time spent schmoozing with the people at NBC, more friends, a bigger life."

Lucas would have loved that too, Georgie acknowledged, recalling a montage of evenings with "the guys" in which one would inevitably make a rude sexist comment about a girl who "could break a few mirrors" or "suck every dick in the company to get ahead."

Late nights on the number six subway train, coming home from these ventures, Lucas would touch Georgie's hand with cold fingers, his breath a puff of alcoholic lime. He'd wobble and grin, hoping not to pass out, slipping into his boyish habit of speaking with a sibilant S, his voice and eyes too lubricated to focus on Georgie.

"Despite her discontent, I was shocked when she asked for a divorce," Ian said. "Let's just say I was the last to know."

"You mean it wasn't precipitated by major blowups, separations, threats, late-night confessions, passionate reconciliations?"

"Is that what it was like for you and your ex-husband?"

"At a much lower volume. Lucas doesn't rant or scream. He has little to confess except for one semiromp at a Christmas party. With him, *passion* isn't exactly the right word. It implies a level of intimacy that is foreign to Lucas. *Energetic* is a better term."

His eyes widened. "Oh, dear."

"Sorry," she said, blushing, appalled at her own honesty. "My marriage to Lucas, other than having Jesse, was wrong, *dumb,* made for all the wrong reasons, which is pretty embarrassing. I was vulnerable. He was game. He's a good enough guy if you're not married to him. You'd like him." She waved away her entire explanation. "Has anyone ever told you you're easy to talk to?"

"As a matter of fact, many felines have. But you're the listener here. Thanks."

"No problem. Can I steal one?" She pointed to the platter of fried dumplings.

"Sure." He passed the plate, having eaten only one.

"I'll just have a couple. Too much fat," she said. Despite this declaration, nerves caused her to scarf up most of the serving. Nice man that he was, he sat in silence, not passing judgment, at least not aloud. Maybe they would end up good pals, veterans of divorce who met every few months to ensure that they weren't fucking around with their exes or calling them more than was merited, bad relationship victims groaning over bitter coffee.

After lunch the rain grew violent, ammunition spit from the sky. Their hopes of grabbing an Italian dessert were dashed as soon as they hit the streets. "Let's head for the subway," Ian shouted as if to elude enemies. Crossing Canal Street with dozens of other desperate travelers, they discovered the IRT subway entrance was boarded up, nailed closed. They stood gaping, two among a gathering of dolts.

Ian glanced left, then right, his hair flinging water. "We're never going to get a cab."

"Let's just walk." She was happy to be confronted with a solvable problem.

"You sure?" His eyes gleamed with admiration. "It's pretty nasty out."

"We'll stop for provisions. Umbrellas for starters. Coffee."

Looking down to avoid the monsoon, they headed north, through a haze of wetness, hugging their coats around them, dodging puddles. On a day like this not a soul was selling his wares; the good merchants of New York had all packed up and gone home. By the time she lifted her head to get her bearings she was lost. Georgie Merkin! A New York City lifer! To her right was a huge futuristic monstrosity with the words PUBLIC WORKS written in steel lettering across its chest.

"I've never, *ever* been here before. Or anywhere that even remotely looks like here. Where is *here*, exactly?"

Ian pointed across the street. "Maria's Bakery of Chinatown."

Before her was a quasi restaurant the size of a parking lot. "Catchy name."

Maria's Bakery affected the style of an institutionalized cafeteria and was divided into two camps—food and dessert—both without waitress service. The tables were bare but for plastic salt and pepper shakers. They felt the glare of eyes on them, the only Caucasians in the joint.

Georgie smiled at a handsome old man in a wool hat with

diamond-sharp cheekbones who was talking loudly to his friends. No acknowledgment. It didn't matter. She'd been transported outside of her life, the now-familiar ache of misery rinsed away by this sudden adventure.

They ordered coffee, almond cookies, and pecan pastry from among the hodgepodge of beige desserts squatting on doilies behind the glass counter. Goodies in hand, they proceeded to a table large enough to seat a family of six. "This is really good," Ian pronounced after biting into his cookie. "This place is like an Asian Automat. My mom used to tell me about them, the kind she went to all the time in Brooklyn."

"Did you grow up there?"

"Until I was six. After my parents' divorce, my mom, my sister, and I moved to Astoria, Queens. Then when I was ten, my mom re-married and we moved into my stepdad's house in West Orange. So, when Stacy and I decided to have a family, we looked at the towns I was familiar with and chose Yantacaw for the same reasons most New Yorkers do." He shrugged.

"Stacy started to hate the place pretty soon after Ava was born; she claims it's full of bourgeois bankers pretending to be artists sup-porting diversity while actually sending their kids to private school by sixth grade."

"Well, there are definitely those who do," Georgie said, thinking his ex could use a visit to an accommodating psychopharmacologist for personality tweaking. "But I can attest to the fact that there are just as many writers and editors using the public schools and having trouble paying their taxes as there are rich bankers."

Ian smiled wanly, looking down into his lap. "I always really liked Yantacaw—another strike against me, according to Stacy, who ac-cused me of being too undiscerning. We sold the house and both got small two-bedrooms. They live in one of the only houses under half a million in Oakdale."

On the lip of the more unwieldy, diverse Yantacaw, Oakdale was a quaint, leafy miniature of a town, devoted to maintaining its or-derly gaslit streets and superior traditional school system. In Georgie's opinion it was a claustrophobic fishbowl of a community that fed off of Yantacaw's medley of tantalizing urban delights—

restaurants serving a potpourri of succulent cuisines, two movie theaters that specialized in independent films, a jazz club, a rare-books store, a shamanic yoga center, a Stott Pilates studio, an array of chic upscale boutiques smelling of lavender and bergamot—without having to bear the burden of its problems.

Ian arranged his expression so that his face had the fresh, welcoming look of a tour director. "How about you? Did you grow up in New Jersey?"

"Upper East Side. I lived in the city my entire life until my divorce. Went to college and graduate school in New York. Never left, which is pathetic. I've been so insulated."

"Just loyal. So what brought you to the Garden State?"

In her last year in the city, she'd become more attuned to urban ugliness and the oppressiveness of the seasons: the dirty mounds of old snow lining the avenues, the urine-soaked garbage, the candy wrappers stuffed in soda bottles sticking out of the piles like flags. Her final summer as a New Yorker, she was acutely aware of the way the buildings incubated the heat so that it felt as if her neighborhood were being steam-pressed, people wilting and going nearly mad right there on the streets as teenagers and college kids rammed into their bodies without regard. The day she decided to move was hideously humid: air sticky, viscous as phlegm, overcast sky.

Her house was only the fourth one the real estate agent had shown her, and she'd fallen in love immediately; spacious with low ceilings and wood beams, it was bathed in a lush, apple green light. The room that with predatory enthusiasm Georgie had coveted as her office opened into the yard through swinging cedar doors. But it was the kitchen that had sold her the moment she walked into the white room with its long stretch of counter space and varnished oak cabinets. Sunlight streamed in from the floor-length windows, bouncing off of the seller's pots and pans with their pewter handles that hung overhead. Pairs of suspended glass vases, stuffed with dried flowers, decorated two walls. The ceramic floor was a montage of porcelain white, pistachio, aqua, and lavender. "This is great!" she'd exclaimed. It appeared to her as cheerful and foreign a place as a child's fantasy.

"Rationally, it was space that brought me to New Jersey," she told

Ian. "But actually it was dirt, noise, and ugly weather. For a year Jesse and I lived in a tiny two-bedroom in Murray Hill." She demonstrated the size with parallel-facing palms. "Incredibly overpriced. I got fed up wasting the Carter fortune on a home the size of a shoe box, while outside the air quality was hideous. I wanted to see how the other, saner half lived." She sipped her coffee. "My favorite cousin, Nina, lives in Summit, which was too suburban-affluent for me and too far from the city. I settled for close by."

"Good," he said. "That was good."

Exchange of smiles, the crackle of desire. *Friends,* Georgie's reasonable side reiterated to herself. *In the shape we're both in, anything more would be totally self-destructive,* she thought. For a while they sat in silence, crunching on their sugary treats.

"This is fun," he said. "We'll have to do this again sometime."

Such a huge promise wrapped in one small adverb.

SIX

"**H**ey! It's Nina. Are we on for dinner tomorrow night? My week is so crazy-busy, I wanted to touch base with you before I lost track of time completely. Wait a sec. Bad reception."

"Hi. Where are you?" Georgie asked, happy to take a break from procrastination. She'd been sitting at her computer, staring out the window at the triangle of light two intersecting trees created, trying to spin out a gauze-light feature entitled "Buff Bottoms."

"The Garden State Parkway. What time is it anyway? Elliot brought my watch in to be fixed last week and I've been late for my entire existence since."

Georgie glanced over at her Lucite desk clock. "Nine fifty-five."

"Lucy Ann is going to kill us! We promised to be really early tonight so she could get together with that pothead boyfriend of hers. It's just as well. I'll swing by tomorrow night around six thirty. Elliot is taking the girls to his folks' for dinner, right, sweetie? If the Audi is out of the shop by then. What a piece of crap that Nazi car is, I swear to God."

"Don't talk about my honey like that," Georgie overheard her cousin-in-law exclaim.

Nina and Elliot began to bicker in that endearing way some couples had, all banter and no bite. They'd never divorce. They seemed to have lined up all the pieces of the Rubik's Cube—marriage, demanding dual careers, two healthy girls, a million-dollar home in Summit, a nanny, a landscaper, a housekeeper, a golden retriever named Siggy, a Siamese cat named Schweitzer, two intact pairs of parents—and snapped it into place. Georgie put them on speakerphone and, for a few moments, listened to them toss out the gentlest of insults (all about chores and who last had taken the car to be fixed, extremely boring).

"Bye, guys," she said, not certain they'd even heard her.

A few moments later Nina's voice—crackling and distant as if she were buried under a pile of dry leaves—emerged from Georgie's speakerphone. "I don't know how much longer I can . . . this from her, Elliot. It's killing . . . am supposed to keep lying?"

Elliot, even harder to decipher, like one of those wireless communications in World War II flicks: "You're not . . . just keep . . . what you're . . . and nod."

Nina: "What if she . . . about Aunt Stellie? This . . . weekend?"

Elliot: Muffle. Muffle.

Nina, breaking up: "I can't . . . lies."

The pros and cons of technology! Nina must have left her cell phone on, while Georgie hadn't pressed down on the TALK button to hang up on her end. Or it could be one of a myriad of electronic faux pas with which Georgie's unsophisticated brain chose not to grapple.

They were obviously talking about Estelle. Her mother had mentioned to Georgie that she was considering a second weekend upstate at a B and B. Georgie imagined her mother holed up in her room—all wicker and dried flowers—in her father's old bathrobe, with a brown bag filled with pink-hatted Sno Balls and her back issues of *JAMA*. For a moment, the urgency with which Nina had spoken chilled Georgie. It was entirely feasible that, through Aunt Lily, Nina knew more details of Estelle's life than she did. But what? Over a glass of white wine and a Cobb salad she'd be forced to confront her cousin.

"What's all this brouhaha I hear about my mother harboring secrets from me? She's okay—healthy, I mean?" she'd ask.

There it was: the little bird of anxiety fluttering in Georgie's chest. Would caring for her one remaining parent now translate into another state of emergency?

They met at a local eatery, Nina insisting that she had business to attend to with a jeweler in Yantacaw before the store closed. They settled on a popular Mexican restaurant painted in explosive oranges and pinks, with trinkets representing the festive atmosphere south of the border cluttering the walls. Their waiter smiled above his starched white shirt and red vest. Nina ordered a margarita and nachos for an appetizer.

"For those five minutes I've allotted between my appointments with my borderline and my recovering anorexic, I have to remind myself to breathe," said Nina, psychologist extraordinaire, her long white hands flying around her face. She was still coming down from her stressful day, all jerky movements, flushed cheeks, and hair that she tried to force behind her ears to no avail. She sat, stood up, removed her sage green jacket, tucked her matching skirt beneath her, and then sat again, exhaling.

Watching her was lovely, a holdover from their childhood, when her tremendous energy would inflate Georgie with good cheer. "Take your time," she instructed, smiling.

"My kundalini yoga teacher keeps telling me I need to learn to breathe correctly. But what exactly does that *mean*? Sometimes I wonder if I'm just on automatic pilot with my life, but then I figure if that's my biggest problem—that sometimes I have to remind myself to breathe—it's not much to complain about." Nina rubbed her temples on both sides with her index fingers and finally focused her gaze on Georgie for a millisecond. "God, what's a good entrée here?"

Georgie pointed to the menu, said nothing.

"Cat got your tongue?"

"Just waiting for a break in the monologue."

"Very funny." Nina leaned her elbow on her fork, causing it to skip off the table. "God, I'm such a klutz."

Nina seemed to be quivering beyond her usual staccato, Georgie observed. "How's everyone? Elliot? The girls?"

"Busy. Kate is bugging us to give her figure skating lessons. She sees herself as the next Michelle Kwan. Franny is making a lot of butt jokes at the expense of the kindergarten boys. Still slapping her sister. How's Jesse? How's my favorite cowboy?"

"With his favorite cowboy. I let Luke take him to a Rangers game—on a school night—against my better judgment. Jesse would much rather stay home tracking storm systems to help avert any new disasters. He refuses to follow any team in any division of anything, much to his papa's and grandmother's chagrin."

Nina leaned in, flipping her hair off her face for the umpteenth time. "He isn't a jock, who cares? If your ex wants a conformist son, he should have thought of that before he married a big jock like you."

"Are you implying I'm a flabby couch potato?"

"No, just that watching a pack of men flinging pucks at each other and growling isn't your cup of tea."

The waiter arrived and presented Nina with her drink. "Ready to order the meal?" he asked, bowing with a flourish.

As Georgie listened to her cousin decide on a chicken burrito with jack cheese and refried beans, an image of the supermodel she'd done a piece on several years ago popped into her mind. "French fries and burgers and garlic potatoes," the model had listed as her favorite foods—Georgie still remembered. Another breed, these women, including her darling cousin.

"What you need to do is start dating, start bringing some nurturing, perceptive male role models into Jesse's life to complement his good-natured but clueless father," Nina said, fiddling with her silverware.

"That's a good one. Where am I supposed to find any of those on this planet?" Georgie asked, stringing Nina along. "Living in Manhattan with their gay lovers? Get real. I plan on living a long, celibate life."

"That's only for married folks. On the other hand, this is the worst possible time for you to hook up with someone," Nina advised. "So how is your social life? I only ask because I can smell something's up. Your pheromones are different."

"That's a rather personal observation. Don't you think hygiene changes are better left unnoticed?"

"You haven't been sleeping with that ex-hunk of yours, have you?" she honed in on Georgie, squinting from the glare of the table's candlelight. "Don't play dumb. I know all about your little indiscretions."

From the first, Nina had warned Georgie about involvement with Lucas Carter, cataloging the myriad of ways she was getting herself into trouble: "Nice guy, wrong for you, worst timing, your head's messed up over your dad, moving in with him, very bad idea."

"Twice, Nina. It happened twice. That was when my dad was really sick." Georgie swallowed down sorrow. Okay, it was more like four or five times—no need to provide specific, intimate details, especially of the last regretful encounter a month before.

"Right. Sorry." Nina took a sip of water and then squirmed in her seat, as restless as her young daughters. "I just wish you'd stop recycling old material."

"Okay, point taken. If you must know, I'm done recycling. I met a sweet guy. I'm just hesitant to speak about him." She felt as if recognition would create a sort of relationship voodoo, causing Ian to fade and, ultimately, disappear from her life.

Nina's eyes glittered, festive as silver bells. She clapped her hands together in glee. "Oh, how exciting. Do tell!"

"He's a vet; he's fairly adorable in his own way." Georgie shrugged, wanting to appear casual. "If it doesn't pan out, he will have been a good diversion from the last few months juggling work and single mom–hood with my bare hands while obsessing about cancer. Speaking of life after cancer," she segued, "what have you heard from your folks about my mother these days? Anything?"

"Aunt Stellie? What do you mean?" Why was Nina blinking so quickly? "Why would I have heard anything special about her?"

"You talk to Lily all the time. Your mom is much closer to Stellie than I am."

Nina was no dope. She'd graduated magna cum laude from Harvard and received her PhD from Columbia five years later. When focused, she detected psychic waves that other human animals missed while blithely chewing their cud. "What are you implying?" she asked, her feet clicking together like castanets.

Shrugging, Georgie nabbed a piece of red pepper off her plate of stir-fried veggies, which had arrived lickety split. Eating now became her diversion from confession. *Sorry,* her shoulders said, *I'm too hungry to speak.*

"If my mom said anything to you, you might as well tell me, because it sounds as if you have some distorted idea," Nina said.

"Idea about what?"

Nina shifted her weight again, and then concentrated on padding her burrito high with fried onions, before funneling a good amount of it into her mouth. She said after swallowing, "Tell me what she said that you've misinterpreted."

"It wasn't your mother. It was you. Your cell phone was still on in the car last night when you were talking to Elliot about lying to me about Stellie."

Nina smacked the heel of her hand against her forehead. The two women grinned at each other. "Okay. Here's the thing. It's not my place. . . ."

Georgie was nodding too emphatically. "Because of my dad." .

"No. This has nothing whatsoever to do with Uncle Adam. I swear. You have the wrong impression." She reached over the table to squeeze Georgie's hand and, subsequently, dipped her sleeve into the salsa. "Shit!"

"Here," Georgie said, offering her napkin.

Nina dabbed the soiled spot. "It's none of my business. I happened to overhear my mom and dad talking about Stellie and I confronted them about something that seemed suspicious."

Georgie's stomach clenched and her jaw set. Her head was bobbing in rhythm with her fear while tears nipped at the edges of her eyes. She felt as if a hex had been put on her family, first father, then mother, and then daughter. "Is she sick?"

"No, honey! You're imagining things. It's another kettle of fish entirely." She turned away for a moment as if to spare Georgie the sight of her internal struggle. "There's someone new in your mom's life. But it isn't a man. Not that kind of man, anyway."

"She's a lesbian?"

"Oh, God! What a riotously funny thought. Estelle out of the closet."

The tension drained out of them and they giggled in unison, hands cupped over their mouths.

"Hey." Georgie touched the two protruding bones on Nina's wrist. "Just say it!"

"Okay. She's been corresponding with someone, that's all."

"Corresponding? Like in chat rooms? My mom is having online sex?" Georgie smiled broadly at this ludicrous suggestion.

"Yes, constantly, can't seem to stop herself, which is why she's come to me for addiction therapy."

"Ha ha!" Georgie said.

"No, she's been writing letters to someone who also lost a close relative to cancer."

"You mean like a bereavement pen pal? A widower?"

"I think it was his mother who died of cancer a few years back. He's younger than she is. It's not a romantic thing; trust me."

Georgie's shoulders slid down from their spot around her ears. Encoded in her body over the last year was a sense of vigilance, a paramount need to keep disaster at bay. At several times during the last few months of her father's illness, she'd wondered if her body might simply collapse from the fatigue of anticipation.

"So? I don't get what the big deal is," Georgie said, awash with relief. "Who is he?"

"That's something for Aunt Stellie to explain," Nina said, smiling wanly. "Do me a favor? Don't tell your mom I told you this. It's silly, but I'm not even supposed to know, and my mom sort of swore me to secrecy."

"Sure. But, I can't see why it even matters. It might be a good thing if my mother has a comrade in her grief."

"Hey," her cousin said. "That someone is you."

"This is better," she said. "A computer pal carries less baggage."

The phone felt heavy in Georgie's hands. It was Estelle's late night seeing patients; Georgie didn't have the courage or the energy to connect with that alert, focused voice anticipating an obstetrical emergency. There would be the switch to clipped impatience when Estelle realized it was only Georgie and said that she needed to make it quick in order to shove her hand up a couple more women's vaginas before heading home. "These days," Estelle had admitted, "I resent them all, these healthy women with husbands and their whole lives ahead of them. Maybe it's terrible of me. But I can't help what I feel."

Although never a Mary Cassatt image of maternity, Estelle had developed a reputation as a kick-ass advocate for her patients; now Georgie wondered if her clients were getting nervous or if they were too caught up in their own physical alterations—expanding girth, flatulence, lack of bladder control—to even notice their doctor's murderous moods.

Jesse was at his desk, head bent over his science homework, the muscles in the back of his neck constricting as he clenched his jaw. Georgie wanted to kiss the knob at the top of his spine, to caress the last vestiges of his baby-soft skin. But she let him work in peace. "Curiosity killed the cat," she whispered even while dialing her mother's home number. A compromise: She'd leave a message and hope that, by the time her mother got it, Estelle would be cheered at the thought of e-mailing her new friend.

"Hello?" Estelle said in a tentative voice.

"Ma?"

Big sigh, momentous sigh, a sigh of the most oppressed, the heads of state fending off world war, of surgeons confronting loved ones with a bad outcome, of East German border guards demolishing the Berlin Wall. "Georgie?"

"Is this a bad time?"

"When is it a good one?"

"You're back early. Isn't this your late night?"

"Catherine offered to cover for me." Dr. Catherine Massie, one of her two partners. "I'm so worn out."

"Sorry about that."

"Yes, well." Her voice grew stronger, emboldened by Georgie's contrition. "I was just looking over some of Dad's things. I would appreciate it if you could come soon and pick up what you want. I really would."

"Okay. I will. Next week." Couldn't his belongings remain in their rightful place for a few more months? Forever?

"I don't know if you'd be interested, but I found some old books of my father's, mostly junk, but some of them are in good condition."

"I'll look when I come, Ma." She snapped off a loose thread dangling from the old jersey of Luke's that she still wore to bed.

"It's strange how much I've been thinking about my parents lately. Resentment and pride were so big in my family, especially with my father. Being a Jew, forced to leave Kiev, he gave up his chance to teach at the university and never got over it. All that shame he harbored and passed down to me. I've been thinking a lot about shame, especially lately," she said provocatively.

Georgie swallowed the pungent taste of onion and chili powder from her stir-fry.

"Did you know that Grandpa never told anyone outside of the neighborhood what he did for a living, never discussed it? You'd think he was in the Russian Mafia, the way he hid his livelihood, this big intellectual owning an appetizer store.

"Once when we were still dating, Adam said, 'Stellie, it's okay about your father.' I didn't know what he meant. I'd always avoided telling him what Grandpa did because my father had ingrained all that secrecy in me. Adam said, 'It's okay that he was in jail.' That's what Daddy thought, that Grandpa Jacob was a felon. He was willing to marry me anyway." She chuckled at the memory.

"Wow," Georgie said, remembering her grandfather lying in the hospital after heart surgery, days away from death, eighty-six years old and still a first-class kvetch.

She'd accompanied her mother to visit him on a night when Adam was on call. Jacob was causing a commotion on the geriatric ward by ranting about his inadequate care. Estelle strode into his room with that "move over, I'm here to fix everything" look on her face, the assertion in the upward tilt of her chin, her steady focused gaze.

"That nurse has a *goyisha kup*," Jacob snapped, still oddly handsome with his Aryan blue eyes and angular cheekbones accentuated by illness. "All looks, no brain. Couldn't they get me a smart person in this fancy hospital of yours?" This last comment was directed at his only child.

"Daddy, the staff here is excellent," Estelle said with restraint. "But I can hire you a private nurse if you want."

"Don't bother wasting your money. I'll be out of your way soon enough."

Georgie had excused herself to hunt down a cup of coffee. When she returned from the fluorescent-lit cafeteria with the broken vending machines and the dirty tiled floor, her grandfather was raging.

"I thought Geulah had more sense than to write this drek." Geulah, the Hebrew name he'd designated for his granddaughter, vowing never to say aloud the goyim moniker her parents had chosen for her.

"Who reads such things? Stupid, empty-headed American women, that's who." In one veiny hand, he was holding up the *Cosmo* that had printed a piece entitled, "Don't Gloss over Your Man: How to Apply Makeup So He'll Notice, Not Protest." "The girl has a master's degree, doesn't she? In my country, she'd be ashamed to use her education for such purposes."

Estelle sighed softly. "You know, Daddy, it's very hard to get published in this magazine."

Georgie had watched from the hall as her grandfather muttered in Yiddish while glaring at the glossy pages. *You're a mean old man,* she thought. *Who are you to criticize a national publication, Mr. Deli Owner?* She'd turned and strode to the elevator, never to see him alive again.

Early Saturday evening, the mid-May sky was a slate gray tarp stretching across the state. The humidity of the day was finally breaking so that a mild wind blew in the faint scent of iris and honeysuckle. Ian picked Georgie up in a burnished-red Camry. "My date car," he joked after opening the door to the passenger seat.

"You must do a lot of dating to justify a separate car."

He laughed and climbed into the driver's seat, his long legs clad in khaki pants. He was wearing a black shirt that he'd ironed too well for the occasion. "Actually, I don't." He smiled self-consciously, and she thought of her queen-size bed that had yet to entertain a male suitor. "My daughter can't stand being in the van. She says it smells of doggy breath."

"How appetizing."

"Exactly."

Backing out of the driveway, he said, "I thought we could try that new Thai place downtown that's getting all those amazing write-ups."

"Sounds good," Georgie said because—sinking into this excursion away from her knotted pain—*everything* sounded good. She shut her eyes and imagined her body being inflated with fresh clean air imported from Big Sky country or Anguilla's coast.

"What's going on with you?" he asked after a moment.

Georgie hesitated to say, not wanting to sabotage any chance with this man. This delicious man, she noted, glancing at his square shoulders, the arch of his neck, his goofy grin.

"Work. Raising Jesse. Same old."

He took his eyes off the road and looked at her askance. "I know you've been through a lousy few months. I was trying to conjure up some madcap adventure as a distraction but all I could think of was the Thai place." He sighed. "Guess Stacy had a point."

"What was that?" Her foot began to tremble.

"She said I was a tree, solid and steady but so rooted that she eventually had the urge to chop me down."

"Nice."

"Yeah. So how is life? Honestly." He took his right hand off the wheel and reached for hers. His skin was rough but pulsated with warmth.

Georgie shot him her confident smile—bachelorette throwing her cap into the wind, à la Mary Tyler Moore with kid. "Hard since my dad died, but I'll adjust. Word of advice: Never go out with a woman going through a crisis."

"Is that what it says in the manual?"

She smiled, watching the houses sweep by. "We should talk about fun things, getting-to-know-you things." Her hands flew up in an emphatic gesture. "I've been brainwashed from all my years writing how-to service pieces for women's magazines."

"Are you still writing those 'how-tos' on romance?"

"No. It was years ago, in my shining youth, along with articles about fashion and beauty. It was a result of the contacts I made in my twenties. Because of my great outward beauty and inner shallowness." She played with the silver chain of her watchband.

When he glanced her way, she added, "Me, your average suburban mother, writing about beauty, hard to imagine, huh?"

"That's not what I was thinking. I just took you for a more . . . academic type."

"You mean deep? *Au contraire*. I was always attracted to the world of artifice. Hearing about ruptured fallopian tubes and episiotomies at the dinner table can make a girl stop studying for life and run to the lipstick counter."

"I'll keep that in mind whenever I have the urge to talk heartworm and feline leukemia in front of Ava. What do you write now?"

"Mostly features. They tend toward the psychological although I still write my fair share off fluff—about makeup and cellulite. Very big in today's market are articles on addicts, foodaholics, alcoholics, shopaholics, rageaholics, breadaholics, women who can't stop eating Brillo pads or tearing out their hair. Right now I'm working on a piece on women who are addicted to plastic surgery."

"Eating Brillo?"

"It's a syndrome. I forget what it's called." Catching a glimpse of his soft mouth, she bit down on her own. "What about you? Did you always want to help sick pooches?"

"That or be an astronaut." As he noticed her dubious expression, his eyes glimmered. "I was obsessed with space until I realized there weren't any Jewish astronauts who got to go to the moon. I settled for trying to heal animals, my second love, and decided to stay here on Earth."

"I'm glad." Suddenly all aglow with endorphins, she peeked in the side mirror and could swear her skin looked positively collegiate.

Georgie recognized these first stirrings of love.

There was a little cafe on Hudson Street where she and her first serious boyfriend used to go at the beginning, when they were all of nineteen. They'd gaze at each other in the rose candlelight. It was winter, and Michael would wear a sweeping Burberry coat with a high collar, which hinted at a long trek through snow. Sometimes he'd don his grandfather's old fur hat and, in this getup, she'd call him "Dr. Zhivago." They'd lean toward each other, so attuned it was as if they were listening to the exact clockwork of each other's hearts. Finger by finger, he'd remove the black leather gloves from his large, square hands. This motion kindled in Georgie a passion for him that felt remarkable: Spoons and forks sharpened in clarity; the aquamarine walls and matching tablecloths grew more vivid. It seemed as if those hands had created everything in her world.

And later they would touch her.

Then in August of 1991, Michael left for Kuwait on an assignment and her father was diagnosed with lymphoma. The light went out of her life and didn't come back until Jesse was born.

Siam in the Suburbs was half a block from the town's center. Sandwiched between a chic coffeehouse and an old-fashioned mom-and-pop pharmacy, the place was injected with adrenaline and kitsch: reed-thin waiters and waitresses in mock tuxedos, jade green walls, a glass enclosure of exotic fish, a Zen garden exhibited on a round table in the middle of the room, a photograph of the Thai chef shaking hands with former president Clinton, the hokey painting of an emerald Buddha.

"Did Ava like her birthday present?" Georgie asked once they were seated and served appetizers.

"She loved it. Thank you for helping me." Ian stood halfway up to kiss her. A quick kiss but there it was, the taste of fried banana on his breath, the fleshy feeling of his lips. "I also bought her a trilogy of Marx brothers videos. I turned her on to them last summer. Important question: Which of the Marx brothers was your favorite?"

"Don't know. I've never watched one of their movies all the way through."

"You're kidding." He widened his eyes in mock horror. "We need to rent some. Make a night of it. I'll give you an entire Marx brothers course in one long night."

"That sounds promising," she said, feeling a tingling between her thighs.

"Good. It's a date."

She smiled at the tablecloth and speared a yam, noting the fibrillation of her heart. "Do you have a picture of Ava?"

"I do." Ian whipped a snapshot out of his wallet and presented it to her proudly. Ava was a bombshell with champagne-colored hair pulled back into a loose ponytail, round blue eyes graced with black lashes, and a wide mouth that would have been prematurely seductive if it hadn't been parted to reveal a missing front tooth.

"She's very pretty."

"She gets that from her mother."

Stake through her heart! "Oh?"

"Stacy is a knockout. I could never figure out what she was doing with me."

The sense of romance flushed out of her instantly. Even in her lavender sweater, she felt drab, not up for the competition. Still, she tried to think of a witty comeback, one that would prove that great beauty ran a poor second to a sharp mind. Instead she excused herself.

The bathroom was the smallest one she'd ever encountered in a restaurant; it seemed built for animated characters that could stretch and slither to fit the shape of any compartment. There was only the narrowest of toilets and a sink that could be used only by standing next to it, as there was not enough room for a body between it and the door. Georgie remembered how early in her marriage, she'd been locked in comparatively sized lavatory on a commuter plane while accompanying Luke on a business trip—for the first and last time. The door had been jammed shut when a stewardess inadvertently wedged the drink cart against the occupied restroom. For twenty minutes, her husband slept while she bleated, "I'm in here," and, "Please let me out." Finally another passenger signaled to a flight attendant and said abashedly, "I think there's a woman stuck in there, calling for help."

She wondered if Ian would neglect her with the same innocent carelessness, the way one forgot an annual appointment with the dentist or to pick up the dry cleaning on the way home from the office. When she returned to the table, he looked at her with bright, attentive eyes that eradicated any possible parallels between him and her ex-husband. She laughed, unexpectedly, as she slid into her seat.

"What is it?" He smiled.

"Oh, I was reminded of this weird thing that happened to me."

When she'd finished the bathroom tale, Ian grinned. "That's unbelievable. How could Luke not notice you weren't in your seat for a third of the flight?"

"He's a very sound sleeper."

"Umm. Those planes bump around an awful lot," he said, unconvinced.

"I know. I hate to fly. It never bothered Luke. He'd pass right out, obviously. Do you like it—flying, not passing out?"

"I do, actually. But to be honest, I haven't done that much of it. Not much business travel required in my line of work."

"Really?" She winked, leaning on her elbows in his direction. "No emergency moose deliveries in Alaska?"

"Nope. Not as many as you might imagine. I've only been out of the country twice, to be honest, and once was to Vancouver, which really doesn't count. The other time was on my honeymoon in Italy."

"What did you think of it?"

"Of Italy? I assume you're not asking about my honeymoon." He craned his neck as if looking for the waitress to rescue him. "It was beautiful. I loved the food and sitting in the churches. To be honest, the endless religious art got to be too much for me, which annoyed Stacy to no end. She accused me of being just another provincial tourist."

"My dad got sick of the museums, too. But he had a love affair with the churches. We went to Rome when I was thirteen."

What Georgie remembered most about that sprawling beige and orange city was the open space of the piazzas and the labyrinth of streets, policemen in coffee-colored uniforms stroking machine guns, old ladies with yellow teeth and knotted fingers, mangy stray cats with sagging bellies, nuns scuttling by in pairs, their skirts swishing around their ankles, the sink in the hotel by the Spanish Steps that stopped up, gargling and reeking of mud. And her father: his minty talc smell after a shower, his half smile and dreamy expression when viewing the seventh-century statues, how at home he was in that ancient country.

"He used to accompany Luke and Jesse and me for Midnight Mass on Christmas Eve."

"Midnight Mass has a magical sound to it."

"It can be magical, especially if you're like me, going for the spectacle rather than the Christmas message."

"Let's do it," he said, reaching for her hand. "This year, if all goes well"—he winked—"let's take in a little Mass with our matzo at the holidays."

It was a bold or naive move, his proposing a plan six months in advance. Long ago a man whose malleable face reminded her of the rubber puppets in her father's waiting room had casually referenced a plan he'd made for them on New Year's Eve. It was late November and only their second date; she was repulsed by his presumption and the way his elastic facial muscles registered indignation when she quashed his enthusiasm. But Ian's invitation felt liberating, like securing a spot in a competitive college the spring before freshman year.

She opened her mouth to agree and was suddenly seized with a bone-shaking attack of nausea, followed by a fierce headache, like a dental drilling directly behind her eyes. Without warning, the bright colors of the restaurant shifted patterns; Georgie grabbed on to the table.

"Hey, you okay?" Ian asked, reaching out to steady her.

Georgie nodded, even as his image appeared blurred, his face, eyes, mouth all drooping, as if the poor man had suddenly developed palsy. "I think I'm getting sick, one of those killer twenty-four-hour viruses that hit you out of the blue. Everyone in town has it."

She shut her eyes in an attempt at balance. It was as if she were trapped on a racing carousel, her palms sweating and legs trembling, no escape as the horses spun around and around.

SEVEN

S tanding barefoot in her bathroom, Georgie was frozen down to her fingertips despite the humid spring weather. Light the color of Chablis shone in from the window, the sun's rays glittering on every surface of the room. Surely such an incandescent morning would prove her premonition wrong. Seized with a clammy queasiness for the third day in a row, Georgie could easily forecast what the stick, dipped into her own urine, would reveal: She might as well scatter any remnants of an orderly, sensible life into her backyard like confetti.

In a daze, she lifted up the white stick gingerly, as if it might burst in her hand. The tip was so pink that Georgie determined the results with the blurred vision of shock. She was as pregnant now as she had been ten years ago, when she let out a wallop and hugged Lucas so hard she almost transformed his ambivalence into jubilation. This time around her first instinct was to peel her skin from her bones the way she would rip the protective hide from an orange. Her gut was churning, but her heart didn't seem to be beating until, finally, it resumed with a startled thump as if defibrillated back to life.

"Damn!" she said. She stood staring at the stick, wooden as a dolt. She was recalling how, the day she went into labor with Jesse, Lucas had just boarded his delayed plane for Bermuda. Outside on Park Avenue, car exhaust created clouds of gray smoke. There was a long honk, then the sound of a vehicle skidding before slamming to a halt. Georgie was in the kitchen slathering butter on a bread stick for breakfast when her water broke, gushing like a milky, warm waterfall.

She'd called Nina, who was living with Elliot on East Eighty-second Street. "I seem to have peed in my pants quite badly," she said, oh-so-cavalier.

"Can you plug it up and get a cab? Can you make it all the way up to Columbia Presbyterian Hospital alone?"

Not as convenient as Lenox Hill Hospital, but she'd be damned if she delivered in Estelle's domain.

"Sure." The contractions had begun, but were mild as second-day menstrual cramps.

"Good. I'll call your doctor. Go ahead and give me the number. What's wrong with your husband? He should be waiting on you like a foot servant instead of soaking up rays in the islands."

"I'm almost three weeks early, and he's on a business trip, not at a bachelor party. I'd love to continue the standard Luke's-no-good-for-me arguments, Nina. Unfortunately, I'm soaking our beautiful marble floors."

In the stairwell and on the street, she fought the waves of intensifying contractions by rocking onto the balls of her feet and easing forward into an awkward bow. But in the taxi there was no remedy. By the time the cabby swerved through Central Park to get to the West Side, Georgie had rolled down her window and thrown up green bile.

When the labor hadn't progressed ten hours later, the baby's heartbeat slowed down, and after much shuffling of feet and hushed, tight voices, a cesarean was deemed necessary by the on-call doctor with the talcum-powder white skin. Weeping and moaning intermittently, Georgie prayed that the dense fog of pain and panic would now clear. She'd clutched Nina's hand, as she imagined her baby being scooped out in one clean gesture, like a dove from a magician's bag. Georgie was transformed into a medical pincushion, a catheter inserted deep into the ache of her bladder, an epidural needle pierced between the vertebrae of her spine. The last sight she saw before her son was thrust into the world was the white throat, thin nostrils, and downward gaze of her beloved cousin.

Now, a decade later, Georgie stared at the white plastic wand. Its tip glared back, a sharp pink line shaped like an accusation. If Luke had been above the Atlantic for the birth of their first child while they were still married, where would he be this time around? Inside of Zoë, most likely.

Georgie shut her eyes and imagined the faces of her friends and relatives, from her son's crestfallen one, to her mother's searing blame, to Nina's loving look of disappointment, to Lucas's blanched expression of entrapment, to Ian's sympathetic countenance hinting of inevitable withdrawal.

"It's impossible," she said, anxiety ballooning in her chest. It had taken three months of concerted effort to conceive Jesse. How had one night of semidebauchery resulted in pregnancy a decade later? Weren't the statistics against her? It simply could not be true.

That afternoon Nina was scheduled to help Georgie sort through her father's things while Jesse enjoyed his Sunday playing video games at his friend Gus's house. Nina insisted on driving once again, which in Georgie's current state was preferable.

"What's up with you?" Nina asked, once Georgie had slid into the passenger seat in faded overalls, with no makeup and mussed hair. "You look like hell."

"Thanks. Stress. Indigestion. The usual suspects."

"Something else is going on." A thin vein at Nina's temple protruded as she peered in Georgie's direction. "You're green as Gumby."

"Thanks. I'm preoccupied. With the guy I'm seeing," she said as a decoy. She'd planned to tell Nina about her pregnancy; of course she had. But shame over her predicament lapped over her, thick as honey.

"What? I *knew* it. He can't be good for you if you look like this! Tell me everything."

Georgie quickly provided a synopsis of Ian's hankering for the ex-wife who'd discarded him nonchalantly, like unwanted dinnerware at a yard sale. "Anyway, this is the worst time to start the first relationship since my divorce a millennium ago."

"Only three years. Let's not exaggerate. Although you do need some time to heal from your dad."

"I don't believe in that. It's just what shrinks say. Who heals from anything really? Knees heal. Scabs heal. People don't."

"Fine." Nina sighed. "Tell me more about this Dr. Ian Weiss."

"Vet, not doctor," she said as if to keep her adolescent promise, sealed with the blood from a pinprick, never to date a physician. "It's confusing. Something about him reminds me of Michael, even though he's nothing like him on paper. Remember Michael Bowman?"

"Michael Bowman?" Nina whistled at his name. "Wow! I haven't heard you mention him in years. That sounds serious."

"Serious? We've been out twice, Nina."

"Don't even bother defending yourself. In what way does he remind you of Michael?"

Georgie hunched over to peel the mandarin orange polish off her thumb. It was an awful color and stubborn as acrylic. "I'm not sure. I'm not sure about anything. I've been out of commission for so long, I'd probably fall for a tree frog if it took me out for drinks."

"I don't think so. You're pretty critical of the usual tree frogs."

"That's because most frogs my age are appalling, fat, and out of shape, or with these gray complexions and graying hair to match. Have you ever really looked at these forty-something hubbies at the gym? Don't even get me started," she railed, relief leaking into her chest—this was safe territory. "Women have so much pressure to keep themselves young and pretty, while men feel entitled to fall to pieces. I should know. I wrote 'Beauty and the Beast: Women's Secret Love-Hate Relationship with Their Less-than-fit Mate' for *O* magazine."

"*Hello?* You're getting off the topic here. This guy doesn't fit any of these descriptions, does he?"

Georgie took a deep breath, the *thumpy-thump* of her confused heart speeding up again. "He's cute, along the lines of Matthew Modine. It could be that I'm dazzled by his decent appearance and moderate level of fitness."

"You're a real hard-ass, you know that, kid?" Nina blew air out slowly, as if performing one of her yoga exercises. "So, where are you with him? Does he know how you feel?"

"We've been on two fucking dates! He knows I have brown hair and that my dad's dog just died. He only knows about my dad because he was Odysseus's vet. Do you think I should confess my undying love for him? That's the pattern with me. My dad gets cancer; I jump into marriage with the wrong guy. My dad dies . . . what am I going to do? Join the circus?"

Get pregnant with my ex-husband?

"Okay, enough! If this Ian Weiss helps you feel happy, great. You deserve it. Just stop worrying about the rest and let yourself experience some happiness."

"Sorry. I didn't mean to take my frustration out on you. Right now I have weightier issues on my mind than dating."

"Like what?" Nina shot her a searing look.

Deciding whether or not to keep this baby, for starters, weighing and balancing the pros and cons on the scales of emotional and psychological justice. An infant would interrupt the already uneven flow of her blitzed life. A newborn would smell like spring air and sugar cookies. A baby would wedge itself between the stable twosome carefully constructed in her home. A sibling might someday act as doppelgänger, support system, or best friend for Jesse.

She averted her eyes and began furiously chipping away at her manicure. "Getting this day over with."

"Stellie won't be there," Nina said. "You can't ask for much more."

But she could ask for more, couldn't she? Her mother morphed into Marmee. Her dad resurrected, his cells clean and shiny as pomegranate seeds. Time rolled back so that the poor little mistake growing inside of her had never been conceived, so that the alchemy of HCG, progesterone, and estrogen would stop its dance of blood and heat.

Nina parked the car in a lot and the two women got out, swaying in the humid Manhattan air like two human equivalents of the Leaning Tower of Pisa. At the corner coffee shop, Nina bought herself a midmorning snack to go, consisting of a gigantic chocolate-chip muffin and a large orange juice. As they approached the familiar skyscraper on the corner of Fifth Avenue, she asked, "How ya doing?" She hooked Georgie's arm so that they were swinging down the avenue as if in a forties musical.

"Just spiffy," Georgie said. "I'll be absolutely peachy as soon as we're done."

Estelle's apartment smelled of Charlene's cleaning, a mixture of citrus and floral scents permeating the hallway, a hint of roast in the kitchen. The granite countertops were free of butter knives and old coffee cups, and the milk container in the refrigerator was closed. The pewter lamps gleamed and the baby grand shone. Good signs. Estelle was back to her neat-freak ways.

But there was nothing reassuring about the brown moving boxes in the center of the living room. Estelle had labeled them with a red Flair pen, *Salvation Army,* and had closed up most of them with gray masking tape. The ones intended for Georgie were left open, the contents folded and tucked away as if Estelle's deceased husband were a desk drawer able to be organized, different facets of him filed under color-coded headings.

As she stared down into a box filled with her father's ancient medical journals, a white-hot wave washed over her. His voice, the slow cadence, the patient tone, was in her ear, warming her skin. "It's okay, Georgie Porgie, we'll figure this out. Meet me at the Alice in Wonderland sculpture after my patients and we'll go for a walk, talk about what to do. You and my number one grandson, you'll be okay." He winked right at her.

"Dad?"

Georgie jolted backward, almost falling. When she looked up, the space where her father had been was just an empty pocket of air, ice-cold. A cacophony of symptoms took over her body: heart pounding like a bongo, sweat bursting from her glands, fear filling her throat with its tangy metallic taste, gagging her so that her breathing became jagged. She knelt on the carpet and held on to the fireplace for support.

"I think I'm having a heart attack," she squeaked in a strange, falsetto voice.

"A panic attack is more like it, honey," Nina said, rushing to her side and massaging her neck. "Breathe slowly and deeply. That's right."

Hunched over, Georgie hugged her knees into her chest. Could her changing hormones be causing such a ruckus? At the thought, fear vanished in a magical whoosh, as if calming progesterone were coating her innards with its greasy balm. Breath returned to her lungs. Time grew languid. Equilibrium resumed.

"I've never had one of those before," Georgie said. "They suck."

"Yeah, they do by definition. Let me go get you a glass of water."

"How embarrassing to have this happen in front of you."

Back from the kitchen, Nina was sitting next to Georgie, gently caressing her hair. "Who cares?" She laughed. "That should be the worst of your problems."

Gulping down her water, Georgie glanced around. The apartment was stagnant again, like the home of elderly people who hadn't changed a seat cushion or bought a new book in decades. Her father was gone. Sadly, she realized that the cancer paraphernalia were the only objects that had given the place life in the last few years.

"I need to grab a few choice things and get out of this mausoleum pronto," Georgie said as she began to rifle through a box. "You won't be needing back issues of *JAMA,* will you?"

"Nope," Nina said. "Especially not from the mid-eighties."

"How about *Sport Fishing* magazine? These are more current."

"Nah. Not that I'm not tempted. Maybe you should offer them to your ex? He'd enjoy reeling in all the fish in the sea."

Georgie's heartbeat sped up but this time she ordered it to steady.

"Here are some old poetry books you might actually want." Nina picked one up and flipped through it. "Wow. They're Uncle Adam's college poetry books, and it looks like he wrote some of his own lines in the margins. Here's a poem he must have written on the last page."

"Don't read that," Georgie said protectively, reaching over and running her palm along the page. "We don't know if he'd want anyone else to see it."

"Well, there's these two books that your mom stuck 'For Georgie' Post-it notes on."

One was a dog-eared paperback edition of *Selected Poems of William Carlos Williams,* the other an old but intact hardback entitled *Women in Medicine* by Carol Lopate. Georgie picked them up and leafed through the Lopate book. On the inside cover, her father had written in his elegant script: *To my magnificent wife, a testament to woman's enduring place in medicine. Your loving husband and most adoring fan, Adam, 7/69.*

"I wonder why my mother left me a present that my dad gave her. She must have some ulterior motive."

"Oh, wow!" Nina exclaimed. "There are some adorable pictures of you in this box."

Georgie joined her cousin in leafing through the photographs. There were a couple of black-and-whites from when Georgie was a toddler, her mother's face so young and beautiful, despite its austerity: eyes large, dark, and slightly haughty, chiseled bones and wide mouth stretched across a broad canvas, a neck so long and noble it evoked the look of American royalty, of Jackie Kennedy or Grace Kelly's long-lost darker sister. One was of Georgie's dad helping her blow out the candles on her second-birthday cake, another of an eleven-year-old Georgie reading on the dock at Lake Willoughby, in her pink bikini with the lace top. Then there was her dad hugging a newborn Jesse near Georgie's hospital bed, her face in the background blown up from labor, as if she were retaining the Hudson River.

"What am I going to do, Daddy?" she whispered, as if her plea could usher a ghost out of its hiding place, as effectively as a magnet galvanizing iron molecules.

"What is it?" Nina asked.

"Nothing. Just this one of my dad with Jess."

"I'm sorry, honey."

"Oh, Nina. It's my dad's old jacket. I love this thing." She lifted up a crinkled rust-colored corduroy coat with beige patches covering the ripped elbows. "My dad wore this until my mother basically threatened him. I guess she didn't throw it out." She rubbed it against her face, the pungent scent of cigar seeped into the fabric. How long had it been since he'd enjoyed one of his fat Bolivars?

Georgie's fingers caressed the deep pockets, the ones in which her father had hidden saltwater taffy and cherry gumdrops when she was a child. She found a packet of Juicy Fruit with one stale piece remaining, and a wrinkled doctor's prescription, not from her father's pad. The doctor's name at the top of the page was Leonard Weitzel, and the date in the right-hand corner was September 9, 1974.

"Can you read this? It's practically illegible."

Nina inspected the piece of paper, squinting as she brought it closer to her face. "Maybe. But what's the difference?" The tone of her voice left Georgie chilly.

"Tell me."

"It looks like Anafranil," she said, reluctantly, avoiding Georgie's eyes, her peach cheeks reddening. "I might be wrong. This prescription is a hundred years old and wasn't even given to the pharmacist."

"You're not a doctor; how do you know what it's for?"

"Sweetie, it's an old-fashioned antidepressant. Big deal. Your dad probably took it to deal with the lymphoma."

Georgie's throat tightened so that she could taste sour saliva. "He didn't have lymphoma in 1974. Unless they were lying about that."

"Hey," Nina said, pursing her lips. "Let's not get paranoid. They just didn't tell you your dad had a prescription for Anafranil that he never even filled. You were what, ten in 1974? Do you think your parents should have consulted you about a bad period in your father's life?"

Disparate thoughts rattled around Georgie's brain in a mad dash to hook up with one another, to form a discernible pattern. She was eight years old, maybe younger. Her parents' voices had awoken her in the purple night, her mother's high and lilting, as if she were singing a lullaby, and her father's moaning, a terrifying animal sound, like game being slaughtered. Wrapped in her scratchy blanket she felt woozy, as if traveling up a sinuous mountain road in the back of her parents' SAAB. She'd reached out for Beauty, her calico cat. But the cat had abandoned her spot on the bed in her usual contrary manner.

Georgie tiptoed down the hall that was the liquid black of ink, no shadows anywhere, holding on to the wall for guidance. Outside her parents' bedroom, she stopped and fondled a small tear in the forest green wallpaper. The light from the lamp on her mother's end table illuminated her father's face, which was white, the color of waves after they'd unfolded from the blue-green ocean and lapped onto the beach. The veins in his neck bulged as if pleading for relief. "Help me, Stellie!" he begged. "It's not working. I'm dizzy, constipated, and sweaty at the office. How am I supposed to function this way?"

Estelle's voice spun a silky thread. "It'll be okay. Give the medication more time, Adam. You haven't given it enough time. Let's wait and see, okay? Can you do that for me, honey?"

She'd waited for her father's response but none came.

"There's nothing to get upset about, not about this," Nina said now. "Except that someone should have had this jacket cleaned in the last three decades. Didn't he ever empty out his pockets? Seriously, you have no context—your dad isn't here to explain—and you won't have a clue about what was going on unless you ask your mom."

Squatting next to the box, Georgie asked, "Do you think she wanted me to find this?"

Nina rubbed Georgie's hand. "Of course not. It's garbage. What could she possibly hope to accomplish by showing it to you?"

Georgie shook her head. Cancer had taught her about the decay of the body, the brittle bones held together by ravaged flesh, the yellow-eyed gaze lacking in recognition, the birdlike heartbeat in a hollowed-out chest. But this was a lesson in emotional humility. All the shadows around her father: Why hadn't she possessed the vision to see them?

"That my dad had major problems I never had a clue about?"

In a reproachful tone, her cousin said, "Don't you think you're letting your imagination run amok?"

Georgie rose to her feet, needing to witness how, outside the window, the world wasn't moving at the speed of light. Inside the apartment windows across the way, families lived happily, easily, within the boundaries of everyday stress and strain, where Tylenol and Sinutab lined the inside of their bathroom cabinets instead of psychotropic drugs next to expired birth control. Inside these homes, parents lived to a ripe old age, gracing their children's Passover dinners with their anecdotes and advice, and daughters woke up in the morning without their ex's bun in the oven.

"You're right. If he suffered for a time with depression, I don't want to even know about it right now. I want to remember him the way he always was with me. Let's look through the other stuff and get out of here."

Estelle's bedroom was a shrine to Adam's clothes and books. They were piled everywhere, leaving no place for her to sleep. On the end table sat a five-by-seven portrait of him encased in a wire frame.

Bearded, bespectacled, smiling his wisp of a smile, no teeth showing, was Adam, the old Adam, a face that felt like coming home after a long, treacherous drive in inclement weather.

At the foot of the bed was a collection of his medical books. Peeking out at the bottom of the heap was a photo album made of cardboard covers jacketed in peeling paper with the look of wallpaper— dancing Victorian children holding kites and umbrellas. Gingerly Georgie eased it out.

"Look at this, Nina. It's ancient."

The album was held together with a dirty white string laced through two punched holes. Inside, the multicolored construction paper was ripped in places and sprinkled with her grandmother's perfect print below photographs of her father's early childhood. The first page said *The Chronicle of Adam,* and underneath his birth announcement was pasted. The infant Adam was almost girlishly pretty with his abundantly curly hair, long eyelashes, round eyes, and pudgy cheeks. And there was Grandma Ruth, who, even in black and white, appeared made up in dark lipstick with her eyebrows drawn, a light-colored kerchief on her head, attractive, her figure the same as always, no hint of fatigue or pregnancy after only three months. Just like Stellie, who'd returned, slim and starched, to medical school only three weeks after delivering Georgie.

Page after delicate page of baby Adam, from nightshirts to jumpsuits and sturdy brown shoes, always with dark eyes, round as cherries, soft curls, and a natural pout. He looked like Georgie as a baby; he looked like Jesse. If she didn't stop the cells inside her from multiplying, would this grandchild also don his grandfather's face?

"Wow," Nina said from across the room, at Estelle's dresser. "Your dad was quite a letter writer."

"But they were always together," Georgie said, turning to see her cousin holding up a stack of envelopes tied together with a silver ribbon, decorative as a Christmas stocking stuffer.

"Oh, how sweet."

Georgie took the liberty of untying the blue ribbon from an old-fashioned box. Inside were six black leather books held closed by thin straps and bronze-colored clasps.

She picked up the one on top and fiddled with the lock, which was broken. She flipped it open; on the inside cover was inscribed: *Estelle Sarah Ackerman, 1956,* in the large, loopy letters of a teenage girl. Georgie skimmed through the slightly yellowed, lined pages, amazed at her discovery. Although tempted to sink onto the floor and peruse her mother's diaries, she fought the urge until she came to the last one, the date of which was 1964, the year Georgie was born. She read:

> Ruth has hired a German baby nurse for us, a woman named Hilda who embodies all the stereotypes. She's about six feet tall, with hips so square she could double as a card table, mousy brown hair, and cool blue eyes that dart around the room, only to rest on the one pile of unpaid bills, or the unwashed dishes in the corner. How embarrassing and intimidating! It's clear she disapproves of a mother leaving her baby to attend medical school. I can't let myself get caught up in guilt. The only consolation is that Georgie seems to like her. Then again, Georgie is undiscerning. She likes everyone. It's astounding to think that I've produced such an easily contented child, that I was capable of such a feat.
>
> Georgia has the most remarkably curious eyes I've ever seen, uncommonly alert in someone of any age, but particularly in a baby. From the time she could lift her head, she struggled to see over my shoulder and out the window into the wild blue yonder. But when her adored father comes home, she stares at his face so long and hard, it's as if she's recording a picture of him into the recesses of her brain. She's certainly Adam's little girl. With all that has happened to me, I hope I can do right by her.

"What are you reading?" Nina asked.

"This is incredible!" Georgie exclaimed. "My mom actually kept a diary!"

"Hey, George, I don't think you should be reading that." Her cousin peered over her shoulder. "I'm not even sure your mom meant for you to be poking around in here."

"Yeah. I'm done. I just read one paragraph. She was describing me as a baby, how much she admired and liked me."

"Of course she did. Your mom isn't a monster."

"But she never expressed her feelings to me. I can't believe there was this whole other side to her."

Georgie's throat constricted. All her life she'd wondered about the intricacies of love, the way her relationship with each of her parents had formed a curve that didn't quite snap into place with the slope of the other. Her father's loyalties seemed doomed to be divided. But why had her mother created the need for division in the first place, when clearly she'd loved her daughter?

She replaced the journal and spotted *Adam's love letters* scribbled in Estelle's handwriting on a Post-it note. This way of labeling seemed cheap, a throwaway, her mother's marking them like some patient's records. Georgie knew her mother would dispute this; she was simply cataloging her husband's devotion in the best way she knew how. It wasn't meant for a trespasser's eyes.

Another pile of letters was edged underneath her father's, all tucked in their envelopes and held together with a rubber band. It was wrong. Nevertheless, she inched one out. It started formally— *Dear Estelle Merkin, I've thought a lot about how to begin this letter*—and ended in the same tone with, *Respectfully yours, Daniel.*

Daniel. Was that her mother's old friend from the Bronx, the one she'd mentioned at the funeral?

"You shouldn't look at these without talking to your mom first," Nina admonished.

"You're right. Let's go," Georgie said, filled with guilt. She replaced the letter carefully. "I just want my dad's old coat, a few of his college texts, and the two books my mom marked for me. I can put them in a shopping bag."

"That's it? Are you sure?"

"Maybe some of Charlene's homemade potato bisque that she freezes by the ton for my mom."

In the car, the motion put Georgie out as if she were a baby. Memory stewed with dream. Adam's voice, plaintive and self-deprecating, wafted into her ear. "We poetic types all have our demons, Georgie. Sometimes a person can be so sensitive that one more sick kid can make it hard for him to breathe. Your mother, on the other hand, could sew a child's head back on without blinking, could save a life that way. How lucky was I to find her?"

Groggy from slumber's gelatinous membrane, Georgie mumbled, "Nina?"

"Umm?"

Nina was driving fast, as always, on the FDR Drive. Afternoon sunlight kissed her freckled cheeks, highlighted the fine lines at the corners of her mouth, rendering the thin skin of her nostrils nearly opaque. Nina the angel.

"Do you ever wonder why your mom and dad stopped trying for more kids? I know your mom had trouble." She shifted in her seat. "I used to think that was a rhetorical question when it came to my mother. I always figured it was my fault, that I was such an unpleasant experience. Now I'm not so sure."

Nina turned, her eyes squinting from the glare. "Well, my mom had the two miscarriages before she had me and was warned not to try again, remember? She was Rh-negative, like Grandma."

"All those miscarriages. But you and I never had any." Maybe this time would be the charm, she thought, sickening herself.

"Just lucky, I guess. Grandma also had a second trimester miscarriage a couple of months before she got pregnant with your dad."

"She did? No one ever told me."

Nodding emphatically, Nina said, "Can you imagine how screwed up her hormones must have been? Can you even imagine Grandma Ruth *having* hormones?" She shook her head in disbelief. "Unthinkable."

"The thing is, she doesn't look screwed up in those pictures. She looks radiant."

"The baby she lost was already almost six months along. Six *months*. Think about it. That's a *viable baby* already."

The phrase reverberated in Georgie's head. When wasn't your own child viable? At three months, at two? "My mother was the only one who didn't have trouble with her pregnancies. How ironic, since she never seemed to like babies much," she said. "That's why I was so surprised at what she'd written about me."

"Honey! Your mom must like babies. Of course she loved you as one."

"I shouldn't have read her journal. It was inexcusable."

"Yeah. You feel desperate to get close to her any way you can," Nina said.

"I'm not sure that's it anymore." Georgie shook her head. "My dad always claimed that her patients loved her, and I figured it was because she was so competent at what she does. They felt safe in her hands. But I remember her telling me how she liked to deliver the babies, but wasn't much interested in them after that, other than that they stayed physically healthy. Funny her becoming a gynecologist, don't you think?"

"Better than a pediatrician. Once they're out of the womb, you're done with them."

"Oh, God." Georgie sobbed, suddenly cracked open like a mango divulging its pulpy center.

"What is it, honey?" Nina cried, turning, a patch of sunlight illuminating the soft skin of her cheek. "What's wrong?"

"If I tell you, you have to promise not to get mad at me."

"Cross my heart and hope to die."

The two women looked at each other and burst out laughing.

"Seems I have a wacky reproductive tract, like Grandma. I managed to get myself knocked up from one little tryst with my ex-hubby."

Nina's complexion lost its pinkish glow and the light faded from her eyes. Without a hint of censure, she said, "Oh, God! What are you going to do?"

"What can I do? I'm not married, not making enough money, can't rely on Lucas financially forever. I'm already raising one boy who would get fucked up if his mom gave birth to her ex-husband's baby."

"Let's pull over somewhere and talk. We can go to a diner." Nina veered into the slow lane, ready to exit off the highway into any northern New Jersey town, on command.

"That's okay. Let's just go home. Face it: My choices here are limited, considering my situation." She shut her eyes in the hope that the answer to her problem would be spelled out like skywriting on the bluest of canvases. Nothing. "I'm not married, and Jess has to come first. I don't think it would be in his best interest to have his single mom popping out his dad's love child. I'm leaning toward getting an abortion."

Georgie imagined the violent severing of a torso, a lung, and a lip from her uterine wall, a few bloody human cells left behind as a reminder. *Stop it,* she thought. *It's only the size of an amoeba.* Yet her mind had jumped the track, picking up speed as it ricocheted from one dead-baby image to the next.

"Wow, are you sure?"

She was anything but sure. Uncertainty jiggled in her belly. Already the baby had seized hold of her, a parasite to its host, a lover to its mate; it was a swerve in the road that could not be reversed.

"Yes and no," she admitted.

They drove in silence. A few miles later Georgie said, "This seems so surreal. How come I'm more fertile now than I was at twenty-five, when I had to make an effort to get knocked up? Am I a medical miracle? Should they do a segment on me for *20/20*?"

Nina said in a gentle voice, "It's not an exact science."

"I'm not a spring chicken, and I did use birth control—okay, not completely correctly. The expiration date on the jelly had passed, but who believes those arbitrary dates, anyway? I've taken expired Advil and it worked. God, listen to me! I sound like some trailer-trash teenager."

Nina reached over for Georgie's hand and gave it a gentle squeeze. "Give yourself a break, kid. Are you going to tell Lucas?"

"He would either get annoyed or superpractical. Remember that fight we had a million years ago about Milgram's experiment?"

Nina turned to her cousin and grinned, color returning to her cheeks. "I can't honestly say I do."

"When I was a teaching assistant at NYU, one of the essays I had to assign was Milgram's 'Obedience to Authority,' and Luke and I got into a stupid fight about it at Le Figaro Café on Bleecker Street. You remember the place, all those waitresses who looked like stoned dancers and took an hour to serve you a grilled cheese?"

"Yeah, I loved that place."

"Me, too, the best melted-cheddar-and-bacon in Greenwich Village," she said. Georgie's right foot seemed to have developed a Parkinsonian tremor. She leaned over to massage it still.

"Anyway, Luke claimed that, unlike the majority of people in the world who liked to cast themselves as heroes and honorable men, he was honest enough to admit he'd probably be one of the sixty-five percent who obeyed authority. I wittily replied, 'Especially if the person telling you to give the shocks happened to be dressed like your mother in her unruffled plaid skirt and emerald green wool sweater.'"

"Excuse me if I'm not making the connection here."

"The connection is that Luke doesn't even pretend to hold himself up to a high moral standard. Even in his business, his only motivation is avoiding scandal and financial ruin. He wouldn't suffer remorse if I got an abortion; just the opposite. He'd easily accept it without a qualm, which would only hurt more."

"Poor Georgie." Nina clucked. "Forget Lucas. As long as he'd keep helping you financially, you don't need anything else from him. Think about what you want. Remember how much you wanted a second child?"

"That was a long time ago, when I thought I could still salvage my marriage." Inhaling deeply to stem tears, she said, "It's not that I wouldn't love another baby in a different circumstance. You know I would! It's that after my being divorced for years, the possibility hasn't even been on my radar screen."

"So put it there. Let's think this through."

"No, please. It's too painful. Having the baby is not a realistic solution. Luke's generosity won't last forever. He was making grumbling noises, before my dad got sick, about not wanting to support me forever. All that pressure to start making real money while still being home, baking brownies by three-oh-five, you know what that's like. Plus, the real glitch is, I can't figure out how I'd explain it to Jesse. If I told him the baby was Luke's, he'd be completely confused and excited. He'd expect us to get back together."

"You could tell him that you've been wanting another baby for a long time." Nina looked in her cousin's direction, the light brightening her eyes, illuminating the narrow forked lines at the corners as she squinted. "You can say you had artificial insemination."

Georgie shook her head and her foot started quivering again. "Nina, he's too smart for that. He'd think his mother was a slut and that the pregnancy was a result of a one-night stand. It's not like I've even had a steady boyfriend since Lucas and I split up."

"There's that nice veterinarian."

"Whom I've barely kissed and have to avoid talking to now."

Georgie cupped her head in her hands. "Ian has probably given up on me already. He called a few hours ago and asked me out for this weekend. I lied and said I had to go away for a couple of weeks to do some research for an article. I felt sleazy lying, but I wasn't about to go on a date while pregnant with another man's baby."

"Did he believe you, that you had to travel for an assignment?"

She shrugged. "Sure, why not? It's not as if he knows my habits well enough to realize that I rarely get off my ass for work. I said that Lucas was staying with Jesse, and he seemed a little freaked out by that, Lucas staying at my house."

"You're not required to explain yourself," Nina absolved her. "You're not even in a relationship yet."

"He's the first man I've felt even vaguely interested in since my divorce, and look what I did to screw it up!" Georgie exclaimed, noting the quaking in her voice. "I slept with my ex-husband, with whom I have no future and a shitty past."

"Stop beating yourself up. It happened before you met this guy and right after your dad died, when you were most vulnerable."

Was vulnerability to blame for her dilemma?

"How about your mom?" Nina asked. "Are you going to tell her? This is one area where she could actually be of help to you."

"No! Absolutely not!" Georgie whipped her head around in fear. "You have to promise not to say anything to anyone, not Aunt Lily, not even Elliot. Not a word!"

"I promise. Don't worry." She squeezed Georgie's hand and they drove in silence for a few beats. "How you holding up?"

Swallowing down the chalky taste in her mouth, Georgie stared out the window at the adobe-style housing complex built yards from the highway. "A part of my brain is just completely numb. Death is becoming a way of life."

EIGHT

A thirteen-year-old Georgie sat hunched over her journal, legs splayed on her bed, creating a wide triangle. Distracted from her newly lithe body, she clamped down on her pen with her teeth. The late-afternoon sky had finally shed its bleak winter suit, and the sun winked as if too happy ever to set. This was following a miserable season; for months the snow had fallen from a gray sky with stultifying regularity, until the city's sharp silhouettes were muted, and the trees hunched over from the weight leaning on their branches. But finally Georgie had cracked open her bedroom window for the first time since summer, the lacy white curtains billowing, the sound of the city, its honks and screeching tires, wafting in like music.

Estelle appeared in the doorway, her face uncharacteristically lax, but her back perfectly straight as if tightly corseted. All that day, transported by her poem, polishing the language so carefully, like a jeweler with a rouge cloth, Georgie had allowed herself to consider a miracle: that her mother—through telepathy or divine intervention—would snap off her rubber gloves and rush home to celebrate this achievement, just the two of them.

"What are you up to?" Estelle asked in her measured voice. "Homework?"

"No, done," Georgie said, nervous excitement fluttering in her torso like moths manic from the light.

"What are you working on then?" She walked closer and bent over Georgie's shoulder, so the girl could smell the spicy oriental musk of her mother's perfume.

"I'm finishing my poem for the contest."

"Yes, I wanted to talk to you about that. I have some bad news." She sighed. "I'm afraid I have to go out of town for a few days and won't be back in time for your performance."

"What?" Georgie exclaimed, awash with disappointment, the corners of her mouth downcast.

"I *am* sorry, but it can't be helped. There's a conference at John Hopkins University that I'm obligated to attend. I've agreed to participate on a panel. Its focus is the ongoing ramifications of *Roe versus Wade* on the medical profession, which is very important to all women of this country, as you know." Estelle smoothed the hair on the nape of her own neck and took a deep breath. "Dad will be at your contest, though."

"I'm one of five finalists in the city and the youngest one, the only eighth grader!"

"Well, that's nice by itself, isn't it?" her mother asked in a falsetto voice.

"Writing poetry is important even if the Supreme Court isn't choosing the winner."

Rejection caused a warm pain to spread through Georgie's chest and belly. Why couldn't her mother even feign understanding? Georgie's current best pals called themselves Sylvia and Anne, after two famous women poets. They wore purple and burgundy peasant skirts, Dingo boots, mood rings that shifted colors from red and black—recording how pissed off they were—and sneaked Kool cigarettes. Georgie never smoked because her mother had shown her an X-ray of a woman dying from advanced lung cancer.

Intrapartum asphyxia, meconium aspiration, fetal tachycardia— these and a myriad of other medical terms were her mother's poetry. The fact that Georgie had read *Jane Eyre* and *Little Women* that autumn was not as impressive as a woman coming through a breech birth unscathed. At her father's suggestion, Georgie had even slogged through *Great Expectations* over Christmas break from Brearley. She would lie on her bed, tangled in her elbow-length hair, book in hand, for hours on end, always hoping her mother would notice.

Estelle's eyebrows arched, and for the first time Georgie could remember—without her father present—she asked, "Well, how about you read it to me now, instead? You could practice."

Georgie shook her head. "It isn't finished." She inched over so that the page from her journal was visible. "You can read it to yourself if you want." She'd been proud of the way the words vibrated and gleamed. She skimmed through one stanza describing her affection for her friend before handing it to her mother. Watching her mother's mouth tighten into a thin red ribbon as she read, Georgie feared she'd been mistaken.

Estelle licked her lips and handed back the notebook. "I don't know if this particular poem is the best one to choose, not with an entire auditorium of people listening. What do you think? Maybe you should pick something less personal, less . . . I don't know . . . romantic. This might embarrass you in front of all those strangers."

A piercing chill infiltrated Georgie's bone marrow, freezing whatever had been warm and flowing in her moments before.

"It's not romantic!" she snapped. "It's about friendship."

"Don't take what I'm saying the wrong way. I didn't mean it isn't written well. The writing is fine. I just meant that some things are meant to be private. This might be better for your diary."

Georgie chewed on the inside of her cheek, lumpy and soft. "Poetry is not supposed to be just for the person writing it. Miss Hamilton loved the first draft of this; she thinks I'm good," she braved, close to tears.

"I'm sure your teacher is right. Poetry is a very nice hobby. Your father used to write poetry as a hobby too when he was your age."

"This isn't just a hobby. It's what I want to do."

"No one can make a living as a poet, Georgia. It's better to do something that involves other people—you'll realize that when you get older—rather than living in your own head all the time. Maybe you'll become an English teacher."

Georgie pinched her nostrils together as if this were the most disgusting proposition, as if her mother had suggested becoming an incinerator operator of medical waste or an embalmer at a mortuary. "I don't want to be a *teacher*. I've told Dad that I want to be poet and *he understands. He's even encouraging!*"

Estelle scowled, creating a crease between her eyebrows, an exaggerated slope of her mouth. "Your father grew up with money," she retorted, her teeth clicking together, a metallic sound like pennies hitting against each other. She sighed and headed toward the door. "Dinner will be early tonight. Dad's coming home in about an hour."

The night sky turned indigo, a canvas for the three-quarter moon whose stream of dusty light was as bright as a car's headlights on low beam, only more magical. If only a moonbeam could whisk her away to a more fitting home where mothers loved their daughters unconditionally. When she heard her father's steps down the hall, she regretted her wish. *Dad loves me.*

Adam peeked his head into her room, his eyes glassy after a long day of cajoling toddlers to let him gently poke their soft bellies. "Mom told me she might have upset you," he said. "About the poem? She didn't mean anything by it, Georgie girl."

"Why does she have to be like that?" she asked from her perch on the bed, her journal still in hand. "Can't she just lie if she doesn't like what I write? What would it matter to her if she lied?"

"Ah, honey. Give her a break. It's not that she doesn't like it. Of course she does. She was just offering you a bit of friendly advice. And anyway"—he winked his conspiratorial wink—"your mother's a hypothesis-and-formula gal, although she specializes in bringing new life into the world. That's a kind of poetry too, sweetheart, if you think about it."

Over two decades later, Georgie was trying to recall the sensation of composing poetry: the galvanizing urge to thrust the words out in a rush, before they dissolved like sugar granules on the tongue: "Ode to a Baby Who Will Never Be Born."

Gallows humor, she chided herself, *tasteless.* But her mother couldn't disapprove on the grounds that her subject choice was too sentimental. She could compose a little ditty on one of Estelle's heartfelt political topics, with not a pinch of romance added. A dissident voice reminded her of what she'd read in Estelle's diary, and a host of contradictory feelings swelled in her at once. Her mother, always such a straight arrow, the epitome of clear masculine purpose and stunning achievement, had once possessed prosaic female doubts about her own mothering abilities, her shortcomings.

Georgie held the phone in her hand, her address book open to her gynecologist's phone number. It was early on a Monday morn ing, over a week after she'd confessed her mishap to Nina. And, still she was procrastinating.

She peered at the telephone before replacing it on her desk. On Google she typed *abortion clinics in New York City and New Jersey.* Compelled to read a comparison of the various procedures with taking the pill, RU486, she felt anxiety dance a wild jig in her brain. Swiftly she printed out a list of providers in the tri-state area, then closed the application on her computer. Nina would accompany her to whichever gleaming white room, repellent with the medicinal smells of ammonia and latex, she chose for the procedure. A women's center in Bergen County seemed like a palatable option. The Web site spelled out its mission in bold alliteration: *kind, caring, compassionate, and confidential.*

She made the appointment for the following week, tempted to barter a free aspiration (seemingly the least traumatic method) in exchange for her writing services. Friday she would see her gynecologist to confirm the pregnancy. She could always change her ever-changing mind.

While she was leaving a message for Nina, her mother's number came up on call waiting. "Georgia, are you there?" Elephantine sigh.

"I'm on the other line; just a second." She clicked back over.

"I've gotta take this call from my mom. Let me know if you can make it on Monday at ten forty-five. I have to check in a half hour before."

Of course Nina would be there. She'd cancel out her entire day to ferry Georgie to and fro. When would it be Georgie's turn to return the favor?

"Hi, Mom."

"Yes, hello. Georgia, my anniversary is coming up. I'd like you to come out to brunch with me. I could use some support, this being the first time in almost forty years I won't be with your father."

A yellow jacket buzzed outside Georgie's office window, right under the sun's gaze. Down below lay her small patch of yard, verdant and untended; a robin redbreast landed near a bunch of clover and then flew off. At the graveyard after her father's funeral, a robin had appeared, stunning them all on that cold March day. "It's Adam," her mother had proclaimed.

Slow and steady exhale. "When do you want me to come in?"

"Sunday is my anniversary."

The day *before* the scheduled procedure. "Okay. Fine."

"Good. I need to ask you a favor. I need for you to explain to Jesse that this has to be just us adults this one last time. I promise that next weekend I'll spend an entire day with him. I so miss that boy. It's just taken too much out of me these last few months, and now delivering babies again. I want to strangle them as they come down the pike." She cackled. "A strange reaction to grief, I suppose. Jesse's not used to that."

"What? Not used to you having urges to commit infanticide?"

Oops! Wasn't *she* the pot calling the kettle black?

"Very nice, Georgie, very compassionate. He's *used* to seeing me strong. I'll take him out to Mars for lunch. He still likes Mars, doesn't he? The restaurant where the waiters dress like spacemen?"

"Yeah. He still likes it. The only problem is, this is my weekend with Jesse. Luke had him the last two in a row."

"Lucas is his father. A couple of hours are all I'm asking for."

"I'll talk to him. I'll work it out." She could already hear her ex's grumbling protestations: "Fair is fair. Zo and I had tickets to see a matinee," or "I promised to take Zoë to Soho to window-shop at Prada," or worst of all, "C'mon, that's the time we'd slated for enjoying her new Victoria's Secret lingerie."

Georgie asked, "Is Lily coming?"

"I don't think so. I think it will just be the two of us."

A moment of jerking panic: What if her mother could detect pregnancy pheromones the way a perfumer could sniff out the perfect scent?

The morning of her parents' anniversary, Adam had been dead for three months and four days. Georgie awoke feeling nauseous but eerily calm, the way a suicide was supposed to feel once the perilous notion tickling her mind congealed into a resolution. The doctor had confirmed what she'd known to be true. She was approximately eight weeks along.

The sky was a perfect blanket of blue-and-white beauty, the sun high and bright. Georgie opened her window shades to the day and peeked into Jesse's room, imagining him asleep at his father's place, droplets of saliva raining on his pillow, the smell of musky skin and sour breath tearing through the membrane of his boyhood. Soon he'd be a young man, without his grandfather around to witness the transformation. She longed to touch his forehead with her lips and breathe him in.

Lucas had begrudgingly agreed to take him to the planetarium, Zoë—much to Jesse's chagrin—in tow. Georgie was free until the evening to meet her mother for brunch; the thought caused an accordion squeeze of her heart.

After a breakfast of crackers and tea to settle her queasy stomach, she called Nina. "I'm afraid she'll be able to tell. She's been an obstetrician for so long, she must be able to home in on all the signs. What if I get nauseous or throw up in front of her?"

"There are these modern inventions called bathrooms. You could always try to use one of those," Nina said, chomping on something loud and crunchy. "Look, I wish I could offer some support, show up unexpectedly and share dessert. But I can't. Franny is in a recital at her ballet school. She has to wear false eyelashes and Super Lustrous Lipstick in Revlon Red."

"Tramp, that little slut. Are you sure she wouldn't rather have a free brunch with her great-aunt Estelle?"

"It'll be fine," Nina said.

"In what parallel universe?"

"Honey, your mom is reaching out. It's what you wanted."

"Not when I'm five minutes from ending a pregnancy."

"I'll pick you up at nine thirty sharp tomorrow morning."

A vertiginous shift to the room. "Right. Thanks, Nina. I love you."

"I love you too."

The Manhattan Café on First Avenue was packed, an open space with a view of their gardens in back, polished wood floors and a baby grand piano in the left-hand corner, no player in sight. The tables were covered with linen tablecloths and graced with vases filled with fragrant creamy white gardenias. Georgie arrived before her mother. Feeling all lit up with neon anxiety, she ordered a glass of chardonnay at the bar. *Bad for the baby,* she thought before remembering: *Not as bad as abortion*. The drink was liquid salve, smoothing out the edges of her cracked nerves. She chewed a very salty cashew and ran her hands over the countertop of the bar. The world was just beginning to slow down when she saw her mother enter. Decked out in a new silk pantsuit, Estelle had shed some pounds and appeared less puffy. She was wearing makeup again, although not well. Her lips were painted a startling purplish brown and her eyelids were smoky gray, as if she were aiming for sultry but missing by about twenty years. Still, she looked attractive in an imperial way—Dame Judi Dench playing Shakespeare's majesty—only with darker hair and brown eyes. Georgie considered escape, her body tugging at its own sleeve, but a mad dash for the door, dramatically passing her mother in transit, did not appeal. "Calm down," she scolded herself. "You're being paranoid. She's not going to notice, and if she does, you'll plead stomach virus."

The hostess—an elegant-looking person in a black silk dress and stiletto heels—gently guided the pair to their table, pulling out Estelle's chair with graceful aplomb. Her eyes were lined in kohl, her hair wispy brown with copper highlights. She was young and pretty, most likely an actress wannabe. *Let's get out of here,* Georgie ached to say. *Tell me your life story.* She imagined strolling with this girl along the avenue, peeking into bodegas with their displays of candy-colored fruit, kiwis and apricots, containers of cut melons and bananas, garnet-red pomegranates.

"I'll have another chardonnay," she said, knowing her mother would never suspect pregnancy if she were drinking alcohol. Georgie had been so careful when expectant with Jesse, following all her doctor's rules unwaveringly.

"I'll tell your waitress." The hostess nodded and glided away.

Estelle stroked her water glass delicately the way one would a small cat. "Well, thank you for meeting me. It's good to be out of the house, with all its memories."

"I'm sure."

"You're having wine this early in the day?" Estelle craned her neck so that Georgie could catch a whiff of her disdain.

It had begun drizzling outside, a sudden spring shower, as if God were peeing on them. "Yes, it's wine."

"Aren't you picking up Jesse after lunch? I don't think you need that second glass you ordered."

The elfin waitress appeared, like Tinkerbell, to save the day.

Throwing cholesterol concerns to the wind, Estelle ordered a Reuben sandwich with extra French dressing while Georgie ordered a Cobb salad and scanned the room. To her left was a table of young women sheathed in sleeveless wrap dresses, laughing and tapping each other in glee. To her right was a couple in their early fifties, decked out in yellows and green, pearls and docksiders, appearing dignified and relaxed. Not an inflated belly among them. Not one in mourning. *Can we join the party?* she longed to ask.

"Listen. There are some things I need to talk to you about, Georgia," her mother began. "I would like for you to call Lily for me periodically. She's feeling very isolated since Adam's death, and naturally I can't be there for her the way she needs. Just check in to see how she's doing, cater a little to *her* feelings, as she's been doing so attentively to mine. She hasn't complained one iota about her own depression during these last six months. But I know how bad she feels; of course I do. She's been wonderful, there for me when no one else was."

"Ma, are you okay?" Georgie asked, reaching out to touch her mother's hand. It felt cool, the fingers starting to knot at the joints.

A sob escaped, then another. Estelle's nose reddened and tears ran into the corners of her mouth. She fished inside her leather pocketbook for a package of tissues. "Of course I'm not okay," she hissed. "Should I be? Do you *think* I should be okay?"

Georgie withdrew her hand and watched as her mother blew her nose.

"Oh, look." Estelle threw up her hands and her tears magically abated, like an accelerated re-creation of the Ice Age ending, the melting and drying up in one big *National Geographic* whoosh. She glared in Georgie's direction. "I wish we could be—I can't explain it— like a big, close-knit family, everyone looking out for each other. Let me ask you something—Nina, of course, is being her usual courteous self—but your cousins Alex or Saul, has either of them called you to see how you're doing, even once since the funeral?"

When Georgie shook her head, her mother nodded triumphantly, chin high. "Of course not! I don't know what's wrong with these people. I guess it's partially my fault. When did I ever want a close extended family before in my life? We were all so self-contained in those days—all the Merkins and me—putting ambition before extended family, putting ourselves first, except for your father, of course. Which would explain why Lily misses him so terribly."

She sighed with full Wagnerian intensity. "Let's face it: Uncle Artie is no Adam, not with that toupee. So call her for me. Okay? When you think about it, it's not too much to ask, is it?"

"No, it's just awkward. Aunt Lily and I aren't exactly close. We don't have a lot to say to each other."

"This isn't a social request. It would be an act of charity. Certainly you can find the time in your busy life to perform an act of charity, can't you?"

"Sure, Ma." She felt nausea bubble up into her throat.

Move, Georgie's brain screamed to her legs, but her legs did not respond. Like logs they remained inert, pushed up under the table. Would they remain paralyzed right through her salad and on to lattes and desserts? No. After a minute, she was able to mobilize her body, to duck into the bathroom until the queasiness passed. On the white porcelain toilet, she took several deep breaths.

When Georgie reemerged, her mother was standing there, waiting by the restroom door. "The food is here," she said curtly.

Alone at the table with her plentiful salad, second glass of chardonnay, and destabilizing hormones, Georgie let her mind wander, imagining her father as part of the scene. She envisioned him smiling forlornly, saying little, even escaping to the john to call for his messages, to shut his eyes, distracted, even worried that he forgot to turn on his answering machine. At some point he would whisper, "Your mother doesn't mean to take it out on you, sweetheart. It's not you she's angry with. It's me, for leaving her. Hang in there; help her out."

Estelle returned to her meal. After a few hearty bites—a dollop of pinkish brown dressing dotting the side of her mouth—her hands began to flutter as she touched her spoon, the prongs of her fork. "There's something else I need to talk to you about. I've been thinking about making some changes."

"Like what?" Georgie gazed down into her salad bowl as if it were a Magic 8 Ball. Perhaps some marvelous fortune would bob up through the greens: *Have the baby and all will turn out for the best;* or, *Wait and see; loss will unite you with your mother.*

"I'm considering cutting back on work and spending more time out of the city."

"Really? You've never mentioned wanting to work less."

"My husband never died before."

Georgie grabbed the skin on the nape of her neck and inhaled deeply again. "Why start leaving New York now? You've always loved Manhattan, and all your friends are here."

Stellie licked her lips and, for a second, her brow furrowed. "Quite honestly, I'm lonely here."

"Where would you go?"

"I thought I'd travel." She shrugged. "I have some friends in other cities, some colleagues, and . . . I don't know. It's just an idea. I hate being alone in the house."

"That's a good idea. Maybe you could go with other people, like a tour." As soon as the words left her mouth, Georgie felt the ineptness of them swat her on the face like a wooden paddle.

"God, no! I'd hate that, all those strangers huddled together on a bus, being forced to discuss the Lake District with some nice old woman who breeds Irish setters." She shuddered as if the desire to breed animals were contagious. "I *would* like to spend time away, but not too far. I've always liked the Boston area. It's something I'm *considering*—that's all."

Georgie's heart and lungs clanked together like ice cubes in a tumbler. When had her mother ever professed a preference for that cold city? It dawned on her: this pseudo friend, this pen pal, might be luring her mother up the long arm of New England. He might be a con man, preying on the vulnerabilities of new widows, planning on taking Estelle for all she was worth, like in a Lifetime television movie starring Melissa Gilbert. *Geez, a little too much imagination. No more drinking for you,* she thought, putting down her glass.

"Have you talked to Lily about this? I bet she'd like to spend time traveling with you."

Away from Uncle Art.

Still smeared with sauce around her lip, Estelle dabbed her napkin into the water glass. More landed on her blouse and she attempted to blot it off.

"I don't see myself taking any long trips with Lily. Don't get me wrong: I love her as if she were my own sister. But it would be too horrible for me being with her without Dad, two old ladies traveling. That just smacks of widowhood. What could be more depressing? I'd rather be alone."

"Well, if it would give you a break."

"I'm telling you now for a reason. I'm going up to Boston a week from Friday for a couple of days. I've rented a car and will be staying at the Marriott. I wanted to let you know in advance and give you the information, the phone number, whatever, in case."

"Okay, Ma. I guess it's best to travel close to home until you feel better."

"When would *that* be?"

Georgie called Lucas from her cell phone to say she was on her way. "Send him down to the lobby. Burt can keep an eye on him." Burt—the beefy weekend doorman who always greeted Jesse with a high five.

When she pulled up outside the skyscraper, Jess shuffled to the car, hunched over, head bent, a boyish Quasimodo with a deformed body and a heavy heart.

"Hey, kiddo, what's wrong?" she asked out her open window. "You look sad."

"I'm stressed." Listlessly he got into his seat, taking a long time to peel off his coat.

"Didn't you have a good time? Buckle your seat belt."

"Good time? Not unless you consider watching Miss MTV lick the cream cheese off her bagel with her tongue ring a good time. She's so incredibly dumb! When Dad was talking about these businesspeople in Toronto, she called Canada a state. Dad's dating someone so stupid she doesn't even know Canada's a country! Canada doesn't even have states! It has provinces!"

Georgie couldn't help but grin as she pulled out onto Park Avenue. "Did you correct her?"

The boy shook his head. "I don't talk to her if I don't have to."

"Did Dad correct her?"

"He *never* does. He talks to her like she's his dog or something, all sweet but like he knows it's completely empty up here." He knocked on the side of his head with his index finger.

"So what did you do? Did you guys go out for lunch or anything?"

"Yeah. So what! I can't stand being with him when he's with her. I'm getting all screwed up. I felt like I was getting hot flashes sitting there listening to them talk."

"Hot flashes? What do you mean?"

"I don't know, Ma. I'm just a kid. I felt all hot and dizzy. It's 'cause I'm getting metathesiophobia."

"Excuse me?" Georgie leaned her head back and gave him a quick glance before focusing on the traffic.

"Fear of changes. Another phobia I'm definitely going to get if Dad marries Toe Ring—that's my nickname for Zoë—is novercaphobia, fear of your stepmother."

"Jess! How do you know these terms?"

"Gus and me have been looking up phobias on the Web."

"Why, sweetie?"

"I'm telling you, Ma. It's because I'm *stressed*. Soon I'll be polyphobic, afraid of lots of stuff."

"Is Gus worried about developing phobias, too?"

"Not really. He just thinks it's cool to know all this weird stuff. Like last time I was over, he asked his mother if she was proctophobic and she got all concerned at first, 'cause she thought she looked sick or something. Then, when she found out what it meant, she got all mad at him."

"Why? What does that mean?" Georgie was no fool; she could see it coming.

"Fear of rectums."

Jesse broke out in giggles.

Even so, in the mirror, it was easy to detect the tension in the upward curve of her son's eyes, the forced, not quite jovial texture to his laugh. All was not right in her little family of two. How could she add unplanned pregnancy into the mix and expect her son to fully recover his innate good nature?

That night in bed, Georgie contemplated how different the architecture of her life would look if the angel of death had never flown over her father's house. She would have fought harder to maintain her relationship with Michael, her hope to become a serious journalist, all of it. She could have convinced her ex-lover not to follow the scent of burning flesh all the way to Kuwait City or—although much more unlikely—she might have trekked through the scorching desert terrain with him, with calloused feet and dust storms blinding them.

In her first dream, her father, the swirling blue cloud of him, the warm, affirming sense of him, surrounded her in the shadows. Grandma Ruth was there. Georgie smelled hints of rose and jasmine, her grandmother's signature Joy perfume, and heard the whispers of her approval, indistinguishable syllables of love, swirling into her left ear.

But then she dreamed that she'd discovered a lump and the mammogram results were ominous. Some cloud on an X-ray, some patch of breast density, something was awry. Rather than going to the radiology center in town, she'd ended up in her mother's office, seated on a cold steel chair, in only a flimsy robe. The sound of Estelle's hushed voice reached her; blood rushed to her head. In a flash she was home, cradling the phone. The weekend whirled by and her mother never called. Nothing was hurried; there was no sense of urgency. Cancers cells might have been mercilessly multiplying in Georgie's body while Estelle cut her chicken into edible bites and sipped red wine. By her side was her mysterious pen pal, a gerontologist working on a cure for aging, a way to ensure that he and his beloved Stellie would live forever.

Georgie could see him only in shadows, his short, muscular trunk, his face a blur except for a pair of glasses and the long nose in profile; someone quick paced and intense, all his energy focused, like a ray, on her mother. There was the sound of buzzing. It was coming from his back, like that of a fly rubbing his wings together excitedly. Her mother and the man were in a cabin on Lake Willoughby, having escaped for the weekend. A vermilion light passed under Georgie's eyelids, then turned lighter, an orangey yellow. She blinked images of the insect man until he was gone.

Speaking to her lover, Estelle declared, "I bring babies into the world. I don't help kill them before they have the chance to be born."

NINE

Georgie awoke to a warm heaviness, the sun's pale arm resting across her cheek. A dream that she'd miscarried the baby—a froglike creature floating, slimy green belly up, in a pool of blood around her ankles—startled her into consciousness. She was groggy, bobbing under like a buoy knocked over by a particularly windy night. Her eyes were crusty and the hair that had curled into her cheek gave off a musky oil smell. *There is still time for the governor to issue a pardon,* she thought, picturing the abortionist administering the lethal injection.

Her mind wandered to another scene: She was weeping quietly in bed next to Lucas, her back to him as he tumbled into sleep, nonplussed after their terse discussion. Only moments had passed since they'd decided to forgo trying for another baby—the state of their union was too rocky—yet already he'd slackened into sleep, his body curled into a small letter G, his mind lulled into a dreamland filled with snips and snails and puppy dogs' tails. A sitcom Georgie had never seen was on television in their bedroom, the laugh track piped in too loudly. By remote control she turned on the mute button and just stared at the moving mouths and farcical gestures of the actors. Outside the window she heard a car skid, then the soothing sound of light rainfall. She'd studied her husband—openmouthed, bare assed, his leg hiked up, his toe nearly pointed in dancerlike grace, while raindrops of saliva wet his pillow, his breath slightly fermented, like cider gone bad—and felt no connection, not even the coarse ache of sex. That was the moment she knew her marriage was over.

Now dread parched her throat, her knees felt tremulous, and the taste in her mouth was chalk. A quick shower did some good, the cool water slapping her upturned face, the dual fragrances of lavender shampoo and oatmeal soap. Afterward she dropped the towel and stood naked in the bathroom, which—other than the one above the sink—was devoid of mirrors. She'd lost even more weight since her father's funeral; she could see it in the sculpted curve of her hips, the slight indentation of her waist. The blue-gray circles under her eyes had deepened in her now sallow complexion, so that they almost perfectly matched the color of her eyes—a weird trick, like some fashion model's outlandish makeup job for a *Vogue* shoot. Her long lashes stuck straight forward like awnings, as if trying to protect her from emotional hailstorms.

Her only feature that seemed to have improved in the last couple of months was her hair; since her mother's comment at her father's grave site she'd let it blossom out of her head without her usual six-week trim, and hormones were already thickening it so that it grew quicker and curlier. She twisted it into a short ponytail, confining it at the nape of her neck. After dousing her face with water and quickly brushing her teeth, she absentmindedly rubbed her hands around her tummy, whispering, "Shh, shh," to the passenger swimming inside of her. Abruptly she clenched her fists, remembering the grim purpose of her day.

Georgie padded into the kitchen to brew coffee before Jesse rose to the soft-shoe shuffle of Monday morning. Caffeine would jumpstart her sorry neurotransmitters and help put her mind to rights. The room was already warming up like a furnace, the stagnant New Jersey torpor on its way although it was only late spring.

Dark roast in hand, she answered her ringing phone. "Hi, honey," her cousin cooed. "Just checking to make sure you're all right. I'll be there as soon as I run one errand."

"I'll be ready," she said through a parched throat.

"You sound terrible. Let me cheer you up with a little comic relief. Guess who was awoken by the piercing screams of her older daughter at six a.m.? That's right! Yours truly. Franny decided to greet the day by giving her sister a nice sharp bite in the ass."

Lowering her coffee mug onto the table, Georgie smiled. Normal life still existed on the other side of the rainbow. "Why?"

"Let's see. Kate was behaving, and I quote, 'like a butthead' to her all day yesterday. I instructed the babysitter no TV." She sighed. "I hope I don't have a degenerate on my hands."

"Nina, she's fine. She's got spunk, that girl."

"The physical crap has to end. I keep telling her to use words to express anger, but she's learned that violence is so much more effective. Especially since Kate has cornered the market on verbal skills."

"It must be hard to deal with sibling rivalry without having any firsthand idea what it's like, you being an only child, like me, like Jess," Georgie said.

"Oh, honey, there's still time to change your mind."

Georgie's chest hurt. She gazed at the chlorinated blue sky, at the sparrow pecking at the dirt in her flowerless window box. Not even an attempt at planting petunias this year. "I have no mind, anymore, to change. You're not seriously worried about Franny, are you?"

"Nooo. But I'm not happy with her behavior either. God, this traffic is crawling."

"Poor Nina. You've become my nursemaid and chauffeur."

"You're going through a very tough time, kiddo, and today's experience is just going to compound things. You realize that, right? There's no such thing as the Evelyn Wood version of mourning."

"That's too bad, because I'm a speedy kind of gal. Normally I hand in my work a week before deadline."

Nina laughed. "Sorry. You can be the best little Girl Scout in the world, but there's no such thing as efficient mourning."

"You know what I discovered? Most people don't agree with you. They don't expect a person to react so strongly to a parent's death, not when you're as old as I am," Georgie said.

Case in point: Sabine Parker, her editor at *Elle*. Right after Adam's death, Sabine had sent her condolences in the form of an expensive gift basket that arrived the day of the funeral, stuffed with pears, cheese, crackers, and chocolate-covered blueberries. But after a couple of weeks, her e-mails regained their breezy, hectic, scribbling-this-over-my-lunch-of-Caesar-salad-and-a-double-latte style.

"And forget abortion, unless you're in college," Georgie added. "I'm too humiliated to talk to my friends about it. This isn't something you're supposed to be stupid enough to have to deal with after the age of twenty."

"That's ridiculous! Accidents happen all the time. Plenty of married and divorced women are in your situation. I've had patients in my practice who were forced to cope with unwanted pregnancies, several of whom were married or divorced."

"But not friends, right? Mine would be too embarrassed even to discuss it. Can you fathom what Charlotte would think after everything she suffered through? She almost lost her life trying to give birth, and here I am choosing to end my child's like some kind of monster. Maybe I should offer to give her my baby, act as a surrogate."

"C'mon, sweetie. Stop it. You can't compare your situation to hers. It's like saying no one should eat a good meal because somewhere in the world, people are starving."

"Now Sabine, her I could see getting an abortion and still being on time for her pedicure afterward. No fuss, no regrets. At least, she'd never express these sentiments—well, maybe years later in a tell-all memoir."

She recalled the last lunch she'd had with her editor, earlier in the year. Sabine had arrived in a black bouclé suit and platform Prada shoes with open toes painted in a brick red, very Rosalind Russell. Her sable hair was glossed back into a tight ponytail, her mouth painted with her signature rose lipstick, her small blue eyes carefully made up with a light coat of mascara and a white shadow applied with an expensive brush. It had turned into a two-and-a-half-hour marathon, during which Sabine revealed that she was a couple of years younger than Georgie, never married, the proud owner of a one-bedroom apartment on West Eighty-eighth Street and a Birman cat whose eye color matched her own.

Georgie knew for a fact that her editor studied fashion magazines for tips the way other women scrutinized the NASDAQ. She had once confessed that, in her line of work, physical presentation was an asset to be carefully honed. Georgie was amazed to find—upon her first visit to Sabine's home—that in her personal life, her editor was a slob. Sabine had opened the door in a cotton dress and dirty Keds to display a dusty, sparsely furnished interior. Now she imagined Sabine with her professional face applied, smoking a slim brown cigarette and reading the copy for the latest issue of *Elle* while lying on the abortionist's gurney.

"I can't see any of my friends who already have children getting rid of their baby."

"You'd be surprised, Georgie. Be careful not to vilify what you're doing or you'll end up with a nice lingering depression."

"Okay, doc. I'd better go make some breakfast. You can shrink me in the car. About Franny—maybe you should just detooth her like you declawed the cat." She hung up the telephone.

"Who needs to be detoothed?" Jesse called from the stairway.

"Jess!" Georgie said, too exuberantly.

"Who was that on the phone?" he asked, his voice softening, riveting all his attention on Georgie with a look she recognized from his one unhappy season in soccer. He'd concentrated with all his might on that ball, terrified that if he took his eyes off it for one moment he'd lose the game for the entire team.

"Just Nina, sweetie. Dumb girl talk."

He yawned and shuffled to the table in his underwear and one of Luke's old pajama shirts. There was sleep in his right eye, and his hair—his lovely sandy hair—was sticking up like a peacock's crown. "Good, 'cause you've been really stressed lately, like in the commercial with the egg and the ladybug, where the egg keeps sighing and the voice says, 'You know when you're not feeling like yourself. You may feel sad, hopeless, you know, lose interest in things.' You need to lighten up."

Nothing like a little psychotherapist for a son.

"Honey, I'm not depressed. Really." She pulled Jesse's head close to hers and anointed it with three kisses. "I love you. Because you're you and you're so easy to love."

My one and only baby.

He squinted, his small nose crinkled up to a pug, and asked, "Ma? You're not going to start singing like that nun in *The Sound of Music*, are you?"

She smiled at him to prevent tears.

The waiting room of the clinic was a Laura Ashley fantasy, wallpapered in tiny red flowers on a blush pink background with immaculately clean white carpeting, a fake fireplace, and plush couches surrounding a coffee table piled high with magazines.

"This place looks like the inside of Cinderella's castle," Georgie whispered to her cousin. "What could possibly upset me here?"

Anticipating the trip had triggered a Pavlovian response in Georgie, who expected an austere hospital setting. In the car, she'd charted all her body symptoms: fractured, panicky, spaced out, or loopy, her life defined by imminent illness or breakdown.

"It does look like they're doing chemical peels and massages," Nina said. "Instead of . . . other things."

The receptionist greeted Georgie with a smile and handed her a clipboard with papers to fill out. She glanced down at the questionnaire, all about insurance and health history, and in that instant the air seemed to quicken around her, the light switched from a golden yellow to a pale gray; her heart stiffened into an angry muscle fighting to spring from her chest walls.

"It's okay," Nina said softly. "In a couple of hours you'll be on your way home. Can we get her a glass of water?"

Georgie shut her eyes, envisioning Jesse's face, scarlet as a plum as it shrieked his first-glimpse-of-the-world complaint, his arms spread wide as a preacher doing the Lord's work. She recalled scenes in movies in which panicky fliers leaped from their seats, pleading to be freed as the plane taxied down the runway preparing for takeoff. She could do that; the brakes were beneath her feet. Instead she sat anesthetized by resolve.

When a willowy nurse with a sad smile called her name, Georgie trembled. She would have to face this part alone, levitating above her feelings and focusing her attention on an innocent object, the door handle or the sink's scrubbed faucets, and away from the silver instruments glistening in their chrome tray, proud and shiny as a jeweler's display.

The procedure was over in an accelerated whoosh of time. It left her with a contracting uterus, a grainy sensation on her tongue, and one eye that refused to stop tearing. The willowy nurse helped her to her feet and into the recovery room, providing her with a heat pack, an oversize maxipad, and a small paper cup of orange juice. "Make sure you get your prescriptions for painkillers and antibiotics when you leave," she said gently. "And no sexual intercourse for at least a week, preferably two."

"Not much chance of that," Georgie said, smiling wanly.

Lying on her cot, she sought solace in the notion that the tissue extracted from her had been small as a blood clot or a moth's furry larva. Yet she felt pummeled and on the precipice of a steep descent into a shadow-filled valley. When Nina peeked into her room, Georgie looked up at her pleadingly. "Take me home."

The burgeoning season made Georgie cry, thickened her tongue, and rendered her legs wobbly. While the rest of the East Coast was reveling in the scintillating sunlight, the arched-open roses exposing their bellies, the dignified irises with their dipping tongues, while her friends and neighbors were anticipating the fake-cerulean pool water, the sticky-bottomed lounging on beach chairs, the luxuriously long days, while her own grieving mother was taking frequent jaunts up to New England, Georgie was hankering for the crisp clarity of fall.

Nights she dreamed of children who disappeared when she reached out for them, their bodies fading into porous material, as if they were dying from lack of focus. Mornings she awoke fragile as an egg, trying to conjure up the specter of her father dancing in the beam of sunlight streaming into her room. The opening line of Auden's poem "Musée des Beaux Arts" sang, like a torch song, in her head: "About suffering they were never wrong, / The Old Masters: how well they understood / Its human position; how it takes place / While someone else is eating or opening a window or just / walking dully along. . . ."

Work had not been its usual salve for months. The sound of the toilet bowl filling with water had been more tantalizing than any ideas banged out on the computer keyboard. Light would spill in generously from the back window, bathing Georgie's home in butter-colored warmth. She'd sit dutifully at her desk and gaze at Jesse's framed artwork hanging on the wall: his five-year-old rendition of two powder blue sparrows flying under a rainbow; a watercolor, done a year later, of a yellow flower with a lime green stem and vibrant pink petals—a hobby enthusiastically encouraged by Grandpa Adam. When he was seven, his teacher recommended signing him up for extracurricular art classes. Up until his grandfather's death, Jesse had continued to paint the physical world in pastels. But in the last few months he'd begun to belittle his own work. Finally he condemned all artists as "losers," and Georgie reproached herself for a litany of maternal mistakes: divorce, distraction, a dysfunctional relationship with her son's grandmother, and now, the worst crime of all, the obliteration of Jesse's sibling, allegedly, *hopefully*, for his own benefit.

One morning, a tropical storm crashed its way up from the Florida Keys to the tristate area, deluging the streets with ankle-high floodwater, drenching basements, licking the curbs with its monstrous tongue. Georgie felt a grateful allegiance to the weather for mirroring her mood and checked her e-mails: a note from a woman she'd recently interviewed and oodles of invitations to buy drugs without prescriptions. She opened her files of notes on plastic surgery gone bad and surgery addicts.

The article was due in three weeks and was long, five thousand words. Her usually copious research notes barely reached two double-spaced pages printed. She opened her journal to find a sprinkling of physicians' and patients' telephone numbers and one, which Sabine had forwarded, of a disgruntled patient scarred by a bad eye lift. Her mother's indictment of cousin Alex at the funeral flew into her head: "What do I care if Alex starves herself? My husband is dead. Adam would have loved to be able to eat these last few weeks. He had no appetite anymore."

She realized, with a jolt, that for once she agreed with her mother's upbraiding. Let these augmented, lipoed, tucked-and-lifted women complain to a more sympathetic listener while the voice of her father, whose condition had promised annihilation, still echoed in her ear.

"I'm sick of all this beauty. I need to focus on something more meaningful," she said, staring out the window at the leaves rustling in the wind and rain. "But what?"

Thirteen days after the abortion, on a warm, breezy evening, Georgie found herself dozing before Ian arrived, NPR on the radio, the cat sprawled on her lap, hazy white dreams floating across her line of vision. Her father's ghost—cheering her up with his soft-shoe—was whisked away by the peal of the doorbell. She blinked and scanned the room, calling out to Jesse before remembering that he was at his dad's for the weekend.

Ian was carrying half a dozen white roses cradled in his arms protectively, like an infant. Georgie's eyes clouded over as the image passed through her mind. It was the second time she'd seen him since the procedure; the first had been the previous Saturday. They'd gone to a movie and she'd feigned the last vestiges of the stomach flu in order to avoid any romance.

After their time apart, Ian looked even more appealing in his slim jeans, work shirt, and scuffed boots. He had a longish, thin face, aquiline nose, crooked teeth, and a nimble tongue that she liked to watch move as he talked. He reached for her hand—his palms chapped the color of a pink peony—and kissed her cheek.

"I feel like I haven't really seen you in months. It's funny, 'cause we haven't spent so much time together, but I've missed you," he said.

They gazed at each other, heat traveling through their skin.

"These are beautiful. How incredibly nice of you, especially since I was sure you'd be eaten up by one of the other hungry divorcées in town while I was incognito," she said, pulling him into the house. "Here, let me put them in a vase."

"The divorcées tried to have their way with me, but I was otherwise engaged." He winked at her. "I was worried about you. How you feeling? Still nauseous?"

She shook her head. In the last week guilt had been like a water stain seeping into elegant brocade, threatening to ruin the romantic longings she'd had for him. "Much better, thanks. And thanks for your lovely card and witty e-mails. You liked all my clever, writerly e-mails, yes?"

"Every one. What did you think of my attempt at veterinary humor?"

Ian's response to her last correspondence:

It has taken many months to track you down, but have done so with the help of my companion, George, the curious monkey, my patient, who I am sending your way with this missive. George is a young chimp that was brought to

> my care by a good-natured if strangely mute fellow who is
> tall of stature and seems almost unnaturally attached to his
> yellow hat. George can attest to my honorable intentions
> through his wily knowledge of sign language. Please keep
> him as a gesture of my goodwill and hope of further
> courtship. He is affable if occasionally incontinent.

"It was hysterical. I love chimps. They make for very neat *and* eco-nomical houseguests." She nodded, appreciation billowing inside her. "Hey, you look very tired. I can make coffee if you like."

When he smiled, all his muscles smoothed out and a warm light switched on under his skin. "No coffee. How about a beer? No beer? Wine?"

"Herbal tea. Orange juice. Even seltzer. Sorry about the lack of alcohol." She grinned to cover her embarrassment. The truth was, she'd barely had the energy to shop for Jesse lately. "This having-adults-over is a new experience for me."

He eased off his leather jacket (*so entirely sexy, so Marlboro man— what a teenager I am,* Georgie thought). "Don't worry. We'll work on it."

Pitter-patter.

Even her simple movements—reaching for her dad's old phar-maceutical mugs from Pfizer and Shire, pouring the bottled water, turning on the kettle—were under his scrutiny. Instinctively she pulled down her blouse to cover her waist as she stretched, not want-ing even a hint of flabby flesh to show, irrationally afraid her belly was swelling.

They settled in the living room with their respective cups of or-ange blossom, Georgie on the sofa, Ian in the maple rocking chair, jit-tery as middle school kids. The cat swished back and forth against this handsome visitor's pant legs until he swooped down and lifted her into his arms; Abby narrowed her yellow eyes in pleasure as he stroked her fur. Ian's cell phone rang, and as soon as he saw the caller ID, he snapped it open.

"Hi, pumpkin. What's the matter? Uh-uh. Did you try talking to her about how you feel? It's important to explain that to her, Avie. Yes, of course. I can talk to her tomorrow, if you want. All right. Put her on."

Ian turned so that his back was to Georgie, his head slightly bent. He lowered his voice. "Stace, yeah. This is a bad time for me. Right. No, I don't think it's a matter of getting away with . . . She's upset. I can't blame her. Yeah, of course I think it has something to do with it, even if she's not telling you directly. She's a kid! Look, I can't discuss this at the moment. I'm in the middle of something. Tell Ava that I'll call her first thing in the morning. Yes. Okay."

He clicked off his phone and looked at Georgie with a mixture of awkward embarrassment and angry distraction.

"What's up? Everything okay?" she asked, gazing at the triangle made by his collarbone and shirt, the few dark hairs sprouting on his chest. It was as if her craving for him had suddenly changed flavor, from a chocolate-sweet dessert to a full meal replete with rich cheeses and wine. It was clear, even from this one brief exchange, that he was a more insightful father than Luke, a fact that elicited an unsettlingly profound attraction in her.

"That was Ava," he said, tapping his foot. "Lately she and Stacy have been fighting nonstop." His eyes looked hooded and slightly puffy. He rubbed above the brows several times, as if to massage his skin awake. "Sorry; I'm a little preoccupied."

"Are you worried about her?" She leaned forward and touched his hand. "I understand, really! Getting a divorce is a bitch, all that guilt."

"That's it partially," he said, and shifted into an uneasy silence.

Pink twilight bathed the inside of the room. Georgie could hear him breathing slowly and with what sounded like some strain. She watched the day drain into the horizon, then shut her eyes for a moment so that the light behind her lids glowed a yellowish red, like flames.

"What is it? You can tell me," she said softly. "Unless it's too personal. I'll understand."

"It's not just the situation with Ava. It was probably selfish of me to come out tonight in the mood I'm in. But I wanted to see you."

"What's going on? Did something happen at work?" she asked, hopeful, envisioning furry creatures laid out on his operating table, stiff as wood planks.

"No. It's embarrassing even to admit that I'm upset about this," he said glumly, examining the wood floor. "The thing is, Levin proposed to Stacy. We're not even officially divorced yet and Stacy's already engaged. It pisses me off, because she wants me to feel demoralized by the whole thing."

Georgie started as if a door had slammed at her back.

"Maybe you're not over her," she said, thinking, *End of story*. It was a fun couple of dinners and a relaxing night at the cinema. But if it was so easy to dismiss him, then why did she feel the fissure in her heart tear further along its fault line?

"That's not it." He extended his arms in Georgie's direction as he might with a frightened animal whose trust he wished to win. "Please don't think that. All those wasted years—being with a woman who lied about her feelings for me—it's just depressing." He grinned sadly. "Her getting engaged brings up all those bad feelings."

"They weren't wasted," Georgie said gently. "You have Ava."

"Yeah, of course. But Stacy's using her against me now."

"How is she using her?"

"She's insisting that Ava is okay about the marriage, but she's not. If she's so okay, how come she and Stacy are fighting all the time?" He shook his head. "It's so like Stacy to try to manipulate me into feeling guilty for how Ava responds to *her* boyfriend, the man she left me for!"

He pursed his lips, amplifying his glaring eyes. "She warned me I shouldn't try to prejudice Ava against Levin, now that he'll be family. *Family*. He's not part of my family."

Compassion jetted through Georgie like a stream of light. "Divorce is so much more complicated than you think it'll be, isn't it?"

"Yeah." He nodded. "Just when you think you've gotten over the final insult, another hits you between the eyes."

"I know what you mean," she said, remembering the antiseptic smell in the clinic's operating room, the gleaming white lights, the sound of the tools clicking together like kitchen utensils—and then the cramping afterward, as if a jellyfish had stung her insides.

"I'm sorry," he said, casting her a guilty look. "This isn't fair to you, all this bullshit. I promise I'll try to keep it under wraps. You see, the love part is over."

Georgie licked her lips and smiled. "That's good to hear. But you don't have to apologize. It's tough to know what's right. You're obviously a great father. Ava has got to realize that if I do after such a short time."

When he rose from his chair the room shifted; heat rose from the floorboards. Shadows fell on the floor, his elongated one on the wall, first moving toward her, then bending down, and then she wasn't looking anymore.

He sat down beside her and took her hand and pressed his lips against it tenderly. "Bad way to begin a date. Can we start over?"

"Sure," she said, her voice cracking, hoarse.

"The thing is, I'm really attracted to you. I have been since the first time I saw you."

"Really? I thought you only had eyes for the pooch."

"No. Just you."

His kisses were greedy, his touch light as that of a virtuoso performing Chopin on her skin, neck, back, and breasts. All those hours caressing the fear out of high-strung terriers and Siamese cats had paid off, she figured.

"Maybe we should wait," she suggested, even as her body craved yielding to his easy dexterity, his lanky gracefulness, his sinewy, strong hands. She cupped her hands across her chest, feeling ridiculous covering herself, as if the abortion had removed breast tissue instead of a budding life. One day. She was only one day from the optimum time to avoid "sexual intercourse." In the name of maturity, she'd left the clinic with a prescription for the pill, which she'd filled the next morning.

"Hey." He caught her by the lip of her jeans. "Don't be shy. You're lovely."

The way he lowered his voice to stroke that adjective unhinged her: knees soft, a quickening between her legs. Georgie led him to her bed, rationalizing that sex would be a tonic for her frozen soul and ragged body.

"I'll just be a minute," she said, dashing to the bathroom, a little fist of reason knocking against her skull. *We just finished discussing his ex. I just aborted my ex's baby. Slow down.*

She chose not to heed its warning. Instead she imagined herself ushered into a dark cave on a rickety boat with Ian, vulnerable to the terrors ahead in the Tunnel of Love.

Ian's muscles on top of hers were taut, his face focused, his hands warm on the inside of her thighs. So much concentrated flesh, tight as an arrow, flung from the bow. Yet his eyes were clouded.

"Hey," she said, touching his face. "Over here."

"Yes," he murmured. His tongue wandered down her neck, clavicle, and nipples. Then they were a jumble of limbs and nerves. She saw hard flank, long torso, and tawny flesh, his full, expressive mouth. She experienced the glorious sense of being out of herself, watching the sheer newness of it all.

For Lucas, sex was sport, an intense, sweaty hockey game when best, a polite match of tennis at its most blasé. His favorite memories of sowing his oats included a brief encounter on a mountaintop in Munich (the girl's name escaped him), a slap and tickle with a college girlfriend on the grounds of the Bronx Zoo (after hours), a quickie in first-class under a blanket (night flight with Georgie). One lovemaking session with Ian warned her that this would require so much more: a drilling into the deeper recesses of her heart, a widening of the muscle, a close attention to the expanding version of herself. It had been so long since physical intimacy had demanded an emotional relinquishment that she wondered if she were still capable of that much elasticity of feeling. She was now, more than ever, acutely aware of her habit to dim the switch of her emotions.

For a few minutes afterward, Georgie drifted. Images from so long ago, of her journalist boyfriend Michael, floated in and out. Naked, Michael was, and rounded over on the bed, clutching his knees, his face hidden in the vee his stomach and legs made, dark and elegant, eternally young. The smell of him, musk behind his ears and down his lean neck, his onyx black hair and chiseled everything—she'd curl up so close to him there was barely room for a molecule to squeeze between them.

Georgie forced her eyes open and pulled the sheets up to her neck, suffering from postcoital bashfulness. The last time she'd bared her breasts to a new man had been more than a decade before, in her shimmering youth.

Ian drew her to his chest, the soft hairs sprinkled across it. "You okay?" he asked.

"Sure. You?"

"I'm great." He gazed down.

She glanced up into his nostrils, his eyes. He smiled so she could see the pinkish red inside of his mouth and tongue. "It's sort of embarrassing to admit this, but you're the first woman I've been with since the separation."

"I hope not the first of many," she said with a stupid little giggle.

"Of course not. It's just this." He drew an imaginary line between them. "It's new, strange, you know?"

"Sure. But pretty wonderful," she risked.

He lifted Georgie up to a sitting position and wrapped himself around her from behind so that his balls were resting against her buttocks. "*Extremely.* I'm glad to be here with you."

"Me, too. You don't think this is too soon? You and me?"

"It's soon. But not too soon."

"So then there is a you and me?"

"Of course. I'm not a one-night stand," he said jovially. "What kind of guy do you take me for?"

All night he stayed. Georgie seemed to sleep above sleep, acutely aware that there was a foreign body in her bed, his intermittent snores slicing through her thin shell of slumber. The smell of sex permeated the air: semen and saliva, musk and sweat, the faintly rubbery scent of penis, which was flopped over on its owner, resting after a valiant night of service. For a moment, on the crest of sleep, she lay next to a composite of all the men she'd ever made love to: Michael, Luke, Dennis Fieldstein, the two boys in between whose faces were permanently out of focus, and now Ian. In that instant, time inverted on itself and her father was still alive, the world a safe and familiar place; then the past collapsed into the present and yet, astonishingly, the sensation of peace remained.

For the first time in weeks, she didn't dream of death.

TEN

The summer that Georgie was twenty, she shared an apartment in lower Manhattan with Michael Bowman and his roommate, whose name she'd since forgotten. As she was still in college, her parents paid the rent, and it was Estelle who sent the checks. Georgie always sensed her mother's pleasure at being able to show possession in this concrete manner. When Georgie married Lucas, some of Estelle's disapproval seemed to come from the fact that the Carters were so immensely rich that her role as provider—her main way of demonstrating maternal devotion—was eliminated.

But that summer, living as a poor student, Georgie found a place that was basically a large studio split by a wall; in the section Michael and she shared, couch to bed was the farthest you could get from the other person without escaping into the bathtub. Days, Georgie worked as a temporary employee in various offices, tedious jobs that stayed with her into her sleep so that she'd dream of typewriter keyboards, the noxious smell of Wite-Out tickling her nostrils. The three roommates wrestled with insomnia, due to the apartment's location; outside their windows the traffic moaned and squealed, a collective noise they'd labeled "the Wounded Elephant." Occasionally they would share a bottle of Zinfandel in the hope that the wine would knock the noise out of their ears. But blue nights were all that mattered back then. Despite heat and the "roomates'" close proximity, Georgie and Michael would make love religiously—at least sixty times that summer—with such conviction that, often during the act, she'd develop vertigo.

In the sweet pink of new day, she awoke now and remembered those nights.

"Ah, youth! Ah, happiness," Nina said, via telephone, when Georgie described her odd jag of nostalgia.

Eight a.m. on a Monday in early July, all these years later. The bold sun splashed through Georgie's bedroom window so that her toes, peeking out from the covers, looked lit from within like angel toes. Snuggling under the comforter, air conditioner buzzing, she cradled the phone under her chin and balanced a mug of coffee on her belly.

"Nina, do you think things could have ever worked out with Michael if I'd been willing to wait it out for six months? It's strange, but I've been wondering about that a lot lately."

"Don't know, kid. He left for the Middle East. It isn't the easiest place to jet off to for a romantic weekend visit."

"He asked me to be patient."

"So what happened?"

"Cancer made me impatient," she said.

Georgie remembered Michael's expression when she drove him to the airport, ebony eyed as always, his gaze unfaltering, the deadpan face that took the world in as a challenge he could meet. At the last moment, pain glimmered beneath his skin's surface, his mouth twisted slightly, his eyes glistened, and his long-limbed body, so at home with itself, stiffened to ward off the blow.

"Who knows how things might have turned out," Georgie said. "I might have a whole brood of children now and a big house with a white picket fence in Jalib as-Suyuh."

What I wouldn't have is a uterus scraped clean of human tissue. What I wouldn't be is a murderer of my own flesh and blood.

"Sounds idyllic," Nina said.

"Why am I thinking of Michael now? I haven't thought of him in years."

"Gee, ever consider that little four-letter word?"

Georgie inhaled. "The L-word has not come up. If that's what you're oh-so-coyly referring to."

"There are lots of opportunities yet to come."

"Nah. I'm just happy that Ian is proving a great distraction. Otherwise I'd be so lonely with Jess at camp."

She thought of her boy gone, for two weeks, to a science sleepaway camp in the Catskills. Lucas had picked him up Saturday morning for the trip, both little men all excited at the prospect—Georgie's first time ever without her son for more than two days in a row. Change, big and small, was a viral eruption running rampant.

"Hey, Nina, I love you. Thanks for listening, as always."

"You'd do the same, my sweetie pie."

Georgie and Ian had planned a minivacation to Vermont, on the pretense of furniture shopping but perhaps to weigh and measure their progress at this, the three-month mark of togetherness. Georgie hoped not. She hoped that their intentions were modest despite the remarkable blend of passion and security Ian's presence in her life evoked. She craved escape—mountaintop and lakefront—leaving her mind at home in New Jersey to wrestle with the pain of loss and guilt while her body was away.

On top of the abortion, she'd been mulling over ideas for more serious articles—writing as therapy—ones without alliteration in the titles, defending single motherhood. She was exploring the guilt-provoking and disturbing trend to avoid divorce, for the children's sake, the cultural backlash against "selfish parents" creating "broken homes." Georgie would replay her mother's insistent warnings during the year that she and Luke were separating. Lately she'd been wondering if her lovely home was leaking and cracked at the foundation. Would the tissue around her son's heart weaken, the synapses transporting serotonin misfire, because of her self-indulgent choices? These thoughts looped around in an obsessive, pernicious pattern. If only she could send her brain out for a tune-up, could roam through the stacks of someone else's mind for a breather, a respite from the ticker tape that ran through her head: *Have you ruined Jesse's life by leaving Lucas? Should you have stayed in a blasé but not abusive marriage, for your child's welfare? Have you smashed your son's chances of finding true love to smithereens?*

She'd begun writing poetry at dawn, like Sylvia Plath. The difference was that her boy was not crapping in his cloth diaper next to his toddler sister, but was tucked placidly into his cot in the Catskills, dreaming of his unfolding day, searching for marsh hawks. *If I think of you, eyes as soft as a chick's down, the malleable, noodlelike nape of your neck, the soft scalp as if God had marked you with his thumbprint, if I think of the snap of the neck, of the whoosh of death accompanied by those dual fragrances, ammonia and latex.* She began the poem the day of her trip with Ian.

She hoped this little venture to the Green Mountain State acted foremost as a stress reliever; her love life would have to graciously bow down in her embattled psyche.

The first half-hour stretch up the Garden State Parkway was peaceful, cars whistling and tooting along and not much in the way of scenery to distract them. Ian popped an old James Taylor tape into the radio and transported Georgie back to Brearley Middle School with "Fire and Rain." She closed her eyes and felt the car bump underneath her. Like a small child, she was rocked into a twilight state by the seduction of movement. Sapphire blue behind the eyelids and the sway of time.

"Wow," she said, having dozed off and woken with a start. She wiggled into a sitting position, as if in sleep she might reveal something monumentally private.

"Pleasant dreams?"

"Not bad for a change. I'm sure it's the company."

They exchanged a cozy look. Ian's eyes were a lighter shade of brown than usual, flecked with gold. He removed one hand from the wheel and encircled hers in its grasp.

"I've been meaning to ask you something, and if I'm prying, you can just tell me to fuck off."

"Okay." Georgie glanced down at his cowboy boots—worn even through July's torpor—then at his face. Kindness shone from his skin like reflected light.

"You don't seem as happy as I feel. I'm wondering if you're okay with us?"

Georgie glanced out the window at the rim of dove gray sky. "I'm so much happier than you might imagine being with you."

While it might be committing relationship suicide to confess her abortion, her mother's behavior proved safe territory, a plausible explanation of what was exasperating her grief. It wasn't entirely a lie.

She said, "It's just taking me a while to deal with my dad's death.

Other than my cousin Nina I don't have anyone to really share the experience with."

A shock of hair fell over his face and furrowed forehead. "Hey, you have me. You can talk to me."

"I know, thank you." She lifted his hand clasped in hers and kissed it. "I meant someone who knew my dad."

"Can't you talk to your mom? I know you said she's a difficult lady, but I'd think she'd be approachable about this topic."

She shrugged. "She's furious at the world for taking him from her, and, unfortunately, that fury gets misdirected at me a little too often. I understand she's grieving but so am I. It's been pissing me off lately."

"Then tell her that!" he declared indignantly, as if he truly believed that love could act like a road map, that if you followed all the thin, sinuous lines, you'd safely arrive at your desired destination.

"I happen to get nervous expressing anger," Georgie said.

"No kidding. I guessed that about you, Miss Stand-up Comedian."

"Are you saying I hide behind my humor?"

"Hey"—he grinned—"everyone hides behind something. Humor is one of the more pleasant masks for the rest of the population."

"Thank you, Dr. Freud. Did they teach you Canine Psychology One-oh-one in vet school?"

"See what I mean?"

Georgie freed her hand and rubbed her eyebrow, the starting point of her headaches.

"My mother hasn't mentioned my dad lately. She's got this new pen pal that she e-mails, apparently, some younger guy who lost a family member to cancer. I'm thinking she feels more comfortable being vulnerable with him than with me. I know it's stupid, my feeling jealous of a stranger. After all, I have you and she doesn't."

He breathed lightly. "I'm glad to be here."

Outside it had begun to drizzle, the spitting sound of water against glass a lullaby. Ian reached for her hand again and a shiver ran through her, slippery as a minnow.

The rain was suddenly coming down hard. Water tapped its frantic code against the windows.

"Shit," Ian said, tensing forward into the windshield. "This was not predicted on Doppler Four Thousand."

"How peculiar."

"The rain?"

She shot him an ironic smile. "Everything."

They arrived in Vermont after stopping for lunch and a respite from the weather. The woman who ran the inn greeted them in a blousy dress with several silk scarves draped around her neck and shoulders. In the parlor were throw rugs composed of marigold and camel spirals, a wood crate filled with coffees and teas for the guests, and a vase of honeysuckle on a cedar hope chest. Their room was small and simple with a double bed, a rocking chair, and a cherry wood table. They rested on the throw pillows, plump, peach, and tasseled. As Georgie got up for their outing, Ian grabbed her by the arm.

"Hey," he said. "I'm sorry if I bullied you about your mom. You should be able to tell me whatever you want without me trying to solve your problems for you. Stacy always said I tried to solve problems rather than just listening."

Georgie bit down hard on her lower lip. *Fuck Stacy.* "I think you're an excellent listener."

"I hate to see you unhappy, that's all. I feel protective." He glided closer and kissed the back of Georgie's neck.

Sighing at the sensation of his mouth and tongue on her skin, she leaned into his chest, her legs instinctively opening. He placed one hand between them and then slid it down, under her shorts. She arched into him and he moaned in her ear, "You're so great."

"Antiquing can wait," she whispered.

They drove to the town center with its clock tower at the main intersection and small homes that had been converted into shops. Ian bounded out of the car like an unleashed wolfhound, pushed his face up to feel the air on his cheeks, and hurled his long, lanky body into the store.

While he chatted it up with the chunky-faced lady at the cash register, Georgie looked at ornate rings, onyx, turquoise, and garnet, under a glass plate. In a slow New England voice the saleswoman said, "Is your wife looking for anything in particular? We have more jewelry in the case upstairs," and pointed to a rickety wood stairway in the back.

Georgie didn't catch Ian's response. She froze with her back to him at the word *wife*.

At another shop, Ian tried to unlock the hands of one clock, literally stuck together by time. He listened politely to the clerk babble on about the history of the town, the history of the clock, and how it came to be broken. Ian called her "ma'am," and talked in a cheerful, easy way, slipping into a New England accent. In a back room, Georgie looked tearfully at a collection of ancient, dusty baby books, circa 1930.

Next they reached a store with a brook running by it and a narrow little bridge stretching from one bank to the next, made of planks of wood softened by rain and years. Inside it was dark and damp, rotten with the smell of moldy, decaying wood. An ancient balding man in denim overalls was standing toward the back of the place, bent over a tape recorder that in an instant burst forth with Bach. At first it appeared that there was only junk, a scratched-up table missing a leg, glassware with pastoral scenes and the word *Vermont* painted on them, tarnished spoons, peeling, wobbly chairs. But then they saw it. Across the room mounted on the wall was a wooden clock with a brass pendulum swinging, glass covering a white face with black Roman numerals and hands that moved to tell time. Georgie's father had had a clock like this in his den when she was a child. "I always loved it," she'd told Ian.

"The long-lost clock," Ian shouted, and did a funny little dance. "After searching through hill and dale, through uncharted land, we've found you."

The old man clicked on his hearing aid so that Georgie could question him about the price. But Ian waved his hand. "A gift from me," he said, ignoring her protests, telling her not to peek while he paid for it.

"She's a lucky lady," the storekeeper said.

Ian answered jokingly, "I think so."

That night they made love like cats marking their territory (rub here, here, and here), on the bed, on the floor, and in the shower. Afterward Georgie's back hurt and her bladder felt full. When was the last time she'd had such good sex that cystitis threatened? Long ago, her first few months with Lucas . . . She drank two bottles of water for good measure and sighed with sheer exhausted pleasure.

Lying with his arms crossed behind his head on the pillow, Ian said, "That was something."

"Sure was." She curled into the nook of his arm, the lime scent of his deodorant tickling her nose.

"I've never had this before."

"You mean good sex?" she joked.

"Not just that. You know this is more than just that."

Her heart beat out of rhythm. Georgie thought of the last time they'd been together, in his bedroom: cluttered and optimistic with two Cézanne prints on the wall—one of a luminous blue water jug, the other of vivid red cherries—an old maple armchair with several days' worth of clothes thrown over it, adjacent to a desk crowded with papers. She loved it there but the rest of the house was in worse disarray; old coffee cups in the sink with the milk having curdled on the top, dog hair on every inch of furniture, red paint peeling from the shutters, window boxes filled with wilted geraniums, the newspaper still encased in plastic on his small patch of lawn.

"A messy male is a cliché in every women's magazine," she'd said congenially.

"I'm not very good at living alone."

She wondered, then, if he'd pair off with the first female willing to enter Eden with him. Or to clean his home.

"Sure, I've been lonely and horny. But it's also that everything feels different than with Stacy," he said through a yawn, clearly on the night train to slumber. "Warmer. She was so hard to please. . . ."

Georgie scampered to sit up and edge away from him, her body stiffening, instantly all bone. "You know, I'd rather you didn't refer to her so much, or compare me to her."

Ian blinked away sleep and a look of bewilderment blanketed his face. He massaged his eyelid with one finger before hoisting himself up on his elbow. "I'm not comparing you to her."

"You are. You do it all the time."

"I do?" he asked, the corners of his mouth downcast.

"Yes. All the time."

"Wow, I'm sorry. I don't mean to. I guess I'm pretty naive for a guy my age."

"Look, I may be supersensitive. It's just that I worry that you're not over her, not really, and that ultimately you two are going to get back together." Georgie leaned over the edge of the bed to retrieve her underwear and long T-shirt.

"That's not going to happen," he said tersely. "She's engaged to another man."

Whacked! The fantasy had reached its expiration date; infatuation's high was gone. In its place more sadness bled. The wound for Stacy would retain permanent residency in Ian Weiss's faithful heart. Georgie would end up alone again.

"That isn't exactly the answer I was hoping for." She slipped both legs through their respective holes.

Ian reached out for her arm and encircled it for a moment until she slipped out of his grasp. "That came out wrong. I'm not interested in Stacy that way anymore."

"Are you sure? Just think before you say anything," she said, twisting around to face him while still keeping her distance.

He covered his face with his hands and rubbed until his burnished complexion turned ruddy. "You've misinterpreted. I'm just used to referring to Stacy out of habit. You talk about Lucas a lot."

"Not in the same way."

"What do you mean?"

She shrugged and lifted the shirt over her head. "I'm not still obsessed with him."

A mixture of pain and concern oscillated in his eyes, the twitching corner of his lips. "It's not what you think. I was with Stacy most of my adult life, so I'm not the most experienced guy in the world," he said, sotto voce.

"If you guys weren't in such constant contact, you'd get over her faster," she suggested. "She calls you too much, Ian. She seems pretty ambivalent about giving you up."

"We're parents. We need to be in contact about Ava."

"No, I know." She was afraid to say more. It was as if they were trying to thread a needle through a barely visible eye, coming close yet just missing. "Let's see what happens. Not talk about this anymore tonight."

"Right." He kissed her chastely. Then he rolled over so that no body parts were touching. A few hours later, she awoke to Ian nuzzling his face into her neck. She loved his natural musk, disliked when the astringent or animal odors of his clients became absorbed in his clothes, his pores. The minute their tongues met, all her nerve endings began to flutter in song. On top of Ian she slid her hands down his sleek, warm body and then grabbed his buttocks, wanting no space between them. He glided into her as effortlessly as if choreographed, as if their bodies were built as complements of each other, meant to bring the other pleasure.

Yet that night, for the first time in weeks, she dreamed of fully formed babies being carved like Thanksgiving turkeys while she watched and did nothing.

The next morning they ate breakfast in an awkward silence, punctuated by the sound of their silverware scratching against the inn's ceramic plates. Georgie pushed her omelet open, dissecting it for the mushrooms and onions and leaving the eggs uneaten. She drank too many cups of coffee, feeding her insecurity with caffeinated fuel. The dining room, decorated to produce abundant cheer—with its honeystained pine furniture and floral peach-and-green wallpaper—only ridiculed her mood. Outside the window lay verdant Vermont.

Ian shuffled the strawberries off his whole-wheat pancakes and began to cut them without much enthusiasm. He didn't touch his cup of coffee. "About our discussion," he said.

"I'm sorry I lashed out at you like that," she said, not wanting a continuation of the previous night's conversation. Following the nightmare she hadn't slept well, and her body ached all over—lower back and upper, gut and temples—like that of a Victorian heroine, suffering for the sin of loving a married man.

"I'm sorry we got on the topic of my ex-wife again. It's not too cool, my bringing her up so much." He reached for her hand. "I won't do it anymore."

"Let me ask you something."

"Uh-oh," he said, cracking a nervous smile. "Fire away."

"If she wanted to get back with you, would you?"

Ian frowned into his food, the kiwi, melon, and two little purple grapes arranged on one side, the main dish in the middle. He placed his mug on the coffee table between them and rubbed the corner of one eye. "Absolutely not."

"Are you sure? Be honest with yourself."

"Yeah, I'm sure."

Georgie jammed her fork into the fluffy eggs. "Do you think we should give it a rest, not see each other for a while, at least until your divorce comes through?"

The veins in Ian's neck protruded slightly above his sharp collarbone, and his eyebrows swam together to form one straight line. "Hey, how did you get from a minor scuffle to a breakup? After last night?"

She contracted into her chair so that the ends of her hair dipped into her coffee cup. "I guess I have trust issues, too."

"Yeah? How come? Lucas didn't cheat, did he?"

She shrugged. "Not that I know of."

"Georgie, I know you're scared. I am too. But there's something I need to tell you anyway."

"Okay." *Whatever it is, stay cool,* she instructed herself sternly.

Quickly, Ian glanced to either side. There were two other couples, so quiet only the click of their silverware, the clang of their coffee cups against saucers, could be heard. He lowered his voice. "I meant to say this to you last night, in a more romantic moment. Better late than never, I guess. God, I'm really nervous." He grinned awkwardly. "The thing is, despite my faults, I'm a pretty good guy. I'm reliable and kind. I can even be witty for a guy who spends more than half his time in the company of animals. I'm not an appetizer like Lucas."

"You don't have to sell me on yourself, Ian," she said, flattered he'd remembered her Luke metaphor.

"Yeah, I do, because I think I'm falling in love with you. There, I said it. Phew!"

Georgie's emotions went into free fall: happiness, anxiety, and doubt together like colors in a child's spin art wheel. "Really?"

"Really."

"Wow." She bowed her head and caressed the embroidered cotton tablecloth. "This is unexpected."

"Not too unpleasant, I hope?"

Georgie looked up.

Don't cry. God, don't have your nose run!

"No. It's very pleasant actually." Her breath caught but she pushed the words out as if they were errant children refusing to do as they were told. "Because I definitely feel the same way."

Was love as contagious as the flu? Would they both come to their senses in a few weeks when their fevers broke, leaving Georgie weak limbed and humiliated? She could not afford to suffer one more ounce of pain.

Still.

They grinned at each other, their words lingering like perfume in the summer air.

ELEVEN

All of a sudden the melody of Georgie's life had changed from a melancholy Schubert quartet to a festive Handel allegro. Every night, while Jesse was at camp, she and Ian would indulge in an orgy of bare-bottomed pleasure: sex and more sex, watching silly video rentals, eating mushroom pizza and chicken chow fun in bed. But in the pearly light of morning, she'd think: *Step on the brakes, girl, before you crash, before Stacy Weiss comes back to call and your heart gets shredded like a trash bag by ravenous squirrels.* Yet she didn't listen, swept away by the torrents of feeling, at last releasing her stronghold on despair, embracing this preferable chaos. *Ian is a good man,* the whisper of reason would admonish the alarmist yammering in her head. *He's not going back with her. He's in love with you.* Still, the only one she told about her new amour was her cousin, figuring, why subject herself to superlatives of joy from all her well-wishers when she might have to awkwardly retract them days later?

"Was I always this mistrustful?" she asked Nina.

They stood in the cafeteria-style line at Au Bon Pain at the mall, having met for an impromptu lunch. Nina was in her coral-colored linen suit and silk blouse, Georgie in capri pants and an oversize T-shirt.

"You've been cynical about men since Michael. But you've gotten exponentially worse since the divorce," Nina pronounced, combing her hand through her hair. "You've been through a lot with the baby on top of everything—typical of post-traumatic stress, which makes it hard to trust that the world is a safe and secure place."

"Okay, enough shrinking." Pushing her tray along the metal

grille, Georgie reached out to grab a prepackaged chicken salad, and then poured a cup of coffee. She exhaled slowly, reflecting on the last year, how it had been like holding on to a kite through a long, windy season. Despite her tight grip, she'd lost her father to the pull of the elements. "How's the bulimic?"

Nina bobbed her head from side to side, equivocally. "Still vomiting, alas. The treating psychiatrist and I are trying her on a different, older medication. Unfortunately, the Prozac didn't work. What about you? What are you working on? Besides raising your endorphins?" She nudged Georgie gently in the ribs.

"The usual frills and candy corn," she said. "Women who love themselves so much they rearrange their body parts obsessively."

Revealing the poetry felt too private, too masturbatory. After all these years, her mother's critical eye was still glaring in her head, despite the surprise of finding the William Carlos Williams book earmarked on the page of "The Widow's Lament in Springtime." Apparently her mother had underlined the opening lines in red: "Sorrow is my own yard / where the new grass / flames as it has flamed / often before but not / with the cold fire / that closes round me this year. / Thirty-five years / I lived with my husband."

Perhaps Estelle no longer viewed poets as the trifling whittlers she'd once compared to that pantheon of great minds, those medical giants incapable of saving Adam.

"Well, not only candy corn," she told Nina. "I'm working on some ideas for more serious articles, but have been a bit distracted of late."

"Thank God for distractions in cute packages. So, how is bliss? 'Fess up."

"Blissful except for all the ghosts, the imminent threat of the ex returning to the scene of the crime."

"Let yourself go for once," her cousin counseled. "Enjoy."

"Oh, I am."

They sat at a small circular table, knees practically touching, and sipped their drinks. Nina's hair fell in a chunk of curls over her right eye. "In light of everything, you're not still planning to make the trip with Lucas up to Jesse's camp on Saturday?"

"Sure, I'm still going," Georgie said. She tore open the packet of

Italian dressing with her teeth. "I miss my boy even more than I'd expected. The sooner I see him the better."

"Won't that be hard for you, all that time alone with Luke?"

"I'm not tempted to be with him, Nina. As for the other thing, a normal person might notice that I'm feeling sad or acting differently. But not my ex." She shrugged. "Even if he did, I can always talk about my dad. It's not a lie."

"You're not still attracted to him, are you?"

"Do you think I'm going to jump his bones in the front seat of the car on the West Side Highway? No way. That ship has sailed. Nothing like a good old-fashioned abortion to rid a girl of infatuation."

"Good," Nina said, in a particularly starchy tone. She worked on her sandwich for a while before asking, "What other news?"

"My mother's off to Boston again this weekend."

"Oh?"

"Yep. Got a message from her this morning while I was showering. Don't tell me this is just some acquaintance based on mutual grief. No one travels to visit a casual acquaintance so frequently."

Nina leaned forward in her chair. "Are you asking me something?"

"No. Should I be?"

"I hate this!" Nina declared, dropping her sandwich onto her plate so that a large slice of meat fell out of the bread, flagrant as a wagging tongue.

"Hey, what's wrong?" Slowly Georgie lowered her fork to the side of her plate. "What do you hate? Nina! What is it? What is it you hate?"

Her cousin averted her eyes, so that only the translucent lids with the tiny blue veins showed. She sucked in her lips as if they were words she wished to take back. "God, I can't stand this secrecy anymore."

"What secrecy?"

"There's more to these trips that your mom's been taking. I didn't want to tell you what's going on because . . . well, partly because of all the other shit you've had to deal with lately."

"How much more?"

Nina inhaled deeply; then her breath caught.

"Is it a big deal?"

"Yeah, sweetie, it sort of is."

The mall was suddenly static, the movement of people and air freeze-framed, the light whitening, a low hum somewhere off to the right, a mechanized sound, an engine running.

"You'd better tell me then," Georgie said through a constricted throat.

Nina's shoulders slumped over so that her blouse pleated in front, the scoop neck revealing her nearly alabaster skin and protruding collarbone. She patted her hair repeatedly. "There's no right way to say this. So, I'll just say it. There is something I haven't been honest about. This person, this man in Boston, he isn't just a casual acquaintance."

Georgie felt feverish, anger flying off her like embers. "Why do *you* know this and I don't?"

"Remember at dinner that time, at the Mexican place? When I told you that I overheard my parents talking about Stellie?"

"Yeah. And?" Georgie was growing impatient with Nina's circular explanations, her dovetailing between subjects like a fighter jet twisting and turning in the air to prove the pilot's dexterity in dodging an enemy plane.

"I didn't give you all the details. My mom was distraught and swore me to secrecy. She was adamant that it wasn't my place to talk to you about this, that it was Stellie's."

Georgie stiffened, as if about to receive a shot of Novocain into her tender gums. "Spit it out. You're killing me here."

"Here's the thing: Your mom, it turns out, has a son. Not with your dad."

The blood went rushing from Georgie's head at a rapid speed. The electrons in the room engaged in a frenzied dance as her cousin's words bounced like light off the table and out into the larger world, too elusive to catch. "What? That's *crazy*. What are you talking about?"

"It's a shock," Nina said, kneading her eyebrows with her thumb and index finger. "But it's true. She gave the baby up for adoption a year before she even met your dad. His name, this man, is Daniel

Kaplan. He lives in Boston and that's where your mother is supposed to go this weekend. That's where she's been going these last few trips."

Daniel. Georgie flipped frantically through her mind's Rolodex to locate the name. There it was: Her aunt Lily had mentioned him the day of her father's funeral. Georgie was staring into the well of coffee, at the milk chocolate–colored liquid inside. When she spoke, her mouth felt dry, as if dead leaves were sitting on her tongue. "How can this be true? All these years, my whole entire life, not knowing, completely clueless."

Nina reached for Georgie's hand and stroked the fingertips. "Stellie didn't want you to suspect anything. The situation is complicated. It's a long story."

"Did my dad know?" she asked, her voice dipping as she bowed her head down.

"Yeah, he did. But it's not his fault. He didn't tell you out of respect for Stellie's wishes. Hey, sweetie, are you all right? You look a little green."

Georgie jumped to her feet. She'd eaten very little, yet the food she'd managed to shove in needed to come out. Au Bon Pain's bathroom was out of order. The mall's ladies room was very far away, around the corner, on the way to Nordstrom's bottom floor with its creamy pastel cosmetics, which, long ago and far away, would have been as tempting as sugar candy. She sprinted, the taste of vomit in her mouth. It seemed some kind of feat to throw up directly into a toilet and not on her shoe or an unsuspecting shopper's wristwatch.

She could hear Nina outside the stall, her heavy breathing and the click of her pumps against the marble floor. After flushing, Georgie sat down on the closed lid, head in hands, the stench crawling up her nostrils, her cheeks burning.

"Hey, maybe I'm still pregnant," she joked once she emerged. "Sorry about that."

"It's just another biggie in a year of biggies. All these changes are hard on the body. Let's get you home," Nina was saying. "I'll follow you, make sure you get there safely."

"That's insane. You go back to work, to your life. You've been taking care of me too much. I'll be fine."

As they weaved their way through the mall, Nina held on to

Georgie's elbow, steadying her. She offered a mint from her bag and bought a Sprite for her cousin near the exit.

She opened Georgie's car door and leaned against the frame. "I shouldn't have told you. It was selfish of me."

"Please," Georgie insisted, fastening her seat belt. "I just need to get out of here. We can talk later."

With that, Nina backed away. Somehow Georgie was able to rely on her primitive brain to deliver herself home, as disoriented as an amnesiac, yet still safe in her skin.

The petal-pink walls of her entryway were welcoming. She headed straight for her bed. For a moment she tried to jar herself into a more alert state by zeroing in on the sight of a violet glass vase on the dresser; "spotting it" the way she had in gymnastics class as a girl, but to no avail. She listened to a chirping sparrow carrying on a one-way conversation outside her window, and then trudged into the bathroom to gulp down two Advils. Her face in the mirror looked wrinkled, lines beginning to sprout around the mouth, a deeper ridge, suddenly, carved between the eyebrows, as if Nina's confession had been etched there on the ride home. She stripped down. In the shower, water spit out of the nozzle and she shut her eyes, lifting up her head into the mist.

She dressed slowly in sweatpants and an old jersey of Lucas's. These kinds of mementos from her failed marriage were thrown in between her T-shirts and sports bras. She held up a sweater of his—which was randomly placed like most of her clothes—and inhaled its fragrance: wool and cloves.

She tried to ward off the onslaught of questions firing haphazardly in her brain. How could this be true? Why hadn't she suspected? Hadn't her father wanted to share his confidence with her before he died? Had he known before he'd married her mother or after? Had he felt angry or hurt by the knowledge that his wife had a baby with another man? Had there ever been a minute, even a passing second, that her mother felt an urge—however muted—to disclose this crucial piece of her history to Georgie? She lifted a photograph of her parents from her dresser and arched forward, scrutinizing her mother's face as closely as she might a Hirschfeld drawing, counting the *Ninas* hidden in the creases of skin and hair.

Nothing conspiratorial was revealed in the dazzling smile she bestowed on her husband, only love.

Who do I love that much? Georgie wondered, and her mind came to rest on an image of Jesse, his hair bleached by the sun, his eyes lightened against his honey-colored tan, his skin sleek as a monk seal's. He might be back at his bunk for rest time before dinner. She might be able to hear his voice. "What is it, Ma? What's wrong?" he'd ask, ever vigilant, his senses sharpened into five needle-thin antennae. It could alarm him, her calling him unexpectedly.

Instead she parked herself on the couch and watched television, one puerile talk show after another. The sepia light of late afternoon was flooding the living room, and she waited for the throbbing in her temples to subside. Finally, toward dinnertime, she realized it had been hours since she'd eaten, and, despite her lack of appetite, she fixed a peanut-butter sandwich and a cup of chamomile tea. Halfway through her meal the phone rang, and Nina's voice on the machine pleaded, "Just tell me you got home okay, okay?"

"I got home fine," Georgie said into the phone, the top layer of epidermis having peeled off, raw. She closed her eyes, the promise of sleep's submarine plunging her into its calm murk. "I'm just whipped."

"I'm so sorry."

"My dad died."

"I know, honey."

"I aborted my baby."

"I know. I'm sorry."

"It's even harder to get my mind around this new bombshell. That's so ironic! It's more startling than even the fact that my dad is dead."

"Well, this comes from out of the blue. Your dad was very sick, so his death was not unexpected."

"I've never felt like I could really read my mother, and now this huge secret. Nina, I have a brother."

"Incredible, isn't it?" her cousin whispered.

"That was the strangest statement I've ever made." Georgie laughed, a tinny sound clanking in her ears. "I can't believe it even came out of my mouth. Let me call you tomorrow."

The sun had begun to set so that the square of evening light looked like a rosy patch of quilt. Georgie cocooned herself in a throw, running her finger over its seashell pink trim. She picked up the telephone and dialed Ian's number. "The weirdest thing happened today," she said. "Can I talk to you about it?"

"I'm here."

During the next few days, Georgie received eight messages on her answering machine from various female members of the Merkin tribe. Apparently, obsessive-compulsive disorder was leapfrogging its way through her family tree at rapid-fire speed. The first call was from Aunt Lily, to whom, Georgie realized, Nina had confessed she'd spilled the beans. Aunt Lily's imagination seemed actively employed conjuring up worst-case scenarios. "Don't do anything foolish, dear," she instructed, a trill to her voice.

Like what? Georgie wondered. *Wander, muddy headed and unkempt, through the streets, guzzling whiskey until dawn?* Her aunt had read one too many historical novels featuring distressed damsels.

When Nina confessed what she'd done and offered an apology, Georgie crooned, "I'll survive this blow, too," as if reciting the lyrics of a pathetic country-western ballad. "Tell your mom. She sounds over the edge."

"Don't worry about her. She loves the drama. Her mind is so underutilized. But I feel extremely guilty for what I did. I never should have opened my big trap."

"I prodded it open. I'm still alive and breathing. The good news is that I finally have material for my breakout book, my confessional memoir."

"This is all my fault," Nina said.

"Enough self-condemnation. I'm just in shock. Maybe I should go for shock treatment."

The third call was from Estelle, demanding that her daughter "pick up the phone" in the alert clinical tone she used when a woman went into preterm labor. Georgie was not home, so she could not respond on cue. In the next call—an hour later—Estelle said, "Lily told me what happened. I am very disturbed by what Nina did. My poor sister-in-law seems to think you're so despondent that you're going to throw yourself into the river. Luckily, you're in New Jersey. There are no rivers, just highways and malls. That was a little joke." She sighed.

When Georgie returned from ShopRite, she dialed her mother's number at the office.

"She's in with a patient now," Carole sang. "Let me ring you through."

"Georgia? I'm with someone now but want to talk with you," her mother said formally, so as not to give away the personal nature of the call. "Is there a good time to get back to you?"

"I'm here all night."

"Good. I'll speak with you later." The phone rattled before Estelle successfully replaced it in its cradle.

But that night turned into the next day. Her mother telephoned, excitedly, from the hospital before Georgie had even awoken. "Listen, serious complications have arisen with my monozygotic twin mother. It looks like the twins are suffering from TTTS, which can be very dangerous," she announced to Georgie's machine. "We'll most likely have to perform a SLPCV, uh, laser surgery to seal off the vessels connecting the two babies so they don't share blood. Never mind. I just didn't want you to think I'd forgotten to get back to you. As soon as my patient's stabilized, I promise to talk to you, Georgie. Try not to take this personally."

"I won't," Georgie responded to the disembodied voice. Yet there it was, the primal affront: At life's most critical moments, there was always some stranger more in need of her mother's attention than she. How could she compete with all those busy reproductive traits?

Early on a silver morning, two days later, the doorbell rang insistently. Wrapped in a towel, dripping and cold, Georgie sprinted down the hall to her bedroom. Just as she reached into her underwear drawer to discover the need to do laundry, she heard her mother's command through her open window. "It's me. Please answer the door. I took the bus out and walked all the way here from town. I've barely slept in seventy-two hours." The knocking began, and Georgie hoped that Mrs. Callahan, her elderly neighbor, wasn't checking out the ruckus through her black-rimmed bifocals.

Estelle bellowed for the entire neighborhood to hear, "Are you there, Georgia? Are you going to let me in?"

She had no right, no right at all, to *demand* such prompt attention, to flaunt her newfound proprietary attitude after years of disinterest, Georgie thought. Head in hands, hunched over on the double bed, she pictured her mother slapping a newborn into consciousness, eliciting its first cry of rage.

She dressed quickly in jeans and an old T-shirt before opening the door. "Mom, you're being too loud. This is a quiet neighborhood."

"It's seven thirty already. We need to have a conversation," she proclaimed. "I'm sorry for the delay. It simply couldn't be avoided." Estelle put out her hand like a school crossing guard. "I know you resented it as a child, all the medical emergencies that took me away from you. But you're not a child now."

"I haven't said anything. I hope your patient is okay." *After all,* she thought, *I'm not heartless.*

"She will be. She came through the surgery nicely; the twins, too, thanks to me, I might add. May I come in?" Estelle asked. She barreled into the hallway without waiting for a response. "I brought two cappuccinos on the walk over. Skim milk with chocolate powder on top, the way you like it." She strode into the kitchen and put the Starbucks bag on the countertop, then peered into the cabinets, searching—Georgie knew—for the sugar she'd forgotten to pack with the coffee.

Georgie glanced out the window at two squirrels chasing each other into the headless tulips. She remembered how, the previous fall, a squirrel had leaped through the window onto the counter, where she'd found him brazenly nibbling on a loaf of sourdough bread. The next time one of the rodents tried to invade her home, he smacked into the screen she'd inserted.

"Look, it's no secret that you feel I've been a lousy mother. All that"—Estelle waved it away, her daughter's former life—"is water under the bridge without your father here."

Georgie walked into her living room, toward the window facing her backyard. *Not to me,* she longed to say, but was rendered mute. Like the Little Mermaid, who was given legs by the octopus witch in exchange for her voice, she had gotten away from Estelle's influence but not without a severe penalty, this feeling of invisibility, of inconsequence.

"It's important that you understand. My not telling you about Daniel . . . it had absolutely nothing to do with anything between you and me."

Estelle leaned on the archway to the room and concentrated on loosening the straps to her sandals before removing them from her calloused feet. She was wearing a black jacquard skirt and a loose-fitting gray blouse, work clothes. "I never told you because—right or wrong—for the last forty years I tried not to think about him. It was part of another life. The pregnancy was unplanned, of course. It happened a year before I met Adam. Your father knew despite my mother's pleas to keep it from him, since what had happened was 'a shandeh,' a shame, a disgrace."

"Dad knew all that time?" Georgie asked, another blow to her perception of her father. Her mind clicked away like a camera's shutter. How many memories would have to be revisited and revised for accuracy's sake?

"Yes. But don't blame him."

"I don't," she said, not thinking clearly.

"My mother agonized over what to do. I wanted to get an abortion, even though they were illegal and dangerous if you couldn't afford a good enough doctor. For reform Jews abortion was acceptable, but not adoption. Adoption was for goyim."

Georgie observed Estelle rubbing the bridge of her nose, presumably to help stave off an impending headache, the identical gesture her daughter made, for the same reason, a trick of genetics. "My mother told me that she had suffered from a botched abortion in her second trimester when I was still a baby," Estelle continued. "She aborted my brother and almost died. After that they gave her a hysterectomy. She was afraid I might suffer the same fate."

"Whoa! Slow down. Why would Grandma have an abortion? Grandpa let her abort his own son?"

Estelle shook her head. "He never knew. He thought she was in the hospital for 'female problems,' a damaged reproductive system, and that she could never give him the son he wanted. Frankly, I was stunned that my mother would be able to pull off such a lie. Good for her for having a spine, when she rarely stood up to my father."

Georgie pictured her grandma Ackerman—the mystery of

whose interior life had died along with her—a small, buxom woman with a soft voice and tiny feet, whose circumscribed existence revolved around her husband and a good cut of brisket.

"I don't think he ever forgave her for that, not having more children, a boy," Estelle continued. "They were dreadfully poor at the time, even more so than in Kiev. My father's stationery store on Canal Street had closed because he could never get along with Sol, his own brother. My entire childhood he ranted 'ganif,' crook, whenever Sol's name came up. They never spoke again, not even when Sol was dying of pancreatic cancer; that's why you never knew your uncle. Your grandfather had grievances with everyone."

Estelle maneuvered her newly bulky body into the rocking chair and placed her coffee cup on the wooden chess table she'd given her grandson. "My parents had just moved into the apartment on Morris Avenue and had borrowed money for the appetizer store. I was less than a year old, and Grandma was terrified to learn she was pregnant again so soon. She was a nervous new mother, overwhelmed. Maybe she had postpartum depression, but there was no such diagnosis or treatment for it. They were so poor at the time that they could barely feed me. Grandma was young and came from a more sophisticated family than Grandpa. They didn't have any real money, but she wasn't used to such struggles. Her parents were intellectuals, socialists, second-generation Americans, not potato farmers in Russia."

"But I thought Grandpa was studying to be a professor in Kiev," Georgie said, feeling saturated by all this new information.

Estelle nodded. "He'd hoped to, but that was before he saw his father get shot by the Cossacks for protesting the czar, before his aunt Shirley hid him and Sol in a gentile's basement for two years, trying to get the boys out of Russia during the Revolution. His twin sisters and his mother were left behind and later killed by the Nazis."

She paused and took the first sip of her coffee. "Where was I? Oh, yes, the abortion. My mother figured she'd have more chances later, when she and Jacob got back on their feet. There were no more chances for her."

Georgie slid onto the couch. Were there any Ackerman women for whom baby making was not filled with turmoil and tsuris?

"What does all this have to do with your . . ." She couldn't say the word *son*. It felt awkward, foreign on her tongue, like all those French verbs she'd conjugated at Brearley. "With Daniel."

"I let my mother talk me into having the baby even though I was sure my father would banish me from the apartment and make me stay with relatives. The problem was, we didn't have any relatives; he'd alienated his brother and cousins with his terrible temper, and Mama's only sister lived in Odessa. She had a few second cousins who lived in Brighton Beach, but she was either too proud or too ashamed to ask them to take me in. So, I had the baby and gave him up to a Jewish adoption agency."

"Where does Dad come into all this?"

Estelle emitted a loud sigh. "We discussed telling you, but we both agreed to keep it to ourselves rather than trouble you with something that would never affect you. Dad always felt that way about you, protective, wanting to shelter you from hurt, believing you were entitled to enjoy your own life. There was no reason to think you'd ever find out, not when you were a child," she said. "Everything was so different back then. Adoption was secretive and final. It should never have involved you. That was our reasoning."

"I'm involved now."

"Yes. That's unfortunate. Nina shouldn't have been the one to tell you. I was keeping Daniel's recent reappearance in my life a secret to protect you."

"Protect me from what?" Georgie asked. "From being included in what seems common knowledge among our family? Lily, Nina, I'm sure Uncle Art knows!"

"To protect you from everything you're feeling. Adam and I discussed telling you when Daniel first contacted me, but we decided not to. Lily and Art have known for years. We spoke to them about it. . . . I don't remember now."

Georgie shut her eyes. Like an anchor, this ballast of her parents' pact sank to the bottom of her being.

"Dad thought it cruel to spring this on you because it was such horrible timing, a terrible joke. I got the letter the same month he got his second diagnosis, and everything was happening at once, spinning out of control. He felt it would be too much for you to digest. It's hard to say what he would have felt if he hadn't gotten sick so quickly.

I think he even forgot about the letter, and I didn't bring it up with him again."

"This is so surreal."

"No, it's real," Estelle said. "His name is Daniel Kaplan." She paused, and a flicker of a smile illuminated her face, as if she were fondly recalling a childhood friend, her eyes glistening. "He lives in Newton, Massachusetts, with his wife and family."

"Wife? There's a wife, as well?"

"Yes. He has a wife and two children. The youngest was born just last year. It was Lauren, his wife, who insisted he get in touch with me when he was still wrestling with the death of his adopted mother two years later. Also, his older brother Paul encouraged him. Paul had sought out his birth mother years earlier and developed a congenial relationship with her."

Daniel, Lauren, Paul, a dead adopted mother, and two as yet unidentified children—the cast of characters was too long for Georgie to absorb in one sitting. "There are all these half relatives out there that Nina and Lily knew about. When were you planning on letting me in on this?" Georgie asked, anger, like cigarette smoke, wafting between clenched teeth. "Would I have even have found out if Nina hadn't squealed?"

Estelle threw up her hands. "I was trying to tell you. I even started to a few times. But your father just died, and frankly I've been overwhelmed."

"I understand that. But I shouldn't have to cope with this news right after my father just died either."

"Not in a fair world." Estelle shrugged. "But the world isn't fair, is it? I am sorry that Nina discovered this before you did. But what can I do now? This is what is. This is what we're faced with, and we have to deal with it. It's really not such bad news, discovering you have a brother, is it?"

"I have no idea," Georgie said. "I'm on emotional overload as it is. I can barely process not having Dad here. Now I have to accept that I have a half sibling out there!"

There was a quaver in her voice that shamed Georgie. Displays of emotion in front of her mother had always felt too intimate, like being caught after a shower without a towel: lax belly and pink areolas exposed. "If you'd included me in these family secrets earlier . . . Dad's being sick, that was my burden, too. This I can't cope with right now, all at once."

"Your burden? You don't know anything about that burden, my dear." Estelle inhaled, drawing herself back up to royal status. "Daniel is certainly not a burden. He's a blessing."

"I don't know if he is or not, at least as far as I'm concerned."

"Do you want to know anything about how this mess happened? Who your brother's father is?"

Georgie shook her head in protest so that her wet hair went flying, a section of it slapping her hard in one eye. "Too much information! Give me a minute to catch my breath here."

"If you want to be included, then you need to listen, not run away and put your earplugs in and escape into your world of magazines and poetry. You can't have it both ways."

"You're talking about when I was a teenager."

"Do you think you've changed all that much? You still hate confrontation, anger, conflict; you always have. That wasn't easy for me, Georgia. I'm a direct person. All that sensitivity of yours . . . Well, your father understood how to deal with it much better than I ever could. I realize now I should have tried harder, not let him do so much of the work."

"I guess not." She bit her mouth to stop the humiliation of tears.

"Just listen. The truth won't kill you. Daniel's father was a college boy. Claudio—that was his name—was the son of a successful Spanish businessman. His father insisted he drop out of school for a year. Claudio was a political rebel. It's a long story."

Estelle paused, heaved herself out of the chair, and began to pace.

"Our meeting was a fluke, at a party in Manhattan. We dated for a while—he was very charming, rich, and handsome—until Claudio's family moved back to Catalonia and he went back to Madrid University. This was all before I learned of the pregnancy. Can you imagine the shame of your grandfather's unmarried daughter getting pregnant, and to a colored boy, no less?"

She burst out laughing. "That's what he called Claudio, 'a colored boy.' I kept correcting him, but my father never listened. After the baby was born, neither of my parents ever mentioned their grandchild again. Not for the rest of their lives, not to me, and I'm certain it was a forbidden subject between the two of them! My parents' powers of denial were astonishing."

She clucked before turning wistful. "George Henry, that's what I'd named him."

"What? You named me after him?"

"No. That's not true."

"If, God forbid, something happened to Jesse and I had another baby, do you think I'd name him Jesse? Jesse two?"

"It wasn't like that." Stellie walked in her daughter's direction, but when Georgie flinched, she retreated. "Don't make it more than it is. I needed a name that began with a G, after Geva, grandma's sister, who was most likely dead in Russia. I picked George Henry because of a boy at school I had a crush on."

She giggled out of nervousness or a return to that youthful state. "I knew the adoptive parents would rename the baby. Don't attribute any significance to this. I was a teenager when I had him, for Christ's sake, and was still a girl in medical school when I had you! We did everything so young, in those days. We were all barely conscious! Maybe it did make me feel better about him and about myself, what I'd done, naming you Georgia. I don't know. I don't analyze everything like you and your father."

"You didn't foresee how it might hurt me if I found out?"

"Hurt? No! I was the one hurting. Having a baby and giving him away. It was hurtful to me!" She poked herself on the chest with her index finger, and then pointed it at her daughter.

"I meant how I'd feel second-rate." What was the difference? Georgie always felt that way around her mother anyway.

"It has nothing to do with you! In those days, adoptions were closed. You spent a few moments with your baby after delivery, groggy and drugged, and they whisked him away. Over the years I'd wondered if he was happy and healthy; that's only natural. But I was resolved that I'd never meet him. It never even seemed a possibility until he wrote to me. I agreed to meet with Daniel because your father had just died and—for the first time—I felt an urgent desire to see the son I'd given up. I couldn't conceive of a future without your father. Sometimes I feel as if I'm in some kind of fugue state. The truth is, being sought out by Daniel is helping me. Try to see things from my point of view for a change."

"Okay. I promise. You do the same." Georgie stood there, trembling, eyes fixated on her Persian rug.

"Fine. We'll both work on that."

Estelle grabbed her coat in one arm and left the untouched cappuccino on the chess table. "If you want to call him or go with me to meet him"—she peered, challenging—"he'd be thrilled to hear from you. He's your brother." She stroked that last word with such loving nuance as to elicit a strange, catlike noise from Georgie.

When Georgie was younger, she'd competed with a conga line of faceless pregnant women for her mother's love. Silly, really. It wasn't the humanity of childbirth that Estelle loved; it was medicine itself, the Hope Diamond of careers. That knowledge had afforded Georgie some measure of comfort. Now she needed to reevaluate her perception. Perhaps it had been Daniel—not as a flesh-and-blood growing person but as an abstraction—who had taken her mother away from Georgie all through her childhood, until, in fact, this very day.

PART TWO

ESTELLE

TWELVE

Light-headed with the freedom that a fib could provide, Estelle was on her way to a party at the house of a girl whom she'd never met, a friend of a friend of Janet's. Her parents believed that—at this moment—she was being seated at the Paradise, excited to be out on a double date and seeing *The Bridge on the River Kwai*. Estelle was wearing her favorite outfit: a charcoal gray sweater dress she'd bought on sale at Gimbel's, with sheer stockings and strapless pumps. Her mother had met her with a disapproving glance—the dress was too tight across the bust. They'd had that argument before, but Estelle had held her tongue.

It was a chilly night, the wind whistling down Lexington Avenue as Estelle and Janet rushed to their destination, arm in arm, laughing and interrupting each other as always. The casual observer would not have guessed that, in fact, these were two of the most studious girls in their class, that their plans surpassed both their parents' and teachers' expectations. Neither one was banking on marriage, as every other female at De Witt Clinton High School, and possibly the world, seemed to be doing. They'd spent hours together mapping out their future; medical school for Stellie, law school for Jan. One would prove to be a great trauma surgeon, the other the first woman on the Supreme Court! But for tonight they were newly seventeen and breaking the rules.

In the Art Deco lobby, a doorman greeted them before ringing up "Miss Martinson," on the twenty-second floor.

"Fancy!" Janet exclaimed.

Estelle nodded. "We're not in the Bronx anymore, Toto."

The apartment had a long foyer, high ceilings, and wall-to-wall teenagers in their saddle shoes and white bucks. The sound of Bobby Darin singing "Mack the Knife" drowned out conversation.   .

"This is so neat!" Janet whispered.

It was! The crimson sofa and matching divan looked expensive, and the large paintings were bold, swirling bursts of color, gold and blues and oranges. A photo of the family—a buxom woman with big teeth, a kind-eyed older man, and two grinning girls with ponytails— revealed a life full of idle moments, adventure. Estelle felt buoyed with the notion that light-heartedness could be as easily embraced as her father's rage and her mother's disappointment, that families could choose kind words over disgruntlement.

"I bet we meet college boys here," Janet said.

But when her friend deserted her for a gangly, loose-jointed guy with a face marred by pockmarks, Estelle busied herself with her gold-plated earring, snapping it on and off, rubbing the spot on her lobe where it clamped down too tightly. *Oh, God,* she thought, *who am I going to talk to?*

"Coke, *guapa?*"

She turned to face the most exquisite young man—for certainly this dark and chiseled person could not be called a boy—she'd ever seen. His hair alone! All those rich black waves.

"Oh, yes, thank you."

"I am Claudio," he said, smiling. White teeth shone against the olive canvas of his skin. His eyes were hooded, liquid onyx. His lashes were so long she wondered if they got caught in his eyes when he blinked. When he gave her the drink, his fingers grazed over her hand, lightly stroking her wrist.

"Estelle. Stellie. My friends call me Stellie."

"Then, I too will call you Stellie," he said, caressing her name with his tongue. "No?"

Oh! Yes!

Cuter than James Dean, she was thinking, once they'd been talking awhile. But *sexier* was what she wouldn't dare admit, even to herself.

"So Papa decides I will leave Madrid, the university. *Político, ¿no? Estuve protestando. . . .*"

"Protesting," she offered in a daze of infatuation.

"Protest-ing, *sí*, against *el caudillo, El Falange*."

"What's that?" she asked, wondering if there was some glaring gap in her education.

Claudio leaned in closer to her, his breath on her face. "Franco. *El gobierno*. They were against the people, the workers. Mine is such a poor country. But for a man like Papa, *rico*, rich . . . I am an embarrassment."

She watched Claudio's mouth move. His lips were fuller than those of any of the boys at school whose faces now paraded through her mind as one long line of sallow, thin-lipped, milky-eyed Americans. This feeling—desire—was unmatched in her limited experience: necking with Sam Finkelstein at Fran Kushner's seventeenth birthday party, kissing Marty Blumberg at the Loews.

"Papa is against me . . . my studies of the law. He is a businessman. With *mi familia* it is always business. It is all they can see." Claudio gestured with one hand, flexing his palm and extending his long fingers. An instant later he relaxed and reached for his pack of Camels.

"Never mind my country is so poor. Workers are starving. That is not his concern, Papa says. This is how it has always been. The name Giron means business." He paused to light his cigarette, and then blew out smoke discreetly, away from her face. "Naturally, he wants for me to . . ."

"Follow in his footsteps."

"*Sí*. Yes. The family business. Textiles. Three factories."

Estelle nodded, not exactly listening but mesmerized, biting down on her lip. Kissing him would be nothing like what she'd done with those other boys. *As different as apples and oranges*, she thought.

"Are you moving back?" she asked, suddenly desperate for this stranger to stay put. "To Madrid?"

"My family is from Catalonia. But me, *sí*, I will go back to the university. Study the law. My father, he will have to let me. He will have no choice. I am a Giron, too. Stubborn." When he grinned his dark eyes suddenly lightened a shade, and she noticed that his front tooth was chipped. The tip of his tongue reached in that space and then darted in, agile as a cat's.

"Don't worry, *guapa*, it won't be for a long while before I go home to Spain. A year. Enough time to get to know each other *¿sí?*"

She grinned back. He wanted to know her for a year! She would have settled for a few more hours! *"Sí,"* she said. *Definitely sí.*

THIRTEEN

The lights were out in the building's vestibule again, the second time that month. Estelle rooted around in her coat pocket for her keys, and then pushed her weight into the door to ensure that the lock wouldn't stick. Since late summer it had been getting increasingly difficult for the occupants to enter the six-floor tenement on Morris Avenue. Although most of them had complained, the superintendent still hadn't gotten around to fixing the problem.

But this evening—with its dreary sky and bitter March winds—Estelle was too weary and frightened to chant her silent mantra, *Soon, soon, I'll be away from here. First City College, then Einstein Medical School, then a one-bedroom in Manhattan, maybe even on the East Side.* This plan could never be openly discussed with Devora and Jacob Ackerman, who—like most of the parents of the girls at DeWitt Clinton High School—believed their only daughter should major in English education and marry a doctor. Estelle didn't know the definition of a gerund or the correct usage of a semicolon. Yet she'd received solid As in both science and math for the last six years. If she had been born a boy, she would have received a scholarship to Brandeis University's premed program.

Now everything had changed in the flash of a moment. Dr. Cohen, with his oily slicked-back hair and his scent of Old Spice, had stuck his fingers deep into her private center as she lay out on an examining table, her tight belly exposed, her knees up, taut legs pried open by a man whose colorless eyes peered above her, omnipresent in her line of vision. After plucking off his glove, he'd shaken his head and pronounced the dreaded verdict in a punitive tone: "Thirteen weeks along. Shame."

"Really? How?" she'd reacted, shocked, to which he responded with an abbreviated choke of a laugh.

"I would hope that if you can get yourself in this predicament, Miss Ackerman, you know something about how it occurs."

Of course she did. But, at eighteen, it had been her first visit to the gynecologist's office. Stellie had to steal the twenty-five dollars from the cash register in her father's appetizer store on Fordham Road to pay for the appointment. She'd considered lying, of telling her mother that she'd been bleeding irregularly when it wasn't her time of month. But robbery took less courage.

The hallway was dank and smelled of Mrs. Rosenblaum's stuffed cabbage. Every Tuesday was the same, as were most nights: Mondays, beef stew; Wednesdays and Fridays, pot roast and cooked carrots; Sunday afternoons, London broil with boiled potatoes. You could close your eyes at the dinner hour and accurately chart the day of the week.

Stellie avoided the claustrophobic elevator that wobbled to each floor. She paused before climbing the four flights of steps, squeezing her eyes tight in order not to cry. The thought that she might be trapped, indefinitely, in her parents' four-room apartment—with its fake wood, folding chairs, and dinner trays perched in front of the television next to her father's La-Z-Boy—forced the tears out. She imagined a small crib set up to face the Motorola so that the baby could focus all of its attention on the screen instead of on its relatives. Just like the rest of the family.

It was impossible! How could this have happened to her, Estelle Sarah Ackerman, one of the brightest girls in her senior class, an honor student, a nice Jewish girl from the Bronx? She wiped her nose against the nubby sleeve of her coat, so that a thin strand of wool glued itself to one nostril. Collapsing for a moment on the stairs, she tried to reason her way out of her situation, find a loophole, anything. But what were her options? It wasn't even as if she could forgo college to marry the boy who'd ruined her life. Claudio was back in Madrid permanently. They'd kissed good-bye at his parents' sublet on Seventy-eighth Street right before Christmas. Well, they'd done more than kissed. For a moment the image of him naked, on top of her, entered her mind. He was sliding his elegant dark body in lizardlike movements, crushing her breasts against his chest, his heavy breath covering her face like a cloud. It had happened only three times. Twice on his queen-size bed and once on Marilyn Shore's pullout couch (a friend of Claudio's whom he'd met at another one of his endless parties); in the Shores' Riverdale basement home. Here was her punishment for liking it so much. She shook her head. Biology, bad luck: These things she knew to be true. Not a God bent on vengeance.

She was Estelle Sarah Ackerman. She believed in science. And look where that had landed her. Trapped in her body. A female, not a doctor, after all.

On Saturdays, her father would leave with the dim light of dawn. Lying in her bed, noticing how the shadows moved through her sheer yellow curtains, Estelle listened for Jacob's departure for the store. She could hear him shuffling around in the bedroom. Soon he'd be wolfing down his toast and eggs and spilling just a patch of coffee on the table, as he lifted his cup for one more gulp before slipping on his jacket and hurrying out.

As hard as it was being with her mother lately, it was dreadful tolerating her father. With his angry silences and flickering sneers, he'd list his grievances at every meal. An elderly customer requesting sugared ham. "It's *traif,* I told her. We're a Jewish establishment." The dog shit that had clung to his new shoes right outside his own house. "It should be illegal, owning those mongrels." The errant superintendent. "That good f' nothing foiler, too busy at the racetrack to tend to his business."

After reading Camus's "The Myth of Sisyphus" her junior year, Estelle imagined the condemned man's stone as her father's rage: Jacob pushed it out into the world, at his wife, his daughter, even his customers, and with all the futility and hopelessness of his labor it would roll back at him. It had not always been this way, not during Estelle's childhood, when her pliability had provided an outlet for her father's frustrations. There had been moments of peace between the two of them, most memorably during the evenings spent with their heads bent down, in mutual employment at the kitchen table.

After Devora had cleared away the dinner plates, Jacob would say, "Come, *Milaya moya*, let's do our figures." He would nimbly draw a column of numbers as long, lean, and inscrutable as the man himself. For two hours every night, Estelle would fret over algebraic equations—laboring to solve the calculations without flaw—chewing on the inside of her lip as her pencil stitched together the fissure between father and daughter. In high school, the ritual stopped at Jacob's insistence. "You are too old for our silly games," he declared, bitterly.

When Devora, in a rare moment of defiance, challenged her husband's judgment—"You are a genius at mathematics, Yakov. Who better to teach your own daughter?"—he countered with, "She is a big shot now. If she needs my help, she knows where to find me." He fastened his gaze on Estelle, his eyes as blue as the Belize sky, he a Russian Jew, with such a wide Slavic face and hair the color of earth. "The only blue eyes in the whole family," he'd often boast.

As Estelle never required assistance with her schoolwork, she chose not to seek her father's help. She knew he wished to teach her more advanced disciplines, like calculus, but it was a desire she refused to meet. She craved the anonymity of college courses in which those searing eyes and tapping fingers would not distract or torment her.

These days her usually invisible mother was making her presence known to Estelle as well: With puckered mouth, clucking tongue, and countless sighs, Devora furiously dusted, swept, and chopped vegetables for stew. Between the two women no meaningful conversation occurred; but apprehension replaced oxygen in their shared space. It seemed as if Devora were holding her breath for both of them.

This morning, the last in March, she knocked on her daughter's door. "Stellie, breakfast."

Estelle had fallen back to sleep and awoke feeling groggy and nauseous. The sky was a pale, aching gray; the sun had yet to grace the bedroom. She waited for her mother to retreat to the kitchen sink. After a few minutes, she realized this wasn't going to happen. "I'll be right there," she said.

She stood in the claw-footed bathtub long after she was done washing herself and the nozzle started spitting out only icy-cold drops. *Nothing in this place ever works right,* she thought in disgust. But although shivering—her arms wrapped around her little dome of a belly—she could not seem to extricate herself from the faded green shower curtain with a picture of a pink flamingo on it. After another in a series of fitful nights, Stellie felt ragged, caged inside her mind, which repeated her dilemma and its no-hope solution without mercy.

She stepped out of the tub and turned the faucet knobs as tightly as possible; as always, a drizzle leaked out. Vapor misted up the mirror so that it was hard to observe herself adjusting her expression into the neutral one with which she faced her parents these days. She noted that her eyes were puffy and the skin around them so translucent she could see one delicate vein inching toward her temple. Still hers was a child's face, white and smooth, with round eyes.

Trying not to track footsteps on the worn beige carpet, Stellie dashed out in only a towel. She closed her door behind her and sank down onto her unmade bed, breathing heavily. She was so lonely; every few days it caught up with her, like a lingering cough.

She'd snubbed her best friend so many times in the last few weeks that now when the two girls passed each other in the halls of De Witt Clinton, Janet quickly glanced away, sometimes snapping her gum as if to say, *See if I care!* After math class, Jan made sure to leave with Sally Rubin, giggling or linking arms in a show of camaraderie, sometimes running her fingers over her new pal's cardigan sweater, remarking on the softness of the wool or the cute pearl buttons. Estelle knew how hurtful her own behavior had been. After all, they'd been inseparable since first grade, when Janet had spilled her milk on Gordie Goldberg's lap and they'd locked eyes, stifling the laughter that would have sent them to the principal's office.

Stellie had lost the energy that a friendship required, not when it took everything out of her just to stay focused on survival, on figuring out how to get rid of the thing inside of her, the logistics of it, a way to ensure safety, not to let shame swallow her into its dark gullet. Forsaking Janet was no more painful than the rest of her present surreal life, even though a voice in her head promised that her friend would help her, would not judge, would turn to her if their roles were reversed. Yet Stellie could not fight her nature, her propensity for solitude during troubling times. Every morning she awoke, her blankets on the floor—having thrown them off in the middle of the night—her armpits wet with this new pungent odor that mortified her, her feet sweaty, her belly just a bit more stretched out than the day before.

Devora was at her usual spot, washing the morning dishes. She turned, her gloved hands still in the soapy water and stared just for a second, sizing up the situation as if she had something important to say. "Do you want an egg or some kasha?"

"I'm not hungry," Stellie said. "Tea would be nice."

Her mother nodded slowly, as she sponged down the counter. "You haven't been hungry much, huh?"

"Yeah. I think I've had a virus or something."

Pulling off her gloves, Devora sighed. Then she wiped her hands up and down her apron and coughed into her fist. "For three weeks? What virus lasts for so long? You are the scientist, the one with all those good marks; you tell me." She clasped her apron tightly and tugged. "Stellie?"

"Yeah?" The girl bowed her head and stared down, sadly, at her bare feet.

"I had a talk with Dr. Cohen."

"What?" Tears welled in her eyes. "That's supposed to be confidential."

"*Nyet*. The law in this country says you're an adult as of your last birthday. I happen not to agree with this law. Dr. Cohen agreed with me: As long as you're living in my house, your business is my business."

"Oh, God!" Estelle said, wishing she were still that headstrong five-year-old who thought skirts were dumb because they made your legs cold and that dolls were good only for haircuts, nothing more.

"You have to see what to do," her mother asserted, staring into the dregs of her cold tea. "There is less time than you think. This you can't get out of with a few hours of study."

"What choice do I have? I can't keep it." She could feel a bubble of hysteria rising in her. "I just can't! I have to find a doctor who will help me."

"And the father? What does he want?"

"The father? He's gone. I mean . . . he lives far away. I didn't tell him."

"I don't understand," Devora said in a tight voice. "He was not a serious boyfriend, this boy who did this to you?"

Stellie squeezed her hands together under the table and blushed. "Yes. Yes, of course he was. It's just that he's not from New York, and his family moved away after New Year's."

"Moved away where? Can't you call him or write a letter?"

"I suppose, but he's far away, and even if he weren't . . ."

"So you don't want to marry this . . . *Khazzer*? Not even if he would agree to such an arrangement?" The sting of accusation caused Devora's voice to swell.

"Oh, no. Why would I want that? I haven't even finished college."

"But old enough, *nyet*?" She gestured to her daughter's belly. "Plenty of girls marry at your age. I took a boat to another country at your age without my mama and papa and stayed with cousins who knew not one word of Russian. I had to learn a new language, work in my cousin Levi's lamp store ten hours a day, never see my little sister, Geva, or my parents again."

"I have to go to college," Stellie pleaded. "Please, Ma."

"Do you want your father to speak with him, with his family, to talk some sense into him? It's his responsibility too. You didn't get this way with just God's help."

"No, please. Daddy would kill me. He's not Jewish, Ma. He's Spanish, from Spain."

After a brief silence, Devora's face drained of color. She was biting down on her lip so that blood sprang through the broken skin. "I have never even seen this boy, not once. You never brought him to the house, never introduced him to us, your parents, yet you have his baby inside you."

Estelle glanced down at her hands; they looked larger than usual and almost transparent, so that all her veins stood out in sharp relief. "I'm sorry."

"I won't raise your baby," Devora said firmly, then touched her bruised mouth with the dish towel. "I'm done with all that. I'm tired."

"Of course not."

"There is no family to send you to, no cousins who will agree to raise this baby. We don't have that kind of people here—maybe back home; I don't know anymore after twenty years." She hunched her shoulders. "So. What do you plan to do?"

Stellie shrugged passively. Hadn't she tediously combed through the possibilities, as if scouting for head lice?

"If you want so badly to go to college, you need to start acting like a woman and not this helpless little child."

"I will, I promise," Stellie said earnestly, as if reciting the Pledge of Allegiance. "I want to get rid of it, Ma. I need help finding a good doctor who will do it right, who won't hurt me."

Devora cleared her throat and cast her eyes down. "It will cost. Where will you get that money except from us, from the store? Your father will find out. Don't think he won't."

"I would work every day after school to pay it back if you could get it for me."

In a small voice, Devora reverted to Yiddish. "*A mol iz der refueh erger fun der makeh.* Do you know what that means?"

The girl shook her head. It was rare for her mother to speak full sentences in Russian or Yiddish to her. Estelle knew only a few idiomatic expressions, the most common phrases, in either language.

"It means that sometimes the remedy is worse than what ails you. Understand?"

"Mama . . ."

"Listen for a change. I have something to tell you." Devora stood up slowly, leaning with her palms over her knees as if she'd aged years that day and, in so doing, had developed bad arthritis in her legs. "What I'm about to say is between you and me, you understand? You can never say anything to anyone, even your father. *Especially* to Yakov. If you want me to help you, you'll respect my wishes, yes?"

"Of course."

Devora looked directly at her daughter, her eyes milky as an old woman's. "This happened, this shameful thing, when you were just a baby and your father and I were very poor, right after he and Uncle Sol closed the store in the city. You wouldn't remember that godforsaken place. You were not even one year old. I was not myself that winter. It was so cold; no matter what I wore I could never get warm. Everything ached, even the soles of my feet, and I was so tired, in my bones and my face—I lost my beauty and it never came back."

She shook her head. "You know I'm not a complainer. I told no one and went about my business. You were not sleeping well and the doctor kept saying, 'You're a worrier, Devora. This little girl is *shtark*. She will out grow it.' Teething. An earache. Growth pains. Every time I would shlep you to his office, he'd say something different, with absolute certainty when he knew nothing, that man. Such a big shot, that Dr. Rosenstein with his fancy degree from a German university before the war. He would talk about Berlin, how he missed the strong coffee and the pumpernickel bread with liverwurst, which the dunces in this country could never make. I felt like saying, 'Go back to your wonderful fatherland if you miss it so much, where the food is good and the Nazis are busy killing our people.'"

Surprised, Estelle smiled. Her mother very rarely showed signs of feistiness. Estelle often wished she would display this defiance around her father.

"I kept my worries from Yakov, as he was in a mood all the time, always with the bills till late at night after working all hours in the new store, cursing God for tricking him into believing it would be better for him here on Morris Avenue than if he had stayed and let the Cossacks shoot him in the back. Finally I went to the doctor to find out what was the matter with me, why I wasn't myself, tired and crying all the time. I felt like a fool not knowing. But I'd just had a baby and was still nursing you before bed. How could this be?"

"You were pregnant?" Estelle whispered.

Devora rubbed her hands together as if scrubbing them clean. "*Da*. It was even later than I thought; the doctor said eighteen weeks. I'll never forget it. I was in shock leaving his office. It was freezing out that day, but I walked with you in the carriage for hours. You barely cried. It was as if you knew that something out of the ordinary had happened to your mama and you needed to keep quiet for a change."

"So what happened?"

"I couldn't think straight. It wasn't like when I was carrying you. Night after night I'd lie in bed, not sleeping, Jacob next to me, and I couldn't tell him, not even in a whisper. I knew he'd figure it out for himself soon. I was getting fat sooner this time. He told me to stop eating so many potatoes; you know how your father hates it when I get fat. My mind never seemed to rest. Always it was working on this problem and never coming up with an answer, me, a clever girl. Did you know that when I was a child in Vinnica I got the highest marks in mathematics in my class?"

Estelle shook her head, mesmerized. Who was this woman suddenly standing so straight, when all her life Estelle had seen her mother stooped over in menial work, an oven, a sewing machine, a sink full of dirty pans, her one pleasure her radio shows played at a high volume.

"My papa used to say I was his *umnaya dochenka*, his smart little daughter." Her eyes filled with tears, and Devora put her hand up to stem their flow. "There I was, no longer clever, no longer a beauty, eyes open, night after night, while you lay in your cradle next to the bed and I knew soon, soon, you would be up and I'd get no peace. You were such a busy baby, always with the doing, never wanting to sleep."

Estelle, feeling as if she should apologize for her transgressions as a baby, said nothing.

"I had it done by a doctor in his office on Pelham Parkway. I got his name from a woman who used to come into the store. Something in her face made me know I could trust her. She was the wife of the doctor who specialized in the blood and liked our noodle kugel, said it was the only one, other than from his mama's kitchen, that he would eat. I didn't tell your father about the operation. I left you with Mrs. Shapiro downstairs and went alone. It was so painful what he did to me, I thought I would die from the pain. He told me that the baby he took out of me was a boy, a son for your father. That night I woke up with even worse pain and blood everywhere, all over the bed."

Devora dropped into the kitchen chair, as if the weight of her story had finally proven too burdensome to carry. "I had never seen your father so scared or so gentle. He took me to Montefiore Hospital and even though I was in and out of it from all the hemorrhaging, I begged the doctor treating me not to tell my husband what had happened. When I woke up hours later, I didn't know if Yakov knew. He said the doctor had told him 'female troubles.' They had to operate to stop the bleeding. After that, I couldn't have another baby. They tied my insides up."

Estelle was staring at her mother at this point. "I don't know what to say, Ma."

"That's why I don't want for you what happened to me. The lady I told you about at the store, the doctor's wife, even she knows of a girl who died from having the abortion. Without money, without knowing the right man to do it . . . and even then it could happen to you."

"So what *should* I do, Mama?"

"You will do the best you can to hide it. I will help you. Then we will find it a good Jewish home. You are Jewish, the mother, so the baby will be Jewish too, no matter that the father is not. It won't be easy when the time comes, giving it up to strangers, your baby. But you have to do it. You have no choice." Devora shook her head slowly. "We can't keep it here. Your father would never let us."

"Okay, Mama." Estelle reached for her mother's hand and squeezed it, the rough skin and enlarged knuckles.

"I'm just saying it won't be easy."

"I know, Ma."

But the truth was, keeping the baby was the last thing Estelle wanted. She couldn't wait to be rid of it, to pass it through her system like a gallstone, like some rotten meal she'd eaten but never fully digested.

FOURTEEN

In mid-April, Estelle returned from school one evening to an apartment so dark it was as if the rooms themselves were sitting shivah. Tuesday was her day to stay late, to volunteer in the freshman-tutoring program, the only activity she hadn't renounced. Immediately she sensed a shift in the atmosphere at home, some palpable change in the molecular construction of the air; her breath contracted into her lungs as she treaded carefully into the shadows. With the stealth and skill of a gladiator Jacob was upon her: eyes glaring, beaky nose flared, jaw locked above a solid, veined neck, his movements as rigid as if he'd been strapped into a suit of armor.

"Are you all right, Daddy?" Estelle exclaimed, startled. Her father was never home this early from the store; for just a moment she misconstrued the situation.

"Me? Suddenly you are concerned with me, with my health?" He laughed extravagantly.

"Oh." She said, understanding. Her mind fought to pull away, to vanish like a balloon released into the vast sky. "Where's Ma?"

"Someone had to take over for me at the store, or would you have liked me to lose my income as well as my good reputation? Imagine what ideas went through my head when *Mamme* showed up today, not to work the register, but to tell me the truth about my daughter?"

"Daddy . . ."

"*Kurveh,*" he spit under his breath, excess saliva gathering at the corners of his mouth.

"Daddy, don't," Estelle pleaded upon hearing the Yiddish word for whore.

"And why not? What's the American expression? If the shoe fits you?" He sprang upon her, and instinctively she backed away. His face was contorted in anger.

"Please!"

"You were so smart," he said with a plaintive cry. "How could this *sheygets* make you lose your sense, make you into someone who is a stranger to your parents? Can you explain that to me, please?"

Estelle shook her head. She slunk past Jacob, hunched over subserviently.

"Did he brainwash you? Is that how he got you to open your legs to him?"

"No. I don't know."

She retreated to her bedroom, where the air was stagnant, the smell of cabbage streaming in through her window, and gently closed the door. She gazed at her dirty beige wing chair with its ripped upholstery; it reminded her of an overcooked biscuit whose top was cracked open. She lowered herself onto her bed, using her hands to anchor herself, and waited for her father to enter. He never did.

After that one brief confrontation, father and daughter tried to avoid each other's wrath, an absurd task within their compact space. They were like warring neighbors pushed together in a boxcar bound for Mauthausen, the Nazi concentration camp constructed especially for Soviet prisoners of war. They could smell the fear radiating from each other's skin even as they turned their heads to the dim slats of fading light.

By June, a few weeks shy of graduation, it was not uncommon for Estelle to arrive home to the sight of Devora at her sewing machine in her floral housedress, brows furrowed, her foot swiftly working the pedal. She'd be replacing a zipper with an elastic waistband on one of Stellie's two poodle skirts or on her slacks. The sight brought the girl to tears. It was the worst time of day, anyway. Her home struck Estelle as particularly oppressive in the weak light that the grayish blue sky afforded. The beige curtains were so dull they reminded her of the bark on a dead tree. Dust particles dotted the air, like a halo, around her mother's bowed head.

"I'm sorry, Ma," she'd whisper, wishing she could say more.

Now, close to her last trimester, she'd become increasingly upset with the unwieldy behavior of her body. Like her mother before her, she was carrying low. She'd gained over twenty pounds despite her doctor's warning—"If you put on more, you may never take it off"—and it was detectable everywhere. Her cheeks were so puffy they gave her eyes the appearance of having shrunken, the area around her triceps had grown flabby, her behind was ever widening so that she feared she would never again fit into a seat at the movie theater. Worse than the loss of her looks was the physical discomfort, the heartburn, the pressure on her bladder, the broken sleep. And all this she knew—from poring over the May issue of *Ladies' Home Journal* at the New York Public Library—would dwarf in comparison to labor.

Estelle had managed to remain in school, despite the whispering that hovered around her like mosquitoes on a lake. She'd done everything possible to cover her growing embarrassment. She'd worn her father's extra-large sweaters over her loosest-fitting blouses, even as the radiators at school clanged right through spring and her eyes watered from overheating. She'd departed from both the science and mathematics clubs, without so much as a whispered explanation, after three years of full participation. She'd slink through the hall, willing herself as illusive as a ghost merely touching down to earth for a brief visit among the living.

One afternoon near the end of the term, her physics teacher, Miss Manly, kept Stellie after class. It was a day so hot the windows were sprung wide open, forcing the stagnant Bronx air to mix with the smell of chalk, dust, and body odor. Estelle was sweating profusely, and the skin under her skirt's elastic waistband itched as it dug its way into her belly, sure to leave an angry red mark. All she wanted was to undress, to shower, to rinse away the sense of entrapment her body imposed on her.

"Dear, I was wondering if we might talk?" Miss Manly asked, arching her pale eyebrows. She was a severe-looking woman, tall with skinny legs, an ample bust, and a tight jaw. "If you'd like to discuss any changes in your plans? You should know I'd be willing to listen." Two beads of perspiration glistened above her upper lip, right where the faint hint of a mustache could be detected.

"Is there something wrong with my work?" the girl responded, head up, eyes glaring into the blackboard in front of her.

How could there be? Estelle had been applying herself with even more determination than usual, as if studying late into the evening would ward off an inquiry like this one. And she found solace in her work; day after colorless day unfolded with only her textbooks for company. During all those lonely months, her resolve had hardened like clay exposed to the high temperature of a kiln.

Now Estelle saw how foolish she'd been, as here was Miss Manly, her favorite teacher, standing before her in judgment. Hands resting on her desk, white with slightly red knuckles, head tilted, her grayish brown hair combed back behind her ears. Waiting.

"I thought my grades were pretty good this marking period," she said boldly.

Miss Manly nodded. "Yes, dear. Your work is better than ever." She was the teacher's highest achiever. With her exceptional grades, Estelle was bound to graduate top five in her class—she, a pregnant girl.

"Good. I'll be starting at City College in the fall. I don't want to leave any loose ends."

The truth was that with the baby due in September, she was going to have to wait for the spring semester to matriculate. Until then Estelle was obligated to work in her father's store every day after school, a witness to his fury, in lips so pursed they turned purple, in his stiff shoulders and proud Bolshevik back—this being part of the bargain if she wished to remain in his home.

Miss Manly frowned, causing her matte red lipstick to crack.

Outside the classroom the janitor knocked his mop against his metal pail and then flung it, sopped with soap, down the hallway. Stellie chewed on the corner of her mouth and observed the dull wooden floor. The backs of her knees and calves were tingling, a recent development. Every few nights a terrible cramping in her legs awakened her, bringing her to tears. Now she worried that the tension in the room would cause her to cry as well.

The right side of her teacher's mouth twitched before settling into a smile. She reached out for the girl's shoulder, giving it a quick squeeze. "You should be proud of your accomplishments, my dear," she said.

"I am, Miss Manly," Estelle said, shutting her eyes, letting her hair hang over her face in order to cover her flushed cheeks, her pale lips, even the irony in her words. "I'm definitely proud of myself."

August was so hot the city seemed stagnant, the good people of the Bronx stuck in their tracks, insects biting the insides of their thighs, their anklebones, bugs turned rabid from the heat. The sky was a sheet of whitish gray without a hint of real blue, and the few visible clouds appeared dirty, like laundry left too long hanging on the line.

Estelle's nights were spent listening to a small fan pushing the stale air around and around while she stared at the ceiling and scratched the hives rising on her belly. In the morning she'd wake with great dots of color splintering before her eyes: reds, oranges, purples, and golds. She needed to take care, to get up slowly, to avoid becoming light-headed, the sensation of the room slanting under her feet.

On this August afternoon, after three bad nights of broken sleep, she sat on her bed, holding a letter from Claudio. Hugely pregnant and nearly sick from the pungent smell radiating from her body, Estelle noticed how clammy her hand felt, how the thin overseas envelope clung to her flesh. She tore it open quickly and skimmed the contents, noting the chatty tone, the idiomatically incorrect English, the references to people and events that could never touch her. At the end, Claudio casually mentioned his intention of returning to the United States for a vacation, sometime around Christmas. Perhaps they could "meet together, ¿sí?"

Carefully she folded the letter back along the three crease lines and slid it into its envelope, then opened the drawer to her night table and placed the letter on top of his other unanswered one. Claudio had not mentioned her failure to respond. An American boy would have confronted her, either out of jealousy or anger or pure male pride. That her Spanish ex-lover was all light and breezy charm proved inconsequential. It wasn't so much that her heart had turned cold as that some grander law of practicality now glared in her head like a cosmic stoplight, alerting her brain to life's unexpected dangers.

She barely thought of Claudio anymore, not with the visceral longing she'd felt when he first left, and not even in conjunction with the visitor in her body. The salty taste of his tongue was becoming as deeply buried a memory as the Sunday afternoons spent at the Museum of Natural History with her father—a ritual that had ended before her thirteenth birthday. What mattered most were her resolutions: to avoid charismatic young men, to prevent another catastrophe; to remain unfettered, catering only to her ambition, childless.

She heaved herself up from her bed, wiped the trickle of sweat off her forehead, and headed to the kitchen to help her mother prepare dinner.

FIFTEEN

FALL 1958

After Estelle's due date passed, Devora started having trouble sleeping. Stellie could hear her mother shuffle into the kitchen in her old furry slippers; once she watched, from the shadowy living room, as Devora boiled tea, and then skimmed the newspaper before staring out at the dull sky, the vague outlines of tenements. Eventually she fell asleep on the couch. It was here that Estelle found her in the early hours of morning on September twenty-second.

"Ma?" she whispered, and her voice quavered. It felt as if a tiny nervous bird was lodged in her throat. She'd been awoken by a tug in her gut so strong her eyes had flown open.

"*Shto?*" Devora asked, still lost in the fog of Russian dreams.

Estelle was close enough to smell her mother's sour milky breath. Her lips were tight, her eyes focused on her hands. "I'm having pains," Estelle said.

"Oh!" Devora sat up quickly, the brown-and-blue patterned sheet tumbling to her ankles. She'd dozed off in her housedress and now pulled it down from around her waist where it had gathered. "Let me brush my teeth and we will go."

It sounded nonsensical, her mother's worry about clean teeth while Estelle's insides were being wrenched apart. Yet Estelle was too terrified to disagree with any suggestion. "Okay."

"Be as quiet as possible. We won't wake Daddy," Devora said conspiratorially.

Estelle waited for her mother, sweating and anticipating the next tug deep within her. When Devora dashed out of the bathroom—a small glob of white toothpaste clinging to her jowl—Estelle was trying to negotiate her movements. She'd hobbled from the living room into the kitchen by bending her knees and lowering her head to stave off dizziness.

"I'm going to write Daddy a note and grab my purse and we will leave," Devora said.

Her mother's words sounded so ordinary. It was as if the two of them were sneaking off to Loews for a double feature or to the ice-cream parlor for fudge sundaes, deliberately excluding her father from the fun.

Devora scribbled, *Gone to hospital,* on the pad she kept next to the telephone. Then she tiptoed into her bedroom, emerging seconds later with her brown flats in place of her slippers.

"Okeydokey," she said absurdly, one of the American expressions she used whenever feigning cheer to cajole her husband out of a foul mood. "I will get my jacket. You too, Stellie. It will be cool out."

But Estelle was concentrating on the wetness in her underpants, now running down her legs. What did one use to wash up amniotic fluid without spending money? she wondered in a panic. Baking soda? Canada Dry ginger ale? She figured they wouldn't offer any helpful hints in *Good Housekeeping* or *Reader's Digest*—her mother's two faithful reference guides.

"Ma," she said.

"I'm coming. Hold your horses!"

"Look! I've ruined the rug."

Startled, Devora glanced at the floor.

"I'm sorry," Estelle said, certain she'd be met with a scowl, a reprimand, a warning to be more careful.

Devora shook her head. She reached out for her daughter and drew her close, as if she were a child again. In a voice from aeons ago, she whispered, "Mama *staboi,* Mama is with you."

When Estelle awoke, her head was filled with cotton, the birth a collage of images, as if someone else's memory had supplanted her own. She remembered pain, but not the feeling of pain. Chaos. Nurses in white shoes and sheer stockings running to the aid of a man in cardiac arrest. The hospital ER had been booming with humanity in harmony with its machines. As the orderly wheeled her into delivery, Estelle had felt the room slant to the right; people gripped with purpose sped by at a breakneck pace. She'd been strapped to a gurney in the emergency room while her mother stood silently, lips curled into whiteness, clutching her bag to her chest.

"Can't she come with me?" Estelle squeaked. "I'm scared to be alone."

The RN attendant had a wide, cheeky face and small eyes. She seemed to be smirking as she said, "Let's go, Miss Ackerman."

In the whirl of movement, Estelle caught sight of a nurse's dimpled thigh where her dress had hitched up, heard the click of the wheels, then a short screech as they turned a corner, smelled a combination of bleach, ammonia, and perspiration. She might have been wailing softly; she wasn't sure. Never before had she experienced such humiliation (her wrists buckled down as if she were a mental patient). A drug was injected deep into her muscles without her permission. "Please don't," Estelle had whimpered when the needle first grazed her skin. But this request went unacknowledged. She might have begun her weeping then, or maybe it was later. Mercifully, she couldn't remember much more, just the clanging of metal objects, the racket of voices mingled together, language indecipherable in the underwater region she'd entered. Her head was a swell of colors and noise, dissonance. Then there was a pull toward black nothingness.

Now she lay just barely awake.

The light outside her window, leaking through the slats of the blinds, was the gray of her school erasers, signaling evening. Had she slept through an entire day? She turned to see her roommate—a hefty girl with a bouffant hairdo—sitting up in her bed, spooning red Jell-O into her mouth. Estelle shut her eyes again, and noted how her own hair was a tangle on her forehead, held down by body oil, how her gut ached.

She must have dozed, because the next sequence of events included a nurse sticking a thermometer down her throat and pressing lightly on her pulse, saying in a British accent, "Dear, would you like a spot of dinner?"

When she looked up, she saw a darker woman with brown lips and a black braid, a purplish mole on her neck. Indian perhaps.

"I can get you some toast and tea if you'd like."

The thermometer was dispensed with into the nurse's pocket or hidden somewhere else, miraculously lost in her starched white uniform.

"Okay," Estelle said, not out of hunger, but out of thanks. This nurse was the first human being to show decency since she'd been admitted to the hospital.

"Very good." The woman smoothed the sheets on either side of the bed, tucking them in tightly. "I sent your mother home to eat her dinner. She's been sitting by your side all afternoon and looked very tired. My name is Mahadevi. I'll be here until midnight."

"Thank you."

Mahadevi rose to leave. She was a slender but solid-looking figure, with a wide nose and black-rimmed eyes. When she smiled, her teeth shone like small freshwater pearls.

"Have you seen your baby yet?" So that was it, kindness prompted by ignorance. "Your boy?"

A boy. The son her mother had never had.

"I'm not supposed to see him," Estelle said, tears—to her dismay—sliding from the corners of her eyes. "I'm not keeping him."

"Yes, dear, I know." Mahadevi nodded, nonplussed. "You should see your baby."

Estelle shook her head and said nothing, not about the shocking invitation or the mere thought of its implication. She recognized that it would be like viewing someone after they were dead. The warrant signed. Life over. This way the dream could exist. Somewhere in the world, her son would be laughing without her.

SIXTEEN

I t was another in a series of airless New York days, Saturday afternoon in late August. Nothing was worse than being holed up with Devora while she prepared their cold "dairy" dinner of cottage cheese, hard-boiled eggs, slices of rye bread, and iceberg lettuce on a platter while listening to Brenda Lee or Connie Francis bemoan the cruelties of love. Sometimes the sound of her mother's tuneless voice singing along with the radio caused Estelle's stomach to knot up. It was so unfair, her mother's wasted life.

Claiming she had research to do at the CUNY library, Stellie headed out for the Cloisters. Lately she'd been using this escape on a regular basis, having discovered a haven away from both school and family in the museum. She found it soothing to sit surrounded by the cool, dark limestone—the pageantry of medieval life whistling in her ear—and imagine her future in the faded, centuries-old wool and silk tapestries on the wall. She didn't like to admit how she felt. It was so girlishly silly. But she romanticized her own fate; she was like the chained unicorn, a captive in her father's home.

The windows in the A train were open, slapping stagnant heat into the cars. Stellie tried to read Chaucer's "The Knight's Tale" for her required literature course, but her eyes wandered to the fat young woman sitting across from her in a cheap orange dress and dirty white Keds. There was black stubble on the woman's bulky calves, as if she'd started to shave and had been interrupted or simply submitted to the pull of apathy. She was holding on to the waist of a wailing little boy in a sailor suit. The toddler's nose was running and his fists were flailing near his mother's expressionless face. *That could have been me,* Stellie thought with a wave of relief.

Stellie closed her eyes, wondering if she was missing something, some primal maternal instinct that would make her long for the baby she'd given up without a proper dose of regret. But the sweltering day wore her out; keeping herself awake was hard enough. At her stop at Fort Tryon Park, she glanced up once more. The mother and child were gone.

The Nine Heroes Tapestry Room of the museum was quiet, with only a few people milling about. Standing in front of the sixth tapestry—*The Unicorn Is Killed and Brought to the Castle*—was a familiar-looking young woman with hair the color of carrot cake and shapely legs highlighted by a red sack dress. She was clutching the straps of her white seed handbag and bending forward to study the artwork before her.

"Don't you just love it here?" the orange-haired girl asked in a stage whisper.

Estelle glanced around. The only other visitors—an older couple wearing matching straw hats and sandals—had wandered into the Gothic Chapel and were examining the tombs. She coughed politely, considering which answer might end conversation before it developed.

"Yes, I do," she said.

"I've seen you here before," the girl said in a quick, high voice. Her eyes flickered with a sardonic intelligence, green to brown depending on how the light hit them, and her smile was full and wide. "I'm Lillian Merkin, by the way. Everyone calls me Lily, though."

"Estelle." She paused. "Ackerman."

Lily extended her hand, her fingers manicured in a pearly white polish. Around her wrist was a charm bracelet composed of silver animal trinkets, a heart, and an open book. "Good to meet you, Estelle. Like I said, I've seen you before." She spread her arms out in a wide wingspan. "Have we met at school, at Barnard?"

"No. I'm going into my junior year at CCNY."

Estelle was sure that if any information would discourage her, the discrepancy in their schooling would. Enrollment at City College exposed her as a poor Bronx girl, which this Lily Merkin certainly was not.

But Lily was nodding her head nonchalantly. "What's your major?"

"Biology. I'm premed."

"Wow. That's impressive. Listen, you want to go out in the gardens for a minute? I could use a cigarette."

They stepped from the cool stone quadrangle into the sunlit pathway lined with heather and wildflowers. Bees hummed and the air sucked them into the flowers' pistils.

Lily unclasped her envelope-shaped bag and removed her pack of Chesterfields and a silver-plated lighter. "Want one?" she asked.

"No, thanks. I don't smoke."

The other girl said nothing as she inhaled deeply, her coral lipstick staining the end of the cigarette, her mouth making a small O.

"It's the scientist in you," she said after pausing for a few drags. "My brother doesn't either. He's in medical school at Columbia. He keeps telling me tobacco will kill me. But I'm a writer, or want to be. Writers smoke." She laughed. "He's lucky I'm not a lush, as well."

Estelle finally eyed the other woman with interest. "What do you write?"

"Nothing of any importance yet. I'm a double major in art history and literature. I'd like to write historical novels, you know, e-ven-tu-ally." She drew out the adverb slowly, as if it emanated with the smoke from her lungs. "I adore European history—the Middle Ages." She swung her arm around, encircling it all—the luxurious floral grounds, the herb gardens, the stained-glass windows, the fresco of Virgin and Child, the Gothic- and Romanesque-style edifices, all behind them. "But I'll probably specialize in the Regency period, the late seventeenth, early eighteenth century." She flicked the ashes of her cigarette onto the pathway so that the charm bracelet on her wrist chimed. "The Napoleonic wars, what was happening in England. The domestic life of the women pining away for their navy men."

Estelle smiled. This creature was so different from the practical neighborhood girls with their plans to receive degrees in education or nursing before marrying. She figured Lily must come from a rich family.

"You really should meet my brother, Adam," Lily said. "He'd get a real kick out of you. I wonder how many girls are in his graduating class in medical school? Two? Three, tops?"

Stellie shrugged and licked her lips. She had no interest in meeting a guy who'd marvel at the oddity of her ambitions.

"He's not what you're imagining," Lily said, and put her hand up before Stellie could protest. "What I mean is that Adam's different. He's gentle and handsome. Girls have always loved him. He's not like other boys. Well, he is in all the important ways. He's going to be a surgeon. He got into all five schools he applied to and really wanted to go out of state, get some new experiences."

She shrugged. "Mom and Dad thought he should aim for an ivy, what with the competition among surgeons. Guess what he'd like to be in a perfect world?"

Estelle smiled politely and said, "I have no idea."

"A poet."

Claudio's letters with their easy, flamboyant language flew into Stellie's head. "I'm not the type to go for poets."

"Yes, I can see that. You're a sensible girl."

Estelle felt annoyed. She'd met this person ten minutes before. "I don't have a choice to be anything but. Unless I want to end up like all the other women on Morris Avenue."

Lily nodded, tapping her index finger against her upper lip. "That's why I think you should meet him. You two would be perfect for each other. Yin and yang."

Now she couldn't help but laugh. "Sorry," she said. "You don't know me. Why would you say such a thing?"

The question didn't rattle Lily. She whittled her cigarette against the trunk of a tree until it formed a perfect cone shape, and then shrugged. "I have this instinct about people. Always have. I can read them really well. Adam says it's a gift."

Adam again. This girl suffered from an infatuation with her brother.

"Have lunch with us next week. You two can talk about medical school, and he can give you pointers on applying."

Estelle glanced briefly into the face of this stranger, at her creamy skin, her plump lips. This was the first thing Lily had said that made any sense at all. "Maybe," she said. "I'll have to see."

How odd it was for Stellie to be at a coffee shop on Third Avenue in the middle of a Saturday afternoon, when she should have been at the library on Convent Avenue or putting in her required hours at her father's store, hours she would have to make up during the following week. Instead here she was sipping her Coke and waiting for Lily, a girl she barely knew, and the girl's brother, a fellow called Adam Delmont Merkin—funny middle name for a Jew. If anyone had asked her why she'd agreed to this meeting, Stellie wouldn't have been able to construct a truthful response. *Curiosity*, she might have said; *I don't have any friends who are medical students*. But if she were honest with herself, this fact made no difference to her either way. It was Lily with whom she wanted to spend more time, Lily with the lilting, staccato voice, the narrow, braceleted wrist, the manicured hands, the wreath of sun-kissed orange curls. There was an ease with which Lily threw her words away, as if, in her world, language was not a weapon to be turned against you. In this different world from Jacob's home, women's ideas and opinions must be valued above compliance—that was the tug, the velvet tie that pulled her toward this stranger.

Stellie saw them approach from her window view: Lily in a sleeveless gored dress and flats, laughing and smoking her Chesterfield, her brother, a tall, slim number with a fantastic head of wavy dark hair that wouldn't sit obediently on his head, a thin face, soft mouth with a full lower lip, and a shy smile. When he walked toward the restaurant, she noticed how long his stride was, how his gait was slightly awkward under his billowing pants.

Despite herself, Estelle grinned into her soda. Although she'd done nothing wrong, there was a touch of the illicit tingling below the skin of her collarbone. Then a quickening in her chest as a reminder of the last time she'd allowed herself this pleasure—and the nearly life-crushing results.

"Hi there," Lily called out, as she swung open the glass door and walked toward Estelle. "This is the infamous Adam, and this"—she pointed at Stellie—"is my new, smart friend, Estelle."

The young man blanched. Yet his half-cocked smile bespoke jauntiness, an ironic sensibility. *Isn't she too much?* it seemed to ask.

"Hello," Stellie said. "It's nice to meet you."

"Likewise, I'm sure," he agreed, but his eyes said, *Aren't we the best, humoring my sister in this way? Who can resist Lily?*

Not Estelle, as it turned out.

"Should we all get burgers?" Lily asked, once she and Adam had taken their respective seats next to each other on the opposite side of the booth. She ground out her cigarette in the platic ashtray, and then clapped her hands together gleefully. "How about burgers smothered in onions and an order of fries to split three ways? Our treat."

"All right," Stellie said. "If you want." She glanced over at this bony girl who could order so much greasy food and get away with it.

"So," Adam said, smiling and fiddling with his spoon, "Lil here tells me you're thinking of tackling medical school. That's great— brave, really."

"Brave?" Stellie was blushing, the heat rising to the surface of her cheeks. When she looked up, she was squinting from the streams of light forming parallelograms on the table and washing into her eyes.

"The admission process is ruthless these days. There's no point denying that it's much harder for women, even though it shouldn't be. Barbara Horowitz and Peyton Rogers, the two women in my graduating class, have had to work twice as hard for every A they've gotten as well as put up with snide comments from professors who think they're a bad investment for the school. The truth is, Bobbi and Peyton are worthier than most of the men, myself included."

"Don't say that, Adam." Lily turned toward her brother and slapped him playfully on the arm. "Why do you say these things?"

He shrugged. "I've told you. It's no mystery. I'm not sure I'm cut out for the job, no pun intended. There are other things I'd rather do than dissect cadavers." He winked at Estelle.

"Well, you don't have to choose pathology," she said.

"Of course." Adam nodded. "But all surgery reminds me of anatomy lab."

"There are other fields." Stellie was leaning over the table now, on her elbows, chin thrust forward.

"Adam will be a great surgeon," Lily interrupted. She lit another cigarette and the gray smoke wafted between the siblings.

"Lil, building cabinets isn't the same as removing an appendix. I admit my sutures would be nice and neat, but that doesn't a great surgeon make."

"So? Why not consider other specialties?" Stellie asked.

Looking askance, he said, "To be honest, it's expected of me. You know, family pressure, being the responsible fella and all."

Stellie shook her head. "If I lived according to my family's expectations, I'd be married by now, have two sons, and be an English substitute until my husband established himself, like all the good girls from my neighborhood. My father's philosophy is, nice American girls marry doctors; they don't become doctors. In Russia, women doctors are a dime a dozen."

"How forward-thinking the Communist party is."

"Not really," she said, reaching for her water glass. Why had she mentioned Russia, that red country, the grudge her father carried on his back, like a vagrant hauling around all his worldly belongings? Still, she persisted, her wish to be understood stronger than her shame.

"The clinic doctors aren't well paid, and those in positions of real authority are all men, same as here. I've tried to explain to my parents that I need to work or I'll go crazy, not just cook, wash dishes, and do the laundry all day like my mother does."

Lily laughed and said, "I hope you aren't quite so blunt. I find it refreshing, but I doubt your mother would."

"Of course I never say that to my mother. I talk to them about how much I love science—especially to my father. He's a whiz at math and science. He's always going on about how well he was educated at the gymnasium. Of course, my father was lucky; most Jews weren't allowed to study there. Anyway, I think it would be fascinating to be a surgeon."

Adam said with gentle equanimity, "I could tell you were smart and fearless. If I were dean of admissions at Columbia, I'd let you in."

Stellie examined the young man's jocular, open face, his soft brown eyes brimming with compassion.

"Thanks," she said.

"Me," Adam said, "I think I'd like being an English teacher." He looked down at his small, square hands. " 'By the road to the contagious hospital / under the surge of the blue / mottled clouds driven from the / northeast—a cold wind. Beyond, the / waste of broad, muddy fields / brown with dried weeds, standing and fallen . . .' "

"What's that?"

"It's the beginning of the poem 'Spring and All,' by William Carlos Williams, the great American poet and retired head of pediatrics at Paterson General Hospital."

"You should try to be like him, a famous poet and the chief of pediatrics."

Adam grinned, his eyes an amalgamation of desire and amusement. "A bit pompous to aim so high."

"No, you *have* to, even if you fail."

With a quick salute, Adam laughed. "If you say so, Sarge."

Lily inhaled deeply on her cigarette, glanced at her brother and then her new friend. She beamed as if to say, *I love being right.*

SEVENTEEN

Sunday afternoon in late October, the sun was a wafer of yellow in a cloudless sky, the air crisp as apples. Estelle shared a subway car with three elderly ladies clothed in bright church dresses and pillbox hats, her history book and notepad stashed into her old tote bag (not an elegant choice, but she needed to fool her mother into believing she was on her way to study). She wore her red pleated shirt, her red-and-white-striped blouse with kimono sleeves, ballet slippers with bobby socks, and only a touch of mascara.

As the Lexington line sputtered south from the Grand Concourse on her way to upper Manhattan, she wished she'd abided Devora's consistent urging to update her wardrobe. She took out her compact from the bottom of her bag and tried to keep a steady hand as she applied her Strawberry Pastel lipstick. She couldn't view her face in full in the small mirror, but the cubist montage belied a slightly stunned young woman with round, dark eyes not accustomed to registering pleasure. "Relax," she instructed herself.

The train lurched to a stop at Eighty-sixth Street, emitting the angry groan of an injured animal. She exited onto the subway platform with shallow breaths. They'd planned to meet at the Central Park entrance, walk as much as the weather allowed, maybe take a ride on the carousel, then get an early dinner. On the telephone Adam had said, "It's not nice, my never picking you up. I can only imagine what your folks must think."

"They know you're a nice Jewish boy, a medical student who's busy with his studies."

In truth, her parents weren't aware of Adam's existence. To her mother she'd dismissed the increasingly persistent caller as a pest from her chemistry class angling to borrow her notes. Panic had swelled in Stellie's throat at the notion of being caught in another lie, but it passed, quickly. Adam was nothing like the slick and glistening Claudio; his charm emanated from his soul, not his gonads. Her parents would recognize her new beau's goodness if and when the time came to meet him.

And there he was: a young man in a tan cardigan sweater, beige slacks, and an open trench coat, reading a newspaper. Above him the trees created a palette of sienna, burgundy, moss, and pumpkin in a final display of autumn's beauty. A mild breeze propelled Estelle along, so that she felt as if she were gliding.

"Hey, stranger!" she said. "Busy?"

Adam looked up, smiling. "Nope. Just getting my daily dose of the presidential campaign." He linked her arm in his after giving it a quick squeeze. "Shall we stroll through the park for a bit?"

"Sure thing."

They walked toward a thicket of trees and two college girls whispering and giggling through their red-painted mouths, their pasty-faced dates following in their wake.

"You watch the fourth Great Debate last week?" Adam asked.

"I overheard the television from my bedroom. I was trying to write a paper for history class."

"This *was* history class! Modern history!"

"Well, I told you I saw the first two. That's plenty of politics for me."

"Ah! I see. What would Mabel say about that, I wonder?" In an imitation of a Boston accent, he proclaimed, " 'In the election of 1960, and with the world around us, the question is whether the world will exist half slave or half free, whether it will move in the direction of freedom . . . ah . . . or whether it will move in the direction of slavery.' " He reverted to his own voice and added, "Forgot a phrase or two, but you get the gist of it. Mabel sure loved that speech of Mr. Kennedy's. She always said that likable Ike was not so likable to the Negro. She's got family in Mississippi, so she knows firsthand about racial injustice."

Jealousy rippled through Estelle's gut like the aftereffects of her mother's fried onions. "Is Mabel a friend from school?"

"Not exactly. She's the greatest girl in the world, someone I've known my whole life."

"Really? You don't say?"

"Oh, definitely. Everyone who knows her just loves good old Mabel."

Estelle removed her arm from Adam's and folded it into her chest. "Maybe you'd rather be here in the park with her?"

He broke into a laugh and reached for her hand, interweaving their fingers. "Silly! Mabel is my family's housekeeper since before I was born. She's over sixty years old."

"Why didn't you say so? It's mean to tease like that!"

"I'm sorry. It's just nice to see you get all bent out of shape. It makes me think you might like me just a little." He gazed at her winsomely, with eyes the color of cognac.

"Oh, no. I'm not about to compliment you after that one, mister."

"Fair enough, but Mabel wouldn't like it. She's very protective of me. I'm second only to Mr. Kennedy in her book."

"Uh-huh."

"Seriously, though, Stellie, I hope you're planning on voting in this election. It's the most important one in your lifetime."

"The *first* presidential one in my lifetime, actually, that I'm old enough to vote in, that is."

"True enough. And it's your duty as an American citizen to do so."

They were ambling down East Drive, past the back of the Metropolitan Museum of Art on their right and Cleopatra's Needle on their left. Two mothers with their babies in identical creamy white carriages strolled by, laughing loudly and tilting their heads toward each other as if they comprised their own private Eden.

Estelle smiled into the glare of sunlight. "You sound like my father when he gets going, although *he's* never satisfied. He complained through both of Eisenhower's terms that Americans were too stupid to know what's good for them. He's so down on Americans and their politics, I don't even know why he bothers to follow the news."

"Is he rooting for Kennedy, too, if you don't mind my asking?" Adam said tentatively.

"Yes, of course. Aren't all Jews? He's from Russia. He can't support the man who accused Stevenson of being a cowardly communist. My father reads our neighbor Mr. Rosenblatt's copy of the *Daily Worker* when he doesn't think anyone's looking."

"Your father a fan of Mr. Khrushchev, then?"

She shrugged. "My father isn't a fan of anyone." She paused to try to diagnose the parasite that was eating away at her father's spirit. "He's homesick for his country, for the opportunities he would have had—if he hadn't been Jewish, that is. Ironic, huh? Here it's less important that he's a Jew than that he's an immigrant." She shook her head. "Never mind. He's just an unhappy man because he never lived up to his potential."

"How long has he lived here?"

"Since thirty-seven."

"Long time."

"Yes. He still talks about going back one day, but my mother refuses even to consider it. She loves it here. She's *so* proud of her citizenship. Don't ask me why."

"Why shouldn't she love it here?"

"Oh, let's not talk about my mother and father!" she said more vehemently than she meant to sound. It was that the image of her mother intruded on this other world, the world of youth and hope, her mother in her housecoat and slippers, hunched over the kitchen sink, graying wisps of hair falling over her softening face, jowls developing, pockets of flesh, the white spongy texture of gefilte fish, appearing below her chin and wiggling under her arms. "Are your parents interested in politics?" she asked.

"Of course! They're members of the New York Society for Ethical Culture; my mother volunteered for the Red Cross during the war," Adam said. "They've given money to the movement to ban atomic and hydrogen bombs and to the NAACP."

"You sound pretty fired up about all this yourself."

"What can I say? I'm a bit of an oddball, a future surgeon—or so my parents presume—who'd rather read poetry or the *Atlantic Monthly* on the Kennedy family."

"Umm. Maybe you can one day remove the gallstones of a famous Washington insider."

Adam put his finger to his lips and said, "Shh. Big state secret: I'm actually considering applying for residencies in pediatrics."

"Like William Carlos Williams?"

When he smiled, fractured points of light glimmered in his eyes. "You remembered."

By the time they reached the carousel, in the middle of the park and twenty blocks downtown, Estelle was happy for the rest. On the way Adam confessed, "It's a lot easier to live the life of the mind when you don't have a practical skill in the world. I didn't even learn to do my own laundry until college, and I still can't turn on a stove."

Stellie laughed and promised to cook him "a mean noodle kugel."

"Ah, a girl who has everything: a great mind and talent in the kitchen. I'll have to keep this one, Ma!"

They climbed aboard the saddles of adjacent horses, their legs carved to be in perpetual motion, their mouths open as if neighing fiercely into the wind. The calliope played the organ music and the wood creatures bobbed up and down on their polls as the merry-go-round circled. Estelle watched Adam's hair rise like a loaf of pumpernickel bread. Over and over, with the movement and music, her mind repeated the phrase "I'll have to keep this one, Ma!"

EIGHTEEN

On the subway ride to meet Adam's parents, Stellie felt her nerves jiggling under her skin. The weather was bright and crisp, a perfect seventy degrees, a few kernels of popcorn clouds, white and delicious-looking, scattered in the sky. A Crayola day. She was wearing the new outfit her mother had splurged on for the occasion, a striped navy-and-white sack dress with a pearly blue cardigan covering her bare shoulders. It was risqué and expensive to have come from Devora, but this was a special occasion. In her hands Estelle held a candy bowl made of carnival glass, also purchased by Devora for more than the Ackermans could afford.

Her mother had explained, "These Merkins must be rich people, living near the park, sending their son to such an expensive school. You need to make a good impression on such a family." She'd wiped the pot roast gravy on her apron as she spoke. "We're not trying to fool anyone, Stellie. You're from a working family, but respectable. It's important for you to look nice and modern with a proper gift."

Estelle had been on her way out, already bathed in the gray shadows of the foyer, when Devora grabbed her wrist. "Please," the older woman had said in a husky whisper. "You can't tell him about it, *nyet? Never*, understand? Adam is a good boy. He will leave you for this *shande*."

Stellie nodded. The secret lay between them like the evidence of a crime.

Now the number six train screeched into the Fifty-ninth Street station and ground to a halt. Estelle left the bowels of New York to enter the hub of elegance, all posh, clean-swept, and ornate. She inhaled deeply the fresh, bejeweled air.

The building on East Sixty-first Street had a doorman in a stiff uniform with gold cuff links and a brimmed hat. A waterfall graced the lobby along with two wingback chairs and a low-hanging chandelier. Stellie thought of the apartment on Morris Avenue, of its dank, moldy hallways, the smells of stuffed cabbage and oniony stew, of home with its four small rooms, the peeling paint, the decades-old sofa with the plastic slipcovers, the tattered gray-and-beige area rug, the dim lighting from the lack of overhead fixtures. Her childhood in the dark.

Adam had offered to pick her up at home, but Estelle had insisted that wasn't necessary. The thought of that formal gesture, his expectant eyes on her during the ride from the gritty old country to this shimmering land of opportunity, would only add to her nervousness. He was waiting for her in the lobby when she arrived, seated on one of the chairs, head bent over a slim volume of poetry. He walked to the door to greet her, a grin of pure pleasure on his face.

In the elevator Adam kissed her cheek with chapped lips. "Don't worry," he whispered into her hairline. "My folks are going to love you." Adam knocked on his front door, winking. "Forgot the key."

Ruth Merkin answered the door looking perfectly lacquered: black hair swept off her high forehead, cool ebony eyes, thin upper lip lined in cherry red, penciled-in eyebrows shaped as sideways question marks, a perfectly fitted black suit with a white blouse, and what Estelle decided must be Italian shoes. Stellie could not envision such a fancy woman volunteering for the Red Cross in a dowdy nurse's uniform and pointed cap.

She extended her hand. "I'm glad to meet you, Mrs. Merkin."

"I guess you'd better call me Ruth now," her future mother-in-law said, shaking her hand lightly, then standing aside for Estelle to enter the apartment.

A few days earlier, Adam had announced his engagement to his family over coffee-ice-cream sundaes at Schrafft's. He had explained their plan. They would wait until they were both settled in the next stage of their careers, he in a residency, she in medical school, and coordinate it so they were both in programs in the same city. Then they'd marry.

A tall, trim man with a significant bald spot and a neat black mustache came forward to introduce himself as Edward Merkin and to relieve her of the package of carnival glass. "Not necessary but very thoughtful of you," he said.

Two columns of blond wood formed an archway to the living room. Leaning against one of them was Lily, all hair and sharp eyes. In the periphery, off in the kitchen doorway, stood Adam in profile, pouring a drink.

Lily winked, as if to ask, *Isn't this a fun game?*

The dining room was the closest to the apartment's entrance and, as such, could not be missed: the powder blue tablecloth, the azure glass vase holding lilacs, the pale blue china with the raised white trim, the sterling silverware, the linen napkins. The scent of the flowers mixed with the sandalwood and musk from Ruth's perfume, along with the delicious smells wafting from the kitchen.

A stout black woman with streaks of gray in her dry, puffy hair served the meal. She shuffled around the table in orthopedic shoes, her small feet a shock when viewed after her ample behind and the rolling flesh of her forearms, upon which she balanced a huge tray of tuna steak prepared with lemon juice, white wine, and garlic with slivers of peaches garnishing the sides of the dish.

"Come, dear. Sit here next to Lily," Ruth instructed her guest, resting a light hand on the girl's back. Mrs. Merkin orchestrated the seating arrangements so that Adam was sandwiched between his father and sister. Estelle recognized that her separation from her fiancé was a test of sorts, but couldn't gauge the spirit in which it was being given.

"Mabel, this is Estelle Ackerman. Estelle, Mabel Butler. Mabel has blessed us with her outstanding cooking for twenty-two years now, haven't you, dear?"

"Yes, ma'am," the older woman said. She bowed her head, rippling her double chin and casting her eyes to the floor.

"Mabel's the best," Lily added. "Aren't you, Mab?"

Slowly the cook lifted her head. "Now don't get sassy with me, Miss Lily Merkin," she said with complete authority.

"Wouldn't dream of it. Just want Stellie here to know that you're part of the family, now that she will be too."

"I'm not so old or so stupid to see it as the same thing. It's not as if I'm the lucky one marrying Dr. Adam."

"Ah, now, Mab," Adam said, putting down his glass of red wine. "That's not fair. I asked. You refused me."

The housekeeper giggled, a sound so startlingly light and youthful it moved Estelle in its earnest musicality. Mabel shuffled over to Adam's side and pinched him on the cheek, clucking. "You're my boy. Always were, always will be."

"And you're my girl," Adam said, massaging the red spot she'd left on his face.

Ruth said, "A toast is in order. Why don't you make it, dear," she instructed her husband.

"Very well," he said, rising from his seat—long-legged, pleated slacks slightly creased—in order to pour the wine into each empty glass, then lifting his own. He cleared his throat. "To Estelle and Adam. May you find happiness and health and a long life together."

"And money and babies, don't forget," Lily added.

"Don't be gauche, dear," Ruth admonished.

"Welcome to the family," Edward said solemnly.

Suddenly and without warning, Estelle fought the urge to cry. How could she marry Adam with this secret buried inside her? She would have to confess the truth about herself to him and hope he could view her past mistake as a misstep of judgment rather than a stain on her character.

"Hear, hear," said Adam, beaming.

"Thank you," Stellie said smiling, even as her stomach clenched.

NINETEEN

All during class torrential rain rapped against the windows of Harris Hall. The glacier blue sky darkened to murky gray. The students in mathematical statistics yawned into their textbooks, gently tapped their pencils, and shuffled their feet as if reviewing the steps of a tap dance. A few strained to keep up with Professor Godwin's lecture on maximum likelihood. He was running overtime again, as he did most Fridays.

Estelle glanced at the clock above the door. She had plans to meet Adam at Bloomingdale's in an hour to shop for a bridesmaid's gift for Lily. It was all that was left for them to do after Ruth's deft and imperious handling of their upcoming wedding. Ruth had booked the hotel, arranged for the rehearsal dinner, guided them to a tasteful selection of invitations and floral arrangements, and even paid for their five-day, four-night honeymoon to Saint Thomas. "We're in serious debt to your mother," Estelle warned her fiancé. "How are we ever going to pay her back?"

Finally Professor Godwin cleared his throat, his signal of closure. He nodded to the class and muttered a quick, "See you Monday."

Estelle shoved her books into her tote, lifted it to her shoulder, and headed quickly for the door. But before she could escape into the savage weather, a hand touched her forearm. She looked up into the sallow face of her professor.

"Miss Ackerman," he said. "Your name came up over lunch with Professor Stevens yesterday."

"Really? Why?"

"He mentioned that he'd written a recommendation for you for medical school and that you'd been accepted. Congratulations are in order."

Professor Stevens, her gaunt chemistry professor with the deep-set eyes and the voice like a radio announcer's, was her favorite instructor at the college. She smiled at the thought that he'd singled her out for a conversation with a fellow faculty member.

"Yes, to Albert Einstein."

"You, young lady, are the only female student who has ever asked him to write a recommendation for medical school. Over the years, a number of our brightest young ladies have gone on to graduate school in the social sciences and some even in the health sciences."

"Guess I'm a novelty."

Professor Stevens's half smile melted into his face. "Did you know that statistics have repeatedly shown it doesn't pay to educate and train a woman for medicine, even a woman as intelligent as you, Miss Ackerman?"

Stellie frowned and glimpsed at her teacher, at his Cro-Magnon forehead and the yellowish undertones that made him look as if he'd been bathing too long under the classroom's fluorescent lights. "But what does that have to do with me?"

"You're a woman and I'm reporting statistics relating to your sex, Miss Ackerman. I'm a statistics professor, after all."

"I don't understand, Professor Stevens. Are you saying I shouldn't go into medicine?"

"It's not you, personally, with whom I have an issue; it's your gender in general. Female students take the place of men, and the ladies quit before they even begin to practice, as soon as they get married and have to keep house for their husbands."

Her face and neck grew warm. "That's not going to be me."

"Meaning you're not going to quit or not going to marry?" He glanced at the oval diamond on her left ring finger. "Of course a pretty girl like you was snatched up before her twenty-first birthday."

"Professor Stevens, with all due respect, I don't think my marital status has anything to do with my becoming a doctor."

"Perhaps you'll prove me wrong and defy the stereotype. Otherwise, some worthy young man will have lost his opportunity to become a physician, and the world will have one less qualified doctor to help heal the sick."

"I plan to devote as much time to medicine as do any of my male colleagues."

He yawned and glanced at his watch. "Who knows? Maybe you'll combine a career in maternal and child health with raising children of your own."

"Actually, I hope to work as a surgeon or in the ER."

"Ah!" He let loose a jangling laugh, revealing his cavernous throat and an abundance of gold fillings. "You like to go where the action is. You're so young. You'll learn like the rest of us how to compromise."

Estelle had never been happier to nuzzle up to Adam's minty talc scent, to take in his half smile and dreamy expression. But two hours in Bloomingdale's made her brain feel filled with hay, like the Scarecrow's.

"Let's get out of here," she whispered while they waited for the salesgirl to finish wrapping Lily's present: red leather gloves.

"I wish I could stop thinking about Professor Godwin's comments," she said once they'd exited the store.

The weather was still dreary but the rain had abated. Estelle dug her hands into her coat's deep pockets as Adam's arm circled around her waist, drawing her close.

"You can't let him get to you this way, honey."

"It's just horrible to be talked to that way. Even a man as sweet as you can't know what that feels like."

"Your math professor is like most men, conventional in his thinking and insensitive to anyone other than knuckleheaded men like him."

She smiled for the first time in hours. "And you? How come you're so enlightened?"

He shrugged. "Maybe because I've always felt a little bit different. I can imagine what it's like to be in the shoes of the underdog." He imparted his most sheepish look on her. "Although it's hard to think of you as an underdog. Professor Godwin doesn't have the advantage of knowing the fierce, determined woman I love."

"You may feel different from other people, but you're only different in the best ways, more sensitive, braver."

"Not braver, more cowardly if anything. I've considered taking the road less traveled, yet here I am fulfilling every Jewish mother's dream of becoming a doctor."

"Yes, but you're marrying me, no Jewish mother's dream for her son, even your liberal mother. I won't be making your life easier like most wives would. I plan on working just as hard as you."

Adam sighed. "Harder, much harder. I'll have to be the one to stay home and have the babies."

Estelle snuggled closer to her fiancé as they walked northeast toward the Merkins' home, where they were expected for dinner. But a chill of fear ripped through her at the mention of babies. It was time to tell him. She couldn't put it off even one more day.

"The point is that you accept me for who I am—which won't win you a lot of friends among your chauvinistic colleagues at Columbia. There is so much about me, in fact, that people would find reprehensible."

"How dramatic!" He beamed at her. "Drama isn't like you! Do tell, my little Ethel Rosenberg!"

She stopped suddenly in the middle of East Sixtieth Street. "I'm not fooling around, Adam. There's something I need to tell you." A misery so deep it felt unbearable clutched at her middle. She was always going to be a prisoner of her fatal error—like one of Shakespeare's tragic heroes that Miss Kingston of Literary Survey loved to discuss with a cluck of her tongue.

"What is it?" he asked, switching to a gentle tone, anchoring her with a hand on each shoulder. "You're not cheating on me or in love with someone else, are you?"

"Of course not." She bit down hard on her lower lip to punish herself for the pain she was about to cause both of them. "I'm so worried that I'll ruin everything."

"Look at me, Stellie. C'mon, look at me. As long as you love me—and you do, right? Okay, then. Nothing in the world that you say could ever change the way I feel about you. Got that? Do you get that, Stellie?"

"Yes," she said softly.

"Good! Excellent. Then we're indestructible. Now, what is it you need to tell me?"

TWENTY

A balmy day in early November 1963—a fluke, Estelle reflected, since the week before had foreshadowed an early winter with its bitter winds and even a snow flurry. But not now. Now, all the windows in her small Upper East Side apartment were cracked open to let in this trick of weather, this spring breeze. It was almost enough to lift her mood. Almost.

Perched on her marriage bed, Estelle folded laundry mechanically, dazed but not surprised by the news she'd received that morning. She'd sat across from Dr. Davies—a gynecologist affiliated with Mount Sinai Hospital, where Adam was in his second year of a pediatric internship—hands crossed in her lap, eyes focused on the patterns of sun checkered on the wood floor. No point undressing and donning the flimsy white gown this time—the blood results were all that mattered.

Sure enough, "Congratulations, Mrs. Merkin," the doctor said from behind his desk. He rose from his chair in order to reach over and pat her shoulder paternally. "You're approximately eight weeks."

How different her treatment was this time around, as a respected member of society, a wife (a resident's wife at that!), herself a medical student, having raced through college in three years. Still, the other Estelle—the one who the nurse with the heavy mottled thighs had disdained—lived on inside of Adam's spouse, squatting down deep.

"Thank you," Estelle had replied, forcing a smile. At least, she thought she was smiling, affecting the appropriate signs of happiness, when actually she'd taken every precaution to avert this disaster by

going on that new Enovid pill and, for extra protection, using her di-
aphragm. But not on her wedding night. She'd forgone the contra-
ception on that night.

She wondered about that lapse of judgment. What would have
prompted such careless stupidity? Had she thought that Adam's magical kingdom of glittering money, of social ease, of acceptance even
for Jews, would somehow protect her cervix, would line it with a
nonporous sheath, stopping all of the millions of jiggling sperm from
entrance? Was a remnant of a girlish fairy tale stuck inside her head,
deep below the rational adult sediment?

On the walk home from Dr. Davies's office, she'd watched the
scarlet and citron yellow leaves twirling off the New York sidewalk,
bowing and arching in their freedom dance. A day so warm and fine
that even this city looked clean, air crackling. But Estelle could not
allow herself to be swayed by such esoteric matters as beauty as she
trudged down Lexington Avenue. Like Houdini, imprisoned in a
sealed chest underwater, she felt all her energy engaged in escape.

Now, sorting the white clothes from the dark, she was still measuring her options. And there were options this time. She thought of
a conversation she'd overheard while waiting for her husband to get
off work, two floor nurses on Adam's unit discussing a friend's "problem." One young woman bobbed her head and said, "Yep. Peg is
going to Dr. Saunder this Monday morning. That so-called boyfriend
of hers wasn't ever planning to leave his wife. What choice does she
have?"

The other girl blanched, glanced left, then right, not wanting to
be overhead. "Dr. Saunder does that?" she asked.

Her friend smirked. "Sure, for the right fee, he does. Won't they
all do anything for a price? Why do you think I'm looking to get
hitched to a doctor?" The nurses laughed together in girlish voices.

Estelle left her cotton underwear in a pile and went to the window. She peered out at Ninety-sixth Street, at the same fire hydrant
that had been there yesterday and the day before, at the Chevrolet
parked too close, sure of being ticketed. Was it possible, she wondered—
older and savvier about her options this time around—to pull off an
illegal abortion without a glitch? There was the question of cash, and
of keeping it a secret from Adam. (His parents were paying for the

rent on their place, since his salary barely covered the rest of their expenses. Estelle's schooling at Einstein was almost breaking them.)

There was the more important issue of her deception. Having chosen a pediatric residency, Adam had confessed, "I finally made peace with the fact that I'm better suited for working with children than cutting up people."

They'd been eating lunch at the coffee shop on Third Avenue where they'd first met. It was a few weeks before their wedding. He had grinned that self-effacing grin of his, soft mouth curved up sadly, as if he didn't deserve a full smile. "I'm good with kids, and I actually like them more than most adults."

"There's less serious illness with kids," Estelle had said. "And maybe time for your poetry."

"It's more than that."

She looked up midbite, her oily tuna fish sandwich with crunchy pieces of celery sticking between her teeth. She nodded tentatively, her heart quickening.

"I know we haven't talked much about our future family. I felt it was a delicate matter after what happened to you." His eyes gleamed with compassion.

"You were really wonderful about that," she said, her voice catching in her throat. "Most men would have made a run for it when they found out I'd been with another man, much less . . . you know, about everything that happened."

"Hey, fair is fair. You know about my brief, uh, dalliance with Katie O'Brien, the Catholic nurse Mom was so crazy about!" he said sardonically.

"That's different!"

"Why? Because I'm a man?"

"Because there was no baby!"

He reached for her left hand, the one fiddling with the unused spoon, and lifted it in his. His hand was small boned for a man's. "Do you want to talk about it? I know it must have been so hard for you, giving him up."

When she pulled back, contracting deep into her center, he said, "Hey, I'm here for you. I don't care what your mother said. She's a great lady, but old world. I'm not going to judge you. He's your son."

"No! He's not."

He nodded. "All right. I know it's a touchy subject for you."

"Please, let's not talk about it anymore."

"Whatever you want, sweetie."

They ate in silence for a few minutes, Adam still holding on to her ring finger and pinkie.

"The thing is," he said, "I've always dreamed about having a lot of kids. For some reason, I figured I would end up with a whole brood. Mom and Dad just had the two of us, and you an only child."

He waited a beat. "What do you think?"

Fear scurried through her like a sewer rat, a dirty underground creature. With as much equanimity as she could muster, she said, "You know how much I want to practice medicine, after putting so much work into it."

"Of course. That's a given. How could you not? You're going to be superb at it, the real Dr. Merkin in the family, unlike yours truly, the charlatan."

"Don't say that about yourself, Adam. *Never* say that."

"I have to go ahead with this pregnancy," Estelle said aloud to the pile of her husband's ribbed undershirts. She'd folded them lovingly next to his socks. She couldn't risk losing Adam. "But this is the last time."

On the street, a dog was tied to a skinny tree while his master scooted into a liquor store. "Good boy," the young man said. "Stay." But the scrappy-looking beast barked anyway, catching Estelle's attention.

"Mutt," she murmured angrily, glancing out the window. "*Shande.*"

PART THREE

GEORGIE

TWENTY-ONE

It wasn't until after Georgie attempted to walk off the effects of her mother's visit that she realized Estelle had left behind a manila envelope on the kitchen counter. It was wrinkled and folded in half like a piece of discarded junk mail bound for the garbage.

Georgie lifted the envelope. It weighed next to nothing, yet its power over her was immediately indisputable. Insides churning, she opened the clip in the back. Other than one short letter, the envelope contained tangible proof of a life, eyes and ears and teeth and fingernails. "Here goes nothing," she whispered, as she flipped through the three-by-five pictures. They told a story, the evolution of a man from babyhood to middle age. How startling the second photo's similarity was to the four-year-old version of Georgie, with her wide eyes and heart-shaped face. Only the coloring and hair texture were different. He was dark to her light; and compared to the pixie cut she'd sported, Daniel's curls were luscious and a rich shade of brown. His recent photograph was daunting—the turn of the lips, his hooded eyes and bushy brows, the longish hair curling around his ears. It was a close-up shot, his seated body not shown.

Georgie walked to the mirror and held the image next to her face. They were no longer look-alikes. Her mouth was thinner and her eyes set farther apart, gray-blue to his espresso brown. When she smiled, her skin creased with age; his appeared supple, thanks to his Spanish father, no doubt.

She could not stop staring. Her emotions—disbelief, glee, and anger—were like puppets in a Punch and Judy show, cursing and clubbing each other.

She studied the last of the batch, a snapshot of a younger Daniel, on his feet, smiling, his arm around an older woman with round cheekbones, gray eyes, a square chin, and a fat black scarf snaked around her neck, her hair pinned loosely in a bun with tendrils falling down on both sides of her face. On the back of the picture was written: *Mom and me, winter 1990.* So, this was his adopted mother. She looked nice, like Georgie's father, both of whom were dead from cancer.

On another was written: *Paul and me, winter 1998.* What a pair those Kaplan boys grew up to be! How odd that two people from completely different gene pools—thrown together through the randomness of the adoption system—should turn out to be so attractive while so completely different in their appearances. There was something almost Scandinavian in Paul's look: the lighter skin, the large bones. His biological parents could be anyone: a Danish princess, a Finnish fisherman, or a Swedish student. In that moment Georgie understood what it must have felt like to be Daniel, raised without a sense of origin, rudderless and unable to ask for direction. "Poor man," she whispered.

She carried the photographs into the living room and plunked down on the couch, still clutching them in her hand. Particles in the air shifted, realigning themselves into new patterns above the lampshade.

The afternoon was spent shipwrecked with an expanse of silky blue sky for company and a capricious cat that preferred not to be stroked. Georgie's thoughts were jostled, her body aching from a muscular weariness as if she'd just run a long distance. Several times the phone whimpered in her ear like an insistent animal. Unless it was Jesse calling from camp, she refused to answer; she needed time to comb through and detangle her feelings. Finally, at a quarter till five, she responded to the phone's frantic peal.

"Hey," Ian exclaimed. "I'm just about to check on Pixie, the Portuguese water dog, my poor spaying victim. Looks like she's waking up. Then I figured I'd run home and take a quick shower to rid myself of the stench of doggy gonads before picking you up. Seven okay?"

"Yeah—oops."

"What's wrong? Did I slip your mind?" He laughed his solid good-citizen laugh.

"No, it's just . . ." She tapped her coffee table with three fingertips.

"Hey, you okay?"

"Yeah. I'm fine. Odd day."

"Oh? Do you still feel up to getting together?"

She hesitated, not wanting to put the kibosh on this gleaming new relationship with her *Peyton Place* life. "Can I ask you a favor? Can you come by here and we can order in?"

"Sure, no sweat. I hope you're not getting sick. I know how much you've been looking forward to going upstate to get Jess tomorrow."

"I'm all right." If only what she felt was the simple pain of a sore throat or a broken bone. "Just tired."

They ate rainbow chicken and pork with jingling bells and wonton soup in the living room, on the floor. Georgie's story required space. She needed to spread out, to stretch her legs and mind around it, as she told Ian about Daniel Kaplan.

"Wow, that's intense." Ian whistled afterward.

Georgie nodded, hanging her head like a supplicant, hair falling into the damp corners of her lips, her hands fiddling with the chopsticks. She skewered a crispy dumpling and dangled it above its pool of brown sauce before releasing it with a splash.

Ian was sloshing his spoon around his bowl of soup without lifting the broth to his mouth. "She hadn't met him, this Daniel guy, until after your dad died?"

"So she says."

He reached out and cupped her knee under his warm palm. "I'm really sorry about this, Georgie."

"Thanks. You want to know what upsets me the most?"

"What?"

"That my dad never talked to me about it, told me how he felt about it. We could have shared that so I wouldn't be alone with this incredible news now."

"Hey," he said, lifting up her chin so that their eyes met. "Your dad did what he thought was right, what he figured would cause you the least amount of anguish."

"My mother can be very persuasive, especially with him."

Ian shook his head and his generous head of hair flew around his ears. Georgie had kissed those ears; they lay closer to his head than Luke's and turned red at the tips when he was incensed. "From what you've told me about your father, he'd never do anything on purpose to hurt you. Whatever he decided, he believed it would be in your best interest."

"Once Daniel's letter arrived, he had to know I'd find out. I wish he'd told me about it at that point." She dropped the chopsticks into the paper carton. "He left all of this for my mother to deal with once he was gone. He did that a lot," she admitted, "left the dirty work to her."

Is my abortion the same kind of secret? Will Jesse find out someday and resent me for it?

"Georgie, honey, he was very sick."

"I know. But he had to realize how this would play out. Even when he was sick, he was thinking straight."

"The man was dying. He had other things on his mind," Ian said softly, without judgment. "Give him a break."

"I guess. I just feel so alone with it."

"You have me."

"I'm sorry."

"For what?"

"For dragging you into this mess. It's not your problem." Georgie stood, plate in hand, and signaled for him to come. "Let's eat at the table, like civilized people."

"Sure," he said, and scooped up his plate with one hand, his bowl with the other. "Listen," he said, sidling up to her in the dining room, "you don't need to worry about being so careful with me."

"I'm not being careful."

"Yeah, you are. You're afraid if you show your feelings I'll get spooked or something." He lowered the cutlery onto the table as she headed back for the containers of food. "I don't know if that was how things were with Lucas, if he didn't react well when you got upset. You've said he didn't go in for emotional displays. Well, I'm not him."

He looked intently in her direction. "I *like* emotions. I want to know all of these details about you, your life and all its complications. I don't see how people can get close to each other if they don't share that stuff."

Gazing down into the oily pork swimming with chestnuts and pea pods in their little pond, Georgie said, "We need to pace things. We can't just spill all our embarrassing family garbage on each other and expect love to grow."

His arm was around her shoulder even as her focus was on a bell mushroom. "Too late," he murmured into her ear.

He stayed the night. Of course he did. Georgie set the alarm for six thirty a.m., since the plan was to take the seven-forty-five train into the city to meet Luke outside of Penn Station at eight thirty for the ride upstate. The sound of Ian asleep punctuated the air with polite, muted snores as friendly as a toy train chugging on its track, occasionally bursting forth with one sonorous boom before subsiding back into puffs of vapor. Lying on her side, with only his sharp toenails touching the sole of her foot, Georgie stared into the purple shadows, the reassuring pool of light by the door; out of habit from when Jesse was home she'd left the bathroom light on. Every time she closed her eyes the photograph of that man, dark skin, hooded eyes, lush hair, invaded her rest. She blinked rapidly as if to wash out a toxin. Thoughts of her mother, legs in the stirrups, moaning and pushing out a miniature version of Daniel, taunted her. As she finally entered the twilight pavilion of near-sleep, the image of her mother was replaced with one of her own body laid out in the abortionist's morgue, gray as granite, a fully formed dead fetus in her arms.

At a quarter past seven the phone rang. Fresh from the shower, wrapped in only a towel, Georgie ran to the kitchen to grab the receiver before her ex hung up. She was certain it was Lucas.

Parallel lines of light shone in through the dining room shades, and the floor felt wet beneath her feet. She pressed down on the talk button without checking caller ID. "Hi," she said, her voice a gust of wind—all excited to see her son, only hours away!

"Georgia," Estelle exclaimed, "it's me."

"Hi, Ma. I have to hurry and get out of here. I'm going to get Jesse this morning."

"I *know* that, Georgia. That's why I'm calling this early. I won't keep you. I tried to reach you last night, but either you weren't home or weren't picking up."

Had the phone even rung? Had they been making love or watching reruns of *Seinfeld* or washing out the dinner dishes and that never-resting miracle of technology had trilled at its furious core, demanding that the beast be fed?

"I didn't hear it."

"I wanted to let you know that I won't be around this weekend, in case Jesse wants to reach me. I'll be in Newton, not Boston. That's where Daniel lives. He works as a senior manager of communications for AstraZeneca, a pharmaceutical firm in the next town," she said augustly. "This is the first time I'll be staying at his house, getting to know his wife—she was so gracious and really charming when I met her at lunch—and his children. Why don't you take down the address and phone number?"

"I have your cell phone," Georgie said, standing at attention, water dripping onto the wood floor.

"Do it anyway."

Estelle was reciting a number while Georgie watched another pesky squirrel jump atop her empty window box. Ian, decked out in only his Scooby-Doo boxer shorts—a present from his daughter—poked his head into the room, hair tousled, having just woken up. He shrugged and pointed to the telephone as if to ask, *What's up?* He mouthed Lucas's name.

My mother, she mouthed back.

"Tell her you have to go have sex with this handsome hunk," he whispered.

Georgie shooed him into the kitchen, pointing to the coffeepot.

"Did you get that?" Estelle was asking. "Listen, this isn't the time. But when you get back and have a minute, there's something I'd like to discuss."

"What is it?"

"It's not for now. B-u-t . . ." She stretched the word out as if it were made of spandex. "I would like to talk about setting up a meeting between you and Daniel in the near future."

"I'm not ready for that yet. When I am, I can certainly arrange it on my own."

"Of course you can. I'm only trying to be helpful. I've told him all about you, and he's very excited to meet you," she said cheerfully. "He's a lovely man. It's impossible not to like him, most likely because I didn't raise him."

Taken aback by her mother's last comment, Georgie felt her body slacken out of its defensive posture and into its natural alignment. "What?"

"Oh, let's be honest. I know what kind of mother I was or wasn't to you. I was busy trying to prove I could be a good doctor, as good as or better than any man; I left the parenting mostly to Adam. The truth is, I never really wanted to be a mother. I didn't see how I could manage both things, the obstacles what they were for women in my profession forty years ago. That's nothing against you, Georgie, nothing at all."

"It doesn't feel like nothing."

"I'm explaining what it was like for me a lifetime ago, before you were even born. I wanted to be a surgeon, you know."

"No, I didn't know that."

"It was the one major barrier in my life that I couldn't break through." She snorted indignantly. "I wasn't admitted to any surgery residencies despite my four-point-oh average. Gynecology was one of the few fields open to women at the time."

Which would explain the incongruity between her interests and her chosen specialty, Georgie thought. All these years she'd tried to ascribe deep psychological motives to a decision based purely on gender discrimination. "You never told me that."

"I've never liked to discuss my failures."

"How was it your failure if the schools shut you out?"

"Anyway, I just never got the knack for combining motherhood with career the way you have. No matter what, you always put Jesse first. I guess you learned that from your father."

"Thank you." Georgie widened her eyes in Ian's direction and he grinned back, obviously perplexed but amused.

"We have a chance to make up for some of those terrible mistakes. That's why I want you to meet Daniel. He's your *brother*, Georgie."

Again, that word startled her. What did it mean to have a

brother? She couldn't fathom it. "Look, I really appreciate you telling me all this. I just can't meet him right now."

"*Really?* You've decided just like that? A snap decision."

"I need to take some time to deal with the shock of everything."

There was a long, critical silence on Estelle's end. "Can I ask you something, Georgia? I know the fact of Daniel is a shock, but it's not such a terrible one, is it? We've always had such a small family, and he's a welcome addition to it. This doesn't have to be a crisis. It can be a happy event. You know Carole, at my office, her friend was adopted and discovered years later that she'd had a twin who'd been given up to another family in Virginia. She was thrilled to find out about her brother. All her life she knew that some part of her was missing, like a puzzle piece, that finally fit inside of her. Let me tell you: It's incredible finding that piece. Carole is so excited for me. . . ."

Georgie's face felt impossibly tight, like when she applied her Dead Sea mask and waited too long to wash it off so that it cracked and flaked into her pores. "Mom, please, give me a break here to process the *fact* of Daniel's existence before I think about meeting him."

"You know, Georgie, that's really an astonishing thing to say after the year I've had."

"I need to cope with this in my own time. Dad just died a few months ago."

"I *know* when my husband died."

"Of course you do."

In a tight voice, Estelle said, "Like it or not, Daniel is your half brother. It would mean the world to him to meet you."

As a child, Georgie had competed with her parents' careers on top of Stellie's causes—female-based medical research, adequate prenatal health care for the uninsured, early detection of reproductive cancers—and her demanding mutability, snapping in cold anger one minute, congenially trying to dominate Georgie's decisions the next. But sibling rivalry was a new game whose rules Georgie had yet to study.

Pulling the damp cold towel closer to her body, Georgie caught Ian looking at her tenderly.

"I didn't know I had a brother until this summer," she said into the phone. "I haven't even wrapped my mind around that fact yet. Now you want me to honor your desires above my own."

"When have you ever done *that*, Georgia?"

"C'mon, Ma. We were having a decent conversation here. There's no need to be nasty."

"Well, I'm sorry. I'm hurt. I thought you might *at least* appreciate how important it's been for me, having his emotional support during this crucial, horrible time. Why can't you give me that?"

"I'm glad you have Daniel's support. But I need you to respect my time frame on this. Listen, I have to go get Jess."

"Right."

As if in slow motion, Georgie pushed down on the talk button and disconnected her mother. Her hand was shaking.

"It would be so nice if, for once, she could see what I need," she said, gazing down at the patch of wet floor near her feet. She turned to Ian.

He embraced her, the warmth of his chest pressed against her, the towel sliding to the floor. "Tell me what you need, sweetie." He kissed her ear. "I'll try to make this easier on you."

"Hey, good-looking," Lucas greeted her as Georgie slid onto the gray leather seat of his BMW M3 coupe. He was squinting from the sun, his fair hair downy across his forehead like a child's, but the lines engraved around his eyes and mouth, his pale complexion finally showing its age. He was dressed in rumpled tan chinos and a beige-and-white-striped polo shirt, moccasins, and no socks. Only the two patches of eczema at his hairline held a clue that there were any stresses in this man's life.

He smiled at Georgie. "How's it going? Ready? Did you empty your bladder at Penn Station?"

It was an old joke between him and Jesse. Mom had to pee every five minutes, making the drive twice as long. How many car trips had the three of them made together? Quite a few, actually, even after the divorce, a perfectly well-adjusted family in which Mommy and Daddy just didn't happen to be married anymore.

For Jesse's seventh birthday they'd flown to Orlando, Florida. They'd booked a room for Lucas and Jess to share at the Walt Disney

World Swan and Dolphin resort and a separate one for Georgie. Twice Luke slipped into her bed after midnight and they'd had sex under a cheerful headboard with painted pineapples on it. He'd crept out before dawn so as not to confuse their son. Then there was the weekend they'd spent in Philadelphia—exploring the Franklin Institute's Weather Center and eating cheese steaks—when Jess was eight. Saturday after eleven p.m., she'd been the one to beckon her ex into her room for a joyful romp in the nude.

Who were they kidding?

Afterward, anxiety and a hollow sense of shame would duke it out inside her gut. They'd always been better suited for an affair than for marriage, but with their boy lacing them together, they'd been unable or unwilling to give each other up. "Ma? Does this mean you and Dad are going to get back together?" Jesse would ask each time they traveled together on vacation.

Big mistake. That she'd ended a baby's life was proof of what a colossal screwup it was.

Georgie envisioned a naked Lucas walking away from her, his tight calves and buttocks, the high arch of his feet, his long, freckled torso. That body . . . she wouldn't see it again. *Good-bye, old friend.*

Filled with a nostalgic benevolence, she said, "I peed right before takeoff, pilot."

"Good." He nodded, patting her hand absentmindedly. After accelerating too quickly out of his parking spot and into the roar of traffic on Seventh Avenue, he asked, "So what's up?"

She sighed quietly. *So much, Lukie.*

"Oh, you know, Stellie's being difficult."

"Gee, that's news," he said with his own brand of sarcasm. "Sarcasm lite," she called it.

"And . . . ?"

"And?" He peered in her direction, crinkly-eyed, a grin on his face.

She shifted away from him, her cotton sundress gliding easily on his slick seat, cool even on this sweltering July day. "I've been seeing someone."

"Someone?" he asked in a tight voice.

"Yes. A male person." She stared out her side window through amber-tinted sunglasses that suffused the day in a golden glow. A taxi nearly cut them off on the right an instant before Lucas swerved out of his way. Her stomach lurched. "Jeez, Luke, watch it."

Once they'd swung onto Eighth en route to the West Side Highway, she inhaled deeply. "What's it to you? You're living with Zoë. Do you expect me to remain loyal to you even as you screw a teenager every night?"

The anger had shot out of her mouth like a naughty tongue. She was tempted to confess to Lucas what had happened, what she'd done to remedy the situation. She didn't want to be a keeper of secrets like her mother. But Lucas was no longer her husband. Who would it serve to open up that door of pain?

"It's not every night." He said as he reached over toward the glove compartment, flipped it open without looking, and took out his Fendi sunglasses.

"Semantics." She smiled to reassure him of her basic good humor.

"Is it serious?" he asked briskly.

He gave her the once-over through his azure blue lenses. When was the last time he had really looked at *her*, Georgie, an entity apart from him, apart from her role as Jesse's mother, apart from being the possessor of pheromones to which his penis responded?

"Getting there, I think. We'll see."

"Has Jesse met him?"

"Yeah," she said. "He's the vet who took care of Odysseus."

"The guy put the moves on you while poor Odie lay dying?"

"It was the other way around, but not until he was already gone. Anyway, what's with the questions? In all of our relationship I've never known you to be so inquisitive."

He bit down on his lip in a gesture of frustration and shrugged. "I got used to things the way they were."

"You mean you getting to have a sexy teenager for a girlfriend and me sitting home on Saturday night with your son playing Parcheesi?"

"Jesse doesn't play Parcheesi. Does he?"

"You missed the point."

"Right, right," Luke said, sulking. "Always have, I guess. You can't blame a chimpanzee for his inferior stature in the primate hier-archy."

"Wow, I can't believe you remembered that. I said that a long time ago, Lukie, a really long time. Hey." It dawned on Georgie slowly, despite her claim to superior emotional acuity. "You're not really, actually jealous, are you?"

"I don't know if jealous is the right word. Maybe proprietary."

"Nice SAT word!"

Luke bounced up and down in his seat and then grunted like a monkey. "Okay, party over. Enough dumping-on-dumb-ass-Carter day." He drew in his breath and in that inhalation, inflated his body to alpha male status: chest out, head high, back straight as a marine's. "As long as Jess is cool with you going out with this guy, I guess it's okay."

Slowly a smile formed. "Gee, thanks for the stamp of approval. Because you know how happy he is with you seeing Zoë the exhibi-tionist." She paused, weary of this battle: He was stubborn and self-ish; she was flip and arrogant. "Sorry. Yeah, dude. He seems cool with it."

Lucas nodded. Gazing straight ahead, he reached for her hand and gave it a quick squeeze. They drove in silence until Fifty-seventh Street, then returned to a safe discussion involving frogs and fish, tel-escopes and computer games, and of what was left between them—that which would link them eternally—their one beloved child.

TWENTY-TWO

Georgie had rented a place in Wellfleet for ten days in August—a part of Cape Cod recommended by her editor, Sabine—without any visuals. The plan was to venture to the Cape with just her boy for the first week of the vacation; for the last three days and two nights, Ian would join them, an experiment in modern living. She knew her palms would sweat profusely against the steering wheel as she navigated more highway driving than she'd previously attempted in her entire city-dwelling life. Since her divorce, summer trips had involved merely short jaunts to the Jersey shore; but this year Jesse deserved a wondrous place.

After seven long hours of light FM, of an endless McNugget-filled Connecticut, of a bladder-engorging, rest stop–free Rhode Island, of Jess chanting, "Is it normal to stay in the slow lane the whole time?" they arrived. As soon as she saw the house, her heart flopped over like a hooked fish, belly up. It was set off the road, surrounded by garbage bins, a stout, sad-looking thing covered in peeling gray paint. The inside was worse, decorated 1970s: a couch the color of Orange Crush soda, a rust-and-yellow shag carpet with God knew what parasites inhabiting its filthy strands, tabletops lined with flaking copies of ancient *Life* magazines, and a damp, moldy basement with a television but no cable service, rendering it useless.

"Nice digs, Ma!" Jess exclaimed sarcastically as he perused the joint. "It's like camping, only without the cool tents and sleeping bags." She nodded. Camping would have been preferable. "Face it, Dad's the one who was good at arranging our vacations, not you."

All was dark and dingy, with a view of the woods and a clothesline out back. By seven thirty, the evening started to close in around them, the dark woods like a tribe that congregated at night in a fairy tale. She called both Nina and Ian to proclaim her failure as a mother. "Just hold your breath. I'll be there soon," her beau promised. "Okay." She sighed, bubbles of excitement caught in her throat as if she were a child eagerly awaiting the arrival of the magician at the party.

By morning reality had set in, along with a lower backache. Jesse had tossed and turned on the bottom of a bunk bed lacking springs, as Georgie lay awake on a narrow sliver of a futon, hoisted on a platform, hard as the floor. She packed up the little they'd unpacked, and in defeat coaxed her weary son into the car. They were on the road scouting for vacancy signs by nine o'clock. They'd made it all the way back to Falmouth Heights—the first town on the Cape—before they found an available place that was acceptable to both of them. The Seaside Inn overlooked the bluff with a view of the horizon—ocean and sky in matching blue outfits—and Martha's Vineyard winking at night, tempting travelers to its beguiling shores only a ferry ride away.

"Ma?"

The sun beat down on Georgie's knees and calves, her upper body covered by an umbrella, her feet buried in the sand. Sinking back into her portable chair, she gazed up at Jesse, who'd just returned from his "quick dip." A quintessential city boy, he swam only in chlorinated water, without the threat that algae or minnows or other fishy creatures would slither past his ankles, "grossing him out."

"Ma?" he repeated, plopping down beside her so that sand stuck to his wet thighs and bathing suit.

"What, sweet pea? What is it? You don't like this place either? You said before that it was cheerful." They'd settled in, had a nice lunch at the inn's adjoining restaurant, and finally hit the beach. "That I proved we didn't need Dad to find a decent hotel."

He shook his head, the tips of his hair throwing off droplets, and squinted into the bright day. "No, it's great. It isn't that."

"Then what?" She reached out and cupped his hand.

He shrugged. "It's just, you know, this Ian guy."

"Oh."

Georgie sucked in her bottom lip, noting a young couple hover-

ing around a toddler in a sundress and sagging diaper who was wad-
dling toward the water on her stout legs. The mother was arched over
so that her bare pregnant belly protruded from her bikini, while the
father smiled at his wife. It pained her, the sight of this woman's
proud display, of the fetus's safe, watery haven, tucked inside its
mother and surrounded by its intact family.

"Are you upset that I'm in a relationship? Or that he's coming on
our vacation?"

"What's the difference?" Jesse asked earnestly.

"Well . . ." Georgie glanced at him—to focus on *her* family—
using her hand as a visor. Jesse's skin had already warmed to the color
of a toasted biscuit; his cheeks were kissed pink. "Ian's being here
makes it more real. At home you haven't really seen him that much
since Odie died."

"Yeah." He kicked sand gently at her legs. "I guess. I already have
to cope with that stupid teenybopper of Dad's. Yuck. It's amazing
that I don't have psychological problems, don't you think?"

She smiled. "I know you're used to having me all to yourself. It's
got to be hard for you, the idea of sharing me." *Good thing you don't
have to share me with a baby brother or sister.* "But you liked Ian the few
times you met him, didn't you?"

Jesse's smirk conveyed the message: *That* was beside the point.

"Honey, do you want me to tell him not to come?" She held her
breath. *He's the boss. What Jesse says goes.*

He lifted his face to the sun, shut his eyes, and jutted out his chin
in defiance. "Nah. You deserve a life, Ma. Anyway, being with him
makes you less cranky."

She laughed. "Gee, thanks, kid."

"You're welcome. It's been tough on you lately. First Grandpa
and now with Grandma."

Head bent forward, Georgie peered over her sunglasses. "What
do you mean, Jess?"

Another shrug; too weary to play this game anymore, he said,
"Ma, I don't know exactly. I'm *youthful*. I'm not supposed to understand all this adult stuff. I just know that things are weird with her
since Grandpa died."

Eagle eyes, but too astute for his own good. Georgie wanted to instruct him to stop watching her, to turn off the Weather Channel, to live only in a kid's world filled with friends, *Star Wars*, *Harry Potter*, Nintendo, and, yes, even baseball.

"Jess, things *have* been tense, but they'll be all right."

"Yeah, yeah. Grown-ups always say that when they don't want to deal with you."

"Honey, that's not true. I *am* dealing with you. We're talking. You can always talk to me about anything: about Grandma, your dad, how you feel about Zoë or my friend Ian, about being the kid of divorced parents and how much it sucks or messes you up. I love you so much, Jess. The most important thing in the world to me is to for you to be happy. You know that, right?"

"Yeah. Ma?"

"Jess?"

"Can I get an ice cream?" He pointed behind them to the Good Humor truck perched on the threshold of the beach.

"Sure," she said, thankful for the tan college student and his preserved frozen treats, for the white-and-beige sand, the scorching luminous sun, the normalcy the day might afford her.

That evening, while Jesse watched cartoons, Georgie flipped through the pages she'd printed off the Internet in the hope that a dynamic theme for an article would crystallize before her eyes like an image emerging from a Rorschach test. Lately, an unprecedented desire to choose more substantial subjects than "Buff Bottoms" had propelled her into a frenzy of ineffectiveness. Expertly versed in pop culture's favorite bugaboo—the link between stress and all the world's ills—she was counting on this vacation arresting her cortisol output, unleashing her endorphins, and leading to creative breakthroughs!

Bored, she checked her voice mail for the second time since lunch. "It's me," her mother announced. "Lily mentioned that Nina said you were working on an article dealing with something, oh, I don't know . . ."—she scrambled for a word, clucking and sighing, as if playing verbal Scrabble with her tongue—"*timely* on the subject of single mothers. Don't lambaste your cousin for telling Lily. I'm only bringing this up because there's an excellent article in my new copy of *JAMA* on poor single mothers and depression. It touches on issues that middle-class women experience, which is probably more relevant for your magazine's readers."

She added, "No offense to you, by the way. I wasn't diagnosing *you* as one of these depressed mothers. Let me know if you're interested in my sending it."

Eyes closed, Georgie massaged the back of her neck, waiting for anger to seep through her pores. When it didn't, she dialed her cell phone.

"Ma? It's me. I got your message. Sure. Send me the article. Thanks."

One silent beat. "*Hello* to you, too, Georgie. *I'm* as well as can be expected. Yes, I'll have Carole make a copy of the article and send it to you so it will be in the mail when you get home. How's Cape Cod?"

"Um, it's nice, beautiful. Jesse seems happy." She held words in her mouth, like olives before spitting out the pits. "Uh, how are *you* doing? I mean, you said you were well . . . ? You busy catching up on work?"

"I'm watching CNN, some moronic evangelical Republican with a terrible case of rosacea and no neck pontificating on the evils of partial-birth abortion."

The room sloped slightly, the oxygen thinning. Georgie felt askew, dizzy with a bubble of nausea rising in her throat. Had Nina divulged her secret?

"These politicians may be idiots, but they're dangerous idiots, and I just hope the country can see through their ploys by the election. The reptiles are clever enough to hide behind this nonissue, pretend it's of pressing concern, which is absurd, since only one-point-four percent of abortions are even performed after the twelfth week of pregnancy, never mind in the seventh or eighth month. The only third-trimester terminations *ever* done at the hospital were because the fetus was so damaged as to stand no chance of survival upon birth. Can you imagine the doctor telling you weeks before you're due to give birth that your baby has no brain beyond a stem?"

"No," Georgie said softly.

This was a familiar rant—not unjustified in Georgie's mind—just producing that unfortunate numbing effect of tedious overexposure to a devastating event. What mattered was that her mother did not know. She swallowed deliberately, as if to pop her ears as the air pressure changed from high to normal altitude.

"Monsters! They vilify women who are already tortured by grief. Now *that's* something you should write about, Georgia. The religious zealots are dangerous; they'll bring us back to the Dark Ages if the country is foolish enough to believe these extremists are compassionate conservatives instead of pawns of the religious right! So many young women don't realize how lucky they are, how hard we had to work to ensure they had the legal right to their own bodies, and what's at stake now."

"I recognize what's at stake, Ma."

"I know you do." She released a self-congratulatory laugh. "You couldn't have grown up in *my* home and not been acutely aware of how imperative *Roe versus Wade* was and *is,* especially now that it may be in serious jeopardy. That's why I think you should write something on this topic. We need all the voices we can get shouting that we'll never go back to the way it was before 1973."

Georgie shut her eyes. She was crossing the bridge to level ground, anticipating the firm, packed earth beneath her feet. Nevertheless, she didn't dare engage in a dispassionate discussion with her mother on this subject, not with the gap of ambivalence widening inside her so that it was nearly impassable. One thing was clear; *she* would never again avail herself of this particular legal right. Still, it was comforting, her mother's position, the old feminist warrior inadvertently defending Georgie's decision.

"I'll think about it," she lied.

Five restful days later, Ian called from his cell phone as he approached Providence. "I should be there by two fifteen or so," he announced happily. "I'll probably stop for a piece of pizza or something, whatever's fastest."

"Great," Georgie said, glancing over at her son, who was playing his Game Boy on his bed after a morning of miniature golf and a quick drive-through meal at McDonald's. Her stomach rumbled, maybe from the snack-size fruit-and-yogurt parfait, maybe from nerves. *It's okay,* she reassured herself. *You've thought this through.*

Researched was more like it. Still crammed in her suitcase was an old *Redbook* magazine with a service piece on dating after divorce, several printouts of iVillage articles, and *The Single Mom's Official Guide to Having a Love Life.* Georgie had been following the rules, more or less, until now. But a sleepover vacation with your boyfriend was not endorsed in any handbook.

Ninety minutes later, Ian's car pulled into the parking area visible from the window. "Hey there!" Ian exclaimed once Georgie opened the door. He let in the celestial sky, the extravagantly fluffy clouds, the streaming sunlight, and the stately hollyhocks alongside the inn, as tall as Jess.

"Hi," Georgie said, smiling in response to Ian's easy grin. She noted that there was something roguish in his looks, his bare legs and toes peeking out of his sandals, his wind-tossed hair a little too long in the front, biceps exposed in his short-sleeved shirt. Handsome. Sexy. For a second a vertiginous sensation whooshed behind her eyes, uprooting her from this man. Who was he again? Then the moment passed. "Come in, come in."

"Hey, buddy!" he called out to Jesse.

Georgie winced, remembering that he'd used the same endearment when referring to the dying Odysseus.

Jess scampered from his prone position on his bed. "Hi," he said, shyly, upright but eyes downcast, the doggy nickname not registering.

A sputtering conversation ensued between her boy and her man while Georgie spaced out with worry. They remarked on the beauty of the day—like two old biddies reaching for a bit of pleasure—but then their talk took a more technical turn.

"Cloud formations are sort of interesting, but the stuff we do in school is really basic," Jesse said.

"Yeah? What do you mean?" Ian had moved closer to Jesse's dresser and was leaning into it, palming Jesse's copy of *The Hobbit.*

"Miss Dempsey has to look up everything in the textbook, like the difference between cirrus and stratus, before she can even teach it." Jess rolled his eyes. "She doesn't even know the simplest things, so forget actually learning anything, like how a hurricane works or how to track one." He nodded slowly, a wise elder. "This was her first year, and she's very naive."

Ian shot Georgie a parental smile: *Smart kid.* "It could be that," he offered. "Or maybe science isn't her area of expertise."

More eye rolling and then flouncing back on the bed. "*Nothing* is her area of expertise."

"Okay. Enough, Jess," Georgie said.

"You *know* I'm right."

"Miss Dempsey wasn't the best teacher you've ever had, but you shouldn't be rude."

"Sure, Mom," he said. "She was so boring that Gus and I would think the day was over and we'd look at the clock and it'd be nine fifteen."

"That's too bad," Ian said. "Especially about science. It's so important, and you're obviously good at it."

"Yeah, I'm okay. My dad got me this cool software on weather—it's not even for kids—since I didn't learn one thing all last year."

"That sounds great," Ian said, not missing a beat. "I know that what I do has nothing to do with weather systems, but if you're ever up for a tour of a veterinary clinic, you're welcome to spend a morning with me. It's scientific in another way."

Oh, God, Georgie thought. *Don't try so hard. Kids smell desperation across continents.*

But Jesse was considering the offer, nose wrinkled. "Maybe. Did my mom tell you I really like animals? We have a cat, an Abyssinian. You know that, though. I forgot."

Ian nodded. "Abby. We've met. She's very social."

"Abyssinians are people cats. The dogs of cats," Jesse proclaimed. "My friend Gus is watching her while we're away. She loves Gus."

"Yes, she's very lovable. And then there was Odysseus, poor guy."

"Odie wasn't my dog; he was my grandpa's. It was like Odie didn't want to live without Grandpa, so he died, too."

"Oh, sweetie," Georgie said, warm tears rimming her eyes.

"But you liked having a dog, even for that short while?"

Here it came: the big surprise they'd planned, *manipulated,* so Ian could win Jesse over, but also to take some of the sting out of the last six months—hell, the last three years since she and Lucas had split up.

"Sure. I love dogs."

"Because there's this lady back home whose yellow Lab is going to give birth soon. The puppies will be ready for adoption by Halloween. I was just wondering if you might be interested?"

Jesse's eyes grew to twice their size. "Ma?" He looked at Georgie. "Yes, sweetie?"

"Is this for real? Did he, uh, Ian, tell you about this?"

"Yep, he did. We discussed it and I thought it would be a good idea."

"Wow! Cool! Really? No. *Really?* I can't wait to tell Gus!"

Night flooded through the curtains, the Atlantic creating a warm breeze. Georgie lay very still in the bed, fingers and thigh touching Ian, actively listening. The twin lamps emitted a pale lullaby of light. "He's going to sleep," Ian whispered.

"Shh. He's not asleep yet."

Georgie's thoughts were a loop of anxiety circling around her brain: *I'm more uncomfortable than when I had sex with Lucas. We've been reinforcing our son's fantasy that we'd reunite. Even Zoë's presence in his father's house hasn't rid Jess of that notion. Who could actually believe that Luke would marry Zoë, though? I mean, whom does he think he's fooling? She's a symptom of a phase he's destined to outgrow, like blue hair or a nose ring. No one marries a symptom, do they? Oh, shut up, for Christ's sake!*

"This is weird," Ian said.

"Yeah. It feels slightly sinful."

"We're not even doing anything."

"Yes, but we're thinking about it. Or at least I am."

She could sense his smile in the shadows. "Me, too. I'm itchy for you."

"It's just that I feel as if he's watching."

"Georgie, he's in the other room. There's a door between us."

"Yeah, I know. But he could hear us. Maybe he's waiting for something to happen in here."

"We'll be very quiet."

"Let's just wait a little while longer. Okay?" She inched over into the heat and musk of his body. She held her breath.

"I think I may have won him over a little today, don't you think?"

"Absolutely!"

"Aren't puppies great? They never fail to do the trick."

"Yeah," she said, flopping over on her back, observing the stucco ceiling above. "Scientists should find a way to bottle their smell as an antidepressant."

"That and babies' heads."

Involuntary tears slid out of Georgie's eyes like butterflies shedding their chrysalises.

"Hey, what's wrong?" Ian asked, startled. He snuggled closer to her, his chest touching her naked breasts, the few lone hairs soft as cashmere.

She shook her head. "I remember that scent so clearly. Jesse had this great mop of yellow hair."

Wiping her cheek with two fingers, he said, "Ava was bald, just a tiny circle of fuzz in the center. We called it her plug. We used to joke that it protected her brain, that little bit of hair."

Another pang. Stacy and Ian, Ian and Stacy. She remembered studying white dwarfs in astronomy class; even though their temperatures were so high, they were dying stars. Was this deteriorating furnace what Ian's love for Stacy amounted to?

"I don't think Luke would even know what we're talking about," she said, rubbing her face dry with her palm.

"Are you sure?" he asked. "He wasn't a doting father?"

"He was in his way. But he's not sentimental and not the most observant fellow you'd ever meet. He preferred the mobile Jesse, the stage after crawling, you know, once the real action started."

"A typical dad."

"I guess."

There was a pause in the conversation, a dip in energy, the mutual holding of their breaths.

"So?" Ian ventured.

"So?" she volleyed back.

Her body grew taut, responding to the mating call, the incense of his skin, the air between them dense with longing, even as she felt her eyes flickering caution like yellow streetlights. She couldn't wait any longer.

The bleating of an animal woke her. Georgie's mind, dense with dreams, could not comprehend how a goat had wandered into the room. She'd been deep into slumber, close to its oceanic floor. Now she struggled awake. What was that noise?

Beside her Ian snored quietly, corpselike on his back, nose in the air. He wasn't the goat.

The digital clock announced one thirty in neon green numbers. Georgie switched on the lamp next to the bed and sat up, blinking. Another insistent bleat. She noticed Ian's cell phone atop his detective novel on his night table and wondered if he was being summoned to some dire vet emergency.

"Hey," she said, shaking his shoulder gently. He moaned but didn't awaken. The machine's urgent cry subsided. Yet, she figured, if it were a true crisis, Ian should be informed. What if there was a message relaying some feline disaster, some canine calamity? Or what if something genuinely awful had happened to Ava, his daughter, in the bowels of the dark?

"Ian! Get up!" She gave him a good push.

"What?" he exclaimed, eyes springing open with the alertness of any seasoned parent.

"Your phone," Georgie said, returning to sotto voce. "Someone has been calling you. It must be pretty important, because it's almost two in the morning."

"Uh?"

"Your *phone*. I thought it might be the clinic."

"They'd never call me here." Scampering up into a seated position, he said, "The service is instructed to give out the number of the all-night animal hospital. Remember, with Odysseus?"

"Maybe it was the wrong number. You should check, because it rang twice, actually."

His eyes flickered. "Really?" He leaned over, so that his naked back faced her, and punched in his secret code.

It was hard to gauge his reaction merely by watching his steady breathing, the expansion of his rib cage. But as he expressed nothing, no expletives, no gasps, Georgie could only wait, patiently, with a sense of foreboding. It must have been quite a message, a long, rambling, incoherent communication. Was there a death in the family, some elderly person trying to articulate grief or condolences in a broken voice? Was it merely the computerized promise of lucky winnings or lower mortgages recorded with effervescent verve? She could only guess that it didn't concern Ava—some horrible accident, a sudden case of appendicitis—as he wasn't doubled over in anguish or jumping into his shorts and heading for the door. No, he was considering something. This his back told her.

He fiddled with the phone, perhaps dialing. Finally he replaced the cell on the table, still without turning around.

"What? What is it?"

He coughed. No answer. Then, swinging his head down, he said, "It was Stacy."

She grabbed his hand. Anxiety, that repeat customer, had invaded her body, ratcheting up nerves and tightening vessels. "Is it Ava? Is she okay?"

"She's fine," he murmured.

"Thank God. You had me worried there for a minute."

"Sorry."

"Hey." Georgie placed a hand on his shoulder; it felt hot. "What's up?"

"Forget it. Let's just forget this. Sorry you were woken up. It was a ridiculous phone call."

"Wait a minute," she said. "That's not fair, shutting me out. It's the middle of the night and your phone rings during our lovely vacation. You can't leave me guessing for the next six hours."

"It's nothing," he said more softly, and patted her thigh as he would a golden retriever's: *Good girl; down, girl.* "Umm. It's stupid. Can't we talk before breakfast? Get some shut-eye? Come here."

"Ian! You can't seduce me into complacency." Nevertheless, she smiled flirtatiously because maybe he could.

"I wasn't," he said earnestly. "I was cuddling."

"Why did she call you here? Now?"

He sighed and coughed again, a nervous tickle in the back of the throat. "She's upset. That's all."

"That's all! It's two . . ." She twisted her head around to read the clock. "One forty-seven. What's she so upset about that she couldn't wait until a decent hour?"

"She had a fight with Levin," he said contritely.

"What? She had a fight with her boyfriend? That's why she called you here at this hour?" Georgie was certain she could hear the whorl of her angry blood, its dangerous momentum. Why did this hideous woman feel entitled to Ian's undivided attention at any time, day or night?

"It was a bad one. Look, don't get all worked up. It isn't worth it. You don't see me calling her back, do you?"

"But you almost did. I saw you."

"Force of habit. Nothing more."

"Why is she calling you? Doesn't she have a girlfriend, a coworker, anyone else she could talk to about her boyfriend problems?"

Ian bent over so that his feet touched the floor. Bowing forward, he spoke into his hands: "I'm sure she does."

"So what's going on, Ian?" she pushed, needing him to show some teeth, not liking this docile reaction to his ex-wife's sense of privilege. "Don't you think it's weird, her calling her ex-husband about her current lover?"

"Stacy wouldn't normally do this," he said defensively. "But this is a big deal. They broke up. They were planning their wedding and he pulled out, had a change of heart."

Uh-oh, the devil on her shoulder hissed in her ear. "That's too bad, but where do you come into this? What does this have to do with you?"

He shrugged. "It's force of habit. I'm the one she's always come to when the shit really hits the fan."

"How convenient for her."

For a moment there was a combustible silence in the room. Then, in the best imitation of yogi calm Georgie could muster, she said, "I don't understand why she can dump you, but then can call twenty-four/seven. I hope she's not expecting you to come running back to her now that she's unengaged?"

"I don't know what she expects." He emitted a generous yawn and drew her close, breasts to chest again. This time she felt self-conscious in her arousal, disapproving of her ripened nipples under her flimsy T-shirt.

"I'm sorry, Georgie," he said, shaking his head awake. "I know this must seem fucked up to you. Obviously, things didn't end as cleanly with us as with you and Lucas. You guys seem to really have it together when it comes to not manipulating each other or getting in the way of each other's lives, letting each other move on. I'm learning, though. Time to set some boundaries with Stacy."

He drew her closer. "I don't love her anymore. I love *you*. *You're* the one who deserves my undivided attention."

"Good. Prove it," she whispered seductively.

He entered her seamlessly, with complete grace, as if this particular move had been choreographed eons ago.

Pleasure burst in her like an orange split open, spurting juice and joy. All that accelerated excitement, an opiate in Georgie's system, releasing fear and doubt.

After they were through and Ian was seconds from sleep, she surprised herself by saying, "There's something I have to tell you. Lucas and I haven't always been the perfect divorcées you think we are."

TWENTY-THREE

Under his summer bronze, Ian blanched. With fierce eyes he stared ahead at the television as if hypnotized. The lamp on his nightstand produced a low-wattage glow, but even in this shadowy light Georgie could see him grinding his teeth as if mashing her confession into chewable bites. Suddenly cold on this impossibly warm night, she reached over to touch his arm.

"Please," he said, recoiling. He retrieved his Jockey shorts and inched them around his waist, then reached for his socks. "I'm having trouble dealing with this."

"I see that. I'm so sorry. Don't leave, okay? Talk to me."

"I think it's better if I cool off for a while, so I don't say something I'll regret."

"Please, Ian. Just stay here and say it," she said, clutching her hands together and tensing her body, the way she had right before the nurse punctured her skin to draw blood. "Get it over with."

He settled back against the headboard, his jaw set, not looking in her direction. "I feel like a chump. You lied to me."

"Not directly. I didn't tell you about it before because the pregnancy happened before I met you."

"We were dating already when you got the abortion."

"We'd only gone on a couple of dates when I realized I was pregnant. I didn't want to ruin things with you. Don't you see?" She appealed to him. "It's not the kind of thing you tell someone you've just started going out with, before you even know if the two of you click."

"You gave me the impression that you and Lucas were these . . .

I don't know . . . well-adjusted, perfectly *divorced* people," he declared. "You failed to mention that you're still in a relationship with him!"

"I'm not, Ian. I swear I'm not. I'm in one with you. I was so embarrassed and ashamed about the pregnancy. My father had just died when I slept with Lucas. It was a mistake, one I've paid a huge price for." She could feel the tears burning behind her eyes, the bridge of her nose, all the way to her browbone. If she had kept the baby, she'd be safely in her second trimester by now.

"What if you get upset or confused again?" he asked in a voice tinged with sarcasm.

"It's not going to happen," she said, shaking her head. "Please believe me. I did it before I met you."

"Half an hour ago you were furious at me because Stacy called me. Here I was feeling guilty and I'm not even fooling around with her!"

"Shh, we have to be really quiet. I don't want Jesse to hear," she said.

"Fine. Let's not talk."

"No, listen, I'm not fooling around with Luke! It won't happen again. Things are different now. Luke and I are just friends. No matter *what*."

"Friends don't sleep together, even casually."

"Who are you, the morality police?" She laughed unexpectedly. "Reverend Dimmesdale? I slept with my ex before you and I were involved." She grabbed the blanket to drape over her exposed chest.

"Reverend who?"

"Never mind. I'm sorry I said that. It just slipped out. But you're holding me up to this high moral standard while you're still on the fence about your not-yet-ex-wife."

"That isn't true! I'm not on the fence about Stacy. I'm certainly not fucking her!"

With his mouth sucked into a thin line and his eyes ablaze, Ian was displaying the dark side of decent: the headmaster who failed to distinguish between spiritedness and insolence, between creativity and insurrection, the stern lieutenant of family values who judged others for their indiscretions while not taking into account his own.

Georgie pulled the covers tighter and felt her face crumble.

Ian turned toward her, his eyes darkened, his breath stale. "You condemned me for my relationship with Stacy when all the time you hid what happened between you and Luke!"

"I know, and I'm sorry. I don't want to lose you. That's why I told you now, because I didn't want you to keep thinking that Luke and I had the perfect relationship. But I didn't think I'd need your forgiveness."

He was silent for a moment and then his breath came out in an extended puff. When he spoke, his voice had softened. "It's hard for me to be supportive; I'm sorry. It hits a nerve, you know? It reminds me of Stacy expecting me to be sympathetic about Levin."

"It's nothing like that, I swear! It's about me and my remorse over the abortion."

"I get that. But I have to tell you something. I've never cheated in a relationship, and I couldn't stay with someone if they cheated on me. I'd leave instantly."

"You wouldn't give them another chance on any condition?" she asked, his statement sending a chill from Georgie's throat to her groin.

"I couldn't deal with it again."

"Okay, I get it. I promise that will never happen. But sleeping with Luke before I met you . . . I didn't do that *to you*. I figured that if I were falling in love with someone, I shouldn't keep such a big event in my life secretive. I didn't want to end up lying for years, like my mother. I was all fucked up about the abortion. I still am." She inhaled back tears, wiping her eyes on the back of her hand.

"You never told Luke about the baby?"

"No. He's not like you; he wouldn't even want to know. He likes his life easy, guilt-free, without too many emotional decisions. It would just stir up more trouble, more complications."

"Because he might have wanted you to keep it?"

"Luke? No way. He didn't want another child with me when we were still married. Why would he want one now, when we're divorced and he's living with another woman—who probably wants a child of her own that he'll have to support and feel ambivalent about having in the first place?"

"It's hard to imagine any man being sanguine if he learned that he wasn't even consulted about such a big decision."

"He'd be relieved that I didn't have the baby, which would have only hurt more. Believe me, he wouldn't be angry with me for not consulting him." Her attempt at a laugh came out as a snort. "You're more upset than he'd be."

Even in the dim light, she saw that his expression was loosening, realigning his features into the mild, kind face of Dr. Weiss, compassionate man, lover of animals. She touched him lightly on the thigh. "I may tell him at some point in the future, once enough time has passed and I'm feeling less upset about it."

"Didn't you want him to be there with you during the procedure?"

"God, no. He wasn't even there for me when Jesse was born." She clucked, still astonished at the story. "He was boarding a plane to go on a business trip. My cousin Nina was with me. She was with me for the abortion, too. That's the point, Ian. Luke was *never* there for me emotionally. He can't stand ruminating over the big issues. His philosophy is, 'Why express when you can repress?' a little witticism he and his work buddies invented one evening over drinks."

"C'mon, that's just a dumb thing guys might say among themselves."

"Luke means it. I'm not knocking him. He's an excellent provider and a decent father to Jesse. But you can go only so far with him and then you hit an impenetrable wall. The sex part . . . it was a mistake. I was so sad and lonely, and he was familiar. That's all. I have no intention of doing it again, no matter what happens between you and me."

His breath made a whooshing sound into the otherwise quiet night. The curtains billowed once and stopped—that was the extent of the wind.

"What are you thinking?" she asked, after a minute listening to his steady exhalations, wondering if he'd fallen asleep.

"I need time to digest this."

"That's fair. I understand that, God knows." She thought of her mother's relentless style, in this case, reiterating the mandate that Georgie contact Daniel.

"I'm sorry about the baby," he whispered gently.

"Yeah. Me too. Thanks Ian."

"For what?"

"For listening and for not leaving. You're a wonderful man, and I'm lucky to have found you." She took his hand and gently touched the soft spot between his thumb and index finger. He didn't withdraw or let go.

Morning dawned, and with it a sinus headache above Georgie's browbone. *Ugh,* she thought. *Great start to the day.* Her eyes burned. Allergies and apprehension brewed together in her head. *Did I do I the right thing?* she wondered, considering her mother, the secrecy she'd embraced for so many years. All her life it had been so tempting for Georgie—the desire to contract, like an accordion, to tuck her feelings into pleats small enough to ignore, to hide in books and words, to let sleep wash over her, soothing and gentle as perfumed bathwater. Had she, unwittingly, become the embodiment of her mother's shame?

The sun pounded through the window. Torpor filled the room like the steam from a sauna, making her skin itch. She sat up with the intention of switching on the air conditioner, before realizing she was alone in the bed. "Ian?" she said too quietly for anyone to hear. Was he gone? On his why home to the Garden State, to his needy estranged wife? Would she be left to concoct some half-assed explanation about complicated adult behavior to her already world-weary nine-year-old? "Trust him, Georgie," she reprimanded herself.

"It's hot as hell in here," she said.

For just an instant the ceiling fan alarmed her, how dangerously fast it whirled, like a propeller. She closed her eyes and forced her mind, racing at a staccato pitch, to quiet down.

In her T-shirt and cotton shorts, she opened the door to her section of the suite. "Hey, Jess," she said to her boy in his underwear, watching the Cartoon Network and chomping on a strawberry Pop-Tart.

"Hey, Ma."

"Good breakfast, packed with nutritional value."

"Hmm, low-cholesterol, too."

She drew his head to her waist and kissed his sweat-scented scalp. He was slouched over, distracted by the television, not plugging into her mood. *Good,* she thought. He hadn't overheard the previous night's concert of anger and confession in a minor key. She'd been certain to check on him before allowing herself to fall into a damp, fitful sleep. "It gets turned off in ten minutes."

"Ah, Ma, it's not even eight," he whined.

"Umm, okay, twenty."

The bathroom door was ajar, the rhythmic drip from the shower leaking into the white enamel tub, as soothing as rain against the window. Her heart rate slowed. Yet pulling open the shower curtain revealed an empty tub.

Gazing in the mirror, at the Slavic semicircles beneath her eyes, the fine engravings tracing the downward curve of her mouth, Georgie registered the fact of his absence. "Jess? Did you see Ian this morning?"

"Yeah, he was on his phone for a little bit; then he went out," Jesse yelled above the grating squawks and honks of the animated creatures on the screen. "Jogging. Said he'd be back in forty-five minutes."

"When was this?" Relief and dread formed balloons in her chest; inflating and deflating like a second pair of lungs.

"I don't know. Maybe half an hour ago."

"Who was he on the phone with?"

"Ma, I don't know. He was real quiet."

"Uh-huh. How'd he seem?" she asked casually, thinking, *Dumb question, Georgie. Confuse the kid. Worry him. Get him involved in your shit, why don't you?*

But Jesse sounded only bored. "The same, Ma. I don't *know* him."

"Right. I'm going to take a shower. Then your turn, okay?" No response. *"Okay?"*

"Huh? Yeah, okay, Ma. Can I watch my twenty minutes now?"

Water sluiced in rivulets down her shoulders, the upward tilt of her jawbone. Suddenly Georgie felt a rip, like a punctured organ, then the hemorrhage of fear into her veins and arteries, winding its way to her pumping heart. What if, at the same moment, his Adidases crunching sand, Ian was panting out more words of compassion to his wife, his cell phone hugged snugly to his ear, triumphant, once again in her good graces? What if he was wrestling with a choice, the name Stacy a whisper on his lips?

"Shhh," she comforted her fretful self. "It'll be all right. He said he loves you." She lifted her head up to the showerhead spewing its amniotic nourishment; with eyes closed, she tried to wash her mind clean.

The hollyhocks bowed and sighed from the air tickling their stems. A squirrel scurried up the triangular roof of the inn. Georgie hiked up the windows, despite the heat, to welcome the grand, turquoise sky, the slow, graceful tempo of the day. How odd that beauty could almost compensate. It helped that her father had died during winter's miserable end.

"Get your bathing suit on, Jess. Let's go to the beach when Ian gets back."

While her son dawdled, reading *The Hobbit,* dragging his feet to the bathroom, she retrieved her messages. Technology, that thief of tranquillity, summoned her. She rested her ear against the cell phone, petite and delicate as a seashell in her hand, and listened to the undulating sounds of what sounded like a one-woman opera.

"Hello, Georgia," Estelle pronounced, a cappella. "It's me, your mother, again. The article from *JAMA* is in the mail. I'm calling to let you know that I'll be home all weekend if you care to call. I'm too exhausted to go anywhere and need a break, as we all do, I suppose. It's good for Jesse's sake that you got away. I've been worried about him."

She paused, and when she spoke again her voice had shifted to a more melodious key. "For some reason I keep thinking about the summer after your divorce, when Dad convinced you to come up to the lake with us. You must have been a wreck to agree to share a house with me." She delivered the last statement with her customary tremor of derision, even though Georgie sensed she was serious. "Remember how Jesse loved trout fishing with Dad on the boat, how amazingly patient he was for such a little boy, and how afraid he was of those giant puppets, horse heads and scary huge faces, at that Bread and Puppet show? What a mistake taking a six-year-old to political theater! We pretended it was for Jesse, but we all knew we were going for your father's sake. He adored that sort of thing."

The pain of memory whacked Georgie in the gut with a wallop: how, the weeks following her divorce, she'd longed to leave her body on the shore and swim unencumbered in the halcyon waters of Lake Willoughby, wedged between mountains rising like humpback whales. But wherever she went her body followed, vulnerable as glass. Watching her father with Jesse—teaching him how to cast his line and reel in his prize—brought her, if not joy, to the edge of joy.

"I don't know what made me think of that," Estelle continued, followed by a melancholic sigh. "An-y-way, I wanted to inform you that I'll be going up to Boston for a few days, over Labor Day, to visit with Daniel and relax a little at the hotel's indoor pool. I'm staying in the Marriott this time, not his house, if for some unforeseen reason you need or want to reach me. You know, without my telling you again, how close you are to Newton up there on the Cape. Daniel— your brother—would love to hear from you, I'm sure."

Disappointment and accusation were laced together in her mother's voice, wiping out the benevolence that she'd momentarily evoked in Georgie. What destructive impulse led her to repetitively bash their relationship into bits?

Georgie erased the message; the next one was from Lucas.

"Just checking to see how my progeny is doing. Call anytime, uh, except meetings all day. Can you believe it, on Saturday? Ha, ha, like that never happens. Oh, and tonight drinks with another couple at Pete's Tavern, then a big shindig at a coworker's apartment on Gramercy Park." He lowered his voice. "Zoë has spent an obscene amount of money on this beaded Versace gown that, as far as I'm concerned, should only be worn as a costume on Halloween if you're dressing up as a flapper. She's a clotheshorse. I never even knew this about her! She absolutely loves to shop. In Soho, on Madison Avenue! Sheesh!"

She hung up, wondering if they were all doomed, as coparents and ex-lovers, to live out the rest of their days in these semiunions with their ex-spouses, incapable of moving ahead unfettered.

When Ian returned, the sweat pouring down his arms and face, Georgie's heart did a quick paddle and roll. She took only a few steps forward before forcing herself to wait, to gauge his mood before displaying affection.

"Hey," she said. "Good run?"

"Yeah. It's beautiful out." He avoided her eyes as he wiped the side of his neck with a towel. "Hey, Jesse."

"Hi," the boy said, still focused on his book.

"We were thinking of going for a walk after you showered. Will you come?"

Ian hesitated, and in that pause, Georgie wondered if he was preparing for discarding her like a snake shedding its skin. Dry and tubelike she'd remain, a scaly shell.

"Sure," he said, and shrugged.

Less than half an hour later they were strolling on the beach under an indigo sky fine as good china. The sun played music on the water, each note glittering like a shard of glass while the ocean tide resembled a rolling carpet of colors, teal woven into sapphire, into moss green, embroidered with white fringe. Georgie felt immersed in a Seurat painting with only the sunbathers' costumes updated to modern day.

"How about Columbine for a dog's name? Or Klebold? Here, Klebold! Fetch, Klebold!" Jesse shouted jovially into the Atlantic. The ocean lapped back indifferently, licking its foaming lips.

"Jess!" Georgie exclaimed, scurrying to keep up with his youthful pace. She watched her son's smooth, toasted face turn away from the sun cracking open the sky. "Where did *this* come from?"

"All the kids talk about it, Ma." He shrugged nonchalantly.

"That's very upsetting, Jess. Why am I just hearing about this now?"

"Be reasonable, Ma. It's really old news. It's not like I'm planning anything."

"Those aren't very feminine names," Ian said casually. "What if the pup you pick out is a girl. I'd think she'd like something more . . . delicate."

Jesse turned and grinned. "How about Hermione, like from *Harry Potter*?"

Once again, a knock on Mom's old noggin: *He's just a kid.* Books and culture, gun violence and fantasy jiggled together inside his budding brain like ingredients in a blender: if not Columbine, then Hermione; if not Klebold, perhaps Padmé Amidala.

"That's a good name," Georgie enthused, jogging to keep up with her boy.

"Okay. Cool." He ran ahead again to the beginning of a breaker and let the wave wash over his feet.

Ian grabbed her wrist. "Let him romp and run free. We need to talk."

She bowed her spellbound head, even as one hand rummaged through her canvas bag for her sunglasses—*the better to see you with, Jess.* The one constant, the one male who would not be abandoning her for a more appealing model anytime soon, her skeptical mind taunted.

"Have you decided what to do?" she asked tentatively.

"About what?"

"Are you staying?"

"Of course I'm staying, Georgie." He turned to her with a look of bewilderment on his face. "What did you think?"

She smiled shyly. "That you might be planning a sudden trip to Iceland or Cancún or Yemen in the near future."

"Well, only for an annual veterinary conference in Qatar."

"Umm. Sounds warm."

"Georgie." He squeezed her arm a little too tightly. "That's not what this is about. It's not about my leaving you."

"Then what?"

"Honesty. Being honest."

She nodded. "Okay. So, my not telling you about the abortion wasn't a deal breaker?"

For a moment he was silent. He burrowed his sandaled foot beneath the fractured pink underside of a shell. "No more romps in the hay with Luke?"

She placed her hand over her heart. "Girl Scout's honor."

Slowly he said, "I want to work things out, Georgie. But I can't pretend that I don't feel more cautious."

"That's okay. Can I ask you a question? Do you think you could get some distance from Stacy? I know you called her this morning. Jess told me you were on the phone."

"I spoke to Ava," he said. "She feels responsible for Stacy's breakup with Levin. She needed to hear that it wasn't her fault."

"Did you talk to Stacy?"

"For a minute." He jutted his chin out defensively. "I did."

Georgie sighed. "Listen, Ian, can we change the subject? Because there's something else that I'd like to talk to you about," she said.

"Sure," he said, his shoulders relaxing, his arms swinging more freely as he walked. "My pleasure."

She kicked the sand with her bare feet, sandals in hand, and gazed out to the horizon, the delphinium blue expanse where sky met water. Her urge to discuss the other "big issue" in her life, the resurrection of Daniel Kaplan, was somewhat fabricated. She ached for a respite in this bucolic beach setting, lover and child within eyesight, no words necessary.

"My mother left another message about Daniel," she said, because her family saga seemed like a sympathetic topic, one that would help reestablish intimacy. "She's obsessed with my meeting him. It's not that I *never* want to; I just want her to respect that I have to deal with the fact of him at my own pace."

Ian turned toward her and touched her face tenderly. "What happened to you has nothing to do with your mother, you know."

Georgie shrugged. "There's a certain poetic justice to my getting pregnant out of wedlock, something very 1950s-revisionist about it."

"It happens to women every day."

"Now you sound like Nina."

"She's right."

"That's not what you said last night."

She waved to Jesse, who was at the water's edge, collecting shells.

"I was angry you didn't tell me you'd slept with Lucas. I'm still angry. That doesn't mean that you made the wrong decision about the abortion or that it has anything to do with your mother. But about this other thing: It's okay to be curious about this Daniel guy. Maybe you should bite the bullet and meet him. You must be curious."

"I am, in the abstract. I don't feel anything about *him* as an actual real-life person."

Okay, not exactly true. Georgie was envious of his sterling-sounding accomplishments—an impressive job at a pharmaceutical giant, how science friendly, how family familiar—and the way he seemed to effortlessly delight her mother.

"I don't know much about the flesh-and-blood person. He's like the Kaplan in that Hitchcock movie *North by Northwest,* a phantom, a made-up man, a symbol."

"How about the three of us take a ride over to the symbolic man's town and look around, see what we can see, spy on him in his own environment," Ian said, rubbing his palms together, imitation evil mastermind.

The suggestion resounded, magnified in Georgie's ears. It could be painfully gratifying to watch her newfound brother without his witnessing her presence, to act the part of the paparazzi ogling a celebrity with a wide-angle lens. She might catch a glimpse of his face, as well as a peek at his taste in motor vehicles or landscaping, and, if she persisted long enough, she could kneel down in the rhododendrons and learn whether he'd married for comfort or beauty, how different his son's features were to Jesse's—thanks to Daniel's Spanish father.

"What would I tell Jesse? How would I explain who Daniel is? I don't feel ready to tell him yet," she said.

"You could tell him something else. Give him another reason why we're going."

"Isn't withholding information the same as lying? I think I've had enough of that conundrum for a while. This trip has tested enough limits: you and Jess being together, last night."

"Umm. Speaking of withholding information, there's something I've been meaning to tell you but I've been sidetracked by our Stacy/Lucas interruptus."

Georgie stiffened. "You guys are getting back together but want to keep me on as hired help?"

"Not exactly." He laughed. "I found out a couple of days ago that my divorce should be finalized by Christmas. The lawyer is promising."

"Really?"

When he nodded solemnly, she purred and leaned his way. "That is good news."

"Hey, Ma," Jesse said, suddenly having appeared at her side, slippery as a shadow. "I was just wondering something."

"Hey, Jess!" Georgie said.

"I was thinking that we could come back here with Hermione, to the beach, you know, when she's not still all new and floppy like puppies are at first, but can actually run around without falling down."

"Sure, I don't see why not. We can bring her to the beach in the spring."

"Great," he said. "That would be really fun."

"It would," Ian agreed. "It sounds promising."

The three of them grinned at one another, good pals, all rooting for the same team.

TWENTY-FOUR

Autumn had always been Georgie's favorite season, with its festival of colors, its cracker-crisp air, the sparkling mornings and waning light of evenings. This October, sloughing off the dead skin of grief—its first layer—she was particularly grateful for the change in weather with all its attendant displays of grandeur. A certain appetite for normality had returned; she no longer wished to smooth out each crisis like a bedsheet, then crawl on top of it and sleep. For the first time in a year she was living outside the liquid swirling mess and noise of her own mind. Most important, when Jesse needed her, Georgie felt fully present. Her relationship with Ian was falling into a groove, as well. She no longer expected him to fetch when Stacy threw the stick his way. He was starting to trust her again, in turn—enough so that he'd agreed it was time for her and Jesse to meet his daughter. Georgie invited them over for an early dinner on a Saturday evening.

"I hope you're not cooking," Jesse joked from her bed where he lay belly down, legs dangling in the air.

Georgie stared into her mirror, applying the last touches of her makeup, cream blush and lip gloss. "Thanks for the vote of confidence, kid. Check out the fridge. I ordered from that catering company Pita's Place, on Bellwood Avenue."

She turned around to catch her son creasing his face into his "yuck" expression. "I'm sure Gus's mom uses it all the time. It's very tasteful . . . and not inexpensive."

"*Tasteful* is not a word kids use to describe good food, Mom. What about us *kids*? What are *we* going to eat?"

Georgie smiled at Jesse's inadvertent pairing of himself with Ava. "Don't worry. I bought a couple of personal pizzas to stick into the oven just in case Ava hates everything else. Ian promised that if all else fails, she loves pizza." She realized—too late—how desperate she must sound.

"Ma, why are you so concerned about what this girl likes? It's not like she's some big magazine publisher or something." He smirked. "Why is *she* so important that you spent a million dollars trying to make her happy?"

Georgie sighed and walked over to her son, cupping his foot in her hand. "Hardly a million. I got one of your favorite meals, too. Honey, you know that making you happy is more important to me. But we talked about this. You promised to give Ava a chance."

"Is it my fault that I know I'll dislike her?"

"You can't dislike her on principle."

"Sure I can."

For a second she felt stuck, as if in an elevator, halting between floors, when whoosh, the lights clicked off, blackness encapsulating her. She reminded herself it was just dinner; she couldn't let the event rise to the level of catastrophe, no matter what the outcome.

"You'll be nice to her and Ian, like you promised, right?"

"May-be. If you buy me Pokémon Gold *and* Blue."

"*Jess!*"

"Okay, okay. I'm going to play video games until they get here," he announced, rolling to the edge of the bed and hopping off. "Your being stressed is making *me* stressed."

She flashed him her fake menacing look. "I'm fine. But go ahead. Just come down as soon as I call you. Don't make me shout up to you."

By the time the doorbell rang, Georgie had changed three times, finally settling on a spruce-green shirt, black jeans, silver-and-jade earrings, and her ballet flats. She was sitting at the dining room table, flipping through a magazine, one foot quivering. When she stood up, her heart hopped like a frightened rabbit. "Geez," she said aloud. "Calm yourself. This isn't a biopsy."

The late-day wind snapped at Georgie, so that "Wow, it's chilly" was the first thing she said to her guests. Ian smiled at her, the tips of his ears rosy as they peeked out from a wave of hair.

"The weather changed all of a sudden," he said, glancing down at the girl beside him, his arm curled around her shoulder. "It was such a beautiful morning at the pumpkin farm, wasn't it?"

Ava averted her eyes at the mention of such a babyish venture—but not before Georgie noted that they were more captivating than in the photograph. Her hair was a darker shade of gold, and her belly just a bit stout under her pleated denim dress with its purple embroidered heart, her legs sturdier and shorter than her father's.

"Come in!" Georgie insisted, gesturing for them to enter. "Please. It's great to finally meet you, Ava."

"Thanks," the girl murmured, blushing.

Georgie experienced a sting of panic—what if Ava remained mute all through dinner?—but then said gaily, "Let me just call my son, Jesse. I know he wants to meet you."

"Good," Ian said with a grin. He walked into the living room, hand in Ava's, with an easy walk that revealed no fear.

Observing father and daughter together, Georgie felt a stinging pleasure at the notion that while Ava's face was stunning, she had not inherited Ian's slender frame; Stacy, therefore, must not have possessed the perfect model's body that she'd imagined.

"Does he go to Lincoln?" Ava asked in a soft, lilting voice, like a young Renée Zellweger.

"Jesse? No. He goes to Richmond."

Ian asked too eagerly, "Do you know someone at Lincoln, honey?"

The girl shrugged, no longer interested. "My friend Lindsay, from riding camp."

"Oh, right, Lindsay. Is she the girl with the red hair?"

Ava rolled her eyes and sat down primly on the edge of the couch. "Brown. You don't need to know who *all* my friends are, Dad."

Georgie smiled and turned to retrieve Jesse, who, she was sure, would enjoy Ava.

Moments later he marched down the stairs and into the room with the obedience of a foot solider. Georgie noted that he'd wet his hair in the front so that it stuck to his scalp.

"Hey," he said, nodding in Ian's direction, conceding acceptance.

The night before Ian had brought them to meet Jesse's new puppy, Hermione, who'd be old enough to take home in two weeks. Georgie had watched her son's blissful face as Ian placed the ball of soft fur with the pleading clown eyes in the boy's arms. It would be worth the hassle of caring for another animal, she'd decided, to witness that face more often.

"Hi, Jesse," Ian pronounced, his voice almost booming, his trepidation finally unveiled. "How's it going?"

The two children exchanged a wary look, the reluctant spectators of the anxious adult world.

"Fine."

"Want to eat?" Georgie asked merrily. "I have so much, you won't believe it!"

"Yeah, it's true," Jesse said in solidarity. "Mom went a bit crazy at the supermarket."

Ian laughed as if this revelation were the cleverest he'd heard in ages. "Great. We're starving."

"Dad!" Ava protested, flushed with preteen embarrassment. "I'm not *starving!*"

Nevertheless, once Georgie and Ian loaded the table with platters, utensils, a pitcher of lemonade, and two bottles of soda, the girl licked her bottom lip, peering greedily at the food. She filled her plate with ravioli and an ample serving of Caesar salad soaked in dressing, piled high with croutons. The adults helped themselves to more modest portions while Jesse secured a heaping mound of ravioli into his favorite bowl. For a while they ate in silence. Georgie, attuned to the different sounds each one's chewing and swallowing made, was uncharacteristically tongue-tied. *So, Ava, what's your dad like when I'm not around? How about your mom? Any chance she's still hoping for a reconciliation?*

Ava sipped her soda, gazing impassively at Jesse across the table. She seemed to be considering something. "How many friends do you have whose parents are divorced?" she asked finally.

Jesse focused his attention on her, as if they were the only two in the room. He seemed taken aback by the question, but not displeased. "None," he answered.

She blinked a few times without comment, and then nodded

slowly, eyes aflutter behind her lids. Hers was the countenance of a patient and wise crone for whom nothing could further shock. "Me, either," she said. "I mean, I know *of* people, but they're not my friends. I haven't been to *their* houses."

Jesse smiled. "Welcome to the club."

"Yeah," she said in a world-weary voice. "I guess so."

It had been an extraordinarily fine month, Georgie noted, right before falling asleep; now, the get-together between Jesse and Ava had proven a success. As she stretched her arms under her pillow and felt her body sink into the cool sheets, she was grateful for the simplicity of the day's conclusion: newly in love but happy to be alone with Jesse in her own house. The wedge of sorrow had lessened, had begun to dislodge from its sharp place beneath her ribs.

Sunday morning she opened her eyes to the first slant of light staining the floor; she smiled at the memory of Jesse's open-palmed good-bye to Ava. "See ya," he'd said. "Yeah," the girl had responded, with the flicker of a smile and a wave as she departed with her dad. Both children had behaved admirably, Georgie acknowledged. They deserved some small token of thanks.

Breakfast would be French toast; Jesse loved French toast. She imagined dunking each slice of wheat bread in egg, then frying it in the pan. A smile crept across her face.

It wasn't until she was filling the Mr. Coffee filter with Nantucket blend that she noticed the flashing red light on her answering machine. Sometime between eight p.m. and eight a.m., the outside world had tried to encroach on her newly minted peace; to prevent just such an interruption she'd gotten into the habit of turning off the ringer. She played the message now.

"Hello. This is Daniel Kaplan," a strong voice pronounced in the erudite accent of a Kennedy with a touch of the Brahmin, a continent away from his Bronx-born natural mother. "I hope my calling you is not an intrusion." He paused, exhaling softly. "Estelle gave me your number and insisted it was okay with you." He laughed gently, a laugh that bespoke intimate knowledge of his subject, their mother. "I wasn't sure."

A chemical heat surged through Georgie and the bile raced for her throat. She certainly hadn't given Estelle permission to dispense any private information about herself to Daniel. And she considered her telephone number private.

"Anyway, I just wanted to tell you that I would love to talk to you, or even to meet when you're ready. The thing is that Stellie invited me to Thanksgiving, and I didn't want to just show up at your aunt Lily's and spring my presence on you in front of all those relatives without some earlier introduction between the two of us. I'd be more than happy to come to New Jersey."

Nervously Georgie lowered the volume. She hadn't heard Jesse stir. Nevertheless, she couldn't take any chances of disclosure, not yet. Quietly, in her bare feet, she dashed up the stairs to check on him. His door was halfway open, showing signs of mess: a dirty sneaker under a standing lamp, schoolbooks scattered about the beige pillows of his old ratty couch, one hanging open off the side, a glass with the remnants of milk in it on his end table, Jesse asleep on his stomach, hair risen to the top of his head like a rooster's crown, his quilt with the solar system embroidered on it lying in a rejected heap on the floor. Forgetting about cooking breakfast, Georgie dialed Nina on her cell, certain her cousin— who began each day religiously at dawn—would be fully awake.

"Hey," she said. "Where are you? Do you have a minute?"

"Sure. Dashing off to do errands before I take Franny to her ballet class. Can you believe I've let her take these ridiculous lessons in the city? I must be a complete masochist," Nina expounded. "This is what happens when your prima ballerina daughter has a recital coming up and you're a guilty working mother, so on the weekend, you try to turn into Susie Homemaker."

"Somehow I don't see you baking bread. We're missing that gene in our family. Speaking of genes, guess who called me this morning?"

"Wait. Back up a minute. How'd it go last night?"

"Great. Better than I expected. But there's no rest for the weary."

"Okay, fill me in later. Who called? Your mom?"

"No. Much better. Daniel Kaplan. My mother gave him my number without my consent."

"Whoa! Bad move. Are you going kill her?" Nina asked.

"I might. He told me that she invited him to Thanksgiving. He thought we should meet beforehand."

"Good idea. Why not get it over with? Lessen the blow by meeting him alone instead of en masse. Make a weekend of it. Go with Ian and leave Jess with dear ol' dad. Mix torture with pleasure."

"I don't consider meeting the guy torturous," Georgie responded, cupping her coffee. "He actually sounded nice. He offered to come down here to see me."

"Really? Aren't you just a teeny-weeny bit curious? I know I'd be dying from curiosity."

"That's what separates us rational creatures from weak-willed ones like you," Georgie joked, rising from the kitchen stool and walking to the refrigerator, the phone cradled under her chin. She took out a vanilla yogurt and flipped open the top.

"Call him, George! It's the weekend. He might actually be home today, raking the leaves or kicking the old ball around with his son, as all male Homo sapiens do come the week's end. Doesn't he have an eight-year-old?"

"Something like that. And a new baby."

"I didn't know. I'm sorry, honey."

"I was trying to train my mother to respect my wishes and give me time to absorb all this information," Georgie said, lowering her voice at the sound of the toilet flushing. Jess was up and activated. "Guess it didn't work. Daniel's all she talks about lately. I even told her about Ian, expecting the usual torrent of criticism. She didn't say a word; I don't think the news that I'm in a serious relationship registered. That's how completely obsessed she is!"

"It's only guilt that makes her go on that way, you know."

"I'm not without sympathy for what she went through. But she's acting like a teenager with a new boyfriend. She's certainly more preoccupied than I am with Ian. It's creepy."

"Oh, Georgie! She's just happy he found her." Nina laughed.

"It's more than that, I swear. It's the way she gushes and giggles about him. I'm sure right now my mom's enjoying another Oedipal morning chatting with Boy Wonder."

"Who?" Jesse asked, having sneaked up behind Georgie, one hundred percent attentive.

"Who what, honey?" She whipped her head around to see her son, crusty-eyed and barefoot, in Luke's *Wall Street Journal* T-shirt and his own little-boy white underpants.

"Who is Grandma having her 'Oedipal' morning with?"

"Nina, gotta go." She hung up, her heart doing the doggy paddle, fast. "Do you know what that word means? Oedipal?"

Jesse's eyebrows shot up. He nibbled his lower lip. "That she has a date?"

"Well, not a real one." Georgie took a deep breath, nice and slow. "Not like with Grandpa. It's just a relative of hers she's been talking to a lot lately. One we've never met."

"Oh." He sounded relieved, shuffling to the fridge for his usual morning inspection. The world spun around on its axis.

Georgie would have to tell her sweet boy soon.

That afternoon Gus came over with his scooter and two video games. "Hey, Miss Georgia." He waved on the way to his best friend's room, his long face and dark eyes, almost Asian, eclipsed by a mound of brown curls. He paused to caress Abby Abyssinian as she brushed against his leg. "Hope you don't freak out when Hermione invades next week," he said.

"Hey, Gus," Georgie replied to this exotically elegant boy, this frequent visitor. "Don't worry. My friend Ian is going to help us train Hermione not to pounce on Queen Abigail."

"That's cool."

While the boys exercised only their thumbs and vocal cords playing video games in the attic, Georgie fiddled with an article. For the first time in days her concentration was shot. On top of her filing cabinet next to her desk sat a pile of magazines; wedged between two recent copies of *Elle* was the brown office envelope her mother had sent with more photos of Daniel's family. Gingerly edging it out of its place so as to not cause an avalanche, Georgie bargained with herself: "I'll just peek at one, then back to work."

With eyes closed, she chose arbitrarily. The photograph was a close-up of a woman with a broad smile, greenish brown eyes with flickers of gold in the irises, and a mass of gray-and-blond hair woven intricately together as if in a tapestry. The woman's eyes were luminous with merriment despite her earth mother haggardness: no makeup and face prematurely lined, most likely from decades of carefree summers spent in the sun combined with too many nights tending wakeful children. This was not a woman who would get her hair cut for her father's funeral.

Georgie eased out one more five-by-seven. In this shot, the woman's head was bent down so that the slopes of her nose and round cheeks were prominent. She was holding a sleeping baby with lovely fair skin and a sprout of chick-yellow hair, no more than a couple of months old.

Georgie sucked in the sides of her mouth as if it had been squirted with lemon juice. Dialing Ian at the clinic, where he was putting in a few hours, she questioned her own motives. Would meeting Daniel give her access to this baby who was a Jesse look-alike? Would holding such a perfect creature act as a tonic for what she'd lost?

"The thing is," she said when Ian got on the phone, "I'm actually considering meeting this Daniel Kaplan, man of mystery, before the holidays."

"Good idea," he said. "Ilene, I'll be right there. Get the Pentothal and isoflurane ready. We'll begin in five minutes. I only have a second before Presley's orchiectomy. Can we talk more about it tonight?"

"I'm sorry. I'm bothering you at work."

"Nah, no bother. I'm just about to perform your average castration."

"That's a relaxing image. Before you go cut the balls off this poor guy, let me ask you something. If Daniel answers my e-mail and it works out, schedule-wise, would you be up for a weekend rendezvous with me in New England? I could leave Jess back home with Lucas."

"Absolutely. Ready, Ilene? Sorry, sweetie, duty calls. I need to go chop off Presley's privates."

"Poor guy. He'll never sing again."

It was as if she were composing a sonnet the way she fussed over this one simple piece of correspondence, three lines long. Finally, before Ian came over with a thin-crust pizza and salad for dinner, Georgie sent her e-mail to the address given to her by Estelle. By nightfall Georgie had an answer: *Please do come whenever is convenient. Have been looking forward to this for a long time. All my best, Daniel Kaplan.*

"Why are you guys going up there again?" Jess asked in the car en route to Luke's place the following Friday late afternoon as they slogged through the gray exhaust fumes of commuter traffic.

Georgie had been staring out the window at the traffic pileup leading into the Lincoln Tunnel, tight jawed, weak legged, and slightly febrile with expectation. *I'll meet my brother in less than forty-eight hours,* she thought, silently testing, awaiting her own response. Her son's question rerouted her anxiety, like roadwork on the perpetually overcrowded expressway in her mind.

Jesse was hunched down, armed with his techno toys, Game Boy in hand, the earphones from his iPod hanging around his neck, his long, muscular legs replicas of his dad's swinging out into the back of her seat, kicking her.

"I told you, Jess, I have some research to do." Was a half-truth a lie? Georgie glanced at him in the rearview mirror to see if he suspected anything awry. But after a long week of school, he was sleepy-eyed as a cat in the sun, his sandy blond hair dirty, too long in the front, a disgruntled frown the only sign of his discontent.

"What's in it for me, the shitty little kid?"

"Hey!" she said, snapping her head back and widening her eyes.

"A fun-filled weekend with your dad?" Ian tried.

"What's gotten into you?" Georgie asked.

"That teenybopper will be there?" Jesse smirked.

"Well, yeah. She lives there now."

"It's not fair. You're going away without me. It's bad enough that you and Dad are divorced. But now there are all these extra people in my life who don't even care about me."

Georgie swallowed hard, the bitter taste of remorse. How unlike Jesse it was to be rude, especially in front of other adults. Was this a sign of comfort with Ian or the unraveling of misery? Before she could respond, Ian said, "I care about you, Jess. A lot."

Her son shrugged. "Well, Britney Spearhead doesn't. She just walks around saying, 'Oh, Lukie' this and 'Oh, Lukie' that."

Georgie would have to have a serious talk with her ex about Jesse's jealousy and Zoë's inappropriate behavior, but not with all the other players around. It was a matter for the two of them, the slayers of their boy's hopes and dreams.

"What if I want to come home?"

Georgie exchanged a quick look with Ian as the thought flashed through her head: *I should never leave him—not even at his father's—until he's ready, broad shouldered and stubble chinned. At the ivy-covered entrance to college perhaps? Graduate school?*

"You can call me anytime on my cell. I'll leave it on."

"You'll come all the way back from Boston? Five hours?"

"If things are really bad for you there, I will. You can sit and watch *Episode I* twice and by the second time it's over, I'll be at Dad's."

"Okay, I guess," he said tentatively.

She said brightly, "Hey, you might have fun."

"Yeah, and Ralph Nader might be our next president."

The adults laughed. "Oh, Jess, you're so clever," Georgie said, as if wit might compensate for sorrow.

Two hours and one tense good-bye later ("What, no kiss?" followed by a quiet command to Luke: "Spend time with him without Zoë; he's feeling really left out"), Georgie was on her guilty way.

"I feel so bad about him and this Zoë thing. Maybe we shouldn't go," she said.

"Jess is with his dad, eating junk food and watching the Cartoon Network. He'll be fine," Ian responded, placing his hand on her thigh.

"You know, I get up almost every night and have to peek into his room to make sure he's okay, like I did when he was a baby. Sometimes I actually check to see if he's breathing. He's almost ten, and all of a sudden my body is doing that maternal thing it did the whole first year."

Ian glanced over at her with sorrowful eyes. "Poor Georgie. It's been harder than you thought, huh?"

Tears flowed as she stared at her booted feet. "Yeah, it has. I feel immeasurably guilty for what I did. I feel like a murderer. I am a murderer."

"You're not. You're a great mother. Jesse adores you. And I know this is probably not the right thing to say, but you can have another baby someday." He nearly whispered the last sentiment.

She let Ian's suggestion slide down her throat like a hard candy, big enough to choke her.

"What am I doing chasing after a brother I never even wanted?"

"Figuring out where this guy fits into your life, and spending some romantic one-on-one time with your lover man."

She nodded and shut her eyes as they rode awhile in silence. Memories of her dad cropped up and shifted in cubist fashion. "C'mon, Georgie Porgie, give me a break here," she imagined Adam's ghost saying. "I kept the secret at your mother's instructions. She wanted it that way from the beginning. No mention of the baby. You know how stubborn she can be, like a dog with a bone," said Adam's ghost.

"Like an ox."

"For you too, kid. I did it for you. See how much more complicated everything is now, knowing about him? I never wanted you to have to go through that. Honestly, I never thought you'd have to."

"Dad, it's not just that. It's everything. Finding out about this was the icing on the cake."

"You gotta know how difficult it was for your mom, keeping her secret bottled up. You have a son, so you have to be able to grasp what it was like for her, a little bit, at least."

"No, no," Georgie instructed her apparition. "I don't want to discuss that. Be on my side; be my pal!"

"Ah, Georgie, can't you see how hard it was for me, juggling my two strong-willed gals for so long? I'm tired now, sweetheart. I need to rest."

His image faded into a silhouette and was gone. But her mind vigilantly excavated bits and pieces, fossilized memories. Decades of chatter about babies and children—could the Dr. Merkins have buried references to Daniel behind an alias, his patient or hers? Were any of the family's New England vacations veiled expeditions, hunts for the boy Estelle had abandoned? Or did she search for him in faces closer to home: the squirming toddler on the number six train, the olive-skinned boy in Central Park? Did Estelle avert her gaze as each new infant slid into her obstetrical arms, or did she purposely memorize their fresh, doughy faces as a form of redemption?

Georgie's emotions were so chaotic, she imagined them pelting one another with Jesse's Nerf guns. She shut her eyes and listened to Jane Monheit implore "Please Be Kind" on the radio. Finally there was comfort in the periwinkle blindness behind her lids, the evening air on her cheek, the journey forward.

Drowsing in Ian's embrace later that night, still gummy from sex, Georgie rolled over into the warmth of his chest, dreaming of the beach. In the dream, lying under the umbrella with her lover fast asleep, Georgie felt a sudden sharp sting shooting up from her toes. A snow leopard cub was biting her feet with sharp feline teeth; and try as she might, Georgie could not wrench free. What was this native of Central Asia, this mountain dweller, doing here on the East Coast of the United States? her dreaming mind wondered. Turning her gaze from the sugary blue sky to Ian, Georgie noted that he was gone, vanished behind the scrim of her consciousness. "I'm not a large-animal vet," she heard him say regretfully, omniscient as the Wizard of Oz, and just as impotent.

At the end of her line of vision, she recognized that familiar form, her mother, mounted at the shoreline. When Georgie called out to her, Estelle's words reverberated inside her head. "I can't help you now. I need to find him in the water. Daniel can't swim."

The cat crunched down hard into the center of her, that old bugaboo of unrequited love. Georgie's eyes sprang open. "Whoa!"

"Umm?" Ian murmured. "You okay?"

"Yeah. In an emergency, do you have the veterinary skills to subdue a lion or snow leopard, a baby one?"

"Uh? You're still sleeping, aren't you?"

"Creepy dream."

He edged closer. "Anyone would be nervous about Sunday." Sunday was D-day, while Saturday was slated for pleasure and relaxation.

"True." Georgie's voice resounded in her ear like a bell.

They slept for a few hours until Ian stirred, his foot hooking hers, the warmth of his thigh touching her hip. She inched down and molded her body into the shape of his: fetal, like twins lying in their mother's womb. Ian's cheek was creased, a bead of saliva shining in the corner of his mouth. She hugged him tight and he sighed.

The continental breakfast was free, but they opted for the decadently expensive room service, $12.95 eggs that came with croissants as bloated as blowfish and candy-red strawberries as pretty as M&Ms'

shells. They'd agreed to use the exercise room and saunas before heading out to Quincy Market and the north end of Boston. So, Georgie felt bad proposing a slight change of plans. Would it be okay if she hopped over to Newton to scope out the "suspect" while Ian enjoyed the womblike undulations of the whirlpool? Would he mind if she borrowed his car?

"Of course not. But you're going to see the guy in twenty-four hours. Why not wait?" His expression was quizzical but not angry. She had not witnessed Ian's self-righteous rage since their fight on Cape Cod.

Georgie shrugged. "Now that we're here, I'm sort of curious to see where big brother lives, since it's only ten minutes away. It's like research. The more prepared I am for our tête-à-tête, the less anxious I'll feel." *Hopefully.*

He gently stroked her back under her sweatshirt. "I'll be happy to go with you."

"No need. You enjoy the fine amenities of our expensive accommodations," she said, springing off the bed. "I'm going to shower and change and I'll be back before noon. We'll have the rest of the day and night to ourselves."

Smiling, he winked. "Good luck, Double-oh-seven."

An hour later Georgie stepped outside into the pastel cold day. She sat at the wheel of the car without moving. "I'm a natural explorer," she said aloud, and then switched on the radio for company, a local map spread out on the passenger seat.

Perhaps because her brain was mired in the fog of disorientation, Georgie took a wrong turn or two once she landed in Newton. The sun was dizzying; suddenly everything had acquired a green cast as she slowed the car down at the curb of a street in a quiet, leafy neighborhood and leaned over the steering wheel. She gazed up at the sign and hung a right. "Where am I?" she asked the rustling of a slight breeze, the imperial oaks. "What am I doing?"

Just like that she saw it, through the slit that two branches made: Adams Avenue.

"Oh, my God," Georgie said, drinking in air. Then she reached over for the street map of west suburban Boston. "Here I go, Dad. You guide me there."

Watertown followed Adams out of this more modest part of town. Lowell followed Watertown, which preceded Otis, a magnificent place filled with Victorians worthy of Scarlett O'Hara before the Yankees won the war. His house—her brother's house—was not as opulent as the plantation next to it, but still a large white colonial, newly painted with glossy black shutters and a slick red door. The lawn was as manicured as a precisely groomed poodle, with a clipped crop of orange and yellow nasturtiums carefully lining the walkway. The cobblestones in the pathway leading up to the door were sparkling like tourmaline crystals.

Georgie parked across the narrow road. She didn't duck or even hunch over. Instead she stared out into the expanse of this stranger's life, the abundant clean fertility of it, home and foliage. There were no cars in the driveway, and the garage door was down. Minutes passed in a haze of stillness. Even the birds stopped warbling.

When a forest green Land Rover approached, she had already started the engine of her car to head back to Boston. Her hand was still touching the key as the skin on her neck prickled. Through her left window she saw him: a tall, olive-complected man with broad eyebrows and a grin on his scruffy face, which was longer and thinner than it appeared in the photograph. He emerged from his SUV and she saw that he was wearing a Red Socks T-shirt, faded jeans with a hole in the left knee, and sneakers but no socks. A few seconds later the door to the passenger side opened and a boy scurried out; he was small with chestnut-colored skin. The man tousled his son's slick ebony hair. Then the two went into the house.

Georgie saw him first, sitting at the coffee shop in the Colonnade at Quincy Market. But then Daniel noticed her with his radarlike gaze and leaped to his feet as if to issue a standing ovation. In an instant he was squeezing her hand. "Georgie," he exclaimed in that same aristocratic voice she'd heard on her machine.

This man was her *brother*. The noun swirled nonsensically through her mind.

On talk shows sibling reunions always began with a gasp, a hand over the mouth and an exclamation of joy, followed by a huge bear hug between the estranged family members. Georgie initiated this emotional love fest by blowing her nose into a used tissue she'd dug out of her pocketbook.

"I recognized you from the picture Stellie gave me," he said, this wiry man who'd developed streaks of gray in his temples since the last picture of him had been taken, but still had an unruly head of ample dark curls and the full lips that Hollywood stars paid good money to duplicate.

Georgie nodded, her face tilted to accommodate the off-kilter movement of the planet upon which she'd landed.

"Sit down. You look startled," he said, exuding an effortless charm. "It was great of you to come all this way, especially after the last six months, how hard they must have been for you."

She watched his expression swiftly changing from disarming pleasure to a mask of gravity, a downward-twisting mouth and deepening eyes as he tried to gauge her mood.

"That's okay. This trip was a nice break for me."

"I'm so sorry about your father. From the way Stellie describes him, Adam sounds like he was a wonderful man."

"Thanks, he was."

To deflect the intensity of the moment, she glanced out the window at the mosaic of colors in the marketplace, then at the young woman in high heels, applying flourishes of rosy pink to her lips and cheeks, at the next table.

"Are you okay?"

"This . . . it feels incredibly surreal." She was as jittery as if this were a first date.

Daniel cupped his head in his palm. "It isn't every day that you meet your sibling for the first time."

He was all people skills, the direct eye contact, the hand-holding, but not for so long as to make Georgie squeamish, yet none of it seemed studied or disingenuous, but rather as if his was a radiant spirit disposed into this robust male body with instructions to treat the less fortunate charitably.

The waitress showed up with a plastic carafe of coffee and a frown. While he ordered his egg-white omelet, Georgie observed his striped maroon shirt—such a bold color—folded up at the elbows in a slapdash way so that the ironed material crumpled.

"I'd like a cappuccino with skim milk," she told the waitress, and to Daniel, "I ate my free breakfast at the hotel."

He nodded and for a moment was quietly observing. "I'm so happy you're here," he said. "For the record, you don't have to worry. I'm basically a nice guy."

"I'm sure."

"What are you thinking about?" he asked, leaning forward.

Such a presumptuous question from a stranger, and yet his tone was hypnotic, like a good shrink's or a genuinely caring spiritual healer's.

"Truth?"

He nodded. "Sure."

"My first impression of you is that you seem really comfortable in your own skin."

"And you're not?"

"Let's just say not as much."

He smiled broadly and tilted back in his chair, away from her in orchestrated rhythm with the signals her body was sending. *What a fabulous gift,* she thought, *when most people just chug along on their self-absorbed tracks.*

"I have a knack for appearing comfortable." He smiled.

"And you're not really?"

"I *am.* Mostly. Plus, I work in corporate communications enhancing the global market's perception of my company. I have to stay on top of the new media technology, but the public relations part I could do in my sleep." He shrugged. "I'm good with people, at ascertaining their concerns and addressing them, at putting them at ease with my ease."

"Did you ever think of going into politics?" She took a sip of the water the waitress had plunked on the table.

"Never." He laughed. "My wife used to ask me the same question when we were dating. I've never liked the law—too dry. I'm an odd mix between a techno nerd and a media junkie." In a mock whisper he added, "The *TV Guide* and *Macworld* are my favorite reading materials."

"That's not much of a confession to a girl who has spent over a decade describing the best shoes to wear to work."

"Here's to popular culture." He raised his water glass between them, jocularly, as if it were a champagne flute.

She clinked her glass with his. "It's an unspoken faux pas in my family, my having such a nebulous career."

"Really? I didn't get a sense of that from Stellie. She brags about your being a writer."

Georgie shrugged, lapsing momentarily back into the role of sullen daughter. "Umm. She likes to put her best face forward. But I freelance for magazines she doesn't respect. I admit they're mostly frivolous pieces. That's what pays the bills. I tried my hand at a couple of more serious essays before my dad died which haven't come out yet, with the long lead time. I'm playing around with the idea of doing more."

Stop trying to sell yourself, she thought. *You sound pathetic.*

"It's funny. Estelle talks about your work with a real sense of reverence. She also mentioned that you're a great mom."

Georgie swallowed, noting how raw her palate felt. "It's interesting that up until my dad died, she hadn't exactly honed her nurturing skills, at least when it came to me. Lately she's been a little better." *As if she's trying to make up for his not being here.* "Not that her opinion should matter anymore, in my old age."

The waitress approached with their order, and Georgie noticed the diamond stud in her nose, her cropped ruddy brown hair, her round, feline face. "Anything else I can get you?" the girl asked in the laissez-faire voice of a student moonlighting as a waitress. She pulled on her shirt, which reached only halfway down her flat midriff.

"No, thank you. We're good," Daniel said, flashing her his cultivated boyish smile, the white panels of his teeth displayed, his eyes shimmering with a contained sensuality.

"You were saying?" He turned his full attention on Georgie once the waitress was gone.

She shrugged. "Nothing important."

"It's important to *me.*"

"Just that our family motto has always been 'Go to medical school,' or 'at least, earn a degree that leads you to serve others honorably,' the exceptions being Dr. Alex and cousin Rich, who took the Hippocratic oath in order to perform face-lifts. You'll meet them at

Thanksgiving, a real treat. They're quite the handsome, if synthetic, couple."

Daniel grinned. "Looking forward to it. I have a bit of a sag I'd love to tighten up," he joked, patting his chin. "My wife, Lauren, will fit right in."

"Why?" Georgie laughed. "Does she need a rhytidectomy too?"

He laughed, a deep, resonant sound. "I meant with the rest of your clan of do-gooders. She's an immigration lawyer working on the Women's Refugee Project in Boston, helping to develop asylum law at the federal level."

"God," Georgie muttered. "My mother must love her."

"I admit Stellie was impressed with Lauren's résumé. But they genuinely seemed to hit it off when they met. I, on the other hand, must take after my biological father. From what I've gathered he sounds like quite a player, or he was forty years ago."

"Are you angry about him?"

"Why?" he asked, sounding defensive for the first time.

"Just that she never told him about you." *She. Our mother.* "Have you tried to contact him?"

"Claudio? Not yet. But I hope to be able to find him, maybe even visit Spain at some point. It's tricky, since he doesn't even know I exist," he said, a shadow over his eyes. "I don't want to give the guy a heart attack with late-breaking news of my conception."

"And your adopted father? What does he think of all this?"

"We don't talk about it in too much detail. I don't want to hurt Dad or make him feel that he was inadequate or failed as a father in any way."

"Wouldn't he just think that you were curious, that you wanted to find your biological roots?"

"Yes, intellectually. But feelings aren't rational. I want to be respectful of how he feels."

She smiled. "They must have raised you well, your . . . parents."

"They did. I was lucky."

Georgie nodded, realizing with a start that—despite a certain slickness—she liked this man with his banter and smooth moves, that in their first meeting she already preferred him to most of her other relatives. What a peculiar revelation!

"What are you thinking?" he repeated.

Georgie shook her head, but then wondered, What danger was there in disclosure? After all, shame and self-censure were not genetic traits like slim hips and left-handedness. Whatever measure of these she possessed were learned from her mother, and now—looking at Daniel—she knew why. For nearly forty years Estelle had safeguarded her secret, and all the while the feeling had festered: that she'd casually, even callously, given her child away. Her heart, already a thicker muscle than most, had become tighter, tougher.

It was sad for her mother, much like the abortion was for Georgie. But she wouldn't allow herself to dwell on that thought. Sympathy for her mother could be tucked away in a dark corner of her mind, to be unfurled for inspection later. Georgie wanted to enjoy the company of the man seated across the table from her, his face receptive to all her words and gestures, so glad of her presence on such a remarkable morning.

TWENTY-FIVE

Georgie awoke two Saturdays before Thanksgiving to the angry roar of a leaf blower, that king of the suburbs, and the irrefutable knowledge that this was the day to enlighten Jesse about Daniel Kaplan.

"Pass the orange juice, honey," she said to him over breakfast at the kitchen table, as she contemplated strategy. Perhaps she should have practiced her nebulous communication on Ian, focusing on a waterstain marring her bedroom wall so that his face was only peripherally in her line of sight. She could have stood straight and spun out platitudes as if delivering a speech on courage and initiative to a troop of Boy Scouts. Instead her mind and mouth felt filled with mush.

Her son—deeply engrossed in his *National Geographic Kids* magazine—did not pass the juice.

"Jess, can you give me a minute of your attention? There's something I need to talk to you about."

Her voice might have been a bit too shrill, because the look in his eyes was that of bystander to a car wreck, as if he'd been staring too long and steadily at the flames. "I don't want to talk about it," he said. "Hermione," he called out to the puppy, gnawing her rawhide bone in the corner. The dog glanced up for a second—her sorrel brown eyes fetching—then succumbed to the greater temptation in front of her.

"What, sweetie? What don't you want to talk about?"

"Dad is marrying that floozy, isn't he?"

Georgie's hand flew to her lips to conceal a smile. "No, no. Where did you learn that word?"

He shrugged. "Gus. He calls Felicia Winston Felicia the Floozy because she likes every boy in the fifth grade, including the fat ones and the really dumb ones, even Nelson."

She nodded and leaned over the table to kiss her son's forehead. "Well, the answer is no. Dad and Zoë have no plans to marry."

Head bowed, he asked timidly, "Is it you and Ian?"

"As of this minute, neither Dad nor I has plans to remarry. If and when we do, you'll be the first to know."

Jesse's shoulders sank back into their natural alignment and the scowl disappeared into his smooth skin like linen being pressed. "Ma, it's not that I don't like Ian, 'cause I kinda do. I mean, he's not like the floozy. He actually pays attention to me and treats me like a person, not just a stupid kid. And he gave me Hermione. It's just that everything is so . . . haphazard." He said this last word carefully, as if testing out its meaning.

"I know it has been, Jess. But you've been great, really handling all the changes in your life so well."

"Nice sentiment, Ma. But false."

"Why do you say that?"

He shrugged. "I'm not as cool as you think. You're my mom. It's your job to think I'm in great shape, that you're not screwing up."

"Am I screwing up?"

He sighed. "What do I look like, a shrink? If you're not getting married, then what is it you wanted to tell me? Cut to the chase."

"Okay. Don't be rude. What I'm about to say might matter to you or it might not. I'm just not sure. It's about Grandma." The alarm was back in his eyes; the bodies in the burning car were visible, the charred bones and hollow skulls. "Honey, she's not sick. Nothing bad has happened to her."

He waited a beat, then collapsed back onto his chair. "Is *she* getting married?"

This time Georgie let her laugh escape. "No, Jess. Who would she marry?"

"I don't know, Ma. I'm not Grandma's social director."

"Nice attitude, kid. For the record, what I wanted to talk to you about has nothing to do with matrimony." Her voice sounded magnified, as if she'd been speaking too close to the microphone. "It's sort of a weird story. Turns out Grandma has been keeping a secret from me because she was embarrassed, I think."

He was listening intently, as if in anticipation of some tall tale composed by George Lucas.

"Something happened to her before she had me, before she even met Grandpa that's just now . . ."—she stumbled—"uh, affecting her and us."

"Huh? Speak English, Ma, the language of New Jersey."

The world, it seemed, was rife with land mines, and the only way through them was to tread carefully while whistling a humorous little ditty.

"Grandma had a baby a long time ago, when she was really young, too young to take care of it. She gave him up for adoption."

"What? You mean Grandma was married before Grandpa?" His face turned an ashy white, as if the person behind it were either in shock or uncomprehending.

"No. This was with a boyfriend, Jess. Grandma was very young and it was an accident. You don't have to be married to have a baby."

"Oh, yeah. I knew that."

"Sweetie, I'm telling you this because the man she gave up for adoption contacted her recently and will be at our Thanksgiving with his family. I didn't want to keep it a secret from you or lie to you, even though you've already been through so much."

There were tears in her son's eyes. "This year? Couldn't he have waited?"

"That's exactly what I thought, Jess. But Grandma invited him. He seems nice. It'll be okay."

He glanced down at his magazine longingly, as if nostalgic for a more innocent time, back when he believed in Santa Claus and two-parent families and a grandmother so tame that she embarrassed him only by singing "The Wheels on the Bus" when he was already old enough to read.

"I don't get how so many things can change in someone's life when they're only a kid. It's like an earthquake flattened everything out the last few months, you know?"

"I do," she said, by his side and hugging him now. "I do."

He was right, her boy. As it turned out, all the clichés were true:

If they were very unfortunate, a catastrophic accident could blot out their existence without their consent and before they were ready. In those moments when righteous anger pumped through Georgie like gasoline—over the cruelty of death or the thorny connection with her mother or the tumultuous changes that had shaken her son's childhood loose at its foundation—the cure would have to consist of Ian and Jesse, Nina and Daniel, the memory of her father's adoration and the righteousness behind her decision to erase the possibility of one child's life to save another's.

It would simply *have* to be enough.

Many hours later, Ian and Georgie lay on her bed, over the covers, as kosher as leavened bread.

"Didn't you say you had to skedaddle? Early breakfast with Ava tomorrow," she asked, to which he sighed and snuggled closer.

"I'd rather stay."

"I know." She noted his erection through his pants. "Nice for such an old man."

"So? Up for it?" He grinned. "Pun intended. We can be quiet as mice."

"I'd love to." She nestled her head under his arm, between his neck and shoulder, and basked in the ocher glow of her Moroccan torch lamp. "You can't imagine how much I would. But unless I have a very talented cat or dog, that was Jess flushing the toilet. He won't be back asleep yet after our upsetting conversation this morning."

"Hmm," Ian clucked. "Poor kid." Contemplatively he stroked her hair and gazed up at the ceiling. A poignant silence enveloped them, the room, the navy blue night with its cluster of jeweled stars gracing them through the open curtains.

"I've been thinking about something," he said in a husky voice. "One thing that could make our relationship a bit less fuzzy for everyone. We could move in together and make it official."

Desire fluttered like gills, propelling Georgie upstream to this fertile place. She kissed his neck, breathed in his tangy skin, a strand of his salty hair.

"I thought you were being cautious because of what I told you over the summer?"

"I was." He shrugged. "I guess you can call me Mr. Optimistic."

"You have no idea how much I'd love to do that. But don't you think it's too fast? You haven't even met my family, other than Jesse."

"Well, who else really matters?"

"It's not that their *opinions* matter. I want you to meet Nina, already; she's going to love you. But you should probably meet my mother before making any commitments." The last sentiment was like a ball volleyed lightly over the net.

He reached for her hand, pressing it to his lips. "You're kidding, right? Your mom could be Attila the Hun and it wouldn't change the way I feel about you."

"Hmm. We'll see about that," she teased. "Seriously, though, what about the kids? Ava's dealing with her mother's crazy relationship with Levin, and Jesse's major fear is of one of his parents remarrying. Our living together might be even more precarious for him. I don't want to make a mistake and hurt him more than he already is."

"What mistake would that be?"

Georgie inched up and smoothed her finger over the crinkle between his brows. "I know the last couple of months have been wonderful between us, but what if things change? I can't risk putting Jesse through that. He just isn't emotionally ready for any more major changes. He's already really upset about his dad living with Zoë."

"He doesn't feel the same about me, does he? You can tell me. I can take it."

"Actually, today he admitted he liked you. I think the dog really clinched it for him." She sighed. "It's the concept of his mom being with a different man from his dad that upsets him."

"That's natural." He nodded. "Ava felt the same way about her mom, at first, when she still liked Levin."

"On a happier note, I get the feeling Lucas is getting sick of his little nymphet. She's become a real pain in the ass, and all her talk of marriage seems to be spooking him."

"Oh." Ian shifted onto his back. "Well, Jesse will certainly be overjoyed if they break up—just like Ava."

There was a long, uncomfortable moment between them. Georgie hooked her leg over his and hoisted herself up, straddling Ian from above. "Nothing is going to happen between Lucas and me again. I only mention it because the happier Jesse is, the better for you and me." She kissed him, drawing her tongue into his mouth, noting the taste of garlic and wine from their dinner of Italian takeout.

Ian moaned. "Umm. Not fair. Put your money where your mouth is."

"Tomorrow afternoon, Jess is spending a few hours at Luke's." She lingered a moment longer, lip-to-lip. "I promise. Speaking of our exes, anything new going on with Stacy and Levin?"

He sighed. "That's a trick question. You don't want me to know the answer. You'll think I'm all chummy with Stacy."

"No, it's okay. I was actually thinking about Ava," Georgie said. "Anyway, I told you about Luke."

"Umm, that's true. Still . . ."

"Ah, c'mon. I won't hold it against you. I promise."

"He misses her, and Stacy's considering going back with him. But she's waffling. She doesn't want to be hurt again by his ambivalence."

"Sounds about right. Poor Ava; she must be so confused." Georgie said. "Isn't love grand?"

"Stacy and Levin have nothing to do with you and me. Ava sees that, and if she doesn't, I'll help her see it."

"I just don't want to rush into anything, with Jesse or with me, when our lives feel so tenuous. I need to go slowly for both our sakes."

Her heart said one thing, but her mind was still spinning like the wheel in a carnival game, unsure which number it would land on, or if it would end up being flung into the haunted house.

His eyes, mouth, whole face, bloomed into a smile. "Deal. I understand how hard it is for kids. But in terms of you and me, don't confuse caution with fear. I love you, Georgie. I want to try to make things work out between us."

Thanksgiving dawned early and cold, the oyster gray sky threatening rain, the trees outside her window stripped of their leafy robes with bark the color and texture of elephant hide. Winter, that dull, scaly season, was on its way. By seven a.m., Georgie was out in the slapping chill, walking mournful-eyed Hermione while Jesse slept, curled up, knees into his chest, as if ready to be shot from a cannon. She checked in on him before dashing out the door with their loose-limbed new pup.

When she got back from zigzagging down the street, walking with an animal that moved as if she'd failed a Breathalyzer test, the phone was ringing. She rubbed her chapped hands together and pulled off her sweater before answering.

"Rise and shine, sunshine," Nina chimed.

"Hey," she said, pouring Science Diet into the plastic dog bowl. "I beat you. I've already been around the block."

"That little cutie keeping you on your feet?"

"Who, the dog?" Georgie asked while measuring Turkish coffee into the filter.

"Touché."

"So. What's up?"

"Not much. Just checking to make sure I'll see you later and *finally* meet this mystery beau of yours. I can't believe it's taken so long."

"Me neither. We'll be there, unmasked and ready for inspection." Georgie bent down to pet Hermione, who was licking her calf, her tail wagging furiously, *swoosh, swoosh*.

"Can't wait. So, did Ian decide to bring his daughter?"

"No. We're coming separately. He's going to have Ava over at his place before meeting us in the city. We're not sure that the kids are ready to share holidays yet."

"But they will at some point. I mean, before the wedding?"

"Very funny. Stop rushing us. You're making me tense." Georgie popped a half an English muffin in the toaster; Hermione stared at her with doleful eyes when no crumbs dropped. "Anyway, how are *you*? How are Elliot and the kids? Franny doing any ass biting lately?"

Nina's laugh was as refreshing as the sun bisecting a patch of bleak clouds. "No. No more violent incidents, although we did have a close call the other day. I brilliantly threatened to pack her off to boarding school if she behaved like that again. Don't you think it's wonderful that Dr. Shrink here should make her daughter cry so hard I had to resort to ice-cream sundaes to make it up to her? Such brilliant judgment on my part."

"Cut yourself some slack. As long as the apology included hot fudge, you should chalk it up to excellent psychological judgment."

"Thanks. So, nervous about your mom meeting lover boy?"

Georgie inhaled deeply. "Yeah. She's been very conciliatory since I went up to Boston. She even asked me a couple of innocent questions about Ian. Guess we'll see if she behaves herself today. I hope so. I have to say, I've been feeling more sympathetic toward her lately; it's good she has Daniel to make her feel better. She probably deserves it."

The ride into the city was blessedly quick and uneventful for a holiday. In the car Jesse listened to the Beach Boys singing "Good Vibrations" through the headphones of his iPod, blithely unaware of his surroundings. The city was oddly still, cleared out, as if all the families had piled into SUVs en route to gatherings in expansive Westchester and Connecticut. The two of them zipped down the West Side Highway, the car bumping and grinding on the poorly paved road like a cheap exotic dancer. Parking proved more of an ordeal than the drive; Georgie circled around the block twice and found the first garage she tried full. Finally she settled for an overpriced lot within walking distance to West Sixty-seventh Street.

Aunt Lily and Uncle Art owned a three-bedroom in a high-rise near Lincoln Center. Rumor had it that Peter Jennings lived in their building, but no Merkin had ever sighted the man in the marble-walled lobby or mirror-lined express elevator. Georgie considered this area the mecca of Manhattan: Pottery Barn on the corner, Loews Cineplex across the street, a three-story Barnes & Noble a block south, Café Mozart with its myriad of fancy coffees and rich desserts a hop, skip, and a jump away. If she'd had any gumption during her marriage, she'd have insisted Luke defy the Carter family conservatism and move across town from stuffy Park Avenue to this more artistic, left-wing part of town. Such an odd choice, really, for her aunt—whose style had evolved into a Madison Avenue socialite of Estée Lauder's generation, old chain-handled purses and wide-brimmed hats included.

On the walk over, Georgie cupped her son's hand. "Don't worry, sweetie. You don't even have to talk much to Daniel if you don't want to. I know you've met enough new people lately, first Ian, then Ava."

Jesse shrugged. "Ava was okay," he said to Georgie's relief.

The hallway outside Lily and Art's apartment was wallpapered in tiny red and green flowers, and there was immaculately clean forest green carpeting on the floor; it reminded Georgie of Christmas at Lord & Taylor. She knocked once and smiled at Jesse.

Lily greeted them at the door, wearing a white pantsuit, a double strand of pearls, and silver mules. She was badly made up—as if suddenly masquerading as a French courtesan—with her usual powder, plus peach eye shadow, an orangey blush, and matte coral lipstick, so that Georgie had to fight the urge to nudge Jess not to stare. But he was barely paying attention.

"Hey," he said, bending his head so his great-aunt could kiss it. Then he slid past the adults into the apartment.

"How's he doing, dear?" Lily whispered, her painted mouth leaving a dab of color on her front teeth.

"He's fine," Georgie said in a taciturn voice.

"Thank God for small favors. I'm looking forward to meeting your young man later. It's very exciting for you." She led her niece by the hand, her own looking fragile, the fingers thin, her wrist birdlike, with her heavy charm bracelet weighing it down.

She's getting old, Georgie thought with a pang.

Following her aunt past the archway to the kitchen, Georgie caught a glimpse of the plastic surgery dream team of Alex Merkin and hubby, Dr. Rich, who'd both flown in from a conference in Paris on breast augmentation and were sharing their newfound wisdom with Uncle Art. "One theory of why capsular contractures occur around the implant is related to the talc that's used to powder surgical gloves. But placement seems to be the more likely culprit," Dr. Rich was explaining, cupping his hand in the air under a phantom breast. "If the implant is placed under the breast gland and pectoralis muscle, capsular contracture rates are greatly reduced to only two to ten percent."

Estelle stood by the fireplace alone, drinking a diet soda. Georgie noticed that her mother looked softer, less menacing than usual. Her shoulders slumped a bit in her crimson blazer, and her hair was frizzier, as if she'd forgotten to style it. She'd lost a few pounds. Despite the reintroduction of Elizabeth Arden's Vintage Red lipstick, she appeared tired and wan, her skin the color and texture of parchment.

When she looked up at Georgie, her eyes appeared momentarily cavernous, as if she didn't recognize her surroundings. It was her first major holiday without Adam.

"Hi, Mom," Georgie said gently.

"Hello. How are you? How's Jesse?"

"He's okay, considering."

There was a careful silence in which mother and daughter were like dogs circling each other before deciding if it was safe to approach.

"I tried to talk to him about Daniel, you know, yesterday when we spoke. Did he tell you?" Estelle asked.

"No. He's sort of clammed up about it."

"Hmm. He probably doesn't want to dwell on it too much. He needs for things to feel normal."

"Yes, he's dealing with enough in his little head," Georgie said. "I think he's on overload."

"Well, I'm sorry about my part in that." Estelle sounded genuinely contrite. "And your friend Ian, was he able to come?"

"He'll be here in a little bit," Georgie said, studying the pearl-colored carpet. "He's spending some time with his daughter first."

"That's a good sign. So, are *you* doing better?"

"Yes, I guess, in view of everything. Coming along."

Out of habit, Georgie waited for Estelle to admonish her, *You have no idea about everything, my dear. I've seen loss. Believe me, you have no idea.* But her mother merely nodded.

"Listen, Mom, there's something I've been meaning to tell you. I like Daniel a lot; I really do." She took a deep breath, gathering her courage. Why was it so hard to be gracious to her mother? Never mind. Like with most things—being close to a man, living without her father—she would get better at it with practice. "And I'm glad he found you. It must have been very hard, what you went through, then not knowing where he was all those years, your own child."

Estelle laid her palm over her breastbone, as if to check that her heart was still beating; her face was flushed and her eyes misty. "Thank you, Georgie."

Georgie gazed at her mother's hands and noted their bulging veins, their knobby knuckles, and the multiple folds around her wrists. When her son had been born, Estelle's hands had been smooth, strong, and ready for anything, of one day performing surgery, of flaunting a diamond ring or a French manicure or a brilliant future. In the unraveling years, all her potential had been realized.

"I was just wondering if you, you know, are considering looking for Daniel's father," Georgie asked, her voice thick. "I talked to Daniel about it and he said he might try." She shrugged. "At some point."

Would Estelle want to disturb her already ruptured life in order to discover whether Claudio had ended up with a quiet country practice, living in a stone villa surrounded by olive trees and an almond grove with his Spanish wife, children, and grandchildren cozily ensconced nearby? What if he'd remained in Madrid after law school, living in a luxury apartment in the city, taking the subway to the Paseo de la Castellana, the business quarter? (Georgie had done her homework.) What if he'd never married and still pined for Estelle? The last choice was unlikely, but remotely possible if one took a romantic view.

Estelle shook her head. "I still imagine Claudio as a nineteen-year-old boy. I don't think I want to upset that image. Daniel, of course, is free to try to find him. . . ."

The doorbell's melodious chime caused Georgie to stiffen, her shoulders jetting up to her ears. She scurried over to Jesse's side by Charlene, who moonlighted for Lily and Art on holidays. A godsend, the housekeeper had employed Jesse's help in serving pumpkin crab quiches and fantail shrimp on a sterling silver tray. Lily let them in, the Kaplan family, the man and boy from Newton and, between them, a woman with masses of blond hair streaked with gray who was holding a sleeping baby wrapped in a woolly blanket.

Estelle rushed to usher the Kaplan clan into the living room to meet and mingle among the Merkins.

"Hey, Jess, you want to come meet Daniel and Ethan?" Georgie whispered in her son's ear.

"Nah, I'm going to see if Charlene will let me sneak some pie," he said.

"You'll be okay if I go say hello?"

"Yeah, Ma. I'm not that lame."

She nodded. As Georgie stepped out of the kitchen's archway, Estelle lassoed her around the waist. "You've met Daniel but not his wife Lauren," she announced majestically. "Lauren Kaplan, my daughter, Georgia."

Lauren wore an embarrassed grin that betrayed a slight, fetching overbite. Her hazel eyes flickered with gold in the irises, and her long, straight lashes reminded Georgie of a llama's. She was without makeup or jewelry; the only hint of a more florid personal style was captured in her multicolored beaded earrings.

"Glad to meet you, sister-in-law." She hugged Georgie until the baby on her chest woke up, squealing. Ethan hung behind her, peering, unabashedly curious, his eyes dark pools that lacked distinct pupils.

"This is pretty weird, isn't it?" Daniel whispered, bending forward, as if Estelle weren't right there listening.

"Very," Georgie agreed.

"It's so exciting for me, finally meeting my whole family," he said, his voice quavering like a fishing rod that had hooked its prey. His eyes shone with an almost manic longing. But then he presented what seemed like a practiced smile and his whole face calmed down, the paragraph lines next to his eyes deepening and relaxing. "This is Ethan," he said, looking down at his son. "And his sister's name is Audrey."

"I have a nine-year-old son, Jesse, who's in the kitchen eating pie," Georgie said to Daniel's boy. "You might want to join him."

Ethan gazed up at his mother, who nodded. "Okay," he said, and Daniel led him by the hand.

A few minutes later Georgie could hear her half brother fawning over Aunt Lily. "I've heard such wonderful things about you from Stellie." Was it Georgie's imagination that Daniel's voice boomed out from the commotion created by the other guests?

"He's sort of a wreck," Lauren confessed.

Georgie turned toward her. "He does seem a little jumpy. He was so laid-back when I met him in Boston."

"He's charming and accommodating, but *laid-back* isn't a term I'd use to describe Danny boy."

Georgie nodded slowly. There was so much she didn't know

about this man who shared her DNA, a whole life, the door of which had creaked open and might spring into full disclosure from a gentle push. She glanced down at the baby and felt another pang. The door had slammed shut on her child's life before the palest shadow of light was let in.

"He said that you're really easy to talk to and that your e-mails are very witty," Lauren said.

"That was nice of him."

The baby whimpered, then let out a wail. "I've got to nurse her. I'm sorry."

"Don't be." Georgie leaned over to examine the blond-headed child. In less than a year's time, this girl could have passed as Georgie and Lucas's daughter. She swallowed hard, and tears sprang to her eyes. The heady scent of baby Audrey had extracted love from her the way breast ducts siphoned milk from wet nurses throughout history.

"Why don't you go in the guest bedroom? You'll have more privacy there," she said, touching Lauren lightly on the elbow and leading her down the hall.

When Ian showed up an hour later, Georgie was parked in a corner, sipping a glass of wine and chatting animatedly with Nina. The sun had finally shown its face and now shot through the window blinds, forming golden bars on the floor, blocking the view of the front door.

Above the din, Georgie heard Ian saying, "It's good to meet you too," his voice bright as a new dime.

"Showtime," Nina said.

A coil of anticipation sprang loose in Georgie, propelling her across the room, her cousin in tow.

Ian had never looked so sumptuously handsome to Georgie; he was wearing a black corduroy blazer, black slacks, a burgundy turtleneck, and his cowboy boots. He was smiling broadly at her aunt Lily, who gazed at him, wide-eyed, hand lightly touching her throat.

"What a cutie! You've been holding out on me on how delicious he is," Nina whispered to Georgie. "My mother's in love with him already."

"Too late. He's taken," Georgie said, nearly bounding to Ian's side. Beaming up at him, she exclaimed, "You made it."

"Yep." He smiled. "Just introducing myself to your lovely aunt."

"Aren't you sweet," Lily cooed. "Oh, Ian, this is my daughter, Nina."

"Well, well," Nina said, extending her hand. "My cousin has been hiding you away for good reason. You're obviously too adorable to share."

"Stop flirting." Georgie elbowed Nina. They were like high school girls vying for this popular boy's attention.

"She talks about you all the time. So, you're either her closest friend or her stiffest competition," Ian joked.

"Let me get you a drink," Lily said. "Would you like a glass of wine or a soda?"

"Nothing right now, thank you. I'm fine. Gotta keep my wits about me." He winked.

"Certainly not for our sake. You're here to relax and enjoy. Oh, you must meet my sister-in-law, Estelle."

All three women quickly scanned the room. Georgie noted that Daniel and Lauren were huddled around their son, Ethan, she wiping his shirt with a wet cloth. Estelle was leaning close to Jesse on the couch, their heads almost touching.

"Let me tell her you're here." Lily nearly gasped and ducked away.

A few minutes later Estelle walked over, grandson tucked under one arm. As they approached, Jesse gave a curt wave.

Estelle arranged her features into a welcome smile, although her gaze remained cool and distant. "Hello, Ian. It's very nice to meet you," she said in a voice filled with exaggerated cheer.

"It's my pleasure, Dr. Merkin," Ian said. "Hi, there, Jesse. How you doing? Hermione keeping you busy these days?"

"I want to let her sleep with me, but Mom said she has to stay in the cage for a while so she doesn't pee in my bed," he said sulkily.

"Give her until she reaches six months and has some more bodily control. Okay, buddy?"

Estelle said wistfully, "A veterinarian. I think my husband, Adam, would have enjoyed being a veterinarian; it would have been his second choice."

"After pediatrician?" Ian asked.

Estelle slowly shook her head. "Poet."

"Like his daughter here," he said, squeezing Georgie's shoulder.

"I'm not a poet," she said in harmony with Estelle's earnest, "Yes."

Startled, Georgie glanced at her mother, whose expression was wiped clean of anger, her eyes glazing over with nostalgic longing. Instinctively she reached over to touch Estelle's hand.

Charlene rang the bell, calling the diners to the afternoon meal. It would begin with her hot biscuits and her famous corn-and-bean salad.

Like a child, Georgie rushed to take a seat next to Ian and Jesse at the oblong table spruced up with vases of red and white petunias. Her nieces' feud over the lone seat near their grandfather, Uncle Art, escalated until Lily placated them by offering to move away from her husband. (Their attraction to Uncle Art was, sadly, purely financial. From their youth he'd been buying their affection with silver half-dollars, sometimes doled out a dozen at a pop.)

"Sorry about the slugfests," Nina said, her voice dipping down into maternal embarrassment. She tore her daughters away from each other and the chair remaining by their grandfather's side.

"Go back to where you were, Mom. They are too old for this kind of behavior, and now," she said sternly to the glowering girls, "they've ruined it for themselves and are stuck sitting with their boring parents."

Jess looked up and shot Kate a sympathetic gaze, to which she rolled her eyes in her mother's direction. Despite closeness in age and frequent family gatherings, the children had never been friends. Georgie found this interchange promising and raised her brows, signaling for Nina to take note.

The doctors clustered together at the head of the table, hunched over their plates as Estelle recounted a difficult multiple birth she'd performed that week. Daniel, as honorary guest, had been encouraged to join this exclusive club, while Lauren and Ethan chose to hang back from the crowd, as far south as possible.

Occasionally one of the plastic surgeons would chime in with a catchy phrase like "vertex-transverse presentation," or "internal podalic version" and the rest would nod, in synchronized understanding, along with Daniel, who Georgie was certain was deftly faking it.

In the past, Nina and she had been the outsiders among their peers. But even Nina—being a psychologist—was a "faux doctor," and therefore tacitly accepted. Georgie's prescribed role as family trifle had its advantages, such as being blissfully ignored.

Which was why it came as a shock when Uncle Art, through a mouthful of dark meat, asked, "So, Georgie, what are you up to these days?"

Her head shot up. "Not much," she said with as much sparkle as she could muster.

"What are you working on?" he insisted. He lacerated another piece of turkey while still chewing. "As a writer, living close to the greatest city in the world, you must have a lot to report on."

Georgie wanted to say, *This and that,* but Uncle Art wasn't going to stand for that the way he had when she was a kid. "A few articles, you know, same old thing mostly."

"Not exactly same old thing, Georgie, dear," Aunt Lily corrected. "Your recent article, 'Mothers of Ambition: Is Superwoman Replacing Her Cape with an Apron?' was certainly a departure from writing about chemical peels and Prada, not that I've ever had any issue with your subject matter." She winked and, for an instant, the years fell from her eyes.

Georgie envisioned her aunt understudying Rosalind Russell in *His Girl Friday:* all cheeky attitude, fierce aspirations, rapid-fire banter, and striped suits with matching hats.

The transformation was momentary; in a blink, Lily was the doctor's wife again, who lived for diamond trinkets and oriental perfume. "Stellie showed me this month's *Elle.* Are you planning on branching out in a more serious direction, dear? I suppose that it would be good for *you,* if not as much fun for me."

"I've always been perfectly capable of being serious," Georgie said to her own astonishment. "I've also had to make a living."

Ian rubbed his hand down her pant leg, upsetting the tablecloth, which tickled her wrist. He grinned at her.

"She's been working on a number of important pieces that have feminist and political overtones," Estelle announced to her public with a territorial air.

"Some people are just shy about their work," Daniel said, winking at Ian. "Unlike yours truly, I'm afraid. I love to expound on the merits of my work. I'm shamelessly exhibitionist." Was he rescuing Georgie or mollifying his own need to belong or both?

"It's true," Lauren agreed, smiling at Georgie. "He's completely lacking in modesty."

Suddenly the conversation was reminiscent of school, as if Georgie's buddies were bartering their smarts to the teacher in exchange for her reprieve. For the first time at one of these family dinners, she felt flush with acceptance.

"How about 'Sex and the Suburbs among the Gay Divorcées'?" Artie goaded. "See? I have a touch of the writer in me, too!"

"Dad!" Nina said. "Why are you picking on her?"

"Who's picking?" He winked at his niece. "We're having a conversation."

"Please don't make light of divorce in front of Jess," Georgie said. "It upsets him."

"Ma, I'm fine." Her son glared, cheeks and tips of ears turning coral.

"Artie, stop being a putz," Estelle said. "She's been through enough, and so has Jesse."

Georgie's neck heated up to her throat, like a beaker filled with boiling chemicals. Was it pleasure she was feeling, a peculiarly painful pleasure?

"I was just fooling around. Waiting for your daughter to toot her own horn a little bit, Stel." Uncle Art peered at his granddaughters, his newfound nephew, then at Jesse. "It's important for everyone to toot their own horn every now and again, if they want anyone else to do it. Remember that, kids. Just a word of advice from an older person."

A sadistic older person, Georgie thought.

"Maybe I don't feel the need to toot," she said, surprising herself.

Daniel stood, holding his wine goblet in the air. "If it's okay with everyone, I'd like to make a toast. I'd like to toast Adam, whom I wish I'd gotten to know."

Georgie glanced at her son. Hunched over, legs akimbo, iPod perched between them, he directed his gaze down, tears in his eyes, all quivering boyish humiliation.

Estelle's tears pooled in the corners of her eyes, not daring to fall.

Georgie lifted her glass. "To Dad." She nodded approvingly at Daniel. "To his life, not his death."

"Hear, hear," Estelle said, her cheeks stained with wetness.

And there he was, shimmering in the corner of the room, neither of this world nor the next. "Time for me to go for good, Georgie Porgie," she heard her father say. "You'll be okay now."

But, Dad, she thought, *I'm not ready.*

With a slight bow at the waist, he lowered his eyes in gratitude, in humility, in love. "Who ever is, sweetheart?" And then he was gone.

What else could she do? Georgie smiled at the others, those still lucky enough to be in the realm of the living. They'd been outwitted by grief, that cunning trickster. It had made them into a family.

ABOUT THE AUTHOR

Nicole Bokat's first novel, *Redeeming Eve*, was published by the Permanent Press in the United States, by Piatkus in the United Kingdom, and by Editions George Vassiliou in Greece. The novel received strong reviews from a variety of magazines and newspapers, including *Publishers Weekly*, *Kirkus*, *McCall's* and *The Bloomsbury Review*. *Redeeming Eve* was nominated for both the Hemingway Foundation/ PEN award and the Janet Heidinger Kafka Prize for Fiction.

Nicole Bokat has a master's in creative writing and a Ph.D. in literature (from New York University) and is the author of the scholarly book *The Novels of Margaret Drabble: "this Freudian family nexus."* She has taught writing and literature at NYU, the New School, Hunter College, and Mediabistro, and has written essays and articles for a variety of national publications. She lives in New Jersey with her husband and two sons.

WHAT MATTERS MOST

Nicole Bokat

This Conversation Guide is intended to enrich the
individual reading experience, as well as encourage us
to explore these topics together—because books,
and life, are meant for sharing.

A CONVERSATION WITH NICOLE BOKAT

Q. Was there a specific event or person that inspired you to write What Matters Most?

A. I was describing the scene of my father's funeral—a terrible moment in my own life—to a friend and I started to laugh. It struck me how people behave in comic ways even during the most traumatic times. I wanted to reimagine the scene with fictional characters. Thus, the idea for the novel was born.

Q. One of the themes of this novel is keeping secrets within a family. What drew you to this topic?

A. Discovering secrets struck me as a good frame for a story about psychological growth. It lent itself to character development and dramatic tension. In the novel I'm working on now, family secrets also play a major role in the plot. I guess this particular theme fascinates me.

Q. The story is seen primarily through Georgie's eyes even though the novel is written in the third person. How "autobiographical" is your novel?

A. I think most fiction writers blend their own emotional responses to the world with those they've observed in other people, along with descriptions and circumstances they've experienced, all of which they inject into imaginary events and characters. For example, Georgie's sensibility is much like mine, as is her sense of humor. I lost my father to cancer several years ago, although not to lymphoma. I have two sons, so I drew upon life experience in my portrayal of Jesse. And my background is Russian Jewish. But the plot and situations are fictional, and the characters are either composites of people I know or imaginary.

Q. *What was the hardest fictional situation to imagine?*

A. Well, one of them was being a single mother. Georgie has it pretty good in terms of her relationship with her ex-husband, Lucas, and the fact that he is wealthy and financially generous. It was a stretch for me because my husband divides most of the child-rearing and/or chores with me and we are not affluent like Lucas Carter.

Q. *You changed the voice and the sequence of events in the middle of the book? Why?*

A. I played around with this section a lot. In early drafts, sections of Estelle's past appeared throughout the novel but, ultimately, this structure didn't work because it gave away too much of the plot. I felt a lot of empathy for the young Estelle and became very interested in the history of women in medicine in the United States. I've read some great books about the subject.

Q. *What writers influence or inspire you the most?*

A. As a child, the greatest influence on me was Madeline L'Engle's *A Wrinkle in Time* because it inspired me to write fiction. When I was ten years old I wrote a hundred-fifty-page novel about time travel; I wrote every day at sleepaway camp during rest time. In high school and college, the writers I read most voraciously were James Joyce, William Faulkner, Virginia Woolf, and Jane Austen. More recently, I read and adored A. S. Byatt's *Possession* and Edith

Wharton's *House of Mirth*. I often return to the poetry of T. S. Eliot, W. H. Auden, and two of my teachers from my graduate school days, Galway Kinnell and Philip Schultz, for inspiration. I admire so many contemporary writers, including Michael Cunningham, Rachel Cusk, Kathryn Harrison, Scott Spencer, Elinor Lipman, Elizabeth Strout, Andrew Sean Greer, Nancy Reisman, and the nonfiction of Lauren Slater, Bonnie Friedman, and Anne Lamott.

Q. *In general, what motivates you to write a novel and what do you find to be the hardest challenge?*

A. Character and theme come to me first. In *What Matters Most*, I wanted to write about loss and its aftermath, the changes in my protagonist's life after her father—upon whom she relies for emotional support—dies. Plot is always the hardest thing for me to sustain. Gradually, I've learned to think more in terms of plot and not just to "superimpose" it upon the characters.

Q. *Is there any kind of novel you'd like to attempt that you haven't yet?*

A. I'm considering writing a historical novel, one that takes place in the late-nineteenth century and deals with themes that interest me—women's burgeoning role in the field of medicine, the mistreatment of woman by society and the medical community, Freud and the dawn of psychoanalysis—but I find the prospect daunting. I wrote one chapter of this novel to which I may someday return, but I found myself bogged down with details like Victorian clothing, plumbing, and the exact routes of the Baltimore and Ohio Railroad! I have literally hundreds of pages of research that I amassed from the Internet or various books. It was exhausting. While I enjoy research, I think I might torture myself over these kinds of specifics. I so admire Tracey Chevalier for what she accomplished in both *Girl with the Pearl Earring* and especially *The Lady and the Unicorn* (which I loved).

Q. What are you working on now?

A. I don't like to give too much away out of some silly notion that it will jinx the writing. But, suffice it to say, it's a novel about two sisters who are very close—one of whom struggled with mental illness and has suddenly chosen to become public with her condition in a manner that offends her loved ones and discloses shocking secrets about her past.

QUESTIONS FOR DISCUSSION

1. The death of Georgie's father is the catalyst for so much change in this novel. In what ways does losing Adam propel Georgie to reevaluate her life and family? In what ways does she mature and come into her own after this experience?

2. Estelle is originally an unlikable character, especially as seen through Georgie's point of view. How did the switch to Estelle's perspective help you understand her better or appreciate her life circumstances more?

3. Georgie considers her role as Jesse's mother the greatest joy of her life. Yet she can't follow through with her pregnancy after her divorce from Lucas. What did you think of her decision to have an abortion? Did it bother you that she never shared the knowledge of her pregnancy with her ex-husband?

4. How did the fact of Daniel Kaplan's existence shape your opinion of Estelle? Did you feel she should have shared this secret with Georgie sooner?

5. Georgie struggles with her own ambitions and identity in the world. She comes from two successful parents and a mother who was somewhat of a trailblazer in her time. Is Georgie really just a "lightweight," as she calls herself, or are other factors impinging on her dreams of writing more substantial articles and her true love, poetry? On the other hand, she has carved out a good career for herself as a freelance journalist. Is her self-perception preventing her from appreciating her own significant achievements?